CO
HEA

ALSO BY STEPHEN EDGER

Dead to Me
Dying Day

STEPHEN EDGER

Detective Kate Matthews Book 3

COLD HEART

bookouture

Published by Bookouture in 2018

An imprint of StoryFire Ltd.

Carmelite House
50 Victoria Embankment
London EC4Y 0DZ

www.bookouture.com

ISBN: 978-1-78681-349-7
eBook ISBN: 978-1-78681-348-0

For my wife and children who warm my heart every day.

ONE

SEVEN DAYS MISSING

'I can't believe it's been a week already,' Mrs Kilpatrick said, as she squeezed back behind her desk. A conservatively dressed woman in her late forties, she had the face of someone who had seen it all and come out the other side to tell the tale. Kate didn't think there was much that could shock her. 'Take a seat,' she offered, pointing at the two chairs opposite her desk, both of which had worn patches where the stuffing was starting to poke through the stitching. 'Budget cuts,' she explained, as she saw DI Kate Matthews eyeing the fabric. 'Can't even afford new chairs, yet they expect me to lose another ten per cent by Christmas.'

The office wasn't very big and along both main walls were cabinets overflowing with textbooks and binders. A large monitor sat in one corner, surrounded by piles of paper and pots of lidless pens. The clock on the wall behind her showed it was nearly seven and a dark, menacing sky enveloped the window below it. The winter blizzard had yet to arrive, but there was no doubt it was on its way.

'We'd like to thank you for allowing us to be in the school today,' Kate said, keen to keep relations with the head teacher as amicable as possible. DS Samir Patel lowered himself into the remaining chair beside her.

'Did you find anything that might aid your investigation?' Mrs Kilpatrick asked.

'The teachers and students we've spoken to have certainly helped us develop a better understanding of Daisy's character,' Kate responded, not wishing to divulge anything pertinent to the enquiry. 'Before we wrap up for the day, we hoped you might be able to share your personal experiences and views about Daisy as a pupil.'

Mrs Kilpatrick's chair squeaked as she leaned back in it slightly and looked off into the distance. 'I don't know what else I can tell you that her tutors haven't already said: she's a popular girl, keeps her head down and achieves strong grades. Her behaviour has never been questioned until…' Her words trailed off.

Kate narrowed her eyes, keen to extract any clue – however minor – to help her understand why fifteen-year-old Daisy Emerson never made it home seven days ago. 'And you're not aware of anything that might have been troubling Daisy in the days or weeks before her disappearance?'

Mrs Kilpatrick's tight dark curls shook with her head. 'I'm sorry, but no. Unfortunately, it's usually the troublemakers of this school who capture my attention. She was a good girl, and I'm afraid that's about as much as I can tell you.'

It was the same message Kate and Patel had heard from everyone they had questioned over the course of the day. The picture being painted was of a girl who was destined to go on to great things; a girl who worked hard, wasn't any trouble and made friends easily. But in Kate's experience, even the most innocent of victims had secrets they kept well hidden.

'Mrs Kilpatrick,' Patel said, picking up on the break in the conversation, 'what can you tell us about Mr Vardan?'

'Ismael?' Mrs Kilpatrick asked, looking puzzled. 'What about him?'

'He's Daisy's form tutor, correct?' Patel asked, keeping his face taut.

The doubt remained. 'That's right. He joined us this year. And a very competent teacher he is too.'

Kate watched her reactions as Patel continued to speak.

'And presumably all his Disclosure and Barring checks came back clear?'

Mrs Kilpatrick looked from Patel to Kate. 'The DBS checks were fine. What exactly is it you are trying to imply?'

'We just want to understand how much you know about Mr Vardan, that's all,' Patel answered, adding a non-threatening smile.

'You're referring to those internet articles, aren't you?'

Kate remained silent, still watching.

'Ismael was very open about all that when he came for interview,' Mrs Kilpatrick retorted. 'We completed our due diligence, and there were no question marks left against his reputation. He's a very good teacher from a difficult background.'

'And you signed off on his approval for the role, didn't you?' Patel pressed.

Mrs Kilpatrick's cheeks reddened. 'I did. He passed all of the thorough checks the county undertakes and those internet articles were proved to be false. I've personally encouraged him to take civil action against the individual responsible for them.'

Kate couldn't blame Mrs Kilpatrick for jumping to the defence of one of her teachers; she would do the same for any of the detectives in her team. But Kate also couldn't ignore what they'd been told.

'The pupil who posted those stories,' Kate said evenly, 'he was one of Vardan's pupils at his last school, correct?'

Mrs Kilpatrick glared at Kate. 'I assume you've read what the boy posted, but he admitted to making up the allegations in order to try and blackmail his teacher into giving him better grades. Ismael was found innocent of *all* of the allegations and handled what must have been a horrific situation with commendable dignity. When he applied to join us here at St Bartholomew's, he wanted a fresh start at a more accepting facility. Thus far, I have no reason to regret my decision to offer him the second chance he craved.'

'What was Vardan's relationship with Daisy?' Kate asked.

Mrs Kilpatrick glared at her. 'He was her form tutor and English teacher.'

Kate sat forward. 'What I mean was: did they get on? Did the two of you ever discuss Daisy Emerson formally, or informally?'

Mrs Kilpatrick sighed. 'We meet every term to discuss his class and any concerns he has over pupils' aptitude or behaviour. He never presented any concerns about Daisy that I can recall.'

'What about your other teachers?' Kate pressed.

'What about them?' Mrs Kilpatrick fired back.

'Did any of *them* express concern about Vardan's relationship with Daisy?'

'What are you getting at, detective?'

Kate glanced at Patel, before continuing. 'I'm simply asking whether any of the other faculty members ever expressed concerns to you about Vardan's relationship with his pupils, Daisy in particular.'

'Nothing that caused me any concern. Forgive me, detective, but if you're alluding to something specific, you'll have to enlighten me.'

Kate folded her arms. 'So that we're clear then, *none* of your staff members or pupils came to you to express concern or worry about Ismael Vardan's behaviour towards, or treatment of, Daisy Emerson?'

Mrs Kilpatrick looked like she wanted to say something, but instead she tightened her lips and shook her head.

Kate didn't like it when people lied to her, but she forced a smile. 'Do you have the paperwork that you completed when hiring Mr Vardan?'

'I do, but I'm not about to hand it over until you tell me why you want it. If you're insinuating that Ismael had anything to do with Daisy running away, I think you need to—'

'I'm not *insinuating* anything, Mrs Kilpatrick,' Kate interrupted. 'But I need to be thorough with my investigation into what could have happened to Daisy. You've seen the kind of media coverage her disappearance has generated already, so I'm sure you understand that I need to dot every "i" and cross every "t". So far, we've yet to establish *why* Daisy decided to run away last Friday. When I'm told that she had a close relationship with a form tutor, a man previously accused of inappropriate behaviour with a pupil, it would be amiss for me not to ask awkward questions.'

Mrs Kilpatrick was doing a poor job of hiding her contempt, but she reluctantly scribbled a note on the pad in front of her. 'It'll take me a bit of time to dig it up. Can I email it to you?'

Kate threw one of her business cards onto the desk. 'You understand that I need this information as quickly as possible?'

Mrs Kilpatrick dropped the card into her desk drawer. 'I'll send it as soon as I can.'

Kate glanced at Patel again, who shrugged to confirm he had no other questions. Kate clapped her hands together and stood. 'Well, we'll be on our way now. I do hope you'll keep us informed of any other rumours you hear involving Daisy? It's only a matter of time before we track her down, and any support you and your staff here can provide will be gratefully received.'

A sudden commotion caused the three of them to spin round as an older man with cropped white hair and a thick, bushy moustache burst through the office door. 'Thank God you're still here.' He inhaled heavily as he tried to compose himself. 'You've got to come with me.'

'What is it, Mr Linus?' Mrs Kilpatrick asked for the three of them.

'The sports hall,' he panted back. 'There's someone in there.'

Kate could see the concern in his eyes. 'And that's unusual because?'

'The hall's been out of use for several months,' Mrs Kilpatrick confirmed, standing and reaching for her coat. 'It's due to be demolished in a few weeks. It's been locked up for some time. Who's in there, Mr Linus? Students?'

He waved a hand in disagreement as he continued to suck in air. 'No, not students… the place is still locked up, but as I was doing my rounds… I looked through the window… and… and… there was a body.'

TWO

Kate hurried along the corridor, surprised at the pace the wiry caretaker was keeping. He'd taken off from the office so fast that Kate hadn't yet been able to confirm exactly what he'd seen. She followed him through a maze of darkened school corridors, only stopping when they reached the set of double doors leading outside. Light from a nearby lamppost flooded through the glass panels in the doors. Fishing into his pocket, a ring of keys jangled as he removed them and searched for the one needed to unlock the fire doors.

Mrs Kilpatrick and Patel joined them a moment later, each wearing looks of confused concern. Linus cursed as the keys fell from his hands and clattered to the floor and Kate seized her chance, stooping to pick them up for him and looking him dead in the eye. 'Just take a moment and tell us what you saw, Mr Linus.'

His hands trembled as she placed the keys into his open palm. 'It was like I said: a body.'

Kate rested her hand on his to steady it. 'Where, Mr Linus? Where was this body?'

He closed his eyes, taking a deep breath. 'I was doing my nightly rounds, you see; checking the school is locked up. I have a routine. I do all the outer buildings first, and then move to the main facility. But when I approached the sports hall... there was something not right... nobody's been near the place in weeks – well, apart from the building inspector and project manager – but someone's changed the padlock on the door.' His story still didn't explain the pallid nature of his face, or the sweat clinging to his temple.

'Go on,' Kate encouraged. 'What next?'

'Well, I know the lock was new, because it didn't have any rust like what the old one did, and none of my keys fitted it. But I swear it wasn't there a couple of days ago when I let the building inspector in. Someone has changed it.'

Kate spun and looked to Mrs Kilpatrick for support. 'Is it possible one of the builders or teachers changed the padlock?'

But Mrs Kilpatrick frowned back at her. 'I don't know why any of them would. There's nothing valuable left in there; we only have the padlock to keep the students getting in. It's not safe, you see – the roof, I mean – that's why it's going to be knocked down. The council can't afford to improve our budget, but it seems they *can* afford to put a swimming pool in its place. Work starts in a few weeks.'

Kate turned back to Linus. 'And where is this body you saw?'

Linus's skin seemed to pale further. 'I continued my check of the building – there's a fire exit and window at the rear – and it was as I looked through the window that I saw her.'

'*Her?*' Kate's pulse quickened.

He nodded ominously. 'It was covered by a cloth of some sort – but the shape... definitely female.'

Kate's mind raced for a satisfactory alternative as to why Linus thought he had seen the outline of a female inside a locked and disused sports hall, but nothing fit. 'Okay, Mr Linus. Take us to this window.'

Once outside, Kate shone the torch on her smartphone through the window into the dark hall, but it was almost impossible to see anything more than ten feet away. Pressing her nose to the glass, she studied the floor inside as she moved the beam around. Then she spotted it. Almost out of sight, a bundle beneath a blanket.

'We'd better take a look inside,' Kate muttered to Patel. She looked back to Mrs Kilpatrick. 'You said it wasn't safe to be inside, what exactly is wrong with the building?'

'Some of the ceiling tiles are starting to come loose. The building inspector and I have been in several times without injury; I have hard hats you can use if you want to go in, but just be careful.'

Kate nodded for her to fetch the equipment, before facing Linus, who looked like he might keel over at any moment. 'Do you have any kind of bolt cutters? Or something we can use to cut through that padlock?'

He didn't respond at first, still staring at the glass.

Kate gently touched his arm. 'Mr Linus?'

He looked up.

'Do you have any kind of tool we can use to cut through the padlock?' Kate repeated.

'Uh… yes, yes I do. I have bolt cutters. They'll work, right?'

Kate nodded. 'Thank you. We'll meet you back at the front door to the sports hall.'

She waited until Linus had moved away from the building. 'Thoughts?'

Patel raised his eyebrows. 'We're in a secondary school as secure as they come. You saw the security cameras at the gate where we entered this morning? A girl is missing and everyone here is on edge. Do I really think there's a dead body in that sports hall covered in a tarp? No, but it'll only take us five minutes to know for sure.'

Kate cupped her hands and breathed warm air onto them. 'Agreed.'

Patel and Kate completed a perimeter inspection of the sports hall building, finishing back at the entrance. Kate shone her light on the padlock. 'It definitely looks new.'

Patel stifled a yawn, and nodded his agreement.

'Here you go,' Mrs Kilpatrick said, as she approached them holding out yellow hard hats. 'I can call the building inspector out if you think it would help?'

'Could you check whether he or any of his team know anything about this new padlock?' Kate replied. 'Between the three of us, I doubt there's anything to be worried about inside, but we'll check to put Mr Linus's mind at ease. Tell me, how long has he been the caretaker here at St Bartholomew's?'

'He's been here longer than I have,' she replied, affectionately. 'He's part of the infrastructure.'

'And is he prone to…' Kate searched for the right word.

'Delusions?' Mrs Kilpatrick offered.

'I was going to say overreacting.'

'No, he knows his job and he carries it out with the minimum of fuss.'

Kate thanked her as Linus reappeared holding a pair of the bolt cutters. As he approached them, Kate was sure she could smell the faint trace of whisky on his breath. He passed the cutters to Patel, who quickly snapped the lock.

'I'd like the two of you to remain out here,' Kate warned Linus and Mrs Kilpatrick, before opening the door and reaching for the light switch immediately to her left. Darkness remained. 'The lights aren't working?'

'Oh, power's been cut,' Linus confirmed. 'Building inspector wanted everything switching off ahead of the demolition. I can find you a torch if you'd like?'

Kate shook her head, flicking the torch from her phone back on and encouraging Patel to do the same. 'Never mind. What can you tell me about the layout?'

Linus pointed ahead of them. 'The main hall is through those doors there. Off to the left there are doors leading to storage rooms where we used to house the vaulting horses and such. Oh, and there is a room to the right where the old gymnasium equipment is now kept; exercise bikes and the like. The window we looked through is at the far side of the hall. I'll see what I can do to get some power back in there for you.'

Closing the door behind them, Kate shone the beam around the inside of the entrance. Immediately to their right were two doors, leading to what would have been the boys and girls changing rooms and toilets. Bypassing those, they pulled open the door to the hall and were greeted by a stale smell of dried sweat and varnished wood.

'The window is over there in the south-east corner,' Patel offered, shining his light ahead of them, 'which means the tarpaulin should be ahead of us here.'

Walking side-by-side, their torch beams slid over the soft wooden floor following the faded painted lines marking out various courts. Kate shuddered as a draught overhead ruffled through her hair.

'This place gives me the creeps,' Patel muttered.

Kate could understand; there was a deathly silence, and their phone lights were throwing strange shadows across the walls where the beams hit PE apparatus on the walls. It was hard not to think of their own kids in a place like this; wondering if they were safe, tucked up at home and waiting for them. They crept towards the tarpaulin, the air suddenly feeling much cooler around them.

'Shall I do the honours?' Patel offered, nudging the material with his foot.

'Together,' Kate proposed, bending and clutching the end of the material. It felt damp.

She waited for Patel to grip an edge, and then the two of them carefully raised it up and over the mound. Kate's phone clattered to the floor as she saw the lifeless eyes staring back up at her.

THREE

Kate stumbled backwards, dropping to her knees, as she scrambled to retrieve her phone and its light.

'A doll!' Patel gasped. 'It's a doll, ma'am. Thank goodness.'

Her heart racing, Kate threw herself closer to the body, her torch in her hand. Lifeless painted eyes stared back at her, and as she took in the pink-coloured plastic skin, painted lips and fake, ratty hair around them she knew he was right.

'It's one of those resuscitation aids, isn't it?' Patel continued, raising his own torch so he could see Kate's face. A small chuckle escaped. 'That explains the outline, I suppose. Should I break it to the caretaker, or do you want to?'

For a moment, when the tarpaulin had first been pulled away, Kate had seen Daisy's face staring up at her from the floor: the short brunette bob, the smattering of freckles on the bridge of her nose, the smooth and taut skin, it had all been there. Her cheeks reddened with embarrassment.

A flicker above their heads confirmed that Linus had managed to reconnect the power as the halogen strip lights buzzed into life, lighting up every inch of the old hall. With the gloomy shadows suddenly evaporated, their own sense of foreboding disappeared just as quickly. Off to their left two treadmills, a couple of exercise bikes and a rowing machine lay idly by, covered in layers of dust.

'Seems like such a waste, doesn't it?' Patel offered, moving over to the equipment. 'I mean, I know this stuff is pretty dated now, but I reckon I could still work up a sweat on it.'

Kate joined him, spotting a punch bag and chain propped up against the wall. 'I should ask the supe whether we have budget to buy it off them. I could just see this punch bag hanging in the incident room for us to work out our stresses.' She paused as a realisation dawned. 'Didn't Linus say all the gym equipment was being held in one of the storage rooms?'

'So?'

'So, why is it out now?'

'Maybe someone moved it ahead of the demolition,' Patel offered, pointing at where some of the dust had been disturbed on the handles of one of the bikes.

Kate looked from the equipment back to the door to the storage room to their right. 'Hmm... maybe.' But then she spotted something else out of place and marched purposefully to the door without another word, using the light on her phone to brighten the red smear that had caught her attention. 'Is this... blood?' she called over her shoulder.

Patel jogged over to where she had crouched, studying the dried stain on the panel above the handle, careful not to touch it.

'Maybe one of the builders cut himself?' Patel offered, always hunting for the most logical of explanations.

'Maybe,' Kate agreed, standing and removing a sealed packet of white forensic gloves from her pocket, and snapping them on. 'Stand back a sec, would you?' she asked, as she carefully took hold of the handle, and slowly lowered it. She paused with the door halfway open.

'Can you smell that?'

'Sickly sweet?' Patel suggested as he sniffed the air. 'Strawberries?'

Kate pulled the door further, stepped through to the adjoining room and immediately wished she hadn't. Her blood went cold as she took in the translucent plastic sheeting lining most of the floor of the former gymnasium, the reddy-brown smears that clung to it and sprayed up the walls, and the strawberry-scented air fresheners that hung all around her. Kate covered her mouth with her arm as she recognised the unmistakeable copper smell of blood beneath their fragrance. She swayed backwards as Patel stepped around her to see for himself. Opening his mouth to speak, he found nothing.

'What the hell…' was all Kate managed to say.

Kate had witnessed many a murder scene in her years as a detective, but only metres from where children had played outside just this afternoon, she knew something truly horrific had occurred.

'Get Scientific Services here now,' Kate commanded, not willing to take a step further, for fear of contaminating the scene.

Unable to answer, Patel left to make the call.

A large white tent now covered the entrance to the sports hall where those few allowed admittance to the scene could change into protective polythene suits. The scene-of-crime team from the Scientific Services Department had arrived twenty minutes ago and were analysing and documenting every inch of the gymnasium, after which they would pack up their findings for further forensic examination back at the lab.

Several portable floodlights had been erected outside the tent so nobody would stumble on the slippery tarmac where a fresh downpour was beginning to freeze underfoot.

'They reckon it might snow,' Patel commented, warming his hands on the mug of coffee Mrs Kilpatrick had made them when Kate had briefed her on why the sports hall was now out of bounds to all staff members and pupils.

A figure in white emerged from the tent and hurried over to them. 'DI Matthews?' the technician said, his eyes wired with worry. 'I need you to follow me, please.'

Kate passed her mug to Patel and proceeded to the small tent, putting on the protective overalls and following the young technician back into the hall. He didn't utter a word as he led her to the familiar face of pathologist, Dr Ben Temple.

He immediately picked up on her surprised look. 'I was at the SSD lab when the call went out,' he explained, 'and you'll be glad I came. Follow me.'

Without another word, he stepped into the small gym, the plastic sheeting crackling as he trod on it, being careful not to disturb the other technicians who were crouched and huddled around the room. Kate stepped where he did, as camera flashes reflected off the blood-spattered walls.

'We found it over there,' he commented, pointing to where some of the plastic sheet was bunched in the far corner, behind the standard lamp. 'It's impossible to know whether it was left there deliberately or by accident,' he continued solemnly, as he stopped where another technician was busy snapping images. Ben gently tapped the figure in white on the shoulder, and the technician stepped to one side, allowing Kate to see what *it* was.

'Oh my God,' Kate whispered under her breath.

The foot was lying on its side, the little toe closest to the floor, the yellowing sole staring back at them.

Kate choked back the urge to retch. 'It's so… small.'

Ben nodded. 'Based on the heel-to-ball length, the narrow instep and the medial and lateral malleoli heights, I'd say we're looking at a female foot.'

Kate was filled with dread. 'And can you estimate the likely age of the victim?'

'Conservatively, based on the size and shape of the foot, I'd say a young adult, certainly below the age of twenty.'

Kate didn't want to jump to conclusions, but a severed foot belonging to a female under the age of twenty found in the school that missing girl Daisy attended was hard to ignore.

'I'll need to take it back to the lab to examine it further,' Ben continued, 'but I saw some blistering on the ball of the foot, which could indicate the victim was regularly on their feet. We'll get a DNA profile created as a priority and let you know the results as soon as we have them.'

Kate glanced around the rest of the room. 'Have you found any... anything else?'

'Looking at the tearing of the flesh above the ankle, I would estimate some kind of electrical circular saw was used to make the cut. It would also explain some of the haphazard spray on the walls. No sign of the tool, though.'

'Electrical?' Kate questioned. 'The place has been without power for several weeks according to the caretaker. How recently do you think the foot was removed?'

'We're talking a couple of days at most, not weeks,' Ben said gravely. 'They could have used a battery-powered saw, I suppose.'

'Do you think you'd be able to find a match?' Kate asked hopefully. 'Might help us narrow down a suspect pool.'

'I'll do what I can,' he promised, silently mouthing, 'are you okay?'

Kate took a deep breath and nodded reassuringly.

Ben continued to study her face, his eyes telling her he was there when she needed him. She gently touched his arm. 'I'll leave you to it. I need to speak to the head teacher and caretaker again. Call me the moment you have news?'

FOUR

Kate couldn't wait to escape the hall, peeling her overalls off in the tent and dumping them in the disposal sack, before heading back out to Patel. She was pleased to see that DCs Laura Trotter, Olly Quinlan and Vicky Rogers had arrived. Beyond them, additional portable lights had been erected by the camera crew trying to capture the unfolding scene, while a reporter shouted questions in their direction.

Kate faced her team and cleared her throat. 'Right, ladies and gents, I need your undivided attention and I need it now. I know the temperature is dropping by the second, but we've got work to do. Quinlan, I want you to get those reporters pushed back and as far from the school as possible. I don't care if you have to close off the entire road, but I don't want details of this making the ten o'clock news. Once that's done, I want you to check the local area for properties with security cameras. It is important for us to establish any unusual activity over the past week or so. High fences separate the car park from the rest of the school grounds and, short of scaling the fence, the only other ways into the grounds are via the school building, or through the students' gated entrance further down the road. The school doesn't have cameras in the actual grounds but there are cameras at the teacher and student entrances, so that's probably the best place to start. I'll speak to the head teacher to get hold of that, and I want those recordings viewed as a priority.'

Quinlan nodded, jogging over to where the reporters were starting to assemble.

Kate glanced at her watch. 'It's late, but we need to get house-to-house enquiries on the neighbouring residential streets started as soon as we can. Patel, I want you to coordinate that. Reach out to Inspector Bentley and ask him to spare as many uniform units as he can. For tonight, you should only approach properties where there is still sign of activity; lights on or noise from within. Everywhere else can be approached first thing. As it's Saturday tomorrow, we might get lucky and make contact with all residents before the end of the weekend. We're looking for any unusual goings-on in and around the school premises. We're looking for unfamiliar vehicles in the vicinity and anyone seen lurking around the perimeter, that kind of thing.'

'What should I do, ma'am?' Laura asked, stepping forward.

'I want you with me when I speak with Mrs Kilpatrick and the caretaker again. Something about all this feels wrong. We know the school would have been closed up when Daisy was last seen, so if – and it's only an if right now – but if she *is* the victim, how the hell did she get into that sports hall, and who on earth managed to get into the grounds and kill her?'

Kate could hear Mrs Kilpatrick talking on the other side of the half-closed door as she approached with DC Trotter. Knocking gently, Kate pushed the door open to find her with her head buried in her hands and a phone pressed to her ear.

'I've got to go, darling,' Mrs Kilpatrick said. 'The police are here now. Yes, I'll keep you posted when I'll be home. Yes, I love you too.' She returned the phone to its cradle. 'My husband,' she added when she saw Kate looking at the phone. 'Oh, I hope that's all right? I just told him there'd been an incident and I wouldn't be home until later. That is okay, isn't it?'

Kate lowered herself into the same threadbare chair she'd been in earlier. 'Of course, it's important to act as normally as possible.'

'I didn't tell him what had happened, just that it was something I needed to see through tonight.'

Kate appreciated the woman's discretion. Keeping a lid on matters was now a priority, and the last thing she needed was to be fending off calls from the press. Ultimately, rumours would escape in time, but the team didn't need the distraction.

'When my DS and I arrived earlier today, we were required to sign a visitors' book. I'd like to be able to take that with me tonight so we can make copies of the names of those who have visited the school in the last week. Is that okay?'

Mrs Kilpatrick was gazing into the distance. 'Sure.'

'And your security camera feeds. I presume you record those somewhere too? We need copies of all footage from the last week.'

'Sure.'

'Mrs Kilpatrick?' Kate asked, forcing eye contact. 'I appreciate what we've discovered this evening must be a tremendous shock. Would you like me to call anyone to be with you? Your husband, perhaps?'

Tears were pooling in Mrs Kilpatrick's eyes. 'No, I'll be fine, thank you. My husband… he-he-he's at home with our children.'

'Is there anyone else who can come and sit with you? A friend, perhaps?'

'No, no, I'll be okay. Do you know yet…?' But her words trailed off as her face contorted into a sob.

'I can't go into too much detail with you,' Kate said, leaning forward. 'All I can say is we have reason to believe that someone may have been killed in the gymnasium, and my team of specialists will need to spend the next few hours processing the scene to try and identify exactly what happened and to whom.' Kate paused, passing over the box of tissues from the corner of the desk.

Mrs Kilpatrick pulled one out and wiped the corners of her eyes. 'I'm sorry… I'm not used to this kind of thing.'

'I understand,' Kate said, offering a supportive smile. 'I've been in the force for nearly fifteen years and you never get used to it. I do need to ask you a few questions, but I appreciate this isn't an easy time for you.'

She blew her nose. 'No, I'm okay now, please ask your questions.'

Kate nodded at Laura. 'This is DC Laura Trotter, who is one of the best on my team. She's going to jot some notes of my questions and your answers. Okay?'

Mrs Kilpatrick nodded.

'Okay, well, first things first: have you seen anything strange in the last week, or anyone acting suspiciously that you can recall?'

'No, not that I can remember.'

'Nobody at the school that you didn't expect, or someone hanging about outside the gates or the fence?'

Mrs Kilpatrick shook her head. 'No.'

'And none of your faculty members have mentioned seeing anything unusual, maybe strange noises, or strangers hanging around?'

'No, but I don't get as much one-on-one time with the staff as I'd like. I can ask, if that would help?'

'That's okay,' Kate offered, 'but if you have a list of your staff members and their contact details you could provide me, I'll have my team reach out to them over the weekend and check.' She paused to allow Laura to catch up. 'Are there regular visitors to the premises who aren't faculty members?'

Mrs Kilpatrick thought for a moment. 'Of course, there's Mr Watkins who tends the grounds, looks after the gardens; that sort of thing. Then there's the postman, but it's not always the same person. There's a third-party contractor who delivers food daily for the school dinners. And we have two cleaning ladies who are here between four and six each night.'

'And presumably each of these visitors would be required to sign the visitors' book?'

'Oh yes.' Mrs Kilpatrick nodded. '*Everybody* signs the visitors' book, apart from the students. Mrs Fletcher is very thorough with that.'

'Mrs Fletcher? The woman who buzzed us through the gate this morning?'

'That's her. I know she can seem challenging when you first meet her, but she's all right when you get to know her.'

'And that's it? No other regular visitors we should know about?'

'Apart from parents coming to visit teachers. Oh, and Chris Jackson, he seems to be here once a week at the moment.'

Kate narrowed her eyes. 'And he is?'

'Photocopy engineer. It breaks down all the time. I've told the board of governors we need to invest in a new one, but there just isn't the funding with the new swimming pool due. Maybe next year.'

'And so, this Mr Jackson has been on the school premises this week?'

'You'll have to check the visitor's book,' Mrs Kilpatrick admitted, 'but it wouldn't surprise me. Oh, but Chris is lovely: he wouldn't harm a fly.'

'I'm sure you're right, but we need to know who was about this week to rule them in or out of the enquiry, and to check whether they saw anything odd. Would you be able to provide me the names and contact information for any regular visitors?'

'I'll email it over to you now.' She stared at her monitor and worked the mouse and keyboard.

'Thank you.' Kate said, standing. 'Is Mr Linus still around? I'd like to go over his exact movements this evening.'

'I expect he is,' Mrs Kilpatrick said, 'he lives on the grounds.'

Kate fired a look at Laura. 'He lives here?'

'Oh, yes,' Mrs Kilpatrick said, sending the email and locking her computer. 'He has a house – well, it's more of a shack – at the far side of the grounds, away from the main building. I'll take you to him now, if you want? I'd like to check how he's doing. Do you need me to hang around for anything else tonight?' she added, unable to stifle her yawn.

'Once we have the footage from the cameras, I think it's fine for you to go home,' Kate replied, 'though we may need to speak to you again in the morning.'

'Fine,' she sighed, locking the office door as she ushered them back into the hauntingly quiet corridor. 'If you follow me, I'll take you to Mr Linus now.'

Kate nodded, the buzz of adrenaline coursing through her veins.

FIVE

Opening a side door, Mrs Kilpatrick led Kate and Laura out, across one of the playgrounds, through a padlocked gate in the wire perimeter fence, to what resembled a small bungalow, hidden away in a thicket of trees, out of sight of the main school.

'How does he get out?' Kate asked.

Mrs Kilpatrick paused before knocking on the weathered door. 'I don't understand your question.'

'I mean, when he wants to go out, to the shops or the cinema or wherever, if the school gates are closed during the day and at night, how does he get in and out of the grounds?'

'Oh, he has his own private exit.'

Kate narrowed her eyes. 'Where?'

'Just round the back of here,' she said, moving away from the door and skirting across the rough and muddy ground to the rear of the building. 'There you go,' she said, pointing.

Beyond Mrs Kilpatrick's finger was a high brick wall separating the grounds from the main road, but built into the wall was a thick iron gate. A digital keypad flashed on the wall next to the gate.

'My team weren't aware of this third exit. We were told there were only two entrances and exits, apart from the main school building itself: the teachers' car park and the student entrance.'

Mrs Kilpatrick looked bemused. 'Well, nobody comes or goes from here, only Mr Linus. He's the only person with the code.'

'Even so, you should have told us about it. Is there a security camera monitoring this entrance?'

Mrs Kilpatrick suddenly looked concerned. 'Well, no, but from here you can only get to the wire fence which leads to the playground and main school building. You'd need keys to get through both, but even then, the sports hall is over the other side of the grounds; there's no direct route to it. If your suspect had come in here, he would have somehow had to make his way through the school building unnoticed and back out the other side. I don't think that's very likely.'

Kate fixed her with a serious look. 'I'll be the judge of that. I'll have one of my forensics experts have a look, regardless. There's mud, so there could be footprints we can use, or possible fingerprints on that keypad.' Kate turned to Laura. 'Can you have SSD check this out while I talk to the caretaker?'

Laura nodded and peeled away, pressing the phone to her ear.

'Anything else I should know about?' Kate asked the head teacher.

Mrs Kilpatrick lowered her eyes, realising her mistake, and simply shook her head.

Linus still hadn't opened his door as Kate returned to the step, so she knocked, leaning closer to listen for movement. 'Are you sure he's in here? Is it possible he's somewhere else on the grounds?'

Mrs Kilpatrick moved away. 'He said he was coming back here. I'll go and check he's not somewhere in the school.'

Kate remained where she was, and banged the door again until it eventually opened, and the caretaker, looking every one of his sixty-plus years, and wearing a flat cap pulled low over his eyes, answered.

'Mr Linus.' Kate smiled supportively. 'Can you spare me a few minutes for a chat?'

He nodded, his movements jittery.

'May I come in?' Kate asked.

He looked uncertain of an answer, but eventually stood to one side and allowed her in. As she passed, Kate breathed in and understood instantly why his eyes looked so bloodshot, and why he'd been so reluctant to let her in.

Kate found herself in an open-plan cabin, a television and armchair in one corner, a small kitchen cooker, fridge and sink facing the school, and presumably a small bathroom and bedroom beyond the two doors at the back of the room.

'Keeps the cold out,' he muttered nervously, as he saw her eyeing the tumbler on the table next to the chair in the corner.

'None of my business, Mr Linus. I'm sure tonight's events have come as a great shock to you.'

He rinsed a mug at the kitchen sink, drying it with the edge of his T-shirt. 'You want a tea or coffee?' he asked, switching on the kettle.

'I'll pass.' She waited for him to finish fixing his cup of coffee, with more than a generous helping of sugar, and retake his seat before she continued. 'Earlier this evening, when you started doing your rounds, had you already had a drink? I smelled it on your breath when you returned with the bolt cutters.'

He placed his mug next to the tumbler and lowered his head in shame. 'I've been stone cold sober for seventeen years before today. But after what I saw...' His words trailed off.

'So you didn't have a drink until you fetched the bolt cutters?'

He shook his head. 'The stupid thing is,' he lifted the bottle of whisky from the floor, a quarter already gone, 'this was a present from one of the children at Christmas. It was so sweet that he'd thought of me that I couldn't refuse it. I meant to give it away, but I guess I forgot and it got put away in a cupboard. I don't usually keep anything like that near me; to avoid the temptation, like. Now look at me.'

Kate couldn't help sympathising.

He allowed the bottle to drop from his hands. 'When you're in recovery, you're told to take it one day at a time. But when something as awful as this... I'm sorry. When I saw that body, I-I-I...'

Kate crouched by his feet, and rested her hands on his, surprised at how ice-cold they felt. 'You don't need to feel ashamed in front of me. The key is not allowing yourself to become dependent again. Tomorrow is a fresh start.'

When he looked up, his eyes were watering. 'It's not right, though... how can something *like that* happen in a school?'

'My team will discover what happened, Mr Linus, I assure you of that. Which is why I'm here. I want you to run me through your actions this evening. When did you start locking up?'

He wiped his nose with the back of his rough and wrinkled hand. 'I start just after six. Most of the teachers have usually packed up and gone by then, especially on a Friday. I went through the gate and across the playground, letting myself in to the school. I stopped to chat to Janice as she was mopping the Year Five classroom—'

'Wait, who's Janice?'

'One of the cleaners. West Indian lady, very friendly.'

'And she was still there after six? Mrs Kilpatrick said the cleaners are usually gone by then.'

'They are usually, but it depends what kind of a state the classrooms have been left in. The teachers are supposed to make sure their rooms are tidy, but some aren't as thorough as others.'

'So, it wasn't unusual for Janice to be here?'

'No.' The first sign of a smile appeared. 'I like to think that sometimes she works slower just so we can have a chat when I come round. Silly, really.'

Kate glanced around the room again. A bookcase was full to bursting with a variety of books, but a thick layer of dust clung to the edge of the shelves. She didn't imagine he had many visitors.

'How long would you say you were chatting?' Kate pressed.

'Maybe ten minutes or so.'

'And what were you discussing?'

He sighed. 'Her plans for the weekend, the cold weather – that sort of thing. She's going to visit her daughter in Nottingham tomorrow. It's her grandson's third birthday.'

'What time did you stop chatting?'

'I waited until she'd finished her mopping and had put her equipment away, and then I escorted her to the school gates and ensured she was off the premises before continuing to check the classrooms and lock the doors. I remember looking at my watch and it was about quarter to seven when I headed out to check the sports hall. I thought if I hurried, I could be back to watch *The One Show*, you see?'

'Did you notice anything strange as you checked the classrooms? You didn't hear or see anything that struck you as odd?'

'No.'

'And you didn't see anyone lurking around either inside or outside of the school?'

'No.'

'What about this week? Has anything struck you as odd – no matter how small – anything at all?'

'I'm sorry, but no.'

'Okay, so you headed out to the sports hall at about quarter to seven. What first alarmed you?'

'It's funny, really, but I don't usually approach the sports hall directly. Usually I check that the fence gate is padlocked, and then go on my way. I don't really know what inspired me to go and check the door to the old building. Maybe it's all the visitors who've been there this week—'

'Visitors?' Kate interrupted. 'What visitors?'

'The building inspector… oh, what's his name? Um… Phillips? Is it Mr Phillips? I think that's his name. Anyway, he's been by a couple of times and a couple of others in hard hats too. They're due to start the demolition in a few weeks. You knew that, didn't you? They're knocking it down to put in a swimming pool. I still remember when they built it and it was considered new. A lot has changed since then. The world moves on.'

Kate jotted the building inspector's name in her notepad to follow up on. 'When was the last time you'd checked the padlock on the sports hall? You said tonight you immediately knew it had been replaced.'

'Probably last Thursday or Friday. As I said, it isn't an everyday thing I do.'

'And when you saw it had changed, what was your first thought?'

'I thought it was odd. I am responsible for *all* the locks and keys in the school, but nobody had informed me that the padlock had been changed.'

'What made you go and look through the window?'

'God, I wish I hadn't looked.'

'But you did, and something drove you to, but what?'

'I was being nosy. Mrs Kilpatrick, she… she plays her cards close to her chest. I wanted to see what progress they'd made on preparing the building for demolition. I assumed that maybe the building inspector had put on the new padlock, but I wanted to just have a peek inside. That window at the back is the only one that looks in on the hall. It was already dark outside, but there was just about enough light to see inside. I couldn't understand what that cloth was on the floor, so I leaned in closer, and that's when I… when I saw the outline.'

'You know now that what you saw was in fact a resuscitation doll, covered in a tarpaulin?'

He nodded. 'Bet you think I'm a silly old fool for rushing to get you. But I swear I thought it was a real person beneath the sheet. The news and papers have been so full of pictures of that little girl who is missing that I-I-I… I must have let my imagination run away from me. I thought maybe Daisy hadn't gone missing like the press were saying and had somehow got into the sports hall, and maybe something bad had happened to her... I don't know. I watch a lot of those crime dramas on the television.'

'Are you aware that we discovered what we believe to be the scene of a murder inside the gym?'

He nodded grimly.

'Mr Linus, I need you to exercise your discretion with that information. We don't want to cause a panic—'

He grunted and waved away her concern. 'Who would I tell, eh? Got no family, or friends to write home about. Most of the time I just potter about here, reading and watching the television. It's a simple life, but easier that way. At least, it was...'

'Your personal gate, Mr Linus: are you the only person who uses it?'

He nodded.

'And nobody else knows what the code is?'

'No, it's for my private use, not that I use it as much as I'd like.'

'Is it possible that anyone else could have discovered the code? Is it written down anywhere?'

'I have it scrawled on a piece of paper in my wallet – memory's not what it used to be – but my wallet is always on me.'

'But if someone managed to get hold of your wallet, they'd have the code?'

'But nobody has.'

'But if they did?'

'Well, yes, then they'd have it, but that hasn't happened. Most of the staff don't even know the gate is there. The students aren't allowed this far back and the property shields the gate.'

Kate wasn't convinced, but SOCO would confirm if there were any foreign prints on the keypad or in the mud soon enough. 'One final question, Mr Linus: does anyone else have access to the gate leading to the sports hall?'

'Only the groundsman who tends the lawn over that side.'

'He has a key to the gate?'

Linus nodded. 'But only for that gate. He still has to go through the school building to get to the fence.'

Kate scribbled a note and straightened up, handing Linus her business card. 'If you remember anything else – no matter how trivial – will you give me a call?'

He took the card. 'You're not going to tell Mrs Kilpatrick about... about *this*?' he asked, eyeing the tumbler.

'It's none of my business, but I'd get yourself cleaned up by the morning.'

His tearful eyes thanked her, and she showed herself to the door, pulling it firmly behind her. Closing her eyes, she allowed her other senses to come to the fore. A bird crowed off to the left, and a car passed somewhere off to the right; the bitter breeze scraped at her cheeks, and the damp smell of the mud and decomposing leaves threatened from behind.

Why here? Of all the places to murder a victim, why a school where security is heightened, and the environment itself is a bedrock of morality and order? Whoever they were now hunting was like nobody she'd come across before, and she already sensed it would take all of her know-how to catch whoever it was.

SIX

Kate paced back and forth in the Scientific Services Department waiting area; anything to keep herself awake and focused. Beyond the hermetically sealed doors, blood from the amputated foot was being compared to profiles on the database. They didn't yet have a sample of Daisy's DNA, and it had been too soon to call on the Emersons this evening; better to rule out other possibilities before putting Daisy's parents through further trauma. But if there was no match tonight, she would have to call on them in the morning. Kate couldn't decide whether she'd rather they find a match or not: an unknown victim versus closure for the Emersons.

It was only two years since she'd come face-to-face with the prospect of losing her own daughter, Chloe. Kate knew first-hand the terror and helplessness the Emersons would be feeling right now, and all she wanted was to put an end to it. Val and Barry had been living the nightmare for a week already, and Kate didn't know how she would cope in their shoes. Chloe's smiling face appeared in Kate's mind; she would be eight in just over a week, and Chloe's dad Rob and his new wife Serena were planning a large party for her at their home in Oxford. Kate had promised Chloe she would be there, and she wouldn't miss it for the world. Things were good now, and Rob had even agreed to Kate visiting Oxford whenever she was free. So far, she'd lived up to all her promises to Chloe.

Kate stopped pacing, and retook her seat, keen to think about anything else. The image of the blood-stained plastic sheet and foot flashed in her memory. She didn't need a forensics expert to tell her what had gone on in that room. The question was whether the victim had been killed there, or whether the school gym was a secondary crime scene. Of course, the other question was whether the victim had been Daisy Emerson.

Kate would know soon enough.

Pulling out her notebook, she began to scribble thoughts and scenarios as they came to her; she just hoped some of the notes would make sense when she met with her team in the morning to direct the investigation.

The sheer volume of blood pooled on the plastic sheeting indicated that the victim hadn't been dead for that long before the cutting began. Or worse, had been *alive* when the cutting began. Kate had seen arterial spray up the walls, suggesting the suspect had probably hit at least one artery, and if the victim had only been dead for an hour or so, then hitting a major artery could cause that kind of spray. But when had the murder occurred? Today? Yesterday? From the condition of the foot, it couldn't have been longer.

Kate's mind wandered back to Daisy. Seven days ago, on the second of February, at quarter past nine, Daisy had left best friend Georgie Barclay's house after a girlie night in. Her phone had been switched off shortly after she'd left the property and, as yet, no witness had come forward to confirm seeing her anywhere along the short route back to her home. It was as if Daisy had left her friend's house and vanished into thin air.

News of her disappearance had hit the press first thing on Monday morning, carefully orchestrated by the police Media Relations unit. Daisy's parents, Barry and Val, had attended the press conference, but neither had found the strength to speak as the cameras had flashed erratically around them. Kate had read a statement on their behalf, begging Daisy to make contact or for any witnesses to come forward. A barrage of false tips and crank calls had followed, but nothing they could use. Statistics indicated that missing children not located within sixty hours of their disappearance rarely returned home alive. But Kate wasn't prepared to accept that; she wouldn't give up hope of finding Daisy until a body was located. Even now, as she waited for the results on the foot, her hope burned bright.

'Penny for them?'

Kate jumped at the sudden sound of Ben's voice over her shoulder.

'Oh, I'm sorry, I didn't mean to startle you.'

She hadn't heard the sound of the lift at the end of the corridor or the lab doors opening. It was as if he had just appeared. 'What are you doing here, Ben? Shouldn't you...' She stifled the yawn. 'Shouldn't you be in your lab, or in bed?'

He stepped forward and pulled her into his long arms. 'I decided to analyse the foot here in the lab as it was closer to the school, and at least someone else is around. The lab at the hospital is quite creepy this late.'

'And? What did you find?'

'Nothing conclusive, but the technician was processing the DNA as I came out, so we should know soon enough whether...' his words trailed off. Although he was used to dealing with the horrors of examining dead bodies, he would never be comfortable with the acts that caused them.

'Whether or not it's Daisy,' Kate finished for him. 'Did you find *anything* that might help identify our killer?'

Ben mused for a moment. 'What I can confirm is an electric or battery-powered saw was used. The haphazard tearing of the flesh is consistent with a small circular saw. I've seen severed limbs and appendages before,' Ben continued, 'and this was not someone in a rush, and I suspect not somebody who was doing it for the first time.'

'So, what, we should be looking for a surgeon?'

'Not necessarily. I think a qualified surgeon wouldn't have left quite the same mess. A surgeon would have used clamps and ligatures to minimise arterial spray, but our killer wasn't worried about mess.'

Kate thought for a moment. 'A butcher?'

'Possibly. A butcher would have a better idea of where to cut and what sort of equipment would be required. Probably not a bad place to start. I should be able to shed some light on the type of saw you need to look for.'

'Great. I'll get one of my team to make those calls first thing,' Kate replied.

Ben brushed a stray hair from her eyes. 'You look tired. Why don't you go home? I don't mind hanging around here for the results and letting you know.'

'Thanks, I appreciate it, but I need to be here.'

'I thought you'd say that,' he replied. 'How about I stick around and keep you company? I don't think we'll have much longer to wait.'

Kate smiled, gratefully. 'I'd like that.'

'I don't know how you do this,' he muttered, staring into the distance. 'It's just too much at times.'

She was just thinking of how she could possibly reply when the lab doors whooshed open, and a technician in a white coat appeared, brandishing a piece of paper.

She braced herself.

'I compared the DNA recovered from the foot to the profiles on the national database, and,' the technician paused, as he turned the piece of paper over for them to see, 'there wasn't a match.'

Kate felt winded by the news. 'Is the foot Daisy's?'

The technician shook his head as he handed her the piece of paper to study. 'If you can obtain a sample of her DNA we can do a direct comparison, but other than that, we have no way of tracing exactly who the foot belongs to.'

Kate passed Ben the piece of paper as she moved across to the window and stared out into the dark sky hanging over Southampton. Daisy Emerson was still out there somewhere, but only time would tell whether they would find her alive, or dead.

SEVEN

EIGHT DAYS MISSING

Watching the team gathering around the dry-wipe board, Kate was pleased to hear the energy in their chatter; it meant they were switched on and ready for the task ahead of them. It was just after seven, and Inspector Bentley had agreed to half a dozen of his uniformed officers supporting her investigation over the weekend, but she was certain it had been the supe's word in his ear, rather than her own plea, that had led to his agreement.

'Morning,' Kate offered, cutting the chatter instantly. 'I take it you all managed to get at least a few hours' sleep last night; we have a busy day ahead of us. As you all know, Patel and I stumbled upon a horrific scene last night at St Bartholomew's school, where missing teenager Daisy Emerson is a pupil. A human foot was located, and as yet we can't be sure whether it was left at the scene on purpose or by accident. Given where it was located in the room, it seems likely that our suspect missed it in the clean-up, but you know my motto—'

'Assume nothing,' the group bellowed in unison.

Kate smiled. 'Exactly!'

'Do we know whose foot it is?' Laura piped up.

'SSD have yet to find a match to anyone on the system, which brings us back to our missing teenager. We know the foot belonged to a female victim, under the age of twenty. I have the unenviable task of visiting her parents this morning to obtain a sample of DNA to compare with the foot. There is nothing, so far, to suggest that Daisy returned to the school after she left Georgie's house on Friday night, but that's an angle I want thoroughly examined. Georgie's house is on Abbotts Way in Portswood, which is a mile and a half from St Bartholomew's.' Kate pointed to a map she'd stuck on the board behind her. 'I've marked the three most direct routes on foot from Georgie's house to the school, and I want one of you to walk those routes today, looking for any evidence that Daisy may have headed that way. I also want you to look for security cameras along the three routes.'

The hand of a young officer thrust into the air. 'I can do that.'

Kate looked at the young PC, and nodded her acknowledgement. 'It's PC Barnes, isn't it?'

'Yes, ma'am,' he smiled, visibly pleased she'd remembered his name. Kate knew he was due to sit his detective examination in the next couple of months and relished any opportunity to gain valuable experience.

'Good,' Kate said, writing his name on the board next to the task. 'There are also three possible routes that Daisy could have taken walking home from Georgie's house. I want two officers stationed at key intersections of each route, showing passers-by the picture of Daisy and asking whether they remember seeing her last Friday. I also want another couple going house-to-house and ensuring we've managed to speak to *every* possible resident who *might* have seen her. I appreciate it's a long-shot, but it will help rule out the possibility that she was snatched by someone on her way home. If you get no answer, make a note of the address and we'll try again tomorrow.'

She paused, reaching for her mug of coffee and taking a gulp. 'Speaking of which, I want two more officers on the university's Highfield and Avenue campuses. Not all students watch the news or read newspapers, so we need to make sure they're aware we have a vulnerable missing child out there. Daisy would have crossed Highfield Lane on her journey home, and that is part of the student route from halls of residence to the clubs and bars in Bevois Valley. We don't have any reason to believe she would run away, but let's be clear, until the evidence points us in another direction, we will continue to treat her disappearance as a runaway. So we need to find anyone who can confirm she actually attempted to make the journey home.'

'I still think there's more to the parents,' DS Phil Humberidge interrupted. 'Nine times out of ten the parents are involved, you know that as well as I do.'

In his mid-fifties, with a full head of white hair, DS Phil Humberidge was counting the days until he could take early retirement and focus on his hobby of painting landscapes.

'We have no reason to believe that any harm has come to Daisy, and until we do, *I* will handle her parents.'

Humberidge raised his hands in mock surrender. 'I was just saying.'

Kate fired him a warning look, knowing that if it was Chloe who'd gone missing, she'd cling to the hope of finding her until the very last moment.

'Do we know if her bank card has been used since Friday?' Patel interjected.

DC Ewan Freeborn raised his hand into the air. 'Nothing yet. The bank has been alerted to look out for any movement on her accounts, and will call us the second they have something.' Freeborn was the latest recruit to the team. He was slightly built with glasses and a quiff that wouldn't have been amiss in the fifties, but he had a good head between his shoulders – a natural analyst – and was already proving himself a useful addition to the unit.

'Good,' Kate acknowledged. 'Where are we with her phone and social media activity?'

Freeborn shook his head. 'As we know, her phone has been switched off since nine twenty the night she went missing, and she hasn't been active on Facebook, or Twitter since then either.'

'And do we know what time she last accessed her profiles?' Kate pushed, hoping it might stretch the timeline of events.

'Ten minutes past nine,' Freeborn confirmed. 'Which ties in with Georgie's statement that Daisy left the house at quarter past.'

'I want someone to go over that statement with Georgie Barclay again. Did Daisy give any clue that she might run away? Was anything troubling her at school or in her personal life? We know she had a boyfriend, but was she seeing anyone else on the side? Was she active in any online groups her parents weren't aware of?'

'I don't mind speaking to the Barclay girl,' Laura offered.

'Thanks, Laura, try and do it today, if you can? Patel,' she said, making eye contact with him, 'I want you to pull in Daisy's boyfriend for a quiet chat. You don't need to arrest him, but bring him down to the station so it's a bit more formal. He's three years older than Daisy, and while I'm not saying he has anything to hide, I think with gentle persuasion he'll tell us a lot more than he has to date. Like, for example, what he and Daisy argued about at the ice-cream parlour earlier that afternoon? We have a waitress who witnessed Daisy in tears.'

Patel nodded his understanding.

'Everyone else is to focus on our new investigation.' Kate stepped to the far side of the board and pointed at the picture of the foot. 'All we know so far is this foot was severed using an electric handsaw with a rotating blade, like a pizza cutter. DC Rogers will be speaking with local DIY and hardware stores today to find a list of purchasers. I want the rest of you to split the list of teachers between you. Make contact with each – ideally face-to-face – and establish if they have witnessed anything unusual or anybody acting suspiciously in the vicinity of the school in the past week. I'm going to follow up with the third-party contractors who had reason to be at the school: the groundsman, cleaners, photocopy engineer and building inspector.' Kate paused. 'Where's Olly Quinlan? Has anyone seen him this morning?'

The sea of faces shook their heads.

Kate leaned closer to Patel. 'Olly was supposed to be on the security-camera footage from the entrance to the school and any nearby businesses. See if you can get hold of him, and find out why he isn't here.' She turned back to Laura. 'How did SSD get on with examining the caretaker's keypad?'

Laura referred to her notes. 'Only one set of prints were recovered from the internal and external keypads, and they've been confirmed as belonging to Mr Linus, who voluntarily provided a sample for comparison. There were no discernible footprints that could be recovered from the ground surrounding that private gate.'

Any potential lead not panning out was a disappointment, but at least in this case it meant the team could concentrate on the two entrances that *were* protected by security cameras.

Kate finished her coffee as she watched the group disperse. It was odd that Quinlan hadn't showed. Watching hours of monotonous security camera footage was one of the worst parts of the job, but it was a vital component in most successful investigations and he hadn't even reported in to say he'd managed to secure the feeds from the school. When he showed, he'd have to have a good explanation for his absence.

'Mrs Barclay said she's taking Georgie to her grandmother's this morning, but will be back this afternoon,' Laura said, snapping Kate's attention back to the office. 'Do you want some company with Daisy's parents?'

Kate had been dreading the possibility that the time would come when they needed to request a DNA sample for comparison. She nodded, welcoming Laura's offer of support.

EIGHT

'Ma'am, you should have turned down there to get to the Emersons' road,' Laura interjected.

Keeping her eyes fixed firmly on the road, Kate gently shook her head. 'We're not going there yet… I want to see Daisy's final route again first.'

Kate had walked, driven and jogged this route several times in the last week already, but Laura would understand why she needed to do it again. Heading through the next set of traffic lights towards Portswood, Kate pulled the car hard to the right up Highfield Lane, before turning left onto Abbotts Way, where Georgie Barclay's house stood. It was such a peaceful road, especially this early on a Saturday morning.

Kate completed a U-turn before pulling up across the road from the Barclay household, but kept the engine running. 'From Georgie's statement, we know Daisy headed north out of the door, in the direction of home. But she never made it. Her road is only ten minutes' walk away, and between here and there, there are plenty of houses with curtain-twitching neighbours, two bus routes, and enough traffic that somebody *must* have seen what really happened to her. Right?'

Laura nodded. 'Do you fancy walking the route she was most likely to have taken?'

Kate killed the engine and the two of them stepped out into the light sleet that was now falling. They crossed the road and stopped outside Georgie Barclay's house.

Kate looked up at the three-bedroom semi-detached. 'According to Georgie's statement, Daisy left here at nine fifteen, having told Georgie she was heading straight home. Can you time this?'

Laura pulled out her phone and flicked to the stopwatch app. 'Okay. Go.'

Kate tried to picture Daisy's movements a week ago as they headed to the end of the road. It had been a dry and cold night. There were no real signs of activity in any of the properties in the narrow street yet, but the chances are there would have been at least a couple of homes with residents awake when Daisy had passed a week ago. Yet nobody had reported seeing a girl in a purple coat walking alone.

At the end of the road, Kate paused. 'Do you think she crossed the main road here, or walked to the pedestrian crossing further up?'

Laura considered the question. 'For me, it would depend on the amount of traffic heading along the main road. If traffic was light, I'd jog across where we are now, but if it was heavy, I'd use the crossing. It's what – fifty metres away? It all depends how much of a hurry she was in.'

Kate turned and headed to the crossing, waiting for the first car to stop, before making her way to the middle. 'If you're a driver who's just let Daisy across, would you remember it?'

Laura shrugged. 'Probably not. Unless she did something unusual, like she was crying, or gave me an angry look, I don't think I'd remember.'

They continued across the road before Kate spoke again. 'There are two obvious routes to her home from here. If she heads left up to the church, she can walk up Church Lane, before turning right onto Welbeck Avenue, *or* she heads right, down to Shaftesbury Avenue, and all the way along until she reaches the opposite end of Welbeck Avenue. There's probably only a minute's difference in the routes, so which does she take?'

Laura looked left and then right. 'According to Georgie they regularly used both routes when walking between their homes.'

'Of course, there is the third option as well: she could have walked down to Portswood Road, and along until she got to Bowden Lane which joins Welbeck Avenue, but that's a good five minutes or so longer, so I can't understand why she'd go that way unless she was stalling.'

'We have no witnesses that identified her on any of the three routes, ma'am.'

Kate sighed. 'Let's head up Church Lane, which is the most direct route. What amazes me, is this route is usually littered with students from the university heading to bars and clubs at that time of night, yet nobody has come forward to say they saw Daisy. Hopefully today's appeal for witnesses on the campus will solve that.'

They arrived at Daisy's house, a three-bedroom semi set back a few metres from the road, behind a small and unloved lawn.

The front door was opened by Daisy's father, Barry. Dressed in a sleeveless vest, the tattoos that adorned both arms glowed green beneath the rich tan of his skin. His eyes looked tired and sad.

'Wondered when you'd make an appearance,' he grizzled, opening the door wider for them to enter and following them into the living room where they found Val glued to the television screen. It took a moment before she realised anyone had entered the room, but as she looked up and recognised Kate, she tensed.

'You've found her?' Val said, clutching the arms of the chair as if anticipating the blow she was about to receive.

Kate glanced at the screen which was showing the BBC 24-hour news channel and then back at Val, whose eyes looked swollen and tired beneath a layer of heavy makeup. 'What makes you say that?'

'It's been all over the news that there were police at her school last night. The reporter said there were forensic specialists going in and out of the old sports hall. It's about my Daisy, isn't it?'

Kate gave her what she hoped was an assured look. 'Right now, my colleagues are processing the scene to determine exactly what happened.'

'W-w-what does that mean? Is she dead?'

At times like this, Kate knew it was better not to speculate and just to stick to the facts. 'The truth is: we don't know. I know you want answers, but at this time I know as much as you do.'

'What you doing here, then?' Barry growled as he joined them, a freshly lit cigarette gripped tightly between his fingers.

Kate was about to answer, when Val suddenly rose from her chair. 'I'm sure she's still alive,' she said, pressing a hand to her wrinkled chest. 'I feel it in here. My little girl is still out there somewhere.'

Kate respected Val's need to stay positive. She paused to summon the courage to say the next part. 'There is something I need to ask you for. In order to determine whether Daisy is connected to the scene at the school, we need a sample of her DNA. This can be anything from a hairbrush, to a toothbrush or a hat she wore. Is there anything you feel comfortable with me collecting this morning to help our enquiries?'

Barry was about to speak, when Val tore from the room. The clump-clump of her footsteps could be heard on the stairs before she quickly returned, thrusting a hairbrush towards Kate. 'This is hers. You can take it.'

Kate thanked her and deposited it in the evidence bag Laura was holding. 'I promise you, Mrs Emerson, I will be in touch as soon as I have more news.'

Barry showed them to the door, and when they were back in the cool air, Kate said, 'I need you to get that back to SSD as soon as you can. Take the car, and then meet me at St Bartholomew's.'

'What are you going to do?'

'I need to clear my head, to get things into perspective. The walk and fresh air will do me good. Tell SSD to process that sample ASAP and compare it to what was generated last night. I want to be called the second they have anything.'

NINE

Hill Lane forms the western perimeter of Southampton Common, stretching the entire length, and is the link road between Lordswood and the centre of the city. St Bartholomew's Secondary School and College sits almost halfway along the road, forming a kind of fulcrum, with residential streets surrounding the area of the school grounds.

The sleet continued to threaten as Kate made her way along the outer perimeter, set up last night several yards away from the school to keep the hungry journalists at bay. One or two called her name as she ducked under the cordon, but she avoided eye contact. The staff entrance to the premises – an electric gate, wide enough for cars to pass through and usually electronically operated by Mrs Fletcher, the administration assistant – was open, guarded by a second officer in a high-visibility jacket, who nodded as he saw Kate arrive. She handed him her identification as he signed her in and allowed her through. Although the school building looked less creepy in the daylight, there was still something intimidating about the way it stretched across the landscape, concealing the horizon. The staff car park was full of police and SSD technician vehicles.

Making her way through the corridors, she wasn't surprised to find a third officer stationed at the door, leading out to the hall. She waved her badge as she passed, and once again stepped out into the bitter chill; the activity out here was far busier and noisier as the scene-of crime-officers went about their duties. Although the hive of activity was focused on the white tent leading into the sports hall, she also spotted men and women in white overalls who were now searching the outer perimeter of the old building, looking for trace evidence that may have been dropped by the killer or victim. Approaching the tent, Kate asked to speak to the SSD lead, who was radioed and met her at the tent moments later.

'Morning, Steve,' Kate offered. 'Been here long?'

DI Steve Hardy stretched his arms over his head, and yawned behind the mask covering his mouth and nose. 'We were here until just after midnight, and then reconvened at seven.'

In Kate's time in Southampton, she'd never met a more thorough and determined Crime Scene Investigator. He knew his stuff and she was delighted to have him directing operations here.

'If you come with me,' he continued, 'I'll talk you through what we know.'

Quickly changing into fresh coveralls, Kate followed him through the complex entrance, noticing the doors to both changing rooms were now open, with camera flashes reflecting off the walls. 'Anything of interest in there?'

'Not so far,' he replied, holding the door to the hall open for her, and then leading the way across the floor to the gymnasium. Hovering at the door, he began to point at areas of the room. 'We believe the victim was already dead before the dissection began. Although the blood loss is considerable, given what we believe occurred and based on Dr Temple's examination of the foot, it is likely that the victim expired late on Wednesday or early Thursday, and that the mutilation was completed on Thursday night or early Friday morning. We believe he rested the body at the far side, as that's where we identified the largest concentration of blood, and where the circular saw would have caused the spray on the walls. The standard lamp is not battery-powered, which means your suspect had power in this room when he undertook this activity.'

Kate's eyes widened. 'He definitely had electricity in here?'

Hardy nodded. 'The lamp was plugged in and the plug switch was on. The blood spatter on the bulb is singed and suggests the glass was hot when the spray landed.'

'But the electricity was off when we arrived.'

Hardy nodded. 'One of my team is examining the cut-off point as we speak. We already have the comparison prints of the caretaker, so we'll see if we can locate a second set, but whoever did this knew how to switch the power back on, and remembered to turn it off before leaving.'

'So why use the lamp and not the overheads?'

'Neither the caretaker, nor head teacher recognise the lamp, suggesting the suspect brought it with him, but it's also worth bearing in mind that the lighting in this building is all on the same circuit. So, if he'd wanted the lights on in this room, he'd have had the lights on in the rest of the complex—'

'And that would draw unnecessary attention to his presence,' Kate concluded.

'Exactly. With the lamp on, and this door closed, there is only minimal light that escapes beneath the frame of the door, and only somebody physically inside the hall would notice it.'

'If he had power then, it's possible the saw he used wasn't battery-powered. I need to report that back to Dr Temple and my team so they don't narrow the search for it. Anything else you can tell me?'

He nodded, and pointed at a cardboard box off to the left. 'We also discovered this box of cleaning products. There's bleach, a brush, scrubbing sponge and a bunch more of the air fresheners that were stapled to this door. We've taken those down and they're back at the lab and being examined. So far, they just look like the sort of car freshener you could purchase at any local petrol station, but we'll see if we can narrow down stockists for your team to contact. We believe the killer brought this box with him, as it was over near the lamp, and might have blocked his view of the foot.'

'He was going to clean up?'

'It would appear so.'

'But he didn't.'

Hardy shook his head. 'There is spatter on the cardboard, bleach bottle and brush, suggesting they were all inside the room during the cutting, but for some reason he never got around to using them.'

'You think someone disturbed him?'

'That would be my assessment.'

'So maybe the foot wasn't left here on purpose.'

'That's our working theory. We think maybe he left to dispose of the body parts, missed the foot, and planned to return and tidy up his mess, but for whatever reason he either didn't make it back or couldn't get back in.'

Kate thanked Hardy and made her way to the tent, her mind whirring with ideas as she disposed of the coveralls.

'There's a Mrs Kilpatrick in her office inside the school,' the officer in the tent advised, as Kate was leaving. 'She's asked to speak to you urgently.'

Kate thanked him for the message, hurried across the playground and re-entered the school building. Mrs Kilpatrick was unlocking her office door as Kate arrived in the corridor. 'Mrs Kilpatrick,' Kate called out. 'How can I be of assistance?'

Mrs Kilpatrick didn't respond but ushered Kate into her office. 'I'm sorry to call you away, but I thought you should know that Mr Watkins is here.'

Kate recognised the name, but couldn't place why.

'Our groundsman,' Mrs Kilpatrick confirmed. 'He was arriving at the same time as I was, so I verified his identity with the officer at the gate. He said it was okay for us to be here, so long as we stayed clear of the sports hall area. I remembered you saying last night that you wanted to speak with him, so I asked him to wait in one of the classrooms down the hall.'

'Thank you,' Kate said. 'Incidentally, what are you doing here on a Saturday?'

'I'm often here on a Saturday. Today I have a meeting with one of the school governors to discuss fundraising. But I also thought you or your team may need me on site to answer any other questions.'

'You're okay to be here,' Kate confirmed, 'but you must not leave the confines of the main building. Is that understood?'

'Of course,' she said. 'Out of curiosity, do you know how long your team will be on site? I mean, do we need to think about closing the school for the immediate future?'

Kate wanted to say yes, but knew it wouldn't be as easy to order the school be closed until the crime scene had been fully processed. That was a conversation she would need to have with the supe at the earliest opportunity. 'I'll let you know.'

'The thing is,' Mrs Kilpatrick pressed, 'we'll have to notify parents, who may need to make arrangements for their kids for any days we're closed, and—'

'I'll let you know,' Kate repeated, as gently as she could, understanding the implications of such a decision, but not prepared to make promises she couldn't keep. 'Which classroom did you say the groundsman is in?'

'Before you speak to him,' Mrs Kilpatrick paused and looked off, as if searching for the right words, 'there's something you need to understand. Neil is… how can I put it…? Neil is a wonderful gardener – don't get me wrong – and I'm proud to have him working here, but… Neil is someone with whom you need to tread carefully.'

Kate's interest piqued. 'In what way, sorry?'

'He's a great guy, and he does an incredible job with our gardens here, but… he can struggle with communication sometimes; use the wrong word or his behaviour can come across as immature for a man of his age. He's perfectly harmless, but I wouldn't want you to misinterpret his behaviour.'

'Are you saying he has a disability?'

Mrs Kilpatrick screwed up her face. 'Not exactly, but… you'll see what I mean when you meet him. He can be wary of strangers, so don't be surprised if he seems withdrawn; it's nothing personal. He knows me, so I'll introduce you, so he understands you're not a threat. He's vulnerable, and we, at the school feel very protective of him.'

'Protective from what?'

Mrs Kilpatrick rolled her eyes. 'Adolescent children can be quite cruel. We've had incidents in the past of a couple of boys taking advantage of him.'

'Advantage?'

'Oh, I really shouldn't be telling you this, as it'll give you the wrong idea about him. A couple of years ago, two of the Year Eleven boys duped him into buying alcohol for them. They told him they were going to a party and really wanted him to come along because he was so cool, or something; anyway they stipulated that they could only get him into the party if he bought a case of beer for them, and for whatever reason he went along with it and bought the booze.' She sighed at the memory. 'The boys' parents complained to the school when their children were ill over the weekend, and we had to investigate what had happened.'

'You allowed him to keep his job, even though it's illegal to buy alcohol for under eighteens?'

Mrs Kilpatrick nodded vigorously. 'I know, I know, but the two boys came clean and admitted what they had done. He was given a written warning and we've subsequently made efforts to keep him away from the children.'

'How do you do that?'

'During the week, he doesn't arrive until the children are in lessons, and is gone before they finish for the day. He works Tuesdays, Thursdays, Fridays and Saturdays. I've made him sound horrid, haven't I? I'm sorry, I just didn't want you to jump to the wrong conclusions.'

'He was here Thursday and Friday this week?'

'Yes, I think so.'

'Then at the very least he may have seen or heard something that could prove beneficial. Can you take me to him?'

Mrs Kilpatrick frowned, before nodding, and slowly standing.

TEN

Neil Watkins was wearing a blue and green woollen lumberjack coat, a fur hat with the ear flaps pulled down, and had squashed himself into one of the Year Seven children's chairs at the back of the classroom. He waved as Kate and the head teacher entered the room.

When he spoke, there was a softness to his tone; he almost sang the words. 'Hi, Mrs Kilpatrick,' he gushed. 'How are you today?'

Kate remained at the door, watching as Mrs Kilpatrick smiled and walked purposefully towards Watkins, keeping her hands by her sides in a non-threatening manner. 'I'm very well, Neil. And, how are you?'

'Cold.' He suddenly scowled, curling his lips down to show his disapproval.

'Yes, it is rather chilly this morning, isn't it?' Mrs Kilpatrick continued, perching on the table nearest him, but keeping her voice bright and alert. 'I see you wrapped up warm, though.'

He rested a hand on the fur hat. 'This is my hat. Do you like it? My mum got it for me for Christmas. It's so warm. Do you want to wear it?' He made to yank the hat from his head.

'That's very kind, but there's no need,' Mrs Kilpatrick replied, her smile widening. 'I'm okay for now. You keep the hat.'

He lowered his hand. 'It keeps my head and ears warm,' he said proudly.

Mrs Kilpatrick waved Kate over. 'Neil, can I introduce you to a friend of mine? This is Detective Matthews. Do you know what a detective is?'

Neil looked warily at Kate. 'Like Sherlock Holmes?'

'That's right,' Mrs Kilpatrick answered. 'Like Sherlock Holmes. You like those detective stories, don't you, Neil?'

His eyes returned to the head teacher. 'Yeah, he's so smart. He solves all sorts of puzzles. I could be a detective. I'm smart too.'

'Detective Matthews would like to ask you a few questions. Would that be okay, Neil?'

He shrugged, keeping his eyes on the teacher.

Kate attempted to mirror Mrs Kilpatrick's reassuring approach. 'Hi, Neil, do you mind if I sit down too?'

'Free country,' he replied, the smile now gone.

Mrs Kilpatrick glanced at her watch, and leaned towards Kate. 'I'd better go as my guest will be here in a few minutes—'

'No! You stay!' Watkins shouted.

Mrs Kilpatrick made eye contact with him again, her tone remaining friendly, but firm. 'It's okay, Neil. I told you: Detective Matthews is a friend. She only wants to ask you a few questions; she wants to know if you've seen anything strange at the school this week.'

'Men. Men at school. Men in white. Policeman at the gate asking who I am.'

Mrs Kilpatrick was about to respond, but Kate got in first. 'The policeman at the gate was a colleague of mine,' she said, moving closer, and tentatively lowering herself so she was sitting on the edge of the table. 'And the men in white are colleagues of mine as well. Did you see them working?'

He looked at Kate and nodded.

'Good,' she continued. 'Being a detective, it's my job to investigate crimes. Can you tell me what your job is, Neil?'

'I tidy the gardens.'

'Here at the school?'

He nodded, still not looking comfortable.

Kate thought for a moment, before pulling out her identification. 'You said you like Sherlock Holmes; would you like to see my detective's badge?'

His eyes widened with excitement. Kate flipped open the wallet and showed him her warrant card and badge. He reached out like he wanted to take it.

Kate pulled it back a fraction. 'Oh no, Neil, I can't let you take it. But I'll tell you what, you said you like puzzles, do you think you would be able to help me with a puzzle?'

He looked up at her. 'You want *my* help?'

Kate nodded for Mrs Kilpatrick to depart, before turning back to Watkins. 'I should warn you, it's a tricky puzzle. You'd need to be pretty smart.'

'I'm smart.'

Kate nodded encouragingly. 'Were you working in the school this week, Neil?'

'I work every Tuesday, Thursday, Friday and Saturday.'

'And you worked this Thursday and Friday?'

He nodded proudly.

'Can you remember where you were working on Thursday and Friday?'

His brow furrowed and he put a finger to his mouth.

Recognising the gesture, Kate leaned a little closer. 'I need you to think really hard, Neil. Let's take one day at a time. Thursday, can you remember where you were working?'

He tapped the side of his head with his palm. 'It gets jumbled.'

Kate tried to remember back to the course she'd taken on cognitive therapy for dealing with memory issues. 'I understand, Neil. Sometimes our memories seem to merge, don't they? I'll tell you what, let's try this another way. Can you tell me what you ate for breakfast this morning?'

He grinned at her. 'Porridge. Hot with lots of honey.'

'That's good, Neil. What about yesterday, what did you have for breakfast then?'

He thought for a moment. 'Toast.'

'And you're sure it was toast?'

He nodded. 'There was mould on the crust I pulled off. Wrote a note to buy more bread.'

'Okay, Neil, what about the day before that. Can you remember what you had for breakfast that day?'

He grinned again. 'Waffles.'

'How can you be so sure you had waffles?'

'I was at Mum's house, and she always makes me waffles for breakfast.'

Kate smiled to show he was doing well. 'I see, so you were at your mum's house. Did you spend the night at your mum's house?'

He nodded, still smiling at the memory of the waffles.

'Okay, so thinking about that morning, Neil, you had the waffles at your mum's house, and then what did you do? You drove to the school, and—'

The door to the classroom burst open. 'How *dare* you interrogate my son, without my consent?'

Kate's head snapped round to see a woman standing in the doorway, arms folded, face glowering with rage.

Kate was about to enquire who the woman was and why she was there when she spotted Mrs Kilpatrick running up behind her.

'Detective Matthews,' Mrs Kilpatrick said breathlessly, 'may I introduce you to Imelda Watkins, one of our school governors, and Neil's mother.'

'Hi, Mum,' Neil cooed, as he waved.

Kate's cheeks flushed slightly. Standing, she made her way to the door. 'Mrs Watkins? I'm—'

'I don't care who you are!' the woman snapped back. 'You have no right to interview my son without me present. There are rules about this kind of thing.'

Kate glanced at Mrs Kilpatrick. 'Perhaps you could sit and wait with Neil, while Mrs Watkins and I have a quiet word outside?'

Mrs Kilpatrick nodded, and moved past them, approaching the table.

'Bye, Mum,' Neil's voice called after them, as Kate followed Mrs Watkins out of the room and down the corridor. They stopped when they reached the school's reception area, twenty yards from the classroom.

'Firstly,' Kate began, keen to calm the situation before it escalated, 'I apologise for what you feel you have stumbled upon. I was merely asking Neil a couple of questions to establish whether he was in the school on Thursday and Friday of this week.'

Mrs Watkins stared over Kate's shoulder to the classroom. 'Why?'

Being careful not to reveal too much about the activity in the sports hall, Kate kept her voice low. 'We have reason to believe that something sinister occurred in the school this week, and—'

'And you saw a groundsman with special needs and assumed he was a suspect,' Mrs Watkins interrupted, shaking her head in disappointment. 'It frustrates me that whenever something goes wrong, all fingers point at poor Neil.'

'No, you misunderstand me, Mrs Watkins. We're asking all faculty members and school visitors if they witnessed anything suspicious or noticed anybody strange lurking about over the course of this week. I'm not accusing your son of anything, I just wanted to establish his whereabouts and whether he may have seen or heard anything odd.'

'And?'

'And, what?'

'*And*, did he?'

'I don't know, Mrs Watkins, I was still trying to establish where he was working on Thursday and Friday.'

Mrs Watkins continued to shake her head in disbelief. 'All his life, people have assumed that because he struggles to communicate that there must be something wrong with him. I had to pull so many strings to get him a job here, and despite that mess a couple of years ago, he's done so well to hold it down. My son is a good person, detective. He loves working outdoors and I'm so proud of the wonderful job he's done with the garden and pitches here. He should be commended for his dedication, not ridiculed.'

Kate could see the years of hurt in Mrs Watkins' eyes. 'I'm sorry if you thought I was trying to accuse your son of anything untoward. As I said, I was merely trying to establish whether he witnessed anything that might aid my investigation into what occurred at the school.'

Mrs Watkins eyed her suspiciously. 'Why? What did occur at the school? Is this to do with that girl who went missing? Uh, what's her name... Daisy?'

Kate chose her words carefully. 'I can't comment on an ongoing investigation, I'm afraid.'

Mrs Watkins raised a sceptical eyebrow. 'Well, before you go linking Neil with *any of that*, I can tell you he's not allowed contact with any of the pupils who go to this school, and on the night she ran away he was at my house.'

'How can you be so certain?'

'Neil has dinner at my house *every* Friday night; he has done since his father passed away three years ago. He comes home to keep me company. We have a fish-and-chip supper and watch the television together.'

'So, he was with you last night?'

She looked almost offended by the challenge. 'Of course! You can ask any of my neighbours and they'll verify his van is always parked outside of my bungalow on a Friday night.' Mrs Watkins unfolded her arms, and brushed her hands down her green cardigan, flattening out a couple of wrinkles. 'Now, if you wish to ask Neil any other questions, I hope you will allow me to be present. He gets easily confused.'

Kate was about to respond when she spotted Laura peering through the glass in the main door. On making eye contact, Laura opened the door and rushed in. 'Ma'am, I'm sorry to interrupt, but can I speak to you in private?'

Kate looked to Mrs Watkins. 'My team will need to speak to Neil again at some point, but I will have them arrange it through you so that you can be present.'

Mrs Watkins offered the first sign of gratitude, smiling thinly before proceeding back towards the classroom.

Kate continued to watch her, before turning back to Laura. 'What's so urgent?'

'Sorry, I tried to call. I've managed to get hold of the building inspector. Mr Phillips? Anyway, he said he is due at the airport at two, but can meet with us *now* if that suits? Are you done here, or do you want me to go alone?'

Kate glanced back along the corridor, spotting Mrs Watkins and Mrs Kilpatrick leading Neil out of the classroom and hearing him proudly telling them he was going to be a detective like Sherlock Holmes.

'This can wait for now. Let's go and speak to this Mr Phillips and find out why he's so keen to get on an aeroplane.'

ELEVEN

The offices of Two Up and Two Down Site Surveyors Ltd. occupied the third and fourth floors of the Norwich House building across the road from the redeveloped Southampton train station, barely a stone's throw from the police headquarters building. It had been home to many a major corporation down the years, ranging from telecommunications to banking, but was now home to anyone prepared to pay the rent.

Kate and Laura presented their identification at the reception desk, which served the community of businesses based in the fourteen-storey structure, which looked more like an inner-city tower block than a cut-and-thrust home for thriving businesses. The old boy behind the desk had a wispy white moustache and eagerly asked them questions about the nature of their visit, not because he had to, but because he was just keen to speak to another person. A television screen in the corner facing the desk showed a muted cooking programme with colourful subtitles bouncing along the bottom of the screen.

He pointed them towards the lift access when it became obvious they weren't going to provide him with the gossip he so desperately craved.

When the doors reopened on the fourth floor, they found themselves in an almost identical atrium, with doors to male and female toilets directly ahead of them, sandwiching a tiny kitchen, and large fire doors to the left leading to the offices. The doors were locked, forcing Kate to press the buzzer.

The intercom crackled a moment later. 'TUTD Surveyors,' a squeaky voice replied.

'DI Kate Matthews and DC Laura Trotter to see Mr Liam Phillips,' Kate replied and the door's unlocking mechanism activated a moment later, allowing them entry into some kind of waiting area, the tub chairs looking sturdy and functional, rather than comfy and welcoming. On the walls hung artistic impressions of famous landmarks from across the globe, including the Eiffel Tower, the Golden Gate Bridge and the Sydney Opera House.

A moment later, a man in his late twenties, dressed in a white, open-neck business shirt, charcoal suit jacket and trousers with a light grey pin-stripe running through them, offered a greeting. 'Hi, I'm Liam Phillips,' he said warmly, a South African lilt to his voice.

He extended a big and warm handshake to both, before leading them along the floor to an enclosed office space, surrounded by satin glass windows. Inside, a large mahogany desk dominated the room, with two monitors on one end and a stack of binders on the other. The large black leather seat on the far side of the desk wouldn't have looked out of place on *Mastermind*.

He invited them to sit in the two reclining leather seats across from him. Kate realised why as soon as they had: his tall build and more upright seat left him hovering above them. 'What can I do for you today?' he asked flashing them an expensive toothy smile.

'I'll stand, if you don't mind,' Kate said, pushing herself back up and moving to the window that overlooked the road running past the building, and beyond it, Hill Lane. 'You're overseeing the swimming pool development at St Bartholomew's, aren't you?' she asked, still looking out of the window.

'That's right,' he said. 'We're due to begin demolition of the old building in the next ten days.'

'Must be pretty handy,' Kate observed. 'The school's what, a ten-minute walk from here at most?'

'I wouldn't know,' he replied confidently. 'I've never walked it. But, yeah, I suppose you're right.'

'How come your company's undertaking the work? Did you bid for it, or did the school approach you?'

The first trace of unease entered his voice. 'We bid for it, and we won.'

'Bit unusual, isn't it?' Kate continued, her breath starting to fog the window slightly. 'I'd have thought a school would use the local council building inspectorate.'

'They were going to, originally, but the job was put out to tender at several development teams across the county. We were the only ones who offered to undertake the building inspections as well as handling the architectural side of matters. We offered the best value for money, I think. It's not uncommon for government-run operations to hire external parties for this kind of work. It's a great opportunity for our company to showcase our talents, and maybe win some other contracts on the back of it.'

Kate turned to face him. 'Other schools?'

'Schools, council properties, private business facilities, you name it. It's an exciting time for TUTD.'

Kate's eye caught sight of a framed photograph on the wall behind him. Phillips was in the foreground laughing and chatting with a stand-up comedian Kate recognised, but couldn't name. 'When was that?'

He looked up at the picture. 'Oh that. My company won the Best Newcomer award at the South Coast Property Awards last summer. It was a great night, both socially and for the company.'

'You own the business?'

'I'm the majority shareholder, and co-founder.'

Kate eyed the framed degree certificate hanging next to the photograph. 'You studied at Southampton?'

'It's why I moved to the UK to study.'

'When did you graduate?'

'In 2013.'

'And then decided to stay?'

'I wanted to give something back. I like it here. Close to the sea, and some of my friends from uni are still local.'

'Impressive,' Kate nodded. Everything inside the office looked impressive, and that's what was starting to niggle at her conscience. Everything had been carefully chosen and reflected a successful, thriving company, but she knew from experience that things were not always as they seemed.

'When did you win the school contract?'

'We signed the paperwork on Guy Fawkes night last year.'

'And completion is scheduled for…?'

'We aim to have the new pool and complex unveiled before term starts in September.'

'That's a lot of work to complete between now and then.'

'Indeed, but nothing we can't handle.'

Kate crossed to the opposite window, overlooking the train tracks, and beyond it a large cruise ship berthed in the docks. 'Do you spend much time up at the school?'

'I am required to keep Mrs Kilpatrick updated with progress. My team are carrying out various checks to calculate the most efficient way to bring down the old building, causing the minimal amount of fuss to the day-to-day running of the school.'

'How often would you say you're up there, then?'

'It varies. Sometimes a couple of times a week, other weeks, not at all. I've probably been up there five or six times this year.'

'Were you there this week?' Kate asked as casually as she could manage.

'Uh… I'll have to check my diary. What's all this about? Has one of my men done something wrong?'

Kate spun on her heel to face him. 'What makes you say that?'

Phillips looked flustered. His voice was awkward as he started to speak, but rapidly calmed. 'Well, I… uh, what I mean is… all this: the two of you asking me about the school contract. I don't understand what we're supposed to have done wrong. It's not every day I'm blessed with a visit from two such stunningly attractive detectives.'

Kate felt sickened by his smile; smarm wouldn't get him anywhere with either of them.

'We're investigating a possible murder in the old sports hall,' Kate said, without batting an eyelid. She knew it was a risk to be so open, but she wanted to gauge his reaction.

Flustered for a moment, he blinked multiple times as his brain registered that Kate wasn't joking. 'Jesus! A murder? Who died?'

'We're still investigating. When were you last at the school, Mr Phillips? I'd appreciate if you would check that diary of yours for us now.'

For the first time, he looked genuinely uncomfortable having the two of them in his office. He began to anxiously type, before swivelling one of the screens for them to see. 'I was there with two of my team on Thursday.'

'Doing what?'

He studied the screen. 'Uh… that's right, we had to test the building's foundations.'

'For what?'

'It's complicated. Basically, before the 1970s, industrial waste materials were used as hard-core infill under concrete floors. But it became apparent that these materials could cause damage to the concrete floors and brickwork below the DPC level of the property due to sulphate present in these materials—'

'What's DPC?' Kate interrupted.

'Damp-proof course. So, for structures of this age, we are required to test for such damage by taking a sample of the infill to determine whether there is any cracking or movement to the floors or walls below the DPC.'

'And this test was performed inside the building?'

'No, all done from outside.'

'Did you go into the sports hall when you were there on Thursday?'

'No, there was no need.'

'You're certain none of your team went inside?'

'No, the two men were with me and Mrs Kilpatrick the whole time.'

'What time was this, Mr Phillips?'

'I think I got to the school just after seven, and was gone before ten, as I had another appointment to attend.'

'You didn't see or hear anything strange at the sports hall, did you?'

'Like what?'

'Strange noises? Evidence that somebody had recently been inside? Anything like that?'

'No, I'm sorry.'

'And you didn't return to the school on Friday to follow up on anything?'

'No.'

Kate observed his body language. He seemed to be perspiring now, but then again the room was warm. She would know soon enough whether his vehicle had returned to the school. 'One final question, Mr Phillips: did you or any of your team replace the padlock on the sports hall?'

He frowned. 'Why would we?'

'I don't know, Mr Phillips, but it seems somebody changed it. You're certain nobody in your team would have replaced it?'

'No, but I will ask around for you. Tell me, detective, is this *incident* likely to delay our start date? We have a lot invested in this project, and any delays to the start date could seriously impact us delivering on time.'

Kate nodded for Laura to rise so they could be on their way.

'We'll keep you posted. Are you going anywhere nice?'

He fired her a puzzled look.

'Your trip to the airport later?'

His eyes widened as he suddenly looked at his watch, before he calmed again. 'Just to Edinburgh, on business.'

'Will you be away long?'

'No, it's a golfing weekend with a potential client. I'll be back on Monday.'

Kate forced a smile. 'Well, I'll probably speak to you then. If you remember anything from your last school visit, please let me know.' She didn't wait for him to offer to show them out, hurrying back towards the lifts. 'I want you to find out everything you can about TUTD Surveyors and Mr Phillips,' she instructed Laura.

'You think he's involved?'

'Too early to say, but he had access to the sports hall, and he seemed mightily jumpy when I mentioned the murder. Also, see if you can find out who the other shareholders are. I want to make sure we don't miss anything vital. Let's get back to the office and see if SSD have the DNA results.'

Laura paused. 'Do you think it could be Daisy's?'

Kate fixed her with a genuine look of concern. 'I just don't know.'

TWELVE

The technician handed Kate the report. 'It's definitely *not* a match with the follicles we removed from the hairbrush DC Trotter gave us.'

Kate let out a guttural groan, unsure if it was relief or disappointment. 'Daisy isn't our victim.'

The technician shook his head in agreement.

'What about the National DNA Database? Still no matches?'

He shook his head mournfully again. 'No hits on the UK version. We're trying to reach out to our neighbours in the US, but it'll take a few days until we have something back.'

Kate pocketed the piece of paper and thanked him for his support, before heading back to the incident room to update the team. If Daisy wasn't their victim at the school then it meant she was still out there. But it also meant they now had a new victim to identify. And there was only one person who might be able to shed light on who that victim was.

Kate was relieved to spot Ben's car in the staff car park behind the entrance to the mortuary, in the basement of the hospital. Given how late they were out last night before they'd gone their separate ways, she wouldn't have been surprised if he'd decided to come to work later. He was stretching his arms above his head as they walked into the laboratory.

He poked his head out from behind the computer monitor. 'To what do I owe this pleasure?' he asked, as a yawn escaped.

Kate raised the cardboard tray of coffee cups into the air. 'Thought you might be in need of refreshment.'

He smiled at the gesture, before moving out from behind the desk. 'How are you? How's the investigation going?'

'I'm okay,' Kate answered. 'Daisy Emerson isn't our school victim. I'm hoping you can give me some clue about to whom the foot may have belonged. Have you had a chance to look at it yet today?'

'I went to bed late but I couldn't stop thinking about it,' he admitted. 'In the end, I gave up trying and came in. I haven't stopped since.'

'And?' Kate couldn't prevent her naturally impatient nature.

'*And* I kept thinking about ways in which we identify victims. Where possible, we opt for one of the primary identification methods: DNA, fingerprints and dental comparison. And then we might use secondary identification features, such as scars, birthmarks and tattoos. Finally, we'd cross-reference this to the victim's personal effects, such as clothing and jewellery. But we can't do any of that with just a foot. And then it hit me: forensic anthropology.' He turned the monitor so she could see. 'Kate Matthews, I'd like you to meet Dr Xander Garcia. Xander, this is the brilliant detective I was telling you about.'

Kate leaned closer to the screen, seeing an olive-skinned man with a jowly face and wearing thick lens glasses. His image blurred slightly as he waved at the screen. Kate nodded at him, and he nervously returned the gesture.

'Xander is a forensic anthropologist,' Ben continued. 'He provided support with a study I completed while at medical school, and we've been great friends ever since.'

'Friends who only speak on the phone or video calls,' Xander interjected, a Hispanic tone to his American accent. 'When are you going to come and visit me over here, Ben? My wife thinks you're a figment of my imagination.'

Ben smiled into the camera. 'You know I'd be over in a flash if I didn't have so much work to do.'

Kate watched the two men exchanging light-hearted banter, surprised that Ben had never mentioned him before, and wondering if there was another reason he hadn't crossed the pond to visit him.

Kate cleared her throat. 'Sorry, can one of you tell me what forensic anthropology is?'

'Do you want to take this one?' Ben asked the camera.

Xander nodded. 'Forensic anthropology is the study of skeletal remains to determine who they belong to and how they ended up in the condition in which they were discovered. I'm trained in anthropology, archaeology, human osteology, and chain-of-evidence procedures. I often support the local PD here in New York with cases of identifying victims. The biological profile derived from skeletal examination has the potential to reveal a victim's personal history. For example, if we discovered an orthopaedic implant in a victim's knee, we might be able to determine that they were an athlete or—'

'So, you might be able to build a picture of the owner of the foot?' Kate concluded, hopefully.

'Hopefully,' Ben replied. 'Xander is an expert in this field, which is why I reached out to him this morning. I hope you don't mind?'

'Of course not,' Kate replied, appreciative of his out-of-the-box thinking. 'This is exactly what I was hoping you might be able to do. So, what have you discovered?'

The smile quickly left Xander's face. 'Skeletal trauma analysis is a time-intensive process. Ideally, I'd need to examine the foot, and in particular the bones, but you'll have to make do with me guiding Ben through the video call.'

Kate suddenly noticed the curtains hanging from the wall behind Xander's head. 'Oh Jesus! What time is it where you are?'

'Thankfully, I'm on the east coast so it's just after six in the morning. I can talk for another hour, but then I'll have to get ready, as I'm guest speaker at a conference later today.'

'Really appreciate your help, Xander,' Ben offered.

'You're welcome. It sure as hell beats listening to my wife snore.' He chuckled to himself. 'Anyway, Ben has sent me some close-up images of the foot, as well as X-rays, which I've been reviewing. I appreciate this is an open investigation, so I will delete the files when we're done here. Are you happy for me to continue?'

What choice did she have? Kate nodded, and Ben pulled the sheet back from the slab, revealing the foot. 'The X-ray showed two stress fractures: one in the second metatarsal, and the other in calcaneus.'

'At the risk of sounding like the class idiot, can you dumb-down the explanation a fraction?' Kate asked sheepishly.

Ben chortled. 'The heel and here,' he indicated, pointing at the two areas on the appendage. 'These are the two most common areas to find stress fractures, and could indicate our victim had recently taken up a new sporting activity such as running.'

'It could also indicate that the victim could have been suffering with osteoporosis or some other bone-weakening disease,' Xander interjected. 'But that can be determined by testing the bone directly, which Ben will do in due course.'

Ben turned the foot over in his hands. 'Before, I identified blistering of the skin around the base of the foot, which could suggest some kind of sudden switch to physical activity. When someone first takes up running, it can often take several weeks for the skin around the sole of the foot to adjust to the new activity. It looks like the blisters were being treated with a moisturiser or cream to aid the healing process.'

Kate couldn't hide her disappointment. 'Gentlemen, while this is all very interesting and information I didn't have before I arrived, it doesn't really help me narrow the pool of possible victims. Please tell me you have something else?'

Ben turned the foot back over, resting the sole on his out-stretched palm. He hovered his little finger near the cut site. 'After I'd cleaned the blood from the foot, I notice this small pattern. Can you see? Last night I took it to be light bruising just beneath the skin, but now I think there might be more to it.' He raised the foot to allow Kate to look at the small pattern.

'What is it?' Kate asked.

He moved it closer to her face. 'Unless I'm mistaken, it's scar-ring left from a tattoo that's been removed by a laser. Recently too. The scarring is fresh, suggesting it was removed not long before the victim died. I'd say anywhere in the last week.'

'What was the tattoo of?' she asked excitedly.

'That I *can't* tell you, I'm afraid,' Ben admitted. 'It seems the tattoo was on the victim's leg, and we only appear to have the end trails of it on the ankle. I can use negative exposure to try and make the image more discernible.'

'It certainly gives us a new direction to follow.'

'I'll send the image over to you as soon as I've sharpened it up. Maybe one of your team can take it around the local tattoo parlours to see if anyone remembers removing it.'

'Thanks. Do you think you'll be able to find out anything else?'

'We'll see what we can do. Xander likes a challenge, don't you, pal?'

Xander's face bobbed up and down as he nodded. 'Even if I don't get to handle that foot, I'll do whatever I can to help you, detective.'

Kate thanked them both, and left the laboratory. Although she didn't yet know Jane Doe's real name, she felt she was a small step closer to solving the riddle.

THIRTEEN

Kate was pleased to hear the buzz of conversations in the incident room as she returned. Unable to see Laura, she called Freeborn over. 'Ewan, Dr Temple is going to send over a digital image of what he believes is a tattoo removed by laser from our victim's foot. When it's in, I want everyone's eyes on it, and for you to contact local tattoo parlours and see if anyone remembers removing it. Dr Temple thinks it came off in the last week, so maybe someone remembers doing it.'

Freeborn nodded, and headed back to his desk.

Patel slid his chair over to Kate's desk. 'I have Daisy's boyfriend, Alfie Caplan, in Interview Room Three downstairs. Do you want to sit in on it, or should I take one of the DCs?'

Kate was about to tell him to proceed without her when she thought better of it. 'I'm sure he knows more than he's told us so far. I want to ruffle his feathers and see what he spills. Can you dig out the witness statement that waitress gave us yesterday? I want to know what he has to say about it.'

Looking like a member of a boyband, Alfie Caplan straightened his sitting position the moment the door to the interview suite was opened. Kate allowed Patel to enter first, giving her extra time to really look at the young man who might hold the key to exactly where Daisy had run off to on Friday night.

Wearing a red and navy checked shirt, with the top two buttons unfastened, she could imagine his slight frame belied his physical strength. With a mane of dark brown hair pushed back and to the side, and hanging over the edge of his collar, he was clearly an individual who took time sculpting his appearance. He had two piercings in his left ear, and a chain of some sort hanging around his neck. He exuded confidence, but Kate had also spotted the rough edging at the tips of his fingers where he'd been chewing at his nails.

Taking the seat next to Patel, Kate offered Alfie a drink.

'I'm fine,' he grunted.

'Are you sure?' Kate pressed, rubbing her hands together and then holding them over the steam of her mug. 'The heating's not up to much in this place at the weekends.'

He folded his arms. 'I'm warm enough.'

Kate nodded at Patel. 'Start the recording when you're ready, DS Patel.'

Alfie suddenly sat forward. 'You're recording this? Wait, do I need a solicitor?'

Kate waved away his concern. 'You're not under arrest, Alfie. You're welcome to call a solicitor if you really feel you need one, but we're just going to chat to you. That's all.'

He narrowed his eyes suspiciously. 'Why are you recording it, then?'

Kate took a moment before replying, allowing his imagination off the leash a little. 'In cases like this, we like to keep an orderly account of all interactions with key witnesses.'

He leaned forward slightly further. 'Witness? Witness to what? I already told you people I don't know where she went.'

'You're a witness to what Daisy was like as a person. I mean, you were her boyfriend so you're probably the best person we can ask about her state of mind on the day she disappeared.'

Patel pressed record and the machine buzzed in to life. Kate introduced the three of them for the recording, emphasising that the interview was voluntary. 'You met up with Daisy on the Friday afternoon, didn't you, Alfie?'

He looked from Kate to Patel, and then back again. 'Yeah, I saw her.'

'What time was that?' Kate asked.

He puffed out his cheeks, relaxing slightly. 'It was after she'd finished school for the day, so maybe around four.'

'Did you collect her from the school in your car?'

'Nah, traffic around there is a nightmare at that time. She caught the bus to Portswood and we went for a coffee.'

'What car do you drive, Alfie?'

'It's a Peugeot 307.'

'A black one, right?'

'Yeah.'

'Is it your first car?'

'Yeah, used to be my brother's.'

'Does your brother live with you?'

He smiled proudly. 'Nah, he's the brains of the family, he's at uni up in London.'

'Yeah? Which one? I used to work in London.'

'Richmond.'

'I remember my first car. A little Fiesta. I miss that car. It wasn't particularly fast, and it only had a cassette player so I had to copy all my favourite CDs onto tapes, but... I don't know, there was something about it. You know what I mean? It was mine, and it was my first.'

He smiled as his shoulders relaxed. 'Mine's got a banging stereo system.'

Kate smiled. 'I'll bet it has.' A pause. 'Was Daisy your first girlfriend?'

The smile vanished from his face. 'No.'

'So, you'd been out with other girls before Daisy?'

'A couple. Nothing serious.'

'Was it serious with Daisy?'

His shoulders were tensing again. 'I suppose.'

'She thought it was serious, didn't she? Her Facebook page showed her "in a relationship". That was with you, wasn't it?'

'I guess. I don't do Facebook.'

'Where did the two of you meet for coffee?'

'What?'

'On Friday afternoon. You said the two of you met in Portswood for a coffee?'

He frowned, trying to determine whether she was aiming to somehow trick him. 'We was at that place that sells ice cream. Can't remember its name.'

'The gelato place, right? The one with the pink neon lights?'

'Yeah, that's the one.'

'We know which one you were in, Alfie, because a witness says they saw you and Daisy in there. But what I don't understand, is why that witness says they saw you and Daisy arguing about something. Why would they say that?'

He shrugged his shoulders, attempting nonchalance, but coming across as defensive. 'Depends who says they thought we was arguing.'

'Oh, so you're saying you weren't arguing?'

Alfie glanced nervously at Patel, who had been scribbling notes since the conversation had started. 'No, that's not what I'm saying… What I mean is, we was talking, but not arguing.'

Kate didn't miss a beat. 'That's not what our witness says. They said Daisy ran out of the place in tears.'

'No, that's not what happened. Sh-she was upset, but that has nothing to do with this.'

'Why was she upset then?'

'She just was—'

'Did *you* upset her?'

'No, I mean, yeah, I mean… I don't know. I can't remember. It was just a silly disagreement.'

'What were you *disagreeing* about?'

'I can't even remember.'

'Did you go after her when she left?'

'No.'

'That's what our witness said, too. They stated you just sat there while your girlfriend ran off in tears. Why didn't you go after her?'

His hand shot up to his mouth as he chewed on a nail. 'She was upset… she was angry—'

'Why was she angry?'

'She was angry with me… I thought she just needed a bit of time to cool down.'

'Why, Alfie? What had you said that made her angry and upset? What aren't you telling me?'

'It was nothing.'

'What wasn't?'

'I just… I-I-I told her I couldn't see her at the weekend because I was going to my brother's.'

Kate wasn't buying it. The phone vibrated in her pocket. 'There's something you're not telling me, Alfie, and I will get to the bottom of it. You saw Daisy that night too, didn't you?'

'What? No.'

Kate monitored his reactions closely. 'Yeah, you did. You'd been together for months, and there's no way you would have left things like that. Did you go to her place? Is that what happened?'

'No.'

'No, of course, because she wasn't at home, was she? She was over at Georgie Barclay's house. Did you meet with her there?'

'No, I didn't see her. I swear to you: I haven't seen Daisy since the ice cream place. I swear to God!'

The phone vibrated again. Kate nodded at Patel to continue as she excused herself and left the room.

FOURTEEN

Freeborn was waiting in the corridor, holding a printed image. 'Dr Temple just sent this over.'

Kate accepted the page and studied the image. 'This is what he managed to recover from the tattoo on the foot?'

Freeborn nodded. 'It's difficult to tell what it is. Claws, maybe? Or the bottom of letters? Do you think it spells something?'

Kate twisted the page in her hand. The scarring was white against the black of the skin where Ben had inverted the colours. She continued to try and decipher the image as they returned to the incident room. 'That definitely looks like the lower edge of a capital "L" or maybe a "B",' Kate suggested, 'then maybe a lowercase "e" or "c", or maybe an "o". Keep playing with possible letter combinations.'

Freeborn pointed at the far area of the image. 'I definitely think these are claws of some type. A crab or scorpion?'

Kate passed the image back. 'Keep checking the local parlours and find out who removed it.'

'Would you ever have a tattoo, ma'am?'

Kate gave him a curious glance. 'What makes you think I haven't already got one?'

Freeborn's cheeks reddened instantly. 'Oh, ma'am, I-I just didn't…'

Kate's lips curled into a smile.

***

Situated between a takeaway kebab shop and a bookies, the windows of the tattoo studio were blacked out, but the studio's name hung above, emblazoned in white lettering.

Freeborn locked the car and hurried along the street after Kate. 'The girl I spoke to on the phone said her boss had removed a scorpion tattoo from a young woman's leg on Tuesday afternoon.'

A bell sounded as Kate opened the door, followed by a warm blast of air from the overhead heating system.

'Be with you in a minute,' a gruff voice shouted from somewhere out the back.

Images of available artwork hung from three of the walls, with the remaining wall covered in floor to ceiling mirrors, with two large barber-style chairs facing them. There were normal chairs against the wall opposite the mirrors, presumably for prospective punters to queue, not that there were any other customers in the shop. Spotting binders with more artwork in a bookcase by one of the mirrors, Kate nodded for Freeborn to grab a couple so they could compare the images with what Ben had produced.

Taking a seat in the waiting-room chairs, they began to flick through the two binders Freeborn had chosen. Kate flipped through page after page of colourful Disney cartoon characters, but nothing came close to resembling the scorpion or any possible letter combinations. Freeborn didn't appear to be having any better luck either, as his pages were adorned with oriental symbols with English translations scrawled in hand beneath each one.

The sound of metal scraping on metal greeted them as a curtain out the back was pulled open and a guy with a large skull tattooed on his shaved head appeared and looked them up and down. 'You want your collar number tattooed on your arm, officer? We offer a ten per cent discount to public servants.'

Kate raised her ID and stood. 'Are you the owner?'

'Yeah.' Distrust and loathing dripped from his expression.

Kate passed him the negative image. 'You recognise this?'

He gave it one look. 'Nope. Doesn't look like anything I've ever inked.'

The curtain hooks rattled as a thin girl, barely old enough to vote, shuffled through, avoiding eye contact, and began to wipe down the three chairs by the mirrors with a cloth.

'Actually,' Kate said, returning her attention to the owner, 'we believe it was recently removed. Do you remember the woman who asked you to remove it?'

He gave the image a second vague look. 'It wasn't removed in here, love. Sorry.'

'But you do remove tattoos as well as create them, right? That's what the poster on the wall behind me says.'

He glanced up with a slight shake of his head. 'We do, but not very often. Most people who come here want more ink, not less.'

The thin girl kept her head bowed as she approached them. 'You want me to do anything else, boss?'

Kate took in her appearance: long, luminous red hair hanging down past her shoulder blades, but shaved on the right-hand side. The strappy top, fully exposing the range of tattoos weaving into each other down both sides of each skinny arm. Her brown eyes were thick with eyeliner, and she had a ring hanging from between her nostrils, and one through her bottom lip.

'Unless the detective here wants to be tagged, you can get yourself off for lunch.'

'Actually,' Kate blurted, 'I do. Ten per cent discount, right?'

The owner pulled an unconvinced grimace. 'Seriously?'

Kate unbuttoned her coat and rested it on the chair next to Laura. 'Why not? But I want *her* to do it.'

He frowned. 'She's still learning.'

Kate scowled. 'I'll take the chance. I'd rather not have a man touching my skin. You understand, right?'

He rolled his eyes. 'Have it your way,' he said, before turning and disappearing back behind the curtain, pulling it across as he went.

Keeping her head low, the girl moved to the barber-style chair closest to them. 'Did you have something in particular you wanted doing?'

Kate passed her the picture. 'How about something like this? I know it's only part of the image, but you know what it is, don't you?'

The girl's eyes widened and she fired a look at the closed curtain. 'Why would *you* want something like that?'

'So, you recognise it, then?'

The girl began to speak, before stopping herself. 'I-I-I don't think you were being serious about getting a tattoo. So, if you're done, I'll go for my lunch.'

Kate reached for the girl's arm. 'Please, don't go.' Kate unbuttoned her blouse and lowered it to expose her shoulders, before climbing onto the chair. 'Please? The woman who had this tattoo removed is dead, and I am desperately trying to identify who she is so I can catch the guy who killed her. You were the one my colleague spoke to, right?'

The girl nodded sheepishly as she shuffled her tools on the work top.

Kate lowered her voice. 'You said on the phone it was your boss who removed it?'

The girl nodded, glancing anxiously back at the curtain again.

'It's okay,' Kate assured her, gesturing for Freeborn to check the boss wasn't eavesdropping nearby. He ducked behind the curtain.

'We're alone now,' Kate said. 'Do you know who the woman was?'

The girl shook her head silently.

'So, you didn't recognise her?'

Another shake of the head. 'Have you decided what you want done yet?'

Kate reopened the binder and began to flip the pages, finally pointing at one of them. 'Is this going to hurt?'

A thin smile finally broke across the girl's face. 'You'll survive.'

Kate closed her eyes and tried to shut out the urge to leave, as the girl began to stencil the design onto Kate's right shoulder. 'What can you tell me about the image that was removed?' Kate asked through gritted teeth.

The girl sighed. 'It's a tag that my boss puts on women who are sent here, but this was the first time I'd ever known someone come to have it removed. She looked so frightened, and was sweating, like she was ill or in pain or something. At first, the boss said he wouldn't remove it, but then he called the guy who he does the work for, who must have agreed, because the next thing I know the woman is in the chair and he's charging up the laser.'

'You didn't catch her name, I suppose?'

'Sorry. It was late on Monday, and he told me to leave them to it and go home.'

'Can you describe her to me?'

'Pretty, maybe in her early twenties. Long fair hair, slim, small feet – I remember she had the most amazing stilettos, red and glittery – and her accent was foreign.'

'Foreign how?' Kate grimaced as the tattoo gun buzzed into life.

'Polish or Russian, I think. Not from around here.'

'Did she say why she wanted the tattoo removing?'

'Not that I heard. I only saw her for a couple of minutes before I went home. Sorry.'

'You described the tattoo as a sort of tag: who sends these women here to receive it?'

The girl didn't answer, suddenly focusing intently on Kate's shoulder.

'You won't get in any trouble, I promise,' Kate encouraged as the needle made contact sending a jolt down her spine.

'You don't understand what you're asking of me,' the girl replied, her voice so much quieter now.

'I don't want you to say anything you aren't comfortable with, but I promise I won't reveal where the information came from. You can trust me.'

Kate gritted her teeth as she felt another sudden jolt of pain. She couldn't determine whether it was par for the course, or whether the girl had pressed harder deliberately.

'This man who brands these women, is he a pimp? Or a drug dealer?'

'I don't know for certain, but…' the girl began, as the needle continued to spike Kate's skin, 'given how these women dress – high heels, short skirts and tons of makeup – I think you can probably figure that out for yourself.'

'I see you didn't chicken out then,' the owner's voice boomed as he suddenly reappeared from behind the curtain. 'Guess I underestimated you.'

Kate saw him grinning at her in the mirror, but there was no sign of Freeborn. 'People have been underestimating me all my life,' Kate glared back, grinding her teeth to stop the pain from showing; she wouldn't give him the satisfaction.

His jaw bounced as he chewed his gum. 'I bet they have. Mind if I sit and watch while she finishes? I want to make sure you get a proper job done.'

Kate could see the panic in the girl's eyes as she continued to move the needle along the outline she'd drawn. Kate calmly watched the owner as he sat down in the seat Freeborn had earlier vacated. Whatever happened from here, she'd got all the information the girl was going to be able to give.

Twenty minutes later, Kate climbed back into the car where Freeborn was waiting. 'What happened to you?'

Freeborn offered an apologetic look. 'When I went through the curtain, I saw the back door had been left open, so I waited there to see if the owner would come back, but there was no sign, so I stepped out. The next thing I know, the door's pulled closed and I couldn't get back in.' Freeborn pulled an empathetic face. 'Does it hurt?'

Kate pressed her hand against the fresh bandage just below her right shoulder. 'Not a word of this to anyone.'

Freeborn mimed locking her lips. 'What did the girl tell you?'

Kate tentatively pulled the seat belt around herself. 'The tattoo is a symbol, like a brand, and means our victim was probably a prostitute, or part of a group operating in the city's red-light district. You'd better get us back to the station. I'll need to feed this new information up the line.'

FIFTEEN

Straightening her shoulders as much as the dressing would allow, Kate rapped twice on the supe's door, and waited for him to call her in.

'Sir,' she said, as she closed the door and then stood behind the two chairs that faced his desk.

DSI Williams lowered the pen he'd been writing with and sat back in his chair. 'Ah, Kate, you have an update for me?'

She nodded, waiting for him to ask her to sit, but it became clear this was to be a quick meeting. She continued, 'It's not about Daisy Emerson, though. I have reason to believe that the foot we found at St Bartholomew's belonged to a prostitute working in a group, possibly out of the red-light district in St Mary's.'

'And?'

'And I thought you'd want to engage with the Organised Crime Team.'

The penny dropped. 'You mean DI Hendrix's unit.'

'Yes, sir.'

'You could have taken this direct to Hendrix without running it past me.'

Kate knew this already, but in light of previous run-ins with the SIO for Organised Crime, she'd thought it best to invoke a mediator first. Not that she would say as much to the supe, though she was sure he'd figured that out for himself.

'Yes, well, I suppose that does put a different spin on things. You want me to hand the case over to Hendrix?'

'No, sir,' Kate interjected. 'I want to pursue it, but I didn't want to be accused of treading on anyone's toes. Although the tattoo we identified ties her to a crew, it doesn't mean she died as a result of their activities. All I want is access to Hendrix's team to establish who she was working for and who she might be. The forensic pathologist is doing what he can to identify her, but it's a long shot he'll be able to confirm much more than that.'

'Very well,' he finally said. 'I will have a word with Hendrix and the three of us can look at the options together. Where are you on the Emerson disappearance?'

'I'm about to go and catch up with my team now. I've had people at both university campuses today and stationed at key points on the route between the two girls' homes, showing pictures of Daisy to see if anyone witnessed her journey home that night. Patel and I also spoke to her boyfriend Alfie Caplan earlier, and I'm sure he knows more about why she disappeared than he's letting on. They were seen arguing five hours before she vanished, but claims it was over nothing.'

'What does your gut tell you: did she run away or did something more sinister happen to her? Should we be looking at an abduction?'

'I'm ruling nothing out yet. We'll continue chasing down leads until we find her.'

'Are you keeping her parents in the loop?'

'As much as I feel I can. I know they're going through so much that I don't want to unnecessarily raise their hopes.'

'God knows, I wouldn't want to be in their shoes.' He reached for the photo frame on the edge of his desk, smiling down at the image it contained. 'There's nothing more important than family, Kate. As parents, we do our best to raise them to be polite and courteous, with a strong moral code, but once they're released into the big wide world, there's no telling whether they'll sink or swim. How old is your daughter now?'

'She'll be eight next week, sir.'

He smiled whimsically, still staring at the frame in his hands. 'Such a precious age. I remember when our Tara was that young. She said she wanted to be a vet; loved animals, you see. But they grow so quickly. She'll be off to university in the summer. She'll be the first doctor in the family, have I ever told you that?'

He had. Several times since Tara had been accepted at Oxford. 'You must be very proud, sir.'

'Seeing those pictures of Daisy in the newspaper last week, it's hard *not* to imagine your own children in that position.' He returned the photo frame and fixed her with a hard stare. 'You need to find her quickly, Kate. I'm being called for updates continuously. To be honest, I'd rather you hand over the amputated foot to Hendrix and focus your attention on tracing Daisy.'

For the first time, she saw clearly just how strained his face looked. The dark rings beneath his eyes were exposed by his receding hairline, which was looking greyer by the day.

'I can handle both, sir.' Kate declared, shuffling uncomfortably. 'I promise, my team are doing everything they can to find her. She's our priority.'

He nodded towards her shoulder. 'Everything okay with you, Kate?'

'Nothing I can't handle, sir. Do you want to attend the team catch-up?'

'I would, but I have a call with the chief super in a minute. Keep me updated with progress, and bring that girl home.'

He sat back down and continued writing, her cue that she'd been dismissed.

Exiting the room, she headed back along the corridor to the incident room. Spotting Quinlan's leather jacket on the back of his chair, she scanned the office for him.

She called Patel over. 'Quinlan's here?'

Patel gave the office a once over. 'He was. I think he might be in the viewing suite down the hall.'

Kate nodded. 'Get the team ready for a brief, and I'll be back in a minute.' She spun on her heel and headed down to the tiny room they used for watching security-camera footage, away from the distractions of the incident room. The blind was down, indicating that someone was inside. Kate knocked twice and poked her head around the door.

Quinlan looked back at her over his shoulder, concern descending as he realised who it was.

Kate didn't wait to be invited in, closing the door behind her and keeping her tone even as she spoke. 'Where were you this morning? You missed the team meeting.'

He paused the video screen, before turning back to face her again, his eyes on his lap. 'I had a family thing. I'm sorry.'

She'd never seen him look so grey. Where was the Olly Quinlan who was the life and soul of every celebratory drink? The Olly Quinlan whose cheeky Irish persona helped keep team spirits up when things were going wrong?

Kate was suddenly certain she could smell stale booze in the air. 'A *family* thing?'

'I'd rather not go into detail, ma'am. I'm sorry.'

Kate could sense there was something on his mind, though he was either too ashamed or stubborn to reveal what it was. 'Is it anything I can help with? You know you can talk to me, Olly.'

His eyes remained locked on his lap. 'No, ma'am. It won't happen again.'

Kate crouched down to his level and softened her voice. 'What you do outside of work is none of my business so long as it's within the ethics and standards of the law, but when it starts impacting an active investigation, then we need to talk about it.'

His eyes blurred with tears. 'I swear it won't happen again, ma'am.'

Kate remained where she was. 'Although I'm your supervising officer, I like to think I've embedded a culture of openness within the unit. You can tell me what's going on. There will be no judgement and I promise to be discreet.'

'I just got some bad news, that was all. I wasn't expecting it and I had a drink. I would never do anything to compromise an investigation.'

But she could feel there was something he was still holding back. 'You can talk freely, Olly. We're alone. Nobody needs to know what we're discussing.'

Their eyes met, and his mouth began to open, before he stopped himself. 'I'm fine, ma'am. It won't happen again.'

Realising she was defeated, Kate nodded at the screen behind him. 'Is that the footage from the school gates?'

He wiped his eyes with the back of his hand and sniffed loudly. 'Aye. I've been jotting down vehicles coming and going.'

Kate straightened. 'Good. Then you can come and share your findings with the rest of the team. Take a few minutes to freshen up and then come and join us in the incident room. Okay?'

'Yes, ma'am. Thank you, ma'am.'

Kate leaned against the door as it clicked shut. She'd seen ambitious detectives go off the rails before, and she couldn't ignore the tell-tale signs Olly was showing. She would try again when the opportunity arose. But she just hoped she'd be able to reach him in time.

SIXTEEN

Kate made eye contact with each of her team, before beginning. 'Let's hear what you've got, starting with our missing teenager.'

DC Freeborn raised his thin arm into the air. 'Still no activity on her phone or social media. Forgive me for speaking out of turn, but a teenager *not* on social media is setting alarm bells ringing in my head. Prior to her disappearance on the Friday, she didn't tend to go more than three hours without accessing the web in some capacity. The site's administrators have finally sent over a log of her activity from the month before she was last seen. Pages and pages of five- to ten-minute checks, during which time she liked or commented on at least one of her friends' posts.'

'Anyone she was interacting with more than others, Ewan?'

'Her inner circle seemed to be made up of Georgie Barclay, their mutual friend Hannah Grainger and Hannah's boyfriend Felix. He shares amusing videos he finds on YouTube and tags the others in them, which usually triggers the response.'

'Anything to suggest we should consider him a suspect?'

Freeborn shook his head. 'Based on his likes and recent comments I wouldn't say so. He's sixteen like Hannah and Georgie, and has continued to be active on social media since the disappearance. I wouldn't say there's been any change in his behaviour.'

'Why hasn't his name come up before?'

'Doesn't go to the girls' school, and is more of a friend of a friend than part of the social group, I guess. You want me to interview him?'

'It won't do any harm, but keep it light for now, and for God's sake, make sure his parents are present when you speak to him.'

'Still nothing happening with her bank account either, ma'am, or any debit card use,' Freeborn continued. 'If she has run away, someone must be housing and feeding her. I went back and in the two months leading up to Friday she'd only withdrawn thirty pounds in total, money her parents had transferred in around her birthday. Ten of it she withdrew on the Friday from an ATM in Portswood just before four, right before she met up with Alfie Caplan. I've checked the camera and she was alone at the ATM.'

It was the biggest indication that this was more than just a case of a girl who had run away from home. But if she hadn't, where was she now?

'Thanks, Ewan,' Kate concluded glumly. 'Laura, what did Georgie have to say when you caught up with her this afternoon?'

'Swears blind she's had no contact with Daisy since that night, and I'm inclined to believe her, ma'am. They were best friends, and if she was in trouble Georgie would have been the first person she'd reach out to.'

'Do me a favour, though: check Georgie's banking activity in the months prior to that night too. Let's just be certain someone else isn't financing this disappearance. Ewan, has Georgie's social media activity changed at all?'

'She's certainly been quieter, ma'am. Very active on the Saturday before she became aware of the disappearance, little on the Monday and Tuesday, but increasing on Wednesday and Thursday—'

'Why not say what's on everyone's minds?' DS Humberidge interrupted. 'It's time to start investigating a murder, not just a disappearance.'

Kate watched him carefully. She didn't want his negativity rubbing off on the rest of the team, but this could be an opportunity to silence his cynicism once and for all. 'Okay, Humberidge.

The stage is yours. Tell us why you're so convinced we're wasting our time.'

Every eye fell on him, but he didn't look concerned by the sudden attention. Pushing off from the desk, he straightened his tie and proceeded to the wallboard. 'Very well. Let's look at Val and Barry Emerson first. Barry's a former boxer – heavyweight – did a few semi-pro fights before he had to retire with a broken eye socket. Set up a business afterwards, restoring antique cars, but the business went bust eighteen months ago and they've been treading water since. Val works as a nail technician in a local salon, but her wages are barely enough to cover the mortgage payment.'

Kate frowned. 'And?'

'I'm not saying that's their motive, but with all the sudden media attention in the last week, and the offers of money for exclusive interviews, it couldn't have come at a better time for them financially. You're all thinking the same as me: if Daisy's alive, where the hell is she? She's fifteen, vulnerable, and from a stable home. How the hell is she going to survive on the streets alone? There's foul play here.'

'Is that all your theory is based on: money troubles and her vulnerability?'

He turned to face her. 'Let me look into them more deeply, then. That girl didn't run away, *ma'am*. In my opinion, someone's taken her and we're wasting valuable time because you refuse to accept it.'

'I remain open-minded as far as this investigation goes.'

He scoffed, as he made his way back to his space in the gathered crowd.

She should have taken him to one side and discussed the matter rationally and without prejudice. But she couldn't bite her tongue any longer. '*I've looked into Val's eyes*, and from one mother to another, I am *certain* she didn't kill Daisy. Until you've experienced the anguish of losing a child, you cannot begin to understand the emotional turmoil it takes.' Kate felt the burning in her cheeks and instantly regretted the outburst, even more so when she saw the open mouths and astonished faces of her team.

'Shall I go next?' Patel offered, keen to move proceedings forward.

Kate nodded for him to carry on.

'We interviewed Alfie Caplan earlier today,' Patel said, addressing the rest of the team. 'He has admitted to a disagreement between him and Daisy at the ice-cream parlour in Portswood, which corroborates what the waitress told us. Caplan wouldn't tell us what the disagreement was about, but we need to verify his alibi just in case. He claimed to be staying at his brother's place in Richmond, West London over that weekend. I agree with DI Matthews that Daisy couldn't have disappeared on her own. Someone must be helping her, and we need to narrow down who.'

'Might it be time for the Emersons to formally appeal to the press?' Laura suggested. 'I know they were at the original conference on Wednesday, but I wondered whether hearing them speak might encourage Daisy to come home.'

'Good idea,' Kate said, composing herself once more. 'I'll discuss it with the supe. Keep looking for her. I have no doubt Daisy is still out there, and it's up to us to find her and bring her home. Now, moving on to our second case. Olly, care to tell us what you've observed from the security tapes at the school where the foot was found?'

Quinlan stared down at his notes. 'I've got footage from the last week, and I'm working backwards from last night. I've been given a list of vehicles belonging to teachers and administrators at the school, so I won't cover those off specifically. The school operates a no-car zone for parents. There are two bus routes that pass the school, and parents aren't allowed to drive into the grounds. Those who insist on collecting their children by car must find one of the limited spaces on the residential streets on either side of the grounds. The hall in question is nowhere near either street, so it seems unlikely that the victim's body was forced over a side fence and then dragged to the sports hall.'

'Any unexpected vehicles on the Thursday or Friday?'

'So far, the Royal Mail van has stopped by twice, each at different times of the morning, but not unexpected. Then there's the works van belonging to Chris Jackson, the photocopy engineer. I'm following up with the school on that to see who called him and to check he was accounted for at all times.'

Kate nodded at Laura. 'Have you managed to get hold of Jackson himself?'

Laura shook her head. 'I've left messages, but no response yet. Uniform have visited his home address, which also serves as his business address, but no answer there either. He could be away for the weekend, ma'am.'

'Okay, keep trying. Sorry, Olly, please continue.'

'The gardener you met this morning – Neil Watkins? – his van arrives just after ten on both days, and leaves again before three. On Thursday afternoon, the school minibus collected and dropped off the football team who'd been playing away at Itchen College, and finally a van delivered food for the school dinners. It's a third-party contractor, which services a number of schools in the city. And finally, Liam Phillips from TUTD Surveyors was there for a couple of hours on Thursday morning.'

'And that's it?'

'Apart from the teachers' and administrators' cars.'

Kate looked at the rest of the team. 'Have we managed to make contact with all the teachers yet?'

'Most,' Patel confirmed, 'though Ismael Vardan wasn't home when we called.'

Kate narrowed her eyes. 'You're telling me the teacher previously accused of inappropriate behaviour with a pupil – and Daisy's tutor – can't be found?'

'You want me to have vehicle recognition search for him?' Patel said.

'I'd like to know where he is and what he's been up to. See what they can find, would you? Vicky, any progress on identifying the make of electric saw and how it was purchased?

Rogers brushed the hair from her eyes. 'We have narrowed it down to two models, but unfortunately it's one of the most popular brands on the market. It's available in all major retailers, and a dozen more online stores. I'll reach out to each for customer names and dates of purchase, but I think this line of enquiry will prove more beneficial when we know who our lead suspect is and can validate his purchase.'

'Do me a favour, get those lists and check it for the names of those we know were at the school: all the teachers, Phillips, Watkins and Jackson.' Kate again looked at each of her team. 'I know it's been a long day and there's nothing more exhausting than heading up blind alleys hunting for information, but all this legwork will pay off in the end. Daisy is still out there, as is the person who left us the foot. Together we will find them both. Overtime is available tomorrow for anyone who wants it.'

SEVENTEEN

Rain lashed against the windscreen as Kate pulled onto her road. After last night's late return and lack of sleep, she couldn't wait for her head to hit the pillow. It had been another tough day, with more questions raised than answered. But she was sure they were doing everything in their power to find Daisy.

Picturing her innocent face out there on a night like this sent a shiver down Kate's spine, suddenly reminding her of the tenderness of her shoulder. The tattoo artist had given her a tub of cream to use to smear over the image, to help it heal.

'You'll experience some skin irritation over the next few days,' she'd warned when she was done. 'But that's just the ink settling into your pores. You should be right as rain in about a week.'

Humberidge's attitude was another irritation she'd have to put up with. She could understand his cynicism; with thirty years in the force he'd seen more than his fair share of horrific crimes and supposedly innocent suspects, but then so had she. But that didn't mean he should question the direction of the investigation in the middle of a meeting. If he had concerns, the time to raise them would be privately, somewhere they could discuss and argue their points. But undermining her in front of the rest of the team was tantamount to mutiny.

Humberidge was from the DI Underhill ilk of police: assume everyone's guilty of the worst crimes until they prove otherwise. Whilst the approach had historically proved effective, there was no place for it in modern policing. With advances in technology, and information on police techniques readily available for all to find, the criminal mind was more advanced than it had ever been.

Kate was certain that Barry and Val Emerson genuinely didn't have any idea where their daughter was, but some of the points the team had made had planted seeds of doubt in her mind. Nobody had seen Daisy walking home, so there was a convincing argument that she hadn't walked home. But no witnesses had come forward to confirm they'd seen Daisy anywhere else either. When someone vanishes into thin air, was it wrong to assume the worst had happened? That someone had grabbed her from the streets?

But who?

Whilst Southampton suffered crime as much as any other major city outside of London, mindless abductions and murders weren't commonplace. But Kate knew better than anyone that serial killers did lurk in the shadows, as she'd experienced more than once.

Kate parked the Audi in her space, and climbed out, darting through the rain to the communal entrance to the small block of flats.

'Kate?' a voice called out from the shadow of a tree in the car park.

Turning and squinting into the darkness, Kate tried to make out who'd called to her, her heart racing at the possibility that Daisy had sought her out.

The figure of the young girl stepped into the light shining through the main door, an umbrella over her head, and a thin denim jacket over her shoulders. Kate continued to watch in shock as the figure moved towards her.

But as the girl reached the steps, Kate realised exactly who it was. 'Tara? What are you doing here?'

The girl's face was stained where her tears had run with her makeup. 'Can I come in?'

Glancing up at the heavy cloud overhead, Kate didn't think twice before opening the main door and heading up the flight of stairs to her flat on the first floor. Once inside, Kate switched on the central heating and set the kettle to boil, showing the supe's daughter through to the living room.

'Hang your jacket on the chair by the radiator,' Kate suggested. 'It'll dry quicker.'

The girl obliged, before edging to the sofa and perching on the end. 'I didn't know where else to go.'

Kate had first met Tara at the supe's birthday barbecue last summer. Only a select few of the team had been invited to the event, held on the expansive lawn behind the supe's house. It had been a beautiful Saturday afternoon, at the height of a long heatwave. The booze had flowed and the party had continued long into the night. It had been the first formal occasion Ben and Kate had appeared as a couple, and despite Kate's initial anxiety, nobody had batted an eyelid. The supe had even commented what a handsome pair they made.

And when Tara had stepped out of the house, resplendent in a faded yellow summer dress, beads around her neck and wrists – souvenirs from her recent holiday with friends on a Greek island – the supe was almost moved to tears as he told everyone that Tara had just been accepted to study medicine at Oxford University. It was a day when everything seemed possible, the horrors of their day jobs forgotten for just a few timeless moments.

Kate lowered herself onto the sofa next to the shivering girl. 'What's going on, Tara? Why are you here?'

'I didn't know where else to go. I'm sorry.' Fresh tears glistened from her cheeks.

'Whatever is the matter?'

But Tara didn't answer, burying her face in her hands.

'Has something happened? Is it your dad? Is everything okay?' Kate pressed, but this only brought more sobs.

Kate returned to the kitchen, as the kettle boiled and fixed two mugs of hot chocolate, adding extra sugar to both mugs, and locating a packet of chocolate digestives in the cupboard. She carried the items through on a tray, not sure how she would get through to the girl she barely knew.

Kate placed one of the mugs on the table nearest Tara, before offering her the packet of digestives. Tara slipped one of the biscuits from the packet and nibbled on it.

Kate retook her seat, sipping from the mug. 'I... I don't want to upset you, Tara, but you need to help me out. I feel like I ought to call your parents and—'

'No,' Tara suddenly interrupted. 'Please don't call them.'

Kate frowned. 'Why not? Have you had a fight with them...? Or... I don't know. I'm sorry, you need to give me something to work with here...'

Tara's brown locks, which were sodden from the rain outside, hung down almost to her waist, her frame slight, and deep brown pools for eyes. Kate could see why Daisy's disappearance was affecting the supe so much.

Tara straightened, closed her eyes and took a deep breath. 'I'm pregnant.'

Kate blinked several times, as she tried to process the information. 'You-you-you're pregnant?'

Tara's eyes remained closed, as if she couldn't bring herself to see the reaction in Kate's expression. 'I did a test.'

But Kate didn't react; she didn't know Tara well enough to express any real emotional response to the news. Her mind was stuck on asking why Tara had chosen to break the news to her.

'These tests can be wrong,' Kate offered, in an effort at reassurance.

Tara nodded, eyes still closed. 'That's why I did five. All positive.'

Kate knew she had to tread carefully here. 'I take it you haven't told your parents yet?'

Tara's eyes opened wide. 'Are you kidding? Can you imagine how my dad will react? You can't tell him, Kate. You have to promise me!'

Kate was taken aback by the outburst. 'Okay, I won't say anything, but you can't keep something like this from them. This really is something you should be discussing with them.'

'I only found out today. I'm not ready to tell them yet. I need to get my head around the news first.'

'Do you know who… I mean, does the father know yet?'

'It's nothing to do with him. It's my body and I need to work out what to do for the best.'

'I know, but this isn't a decision you should take lightly, and it isn't something you should decide without speaking to those involved and those who care for you the most.'

'You can't tell them, Kate.'

'I said I won't. But you can't keep something like this from him. Or your mum.'

'I'll tell them, but when *I'm* ready.'

Kate suddenly remembered the time. 'Where do they think you are now?'

'I told them I was going to stay with a friend, so they're not expecting me home. I don't suppose…?'

The last thing Kate wanted was to be caught in the middle of this drama, but she couldn't send Tara back out into the rain either. 'You can sleep in my daughter's bed. But tomorrow you need to speak to your parents.'

Tara reached out and pulled Kate into an uncomfortable embrace. 'I knew you'd understand. Dad always says how great you are. A real role model.'

Kate wasn't convinced the supe had ever described her in that way, but gently rubbed Tara's back, hoping Chloe would never feel too scared to tell her anything.

EIGHTEEN

NINE DAYS MISSING

'A package for me?' Kate murmured into the phone.

'Delivery driver says it's addressed to you specifically, care of this address,' the constable on the front desk replied. 'You want me to send it back?'

Kate nodded towards Patel who had just arrived in the incident room wrapped in a thick grey coat and dark scarf. He mimed the action for a drink and she thrust her thumb into the air. Although she'd already had two cups since she'd arrived just after six, she had a feeling it was going to be another long day.

'Who's it from?'

'There's no card with it. You want me to open it?'

Kate sighed, annoyed by the interruption. 'No, I'll come down. Tell the driver to wait.'

Kate hung up the phone, and made her way across to Patel.

'You're in early, ma'am,' he commented as the coffee machine whirred to life.

'Couldn't sleep,' she lied. 'I wanted to have another look at the statements we took from Daisy's teachers. I have a feeling there's something we're missing, but I can't put my finger on what.' She thanked him as he handed her over her mug. 'Be honest, Patel, do you think I'm wrong in treating this as just a runaway case? Do *you* think something bad may have happened to Daisy?'

He considered her for a moment. 'You're the one always telling us not to accept everything at face value and to explore *every* investigative lead. Humberidge is a pessimist, but there's some truth in his point worth exploring.'

'You think Val or Barry Emerson has killed her?'

'No... well, not necessarily them. But it just strikes me as odd that *nobody* has seen her since she left Georgie Barclay's house.'

'What about Alfie Caplan?'

'Honestly? No, I don't think he has it in him, but then nothing would surprise me these days.'

'If not the boyfriend, the best friend? Could Georgie Barclay be lying about when Daisy left her house?'

'We only have Georgie's word for it. Daisy was supposedly there from 6 p.m., but what if she didn't stay long, what if she didn't stay at all? Perhaps we should expand the current time window.'

'But her mobile phone signal has her in Abbotts Way until twenty past nine.'

'Maybe she left it with Georgie to throw us off the scent.'

Kate wasn't convinced. 'Doesn't explain why nobody's seen or heard from her since.'

'True.' Patel paused to sip his coffee. 'Back when I was just starting as a DC here, there was an incident where a teenage girl was grabbed on her way home from a pub. Not far from where Daisy was last seen, actually. We managed to trace the guilty party back then, and I'm not suggesting the same person is involved, but maybe an opportunist predator driving around saw her and attacked?'

'Would you mind following up on that for me? Check the open Missing Persons database and look for profiles similar to Daisy's: young and vulnerable.'

She headed for the door.

'You want me to prepare for the morning's brief?'

'I'll do it in a minute when I'm back.'

'Where are you going?'

'There's a package for me at the front desk, apparently.'

'Secret admirer?'

She grinned. 'Who knows? Let everyone know to wait for my return before getting on with their assignments.'

*
**

Kate hurried down the corridor, ignoring the lift and taking the stairs down to the ground floor. The constable she'd spoken to moments before buzzed her through to where the delivery driver was standing, bearing a brown cardboard box, big enough to hold something like a motorcycle helmet.

'I'm Kate Matthews,' she said, showing him her identification.

The guy looked barely old enough to drive, his cheeks brimming with acne and a wispy beard looking like a chin strap. 'I was supposed to deliver it yesterday, but my van broke down. Better late than never, huh?' He held the box out for her. 'I'll need you to sign for it.'

She rested the brown box on the counter and signed her name on the driver's digital pad. She watched him leave the building, climb into his van and drive away, before lifting the box and giving it a little shake.

It didn't weigh a lot, and whatever was inside rolled slightly as she moved it from side to side, and gave off a floral, fruity smell.

She smiled to herself. It had to be a gift from Ben. 'Can you pass me some scissors?' she asked the desk constable.

He did, and she cut through the parcel tape sealing the flaps of the box. She found a second box inside, this one wrapped in colourful wrapping paper: white with little pink hearts in glitter. Some of the glitter fell from the paper as she rested the second box on the desk.

'Someone has a secret admirer,' the desk constable teased. 'Is there a card?'

Oh Ben. The romantic fool didn't know what kind of trouble such a gesture could get her in. She did the maths in her mind, working backwards to try and calculate whether she'd missed a significant anniversary since they'd started dating, but came up with nothing.

Kate turned the box over in her hands. 'Doesn't look like it, but I think I know who it's from.' Reaching for the scissors again, she carefully cut through the Sellotape sealing the wrapping paper and slid out an old cardboard box which had once been used to hold packets of printing paper. The sickly-sweet scent of flowers and strawberries grew nauseating as she slowly began to lift the lid, the first tinge of dread trickling through her. She looked inside and dropped the box in horror.

NINETEEN

'Get SSD down here now,' Kate shouted at the constable.

He looked at her curiously. 'What is it?'

Kate stepped away, fighting the urge to bring up her breakfast.

'Just get them down here,' she managed to blurt, as she desperately tried to control her breathing.

'Okay, okay,' the desk constable replied, picking up the phone and dialling the extension. 'What should I tell them?'

Kate edged back towards the counter, daring herself to look again then reaching for a pair of latex gloves in a box on the desk. She took a deep breath before lifting the lid slightly once more. Nestled within the box, surrounded by stained rose and strawberry-scented car air fresheners, was a grey and shrivelled heart.

'Tell them someone has sent me a heart and that I need to know whether it's human.'

The desk constable leaned forward, not quite believing what he was being told, but as soon as he saw the greying tissue, he grabbed the phone and started repeating Kate's instructions.

Kate used a pen to prod the organ, and as she did, she noticed something scrawled on one of the strawberry-scented air fresheners. Careful not to disturb the organ, she lifted it out and read the message. '*I'm sorry.*'

***

Ben lowered his face mask. 'Well, it's definitely human.'

Kate took a step backwards, her worst fears confirmed. 'Can you tell when it was extracted?'

'Based on my initial observations, the lack of blood within it and its temperature, we're talking a few days, maybe a week since it stopped beating.'

Kate braced herself for the answer to her next question. 'Is it Daisy's?'

'I can say with one hundred per cent certainty it isn't.'

Kate breathed out a huge sigh of relief, but caught herself as the reality of what he was saying bubbled to the surface. 'So, if it's not Daisy's, is it a match to our foot victim?'

'No, it isn't. I've passed the bloodwork to SSD to process and compare against DNA profiles in the system, but in the meantime, I can tell you that it belonged to a man in his late thirties or early forties.'

'Male? How can you be so certain?'

'The size and mass are the clearest indicators. A woman's heart is about two-thirds the size of a man's, and as a result weighs an average sixty grams less. This particular heart came in at about 178 grams, which is pretty average for the sex. Then there are other tell-tale signs such as the thickness of the veins, and the sensitivity of those veins too. We're looking at a male heart for sure. Given the state of the tissue, there are preliminary signs of degradation, which led to my prediction of the age, but what's also interesting is this heart was once attached to a pacemaker.'

'A pacemaker.'

He nodded, stepping back to the table and lifting a flap of tissue. 'If you look here, you can see leads that were used to send electrical impulses to the heart muscle to maintain a suitable heart rate and rhythm. I would guess that your victim suffered with bradycardia: when the heartbeat is slower than normal.'

'But I thought pacemakers were something people had fitted after heart attacks and the like. You said he was a reasonably young man.'

'Of the pacemakers installed each year, the vast majority are fitted to those over the age of sixty-five as you observed, but a small percentage are also installed in younger people suffering with certain conditions. It will take further examination to determine exactly why the pacemaker was fitted in this individual, but it should certainly help narrow your list of possible victims.'

'But what does this mean? It seems too coincidental that a heart is sent to us in the same week we find a severed foot. Are they connected?'

He considered her question. 'Whoever extracted this heart from the victim didn't use surgical tools to do it. The vena cava, pulmonary arteries, and pulmonary trunk were cut using some kind of shearing instrument; maybe scissors? You can tell by the tear in the tissue. A scalpel would have left a different indentation. The reason we use scalpels for making cuts and incisions is they offer greater control and cause less damage to the tissue. Whoever made *these* cuts wasn't worried about preserving the organ for further study. It was quite heavy-handed, shall we say. Given the type of saw used to remove the foot, it's possible you could be looking for the same individual, but there is nothing concrete to tie them together.'

Kate pulled off her face mask as she headed for the door. 'Call me as soon as the bloods are done. And thank you.'

Kate paced in front of the gathered team of detectives who'd heard the rumour of what had been discovered and were eagerly awaiting confirmation.

'I want one of you at that delivery depot immediately,' Kate began, without breaking her stride. 'I want to know exactly who deposited that box with them. Get me any security footage they have too, because we need to nail the person responsible for this as soon as possible.'

DC Freeborn raised his hand. 'I'll go, ma'am.'

'Thanks, Ewan. Don't let them give you any shit about confidentiality laws, and don't tell them why we need the information. The last thing we want is this leaking to the press. And that goes for you lot as well. I know the local journos will pay through the teeth for something like this, but this one stays under wraps. Is that clear? If it gets out, someone will hang for it.'

Freeborn grabbed his coat and made for the door.

'The killer scrawled an apology,' Kate continued. 'It was written on a strawberry-scented car air freshener, identical to those we saw in the gymnasium on Friday night. These air fresheners are common, so I don't think we should waste too much time trying to identify where they were purchased. Kate stopped and fixed the room with a serious look. 'We have to act before this sicko gets a chance to strike again. It seems more than a little coincidental that the same rose and strawberry-scented air fresheners were used at the school and in this package. Let's not rule anything out, but I also want you to investigate any links between the crimes. This heart belonged to a male victim, the foot a female. How many other victims' body parts are going to turn up? *If* there is a new serial killer on our patch, we're not going to stop until we catch him.'

TWENTY

With everyone's duties assigned, Kate was about to log onto the Missing Persons database when her desk phone startled her.

'Matthews.'

'Ma'am, it's Jenson on the front desk again—'

'Tell me there isn't another delivery,' she interrupted, her shoulders tensing.

'Not exactly. There's a young man down here, wanting to speak to you. He says he's Daisy Emerson's brother.'

Kate had yet to meet Richard Emerson as he was away at university but she had seen pictures of him in the family home, and Val had mentioned that they'd told him to stay where he was and concentrate on his studies. Kate had been meaning to send one of her team down to Exeter to speak to him, but there hadn't been time yet. Looking around the office, the team all seemed busy.

'Can you put him in the soft interview room and I'll be down in a minute.'

Locking her screen, Kate fixed two coffees, and headed down the stairs.

Richard Emerson wasn't what she expected. In the photograph she'd seen of him, he'd had big stocky arms and shoulders, thick, curly hair and an early onset middle-aged paunch. But the young man perched on the edge of his seat was trim with shaved, short hair; gone was the excess weight around his face and neck, and there were defined muscles beneath his shirt. Here was a young man who looked like he'd spent a lot of time in the gym.

Kate placed the mugs on the table between them, and offered her hand. 'I'm Detective Inspector Kate Matthews. You must be Richard?'

He leaned forward and shook her hand, his palm clammy.

'Are you just back from uni for the weekend?' Kate asked.

When he spoke, Kate could hear the raw emotion in his voice. 'My professor told me I should come home and be with Mum and Dad.'

Sensing his anxiety, Kate said, 'Remind me, Richard, what are you studying?'

'Computer Science.'

'At Exeter University, right?'

'Yeah, I'm in my final year.'

'And what next when you graduate?'

'I've got a post-graduate internship lined up with IBM.'

'Your mum and dad must be thrilled!' She paused. 'How are they coping?'

He looked away. 'How do you think? They're devastated. They just want Daisy home. We all do.'

'As do I, and my whole team are working non-stop to bring her back, I assure you.'

'But what are you lot actually doing?'

Kate had expected him to be upset – given the circumstances anyone would be – but she hadn't anticipated anger. 'We are appealing for witnesses who may have seen where Daisy went—'

'Don't be ridiculous! My sister didn't run away from home. Why can't you lot see that?'

Kate kept her tone even in an effort to diffuse his anger. 'We are exploring *every* possibility.'

'Bollocks! It's obvious what happened, why won't you just admit it?'

Kate narrowed her eyes. 'What exactly do you think has happened to your sister?'

'It's obvious! Some dirty paedo has snatched her. You'd be better off rounding up all the perverts on the sex offenders register and checking where they were that Friday night. You'll soon find out which of them snatched her.'

'I'm sorry, Richard, but we have no reason to believe any kind of sex-motivated crime has—'

'Don't give me that! You read about it in the papers all the time. I get that you don't want to say it in front of my parents, but I can take it. She's dead, isn't she?'

The question threw Kate. 'What on earth makes you think—'

'Common sense. I know she wouldn't run away; she was a good girl who worked hard and kept out of trouble. I spoke to her on the Wednesday before… and there was no way she was planning to run away. And nobody has heard hide nor hair of her for over a week, so what other conclusion is there?'

'In my experience, these situations are never as simple as they first appear.' He was about to interrupt her again, but she raised her hand to cut him off. 'I will not believe that your sister is dead until I have incontrovertible proof. Every day my team move closer to discovering what happened.'

He shook his head with an angry smirk. 'You're kidding yourself if you think you'll ever find her.'

Kate didn't like where the conversation was headed, but she wouldn't allow herself to return his volleys of anger. He was grieving.

'You and Daisy were close, right? So, you probably know more of what was going on in her head in the days leading up to her disappearance. What did the two of you discuss when you spoke on the Wednesday?'

'I don't know… I can't remember.'

'Did you call her, or did she call you?'

'I called her. There's a band she really likes, and they just announced they're going to do a gig down in Exeter. I phoned her to let her know that I was going to buy her a ticket for her birthday. I figured she could catch a train down, I'd meet her at the station, we'd go to the gig and then she could crash in my room before catching the train home the next day.'

'That's sweet. How did she react to the news?'

'She was excited. She asked whether I could get a ticket for her friend Georgie too, and that she'd get Georgie to pay me back. I said that was fine, and she could give the money to Daisy to pass on.'

'And Daisy didn't say she was unhappy about anything? Or give you reason to believe she was upset?'

'No. She was her usual self. In fact, she was even more excited than usual because of the birthday present. That's what I'm telling you: there's no way she would have run away.'

'Did she hint that anything might be wrong between her and her boyfriend Alfie?'

He paused and watched her. 'No. Why? What's *he* got to do with this?'

'Nothing, we don't think. But a witness in a café said she saw them arguing on the afternoon she disappeared. We're trying to determine what the argument was about, but Alfie's not saying.'

The anger boiled in his eyes. 'You think he hurt my sister?'

Kate widened her own eyes. 'No. But we want to establish whether the argument could be a contributing factor to her running away. I take it you're not Alfie's biggest fan?'

He snorted. 'She could do so much better than that lowlife.'

'Why do you say that?'

'It's not right, is it? An eighteen year old dating a fifteen year old. He's got no prospects, and he's just going to end up holding her back. She'd be better off getting rid and concentrating on her studies. She has her GCSEs to sit in a couple of months.'

Kate was relieved he'd stopped referring to his sister in the past tense, though she wasn't sure how long the resolve would hold out. 'Was Daisy sleeping with Alfie?'

The question was raised innocently, but it pushed Richard over the edge. 'I told you: she was a good girl. She wasn't stupid enough to sleep with him. Wait, do you know something I don't? Was he forcing her to have sex?'

Kate quickly backtracked. 'No. There's nothing to suggest—'

'That's rape, though, isn't it? If he pressured her to have sex, as a minor, that's rape. Why haven't you arrested him?'

'Calm down, Richard. I was merely asking. We haven't been told that your sister is sexually active, I just thought she might have confided in you, her big brother.'

'If he laid a hand on her, I'll—'

Kate raised both palms in a calming gesture. 'Whoa there, I don't want you going anywhere near Alfie Caplan. The last thing your parents need is you getting yourself into trouble with the police. Let *us* handle the investigation.' She pushed the spare mug of coffee towards him. 'Have a drink and calm down.'

But he wasn't listening, brushing the mug away with the back of his hand, so it hurtled into the wall where it smashed in an explosion of light brown liquid. 'Why haven't you lot done one of those *Crimewatch* reconstructions yet? You want to appeal for witnesses? Then get my sister's story on the television.'

Kate looked at the mess on the wall, and took a deep breath. 'We're considering all of our options.'

Richard stood, sending his chair crashing into the wall behind him. 'If you lot won't do what is necessary, I'll do it myself.'

Kate was on her feet in a second, her voice loud and firm. 'I understand you're worried, but if you do something that inter- feres with this investigation, I won't hesitate to arrest you. Am I making myself clear? Leave this to the professionals, and we will find out what has happened to Daisy.' She exhaled, lowering her voice. 'Would you like me to arrange for someone to give you a lift home?'

He moved away, yanking open the door. 'I can look after myself.'

Kate hurried after him, but he wasn't willing to speak to her, banging the door impatiently until the desk constable buzzed him out. Kate watched as Richard slipped out of the station and down the stairs, fearing this wouldn't be the last she would hear from him.

TWENTY-ONE

'You wanted to see me?' Kate asked, poking her head around the lab door.

'Come in, come in,' Ben ushered, lowering his face mask.

'Do you need me to change?' Kate asked, pointing at her unprotected clothing.

'No, the foot is away.'

Kate continued further into the laboratory. 'What is it about?'

'Xander Garcia phoned me back after his conference, and we think we may have something else to help you.'

Kate looked casually around the room for a computer screen. 'Is he…?'

'No, no.' He looked at his watch. 'He'll probably be fast asleep as we speak. No, it's just me here.'

'Okay, so what have you got for me?'

'Based on the tests Xander proposed, I estimate the victim was aged in her early to mid-twenties, but I now believe the blistering I mentioned to you yesterday *wasn't* caused by sudden sporting activity, instead an extended period on her feet in uncomfortable shoes.'

Kate considered the statement. 'There's evidence to suggest she may have been a prostitute. That tattoo scarring you found links to a crew operating out of St Mary's. I take it you haven't found our killer's DNA or can give me any clue what he might have done with the rest of the victim's body?'

He shook his head sadly. 'Sorry.'

Kate dangled her notebook. 'Not to worry, I'm sure this will help. Thanks, Ben.'

Kate returned to the incident room and was writing Ben's findings on the board when DC Freeborn hurried into the office.

'Ma'am? Can I have a word?' he asked.

Kate returned the lid to the pen and followed him down to the viewing suite, where he was inserting a DVD into the machine. Four security feeds appeared in each corner of the screen, showing different angles of the parcel delivery depot. 'You found who left the heart?' she said, the excitement rising in her voice.

'Not exactly.' He paused the playback, and offered her a sheet of paper. 'This is a print out from their system showing the name and address details provided by the person who deposited the box, however, as you'll see, he's given what I can only presume are fake credentials.'

Kate read the page. 'Joe Bloggs. Is this a joke?'

Freeborn shook his head. 'Apparently, they don't ask to see identification for deposits, only collections. I asked the guy on the counter if he remembered who left this particular box, but he said he sees hundreds of faces every day and hundreds of boxes so has no memory of who left it.'

'And this address?'

'Is just around the corner from the depot, so I decided to stop by there on my way back: it's a library. Best guess is the killer walked past the library on his way into the depot and clocked the address. Their computer system searches for addresses from postcodes, and the customer is then asked to confirm which number. It wouldn't be too difficult to find the library's postcode online.'

'Didn't they question it when he gave them the library's address?'

He shook his head. 'The guy I spoke to said as long as the computer doesn't flag the address as incorrect, they don't ask any further questions.'

Kate's frustration was growing. 'They didn't mind you taking their security footage with you?'

'They ran me off a copy,' he said, starting the player again. 'Not that it's going to be any use. Here we have the view of four of the firm's cameras. They have twelve in total around the site, the majority of which are out the back watching their employees, rather than the desk. Apparently, they had a spate of thefts last year and so they set up the additional cameras to catch the employee responsible. They got him in the end, but the site manager is still paranoid about someone else repeating the offence. So, anyway, the twelve cameras go to one box in his office, but are on a loop.' The four images on the screen changed to four new locations. 'Each rotation lasts approximately thirty seconds, before switching.' He paused the playback. 'Note the timestamp in the bottom corner. According to the print out, our perpetrator deposited the parcel at 11:01 yesterday morning. The image in the top left corner is the main door to the collections office, and the one next to it is the counter.'

He started the playback, Kate's eyes darting from the time-stamp to the two images at the top of the screen. Just as the clock changed to 11:01, she saw the door to the room opening, but in that moment, four new images appeared on screen.

'The rotation of camera views occurs at zero, thirty, and sixty seconds into the minute.' He skipped the playback through the next rotation, slowing it as the clock turned to 11:02.

Kate stared at the two top images as they changed back to the front door and desk. 'Wait, where is he? The room is empty.'

Freeborn pointed at the bottom left image. 'You can just see the guy on the counter carrying the box out back. He's gone.'

'Gone where?'

Freeborn shrugged apologetically. 'He had a sixty-second window to get in and out of the office before the camera returned to him.'

'Sixty seconds isn't long. How did he manage to give all his details in that time?'

'He pre-booked it online. Then all he needed to do was go in, give his order number and leave the item.'

'So, this footage is—'

'Pretty useless, ma'am.'

Kate's head dropped. 'I don't suppose they have a camera in their car park?'

'They do, but it's part of the same loop. In the thirty-second view of the car park leading up to his entrance, no new cars arrive, and none leave when the view returns. That's why I think he arrived on foot. The Bitterne train station is only a five-minute walk away, and there are multiple bus routes passing the library too. I've already contacted the bus company and station to see what feeds they can give us. Waiting for a call back, but thought I should get this here for logging.'

'So, somehow our suspect managed to avoid detection when depositing the box.' Kate stood, keen to sustain his motivation despite the lack of usable footage. 'Can you keep me posted about what the public transport people say?'

Ejecting the DVD and returning it to its case, Freeborn nodded.

TWENTY-TWO

Kate called Patel over as she returned to the incident room and took a seat. 'Ben says we're looking for a woman in her early to mid-twenties. And our tattoo artist tells us she had fair hair and possibly worked as a prostitute out of St Mary's at one point or another. Why did he target her?'

'Maybe he was one of her punters?'

'Maybe. Did he target her because she was vulnerable or because she was a prostitute? Or did he happen to see her walking and pounced opportunistically?'

'And what did he do with the rest of her body?'

Kate sighed, pulling out her phone as it beeped in her pocket. Opening the message, she quickly stood and moved away from Patel. She hurried to the safety of the bathroom, before daring to read the message. It was from Tara, thanking Kate for putting her up for the night, and advising that she was heading home to face the music. Kate was tempted to remind Tara not to mention her own involvement, but settled for a 'Good luck'.

Kate's mind was racing, as she retook the seat next to Patel.

'I keep asking myself what would drive Daisy to run away, assuming that's what happened. We've exhausted the possibility that she was unhappy with her life. Every friend and teacher we spoke to said she's an intelligent and well-liked girl. Even her brother couldn't give any insight into what would have made her want to run away.'

'I'm the last person who can offer an insight into the mind of a teenage girl.'

Kate thought about the message she'd just received, and how terrified Tara had been last night. She'd said the words before she could stop herself. 'What if Daisy was pregnant?' she whispered to him.

He mouthed the word 'pregnant' back to check he hadn't misheard, and she nodded quickly. 'If she was too scared to tell her parents what had happened, or even her best friend, what does she do? Under pressure to pass her exams, but not wanting an abortion.'

Patel frowned. 'I think you're reaching, ma'am. We have Caplan on record saying he wasn't sleeping with her, and none of her friends, teachers or family have even hinted at the possibility. I know you're desperate to figure out where she's gone, but I think that's too big a leap, even for your instincts.'

She knew he was right, and had virtually dismissed the idea the moment she'd said it, but even so, it had triggered something in her mind. 'Think about it: she's fifteen, so if it was revealed that she *was* pregnant, her boyfriend Alfie would be in trouble with us, she'd be terrified of messing up her academic potential, and the possible shame it would bring on her family. I'm not saying Barry or Val wouldn't have supported her, but at that age, you assume the worst, right? I don't know, maybe I am just seeing links where there aren't any.'

'I suppose that could explain what the argument with Caplan was about earlier in the afternoon. And the reason why he didn't want to tell us what they'd been arguing about.'

'Of course. He's eighteen, and she's only fifteen, but he expects us to believe that they weren't sleeping together.'

'But something that big? You really think she wouldn't have told anybody?'

Kate narrowed her eyes. 'Georgie Barclay is her best friend; there's no way she could have kept it a secret from her.'

'You want me to come with you?' Patel asked, already knowing where Kate's next stop would be.

'No, you keep reviewing our Missing Persons and see if you can find any links between them. It'll be easier if I speak to Georgie alone.'

*
**

Kate couldn't ignore the fact that her recent experiences with Tara were what was driving this new line of enquiry. But there was some relief in the possibility it might have been the reason Daisy had run away from home.

Kate had yet to meet Georgie Barclay, or her parents, and she wasn't sure calling round unexpectedly on a Sunday afternoon was the best way to endear herself, but she couldn't waste any more time. Kate was certain Georgie wouldn't open up with her parents around, so would need to find a way to get her alone for an off-the-record chat. If anything came of it, she would arrange for Patel or Laura to take a formal statement.

Kate was just pulling up at the kerb when the front door to the Barclay house flew open and Georgie emerged, pulling a dark hoodie around her shoulders.

'I'm going out,' Georgie shouted as she stomped down the path to the small wooden gate.

A harassed looking woman wearing an apron appeared at the door a moment later. 'What time will you be home? For dinner?'

Georgie paused long enough to scowl back at her. 'I'll be back when I'm back. Stop fussing.'

The woman, whom Kate guessed was Mrs Barclay – Georgie's mother – looked like she wanted to say something else, but gave up and went inside as Georgie disappeared out of earshot.

Edging the car forward, Kate couldn't believe her luck as she wound the window down as she arrived at Georgie's side. 'You want a lift somewhere?' she asked, holding her identification out so Georgie knew she wasn't a threat.

'I'm supposed to be meeting someone,' Georgie countered, without dropping her pace.

'You wouldn't be meeting up with Daisy, would you?'

Georgie stopped still. 'Do you really think if I knew where she was, I wouldn't have told her mum and dad?'

'Where are you off to in such a hurry, then? Come on, Georgie, we both know there's something you've been keeping from my team. Get in now and tell me and then I'll drop you wherever you're going. What do you say?'

Georgie didn't move.

'Alternatively, I can go back and drag your parents down to the police station with us, which I'm sure is the last thing they want to do on a Sunday afternoon.' Kate softened her tone. 'Please, Georgie, I just want to talk off the record.'

Georgie rolled her eyes before opening the door and climbing in. 'Fine. I don't know what else you think I can tell you.'

Kate pulled away from the kerb, keen to put some distance between them and the house. 'You going somewhere nice?' Kate tried, keen to establish an open conversation.

Georgie shrugged, focusing on the raindrops starting to catch on the window.

'It looked like your mum was baking something.'

Another shrug.

'Do you bake?'

'No.'

'Me neither. I tried a couple of times when I was younger, but just couldn't get the hang of it. I think people either can or they can't.'

Georgie remained silent.

Kate needed a way to get through to her, but engaging with teenagers was not one of her strengths. 'I bet you're missing Daisy.'

Still no response, but Georgie's hand shot up to her face as she discreetly tried to wipe away a tear.

'Have you two been friends for long?'

'Forever,' she said, her voice cracking under the strain.

'I'm sorry, Georgie, you must be just as terrified for her. How are you coping?'

Georgie shrugged again.

Kate sighed loudly. 'I wish I knew what had triggered her to run away like that. It just seems so out of character. If only we knew why she went, it might help us find her.' Keeping her eyes on the road, Kate glanced occasionally in the rear-view mirror to see Georgie's expression. 'I'm sure you feel the same.'

'I just want her home,' Georgie admitted, wiping a second tear from her face.

'I know you've already given us a statement about that night, but is there *anything* else that you've remembered? Did Daisy give *any* clue that she was planning to run away? Anything at all?'

'No.'

'And you don't know where she would go if something was troubling her?'

'Her brother's, maybe.'

'No, we've spoken to him and he's as worried as you are.' Kate sighed audibly again. 'I just worry that she's out there all alone in danger. Was there anything playing on her mind? Were things between Daisy and Alfie okay?'

Georgie fired Kate a look. 'Ask him, how would I know?'

'You were her best friend, right? Did the two of you not talk about things like that?'

Georgie hesitated. 'Of course, b-but there isn't anything wrong between them. She loves him.'

'I still remember the first boy I fell for. Do you have a boyfriend, Georgie?'

'No. Not at the moment.'

Was that a hint of jealousy? Kate couldn't be sure. 'My first boyfriend turned out to be a bit of a snake, actually. All the time I thought he was the one, it turned out he was carrying on with a friend behind my back. I was probably about your age. All I'm saying is, you have plenty of time before you start worrying about those things.'

Georgie's gaze was on the window again. 'I'm not worried.'

'Good. Quite right. And Daisy wasn't worried about Alfie? We've been told they argued earlier that day. Did Daisy mention the argument to you?'

'No.'

'Do you think whatever they argued about caused her to run away?'

'Look, I don't know why she ran away, okay?' Georgie suddenly blurted, startling Kate.

'I'm sorry to keep asking the same question, but if I'm to stand any chance of bringing her home, I need to understand why she left. At the moment, the only thing that seems to have been out of place in her life was that argument with Alfie. Do you know him well?'

Georgie was glaring at Kate. 'No... what I mean is, I knew him through Daisy, that was all.'

'Do you know if they were sleeping together?'

'What? No.'

'Are you sure? I know she is only fifteen, but he's older and—'

'They weren't sleeping together!'

'How can you be so certain?'

'I just am, okay?'

'She would have told you?'

'Yeah.'

'So, it's unlikely she was pregnant then?'

Georgie snorted. 'You're kidding, right?'

'I promise, what you tell me now won't go any further, but I need you to help me.'

'I'm not lying! Daisy didn't want to have sex with Alfie; she was saving herself. She liked Alfie, and she liked the attention he gave her, but she didn't think she loved him. She thought she was too young to understand her feelings, so wanted to keep things relaxed with him.'

'And he was happy with that? At eighteen, his hormones must be running riot.'

Georgie's attention returned to the window. 'You'd have to ask him about that, but trust me when I say she wasn't sleeping with him, and she wasn't pregnant.' Georgie's attention was diverted by a text message, to which she quickly replied. 'Listen, I've told you everything I know. You can drop me here and I'll make my own way back.'

'I thought you were meeting someone.'

She lifted her phone. 'Not anymore.'

'Then let me drop you back home. It's raining and so cold, and—'

'Thanks, but I'd rather walk.'

Kate indicated and pulled over when it was safe to do so, and watched Georgie as she left the car and walked off into the distance, her head dipped. She was sure there was still more going on, but couldn't put her finger on what.

TWENTY-THREE

'Georgie swears she couldn't have been pregnant,' Kate whispered to Patel, when she was back in the office.

'Well, that's something, I suppose,' he muttered.

As a mother, Kate could understand how difficult Patel had to be finding the investigation, given he was a father of two young daughters. 'You okay, Patel? I can get someone else on this if it helps?'

He glanced over, appreciating the offer. 'Thanks, ma'am, but I'm okay.'

Kate smiled, he was always a professional to the end. 'Well, if that changes, you know where I am.' Kate answered the desk phone on the second ring. 'Matthews.'

'Come to my office immediately,' the supe said firmly, a command, rather than a request.

What now? she wondered.

Unless…

Kate felt for the phone in her pocket. Nothing new from Tara.

'Supe wants an update on the case,' Kate advised Patel as casually as she could muster, before standing and heading to his office.

Taking a deep breath, she knocked twice, and entered. The supe sat with his back to her as she closed the door. 'You wanted to see me, sir?'

He swivelled his chair around, and blinked as if trying to remember why he had summoned her. He looked terrible; his tie had been pulled down and the top button of his shirt unfastened. 'Ah, Kate, I wanted to check on your progress. I have a meeting with the chief super in half an hour.'

He didn't look himself, and Kate knew it was wrong to pry, but she just couldn't help herself. Sitting down across from him, she tried a tentative, 'Is everything okay, sir?'

He looked startled, then relived. 'Is it that obvious?'

'I wouldn't be much of a detective if I couldn't spot it. You can tell me to mind my own business if—'

'My daughter,' he interrupted matter-of-factly.

Kate tried to rearrange her face to disguise how much she already knew. 'What about her?'

'Oh it's… it's nothing. Forget I said anything.'

'I think we've known each other long enough to know that what is said in this office stays in this office.'

He narrowed his eyes. 'You'll learn soon enough how challenging teenage girls can be. Your daughter is a picture of innocence now, but just wait, as soon as she becomes interested in boys and growing up, that will all change.'

Kate swallowed audibly. 'Has something happened to your daughter, sir?'

'I shouldn't be burdening you with my personal problems.'

'I wouldn't have asked if I didn't care, sir. A problem shared…'

'If only it were that simple.' He sighed again, this time deeper and longer. 'I think the pressure of exams and leaving for university has been taking its toll. On us, as well as Tara. Things at home have been… difficult recently and then she left the house last night, without a word of where she was going. Judith – my wife – and I were awake until the early morning waiting to hear whether she'd come home… and then she messaged just after nine this morning to say she'd been staying at a friend's house.'

Kate could feel her cheeks reddening. Tara had lied to her; her parents had no idea she wouldn't be home. 'At least she was safe; all's well that ends well. I'm sure she'll come home with her tail between her legs when she realises how much worry she's caused you.'

He nodded towards the phone. 'My wife just phoned. Tara *is* home, but they've just had a blazing row about her not calling. With everything going on with the Daisy Emerson disappearance… well, it's difficult not to overreact.'

'Does Tara have a boyfriend at all? I mean, maybe she was staying with him.'

But the supe shook his head. 'She isn't interested in boys… not like that, anyway. I mean, she's had boyfriends before, but she's focused on going away to university and doesn't want to commit to a relationship when Oxford is so close.'

Kate clenched her teeth to keep her mouth shut, wondering how much Tara had actually confessed to Judith during the row.

'I'm sorry, Kate,' the supe offered, 'I can see how uncomfortable this is making you. I'm sure everything will work out for the best, like you said. Back to business: you were going to update me on your progress with the Emerson case?'

Kate couldn't hide her relief that he wanted to change the subject. She was about to speak when a knock at the door interrupted her.

'Enter,' the supe declared, straightening his tie, suddenly aware of himself again.

The door opened and DI Naomi Hendrix peered around it. 'You wanted to see me, sir? I can come back if —'

'Please come in, Naomi. This concerns you, too.'

Hendrix closed the door and took up the seat next to Kate. Neither woman acknowledged the other. Although both reported in to the supe, it wasn't often that their paths crossed, but when they had in the past, it hadn't gone well. Hendrix's parents had escaped apartheid and moved to the UK when she was only four; her stunning looks and short cropped hair perfectly shaped her formidable attitude. Hendrix had a reputation as a tough-talking and committed copper, but it didn't make her less-than-affable attitude any easier to live with.

'DI Matthews is looking for a girl – a prostitute – working one of your patches,' the supe said. 'Kate?'

Kate resigned herself to the ambush. 'She is aged between twenty and thirty, fair haired, and had some kind of scorpion tattoo on her lower leg. We believe she worked the St Mary's patch, but her foot was found severed in a room covered in blood-spattered plastic.'

Hendrix turned to face her, studying Kate's features for cracks as she pulled out her own notebook and made a show of noting down the information. 'I'll speak to my team,' she said, her voice showing no emotion. 'Branding isn't uncommon in that neck of the woods. Can you describe the tattoo to me?'

'It was removed in the last week. I can show you the parts of it we've managed to identify, but—'

Hendrix suddenly looked up. 'It was removed?'

Kate nodded. 'By laser, according to the pathologist.'

'If it had been removed that would suggest she'd bought her freedom. Leave it with me. I'll find you a name.'

Kate was taken aback by the lack of argument or disagreement. 'Uh, thanks.'

The supe clapped his hands together. 'Splendid. If you would both excuse yourselves now, I'm expecting a call from the chief.'

Following Hendrix out of the door, Kate hurried to catch up with her. 'Hey, Hendrix, I just wanted to say thank you for not challenging me in there.'

Hendrix paused and turned to face Kate. 'No matter what I think of you as a person, if some sicko out there is attacking the ladies on my patch, then I will do everything in my power to stop him. Fair enough?'

Kate was about to nod her acknowledgement when Patel came bounding down the corridor. 'Ma'am, thank God. It's Daisy's Facebook profile: someone just accessed it.'

TWENTY-FOUR

All eyes fell on Kate as she burst into the Incident Room. 'Talk to me, people. Where is she?'

'Working on it now, ma'am,' DC Freeborn said, a phone pressed firmly to his ear.

Kate headed to the board so all the team could see and hear. 'Tell me how it happened.'

Laura stepped forward. 'I took the call from the Emersons. They'd been phoned by a friend of Daisy's asking them if she was now back home. Long story short, the caller told them that Daisy had just liked one of her Facebook posts, which is what had made her think Daisy was back.'

'Who was the caller?'

'Hannah Grainger, ma'am, a friend of Daisy's.'

'And it was her post that was liked? What did the post say?'

'It was an image of Hannah, Daisy and Georgie, taken about a year ago. Hannah had uploaded it with a message saying, "Missing You x", and approximately ten minutes later Daisy liked the post.'

'She didn't comment, just liked it?'

'That's right, ma'am.'

Kate made eye contact with each member of the team. 'This could be the confirmation we've been searching for that Daisy *is* still alive, and is trying to, or is ready to communicate. Did she like anything else while she was logged in?'

Laura looked over at Freeborn, who was in deep conversation with someone on the phone. 'As soon as the call came in, I told

Ewan, ma'am, and he loaded up Daisy's profile, but it doesn't look like she did anything else. He's now talking to the UK-based office for the website, trying to get more detail.'

'Why weren't we aware of this sooner? It doesn't look good when we have to rely on the victim's parents to supply us with news. We need to be better than this.' Kate paused. She hadn't meant to take out her frustrations on the team. As she looked at each one of them, she couldn't escape how tired they all looked; each had put in way over their contracted hours to progress the investigation.

'We don't know for certain that Daisy accessed her own profile,' Humberidge sneered. 'For all we know her abductor is just toying with us.'

Kate had wanted to raise the possibility more sensitively. 'Humberidge makes a fair point,' Kate said evenly, taking a mental note to speak to him about his tone in meetings. 'For all we know, Daisy wasn't the one to like the post. We need to identify where the profile was accessed from and narrow down exactly who is responsible. Hopefully, it will be Daisy and we'll have great news to share with the Emersons, but let's not get ahead of ourselves.'

Kate dismissed them with a nod, and made her way to Freeborn's desk, hovering over his computer as he spoke on the phone. Taking his mouse, she scrolled across Hannah Grainger's page, opening the photo of the three girls and studying it for any clue as to why Daisy had chosen to like it now.

The girls were dressed in their school uniform – navy blue skirt and blazer, with paler blue blouse – but it must have been taken later in the day, as Daisy had removed her blazer and tied the ends of her shirt in a fifties-style knot. The girls were grinning inanely, clearly enjoying the moment. Daisy was in the middle of the two other girls, and Hannah was the one holding the selfie stick. Kate couldn't escape how similar the three girls looked. Beneath the photo, Daisy was listed as liking the image at 18:45.

'They've put me on hold,' Freeborn said, lowering the phone.

'What are they saying? Can they confirm if Daisy accessed the profile, or someone else?'

'They've confirmed that her email address and password were used to access her profile, but they are currently looking for the IP address. That should confirm whether she used her phone to access the profile or whether it was a computer terminal.'

Kate clicked her fingers at DC Quinlan. 'Olly, get on to the mobile provider and find out if Daisy's phone is switched on, or has been in the last hour.'

He offered her a thumbs up in response, putting the phone to his ear.

'The IP address should also narrow down the location of where the profile was accessed too. That should tell us what part of Southampton she's in.'

'Keep on at them. This could be the breakthrough we've been waiting for, Ewan.'

He raised the receiver as the hold music ended, and Kate walked away from his desk, collecting her coat and car keys and calling Patel over. 'I'd better go and visit the Emersons. They're going to want to know what's going on.'

'You want support?'

She patted his arm in thanks. 'This is something I'd better do alone.'

Kate noticed a difference in Val Emerson the moment she opened the door. Gone were the tears, the aching heart and eyes that begged for positivity. In their place was excitement, hope and anticipation. Kate didn't want to be the one to temper it, but she didn't want to encourage false hope.

'Can I come in?' Kate asked.

Val stepped to one side, and indicated for Kate to enter, but at the last minute pulled Kate into an uncomfortable hug, whispering, 'I knew she was still alive.'

Kate followed Val to the living room, and it soon became clear that Barry Emerson hadn't taken the news as well. He paced the room extinguishing one cigarette and lighting another without missing a step.

'Would you like a cup of tea, detective?' Val asked, encouraging her to take a seat.

Kate thanked her, suddenly realising how thirsty she was and following Val out to the kitchen, eager to get away from the cigarette smoke. 'Val, before—'

'Do you take milk and sugar?'

'Milk, no sugar, thanks.' Kate watched Val as she busied herself, moving to the fridge and removing the milk, pouring it into the cups, and then shuffling back to the fridge. 'Val, please, there's something I need to—'

'I'll just go and see if Barry wants a drink too,' Val interrupted, heading back into the living room and returning a moment later.

Kate continued to watch her, knowing that Val was stalling the awkward conversation Kate was trying to start. She eventually sat down at the table across from Kate, placing a chipped mug in front of her.

Kate reached out and placed her hand on top of Val's. 'There's something you need to consider, Val.'

Val pulled her hand away and was on her feet, heading for the cupboard. 'I forgot to offer you a biscuit.'

'Please, I know you don't want to hear what I have to say, but I wouldn't be doing my job properly if I didn't. Please sit down and let me finish.'

Val remained where she was, her back to Kate and the biscuit tin in her hand.

'I desperately hope that it *was* Daisy who went online this evening,' Kate began, willing Val to turn and retake her seat. 'But there is a possibility that it wasn't Daisy. I want you to be prepared in case that happens to be the situation.'

Val remained facing the cupboard, her shoulders slightly dipped. 'Don't be ridiculous. 'Course it was her. Who else would know her email address and password?'

'My team are working to confirm where the site was accessed from and that should put us a step closer to finding out whether it was, in fact, Daisy. We won't stop until we know for certain.'

'Why you got to go and say something like that? This is the best news we've had since… since that awful night, and now you want to pour water on it.'

Kate's heart ached as she spoke. 'That's not what I'm doing, Val. I'm trying to prepare you for the worst, in case things don't turn out as we all hope.'

Val spun round, tears ready to spill from her eyes. 'Why would you wish that upon us? Don't you believe that if you think positively, positive things will come to you? Think the worst and you'll bring trouble to your door. That's what my mum always used to say.'

Kate's mother had preached the same, but Kate had witnessed too much pain and suffering on the job to believe in the power of positive thought.

'Once we know the IP address that accessed the account, we should be able to pinpoint the location, and then it's a matter of looking for any security camera footage and witnesses. As with everything else it should put a step closer to the truth of what happened that night.'

'Everything okay, Mum?' Richard Emerson asked, standing at the kitchen door behind Kate.

Val wiped her eyes with a tissue and forced as big a smile as she could manage. 'The detective was just telling us about your sister going on Facebook.'

Richard stepped in and wrapped his arms around his mother's shoulders, allowing her to bury her head in his broad shoulders. 'Even more reason for your lot to double their efforts,' he said, glaring at Kate, clearly still angry about their earlier exchange.

'We're doing everything we can,' Kate said, standing, suddenly feeling like an intruder in what was a family situation. 'I'll call you, Val, as soon as we know more.'

But Val wasn't listening as she gently sobbed into her son's arms.

TWENTY-FIVE

Holding the takeaway bag in her hand, Kate's mouth began salivating as she closed the door to her flat with her bottom. She hadn't felt hungry when she'd called in at the drive thru, but now her stomach was grumbling as the smell of the food filled the room.

Flicking the kitchen light on, she dropped her bag and coat on the breakfast bar and removed a plate from the cupboard. Eating the burger and fries out of their packaging would have saved washing up, but she wanted to eat in the living room, and a plate was the safest option. Squeezing more ketchup into the burger and splashing a dollop of mayonnaise on the edge of the plate, she carried the feast through to the living room, turning on the lamp on the coffee table.

She screamed when she saw the figure dozing on the couch.

Tara rolled over and blinked against the sudden light. 'Oh, Kate.'

'Tara, what the *hell* are you doing here? I thought you'd gone back to your mum and dad's.'

Tara sat up and let out a yawn. 'I did, but the second I walked through the door Mum started having a massive go at me.'

Kate remembered the version of events the supe had painted earlier, wondering how much of what Tara was about to tell her would be factually accurate. Kate decided she would give her the benefit of the doubt. For now.

'How did you get back in here?'

Tara sheepishly reached into her pocket and pulled out the set of spare keys Kate kept in the drawer of the unit nearest the door. 'Sorry, I borrowed them… just in case.'

Kate narrowed her eyes as she picked up the chips that had scattered to the floor in her shock. 'So you knew that things wouldn't go well at home? I can't help you if you lie to me, Tara.'

'You don't understand what she's like and I figured you wouldn't mind. You said yesterday that you wanted to help.'

But Kate wasn't buying it. 'I *do* want to help you, Tara, but not by becoming a wedge between you and your parents. I said last night you could spend the night as it was too late to get you home. You told me that they knew you were staying out, but your dad says differently.'

'You promised you wouldn't speak to him.'

Kate sighed. 'I didn't… what I mean is *he* spoke to me. What do you expect? We work in the same building and I report to him. This is why you staying here *isn't* a good idea. Don't you see the position you're putting me in here?'

Tara began chewing the sleeve of her jumper. 'What did he say?

Kate put the plate down on the coffee table. 'He claimed they were up all night, worried sick about what had happened to you. They said you hadn't told them you wouldn't be home.'

'I sent Mum a text, but she never has her phone on. I don't know why she has it, to be honest.'

Kate cocked an eyebrow. 'Why not just call the house phone, then?'

Tara's cheeks reddened, and although she opened her mouth, no words came out.

'Staying here last night was part of something else, wasn't it?' Kate continued. 'You wanted to make them worry?'

Tara scowled at her. 'Not worry, but I wanted them to accept that I'm not a little girl any more. I'm supposed to be going off to university in September, and they won't have a clue where I am or who I'm with when I'm there. I certainly won't be phoning every night to let them know I'm safe.'

Kate recognised the rebellious streak from her own adolescence, and could recall having a similar disagreement with her own mother. She could empathise with Tara's feelings, but as a mother herself, she knew whose side she was really on.

'If you want to be treated as a grown-up, you need to behave like one,' Kate said, without judgement. 'Believe me, I understand what you're going through, but you need to try and see it from their side too. There's a fifteen-year-old girl who disappeared from the city just over a week ago. Your dad and I are working night and day investigating what's happened, and so when you suddenly didn't come home, you can't be surprised at how your parents reacted. Can you? Of course they were going to fear the worst. I know I would if my little girl went missing.'

'So why have a go at me? If they were that worried, she should have been pleased to see me, not go ballistic at the first opportunity.'

'Maybe not, but it all comes from a place of love. Until you have a child of your own...' Kate's words trailed off, as she remembered the reason Tara had turned up originally. 'Did you tell your mum about...?'

Tara shook her head. 'She didn't give me the chance. She accused me of not taking my studies seriously, as if I'm not under enough pressure already.'

Kate turned back towards the door. 'Get your coat on, and I'll take you over there now. I'll stay with you and make sure they hear you out.'

Tara squirmed awkwardly. 'No, I'm not going back there tonight. I don't need the stress. Not with...' she gestured to her belly. 'Besides, your dinner will get cold.'

'I can warm my dinner in the microwave after. You need to speak to your parents about what is going on with your body.

They're the best people who can offer you the advice and guidance that you need right now.'

'Mum needs to cool off a bit first. Please? It's late and I'm exhausted, and if they were up all night, I'm sure they're tired too. I have college first thing, but only until lunchtime, so I'll go back then.'

Kate stared her down.

'And I will tell them everything,' Tara added. 'I promise. Please, Kate, just let me crash here for one more night and then I'll break the news to them.'

Kate sighed, taking a seat on the sofa opposite her and resting the plate of food on her lap. 'Do you want to share this?'

Tara turned up her nose. 'Just the thought of a burger is turning my stomach, to be honest. I had some toast earlier, and I'm fine.'

Kate took a bite. 'Have you had any contact with the father?'

'He was just some guy I met in a club. All you need to know is he's out of the picture.'

Kate sensed there was more to that than Tara was prepared to say, so she let it pass. 'And have you decided whether you want to keep the baby?'

Tara collapsed back into the cushion. 'I don't know. When I think about bringing a baby into the world, and the disruption it would cause to my life, my education, my parents' lives… I just think I should have an abortion. But then I think, how can I kill a living baby, my child? Would I one day regret the choice? I don't know what to do for the best.'

'This is why you need to talk to your mum and dad.'

'What would you do in my situation?'

Kate finished the burger, buying herself time before she had to answer. 'I can't tell you what you should do.'

'Yeah, but that's not what I'm asking. I mean, you're a mother, do you regret having your baby?'

'Absolutely not! There was a time... I suffered with post-natal depression after my daughter was born and I was gripped with fear that I'd never be good enough to be the mother she needed and deserved, but I can hand-on-heart say I don't regret having her for one moment. What I regret, is not being a better mother. But I'm working to improve that every day.'

Tara yawned again.

'But I wasn't pregnant when I was seventeen,' Kate continued. 'I was married, had a good job and a mortgage on a house. Our situations are quite different and you shouldn't allow my personal experiences to guide you. Can you not speak to the father and see what he thinks? Maybe he would want to support you through this, regardless of the decision you make.'

'I told you: it's nothing to do with him. Please can we change the subject? I've spent all day thinking about nothing else. All I want is a moment of normality before sleep.'

Kate nodded. 'Okay, but I want to see you phone your mum and dad and let them know you'll be back tomorrow. They deserve that much.'

TWENTY-SIX

TEN DAYS MISSING

'I made you a cup of tea,' Tara said, startling Kate as she emerged from the steam-filled bathroom with a towel wrapped loosely around her.

'Oh, thanks,' Kate said, accepting the mug.

'I didn't know if you'd have sugar in it or not, so I didn't put any in.'

Kate took an enthusiastic sip. 'It's great, thanks. Do you want me to drop you at college on my way into work?'

Tara shook her head. 'My bus goes past the end of your road, so it's fine. Thanks, though.'

An awkward silence fell between them.

'I'd better get dressed and on my way,' Kate eventually said, nodding towards her bedroom door.

'Oh, yeah, I should get out of your hair too,' Tara said, heading towards the door and then stopping. 'I really appreciate you letting me stay again. And I'm sorry if my being here has made things at work difficult for you.'

And in that moment, Kate recognised the fear in Tara's eyes; facing an impossible choice, with life-changing repercussions. Kate wanted to hug her, but felt too self-conscious with only the towel on. 'Will you let me know how you get on? When you talk to your mum and dad, I mean.'

'Sure, and I promise I won't drop you in it with my dad.'

Kate offered her a warm smile, and waved as Tara showed herself out of the door and disappeared from view. Kate remained where she was for a moment, picturing how the supe and Judith would react to the news, and hoping the three of them would remain patient with each other.

Kate headed into her bedroom, and threw on her clothes, but as she finished her tea, she reached for her phone, unable to shake the unbearable need to make a call.

'Hi, Rob,' she said when the line connected.

'Kate? Is everything okay?'

'Fine, sorry, I just wanted to say hi to Chloe. Is she still there? She hasn't gone to school already, has she?'

'You're in luck, I'll just get her. Don't be long, though, we need to go in a minute.'

'Mummy?' Chloe said, taking the phone from him.

'Hi, sweetie, how are you?'

'I lost another tooth last night,' she said proudly.

Kate felt her eyes filling up. 'Did you? Well, I hope you're going to put it under your pillow tonight so the tooth fairy can collect it.'

'I will. Are you coming up this weekend?'

'Just you try and keep me away.'

'Mum? Dad says we have to go.'

'That's okay, sweetheart. You'd better do what he says, because you don't want to be late for school. I love you, Chloe.'

'Love you too.'

Kate couldn't stop the tears escaping her eyes as the line disconnected.

*
**

'Holland?' Kate exclaimed, exasperated by DC Freeborn's latest update.

'Amsterdam to be exact.'

Kate still couldn't believe what he was saying. 'Daisy Emerson is in Amsterdam? Are they certain?'

He nodded, showing her the email the Facebook team had sent, on his screen. 'They finally managed to pull out the IP address that had accessed her profile, and it came from Amsterdam. Might explain why we can't find her anywhere local.'

Kate frowned. 'If anything, this lends itself to the likelihood that she hasn't run away. I'm sure her mum said they still have her passport. Do we have an exact address for where the IP originated?'

'Working on that now,' Quinlan piped up. 'I'm waiting on a call back from our Dutch counterparts. They should be able to narrow the search and let us know what they find.'

'Good, but if you haven't heard back from them in ten minutes, call again.' She turned back to the rest of the team. 'While those two work on that, let's have your thoughts on what Daisy could be doing in Amsterdam, and how she got there.'

'Choosing the path of least resistance,' Laura piped up, 'maybe she borrowed a friend's passport and hitched a ride on a boat. If she wanted to disappear, she'd know we'd check her passport, but probably not one of her friend's.'

'In that case,' Kate countered, taking on the role of devil's advocate, 'how did she pay for her ticket?'

'Borrowed the money from someone?'

'Who?'

'Maybe the same person who loaned her the passport, ma'am.'

'Hmm, maybe,' Kate mused, considering it. 'But if she wanted to disappear, why log in to Facebook where she could be traced?'

'Maybe she didn't think she could be traced,' DC Rogers suggested. 'Or maybe it was her way of letting her friends know she'd made it there safely.'

Not a bad theory, but Kate's gut wasn't buying it. 'Wouldn't she just message them privately, though? Nobody would have been any the wiser if she had. By liking the post, she's making her reappearance public. And it still doesn't tell us how she got to Amsterdam.'

Laura raised her hand. 'Could Daisy pass as either Georgie or Hannah? In the image she liked, they all look so similar. In the dark and with a bit of makeup, would passport control be able to say for certain that one wasn't the other? I know it seems a bit of a stretch, but probably worth checking out. We could ask the other girls to bring in their passports, and if one can't, that would be pretty damning.'

Kate pointed at Laura. 'Follow that up for me. Anybody else? What's she doing in Holland?'

'Maybe she was grabbed by someone and taken there,' Patel offered, picking up the baton. 'She wouldn't be the first one.'

'Do me a favour, Patel, and speak to Hendrix's Organised Crime Team. Float the theory and see what they suggest. Find out if they're aware of any groups actively involved in trafficking in this county and beyond.'

Rogers coughed. 'Ma'am? If someone did snatch her with the intention of selling her on the black market, why would they let her log in to Facebook and like a picture?'

'You have an alternative theory?'

Rogers looked nervously at her colleagues' faces. 'Maybe DS Humberidge is right, and this is just a killer's way of toying with us. While we're chasing our tails trying to discover whether she's alive or if she's in Amsterdam, he's secretly laughing at us.'

'Vicky, if that is the case, then Daisy's body is probably still in the UK, possibly in the city. So get out there and find her.'

Rogers lowered her eyes and nodded.

Kate wrote the word 'Amsterdam' on the board in bold letters, and dismissed the team. Something didn't feel right. The IP address being linked to Holland just didn't fit with the picture.

'Ma'am?' Laura called over. 'Ben's on the phone. He says he's ID'd the owner of the heart.'

TWENTY-SEVEN

'Talk to me,' Kate said, when she'd signed in to SSD, and been escorted to the lab Ben was once again working out of.

Ben slid the laptop over to her. 'His name was Petr Nowakowski.'

'Polish?' Laura asked, joining them.

'Parents were,' Ben confirmed, 'but both Petr and his younger sister Ana were born in the UK.'

'How did you identify him?' Kate asked, trying to skim read the report in front of her.

'DNA matched his profile in the system, and I did a bit of extra digging to be certain: as a teenager, Petr was fitted with a pacemaker after being diagnosed with bradycardia.'

'So, it's definitely him, then.'

Ben removed his latex gloves and protective suit, depositing them in the sanitary bin. 'I'm afraid so. Good news for you is you have a name and last known address.'

'Anything to indicate *how* he died? I'm doubting it was natural causes.'

'I wouldn't be so certain. Given his medical history, I wouldn't rule anything out. There was sufficient damage to the muscle to suggest it had come under recent strain. That could indicate that he was in a stressful situation immediately prior to death, or that his pacemaker was starting to fail.'

'Fail?'

'Pacemakers run on batteries, and they don't last forever. In fact, most pacemakers are replaced every seven years, and it had been almost that long since he'd last been under the knife according to his medical records.'

'You seriously think he had a heart attack and what, removed and posted me the heart himself.'

'Don't be facetious, Kate. All I'm saying is you shouldn't rule out natural causes. Who and why someone sent you the heart as a souvenir is beyond me.'

She nodded her understanding; it wasn't his fault there wasn't more to go on.

Ben sighed. 'I'm going to get myself a drink; do either of you want anything?'

'No, thanks,' Kate said for them both, returning her eyes to the screen.

Laura, who had been reading the screen over Kate's shoulder, suddenly gasped. 'I remember this guy. I interviewed him with Patel... must be three years ago maybe... yeah, that's him, charged for his involvement in an armed robbery.'

'Armed robbery? And out already?'

'From memory, he was given a reduced sentence for cooperating and giving up the rest of the gang. His evidence helped secure convictions against the other five members.'

'Revenge attack, then?' Kate suggested. 'One of the other gang members?'

'I wouldn't be so sure,' Laura said, taking control of the laptop and running a search. 'Look here: the rest of the gang are still behind bars. I remember the case now.' She began to read, sharing the salient points. 'Nowakowski was the getaway driver... but was only brought along at the last minute when the original driver wasn't able to make the heist... The original driver was being questioned in relation to something separate, but the job they were planning was time sensitive, so they proceeded with Nowakowski... The raid was on a security depot in Fareham.' Laura paused and looked up at Kate. 'It was a couple of months before you joined the department, ma'am. I was still in uniform back then.'

'Explains why I don't remember it, then. What else can you recall?'

Laura focused back on the screen. 'They kidnapped the depot's manager and her family, and forced her to help them gain entry... The leader escorted the manager into the building – signed in as a visiting regional manager or something, I think – while the others waited in a lorry to take delivery of the cash trolleys. Nowakowski was supposed to be waiting in a fast car in case something went wrong, but he was running late and got pulled over for speeding...'

Laura stifled a chuckle. 'They'd hit the place on a Wednesday, oblivious to the fact that the depot was due to test its fire evacuation procedures that day. Suddenly the fire alarm sounds and the workforce spill out and gather at the muster point, which just happens to be outside the loading dock where the gang are filling the lorry.

'The patrol car following Nowakowski has now sussed what's going on and called for backup. Within minutes, the place is surrounded by blue lights. Nowakowski confessed everything he knew, wanting to spare himself hard prison time... According to this, he served eighteen months of a four-year stretch.'

Kate didn't see the funny side. 'Was anybody hurt?'

Laura composed herself before continuing. 'No, ma'am. I think everyone involved was pretty shaken, but the gang saw sense before shooting anyone.'

'Just because the rest of the group are inside, doesn't mean they couldn't arrange for someone on the outside to complete the deed. You know what modern prison is like: operations are still run, regardless of whether the leader is inside. I think our first port of call should be the front runner to see what he has to say about it.'

'So why send you the heart? You weren't involved in the arrest.'

'He grassed them up, so maybe the heart is symbolic of him turning on them… I don't know. But they wanted us to know that they'd got to him, and I guess it sends out a message to the criminal underworld: grass and you know what'll happen to you.'

'So, where's the rest of him?'

'Your guess is as good as mine: burned; buried; chucked in a river. Who knows? We may never find the rest of him if this gang were involved. We'd better brief the team. I'll send Patel to the prison to speak with the crew.'

Ben was just returning as they were leaving, and held the door open.

'Thanks for this, Ben,' Kate said. 'Can you email me what you've got?'

He smiled. 'Of course. Glad I could help.' Moving closer to her, he whispered, 'Come to mine for dinner tonight?'

After the last two nights of worrying about Tara, nothing sounded better. 'I'll bring wine.'

TWENTY-EIGHT

'You think she's home?' Laura asked, as they pulled up at the mid-terrace property.

Kate looked at the overgrown lawn beneath the windows, which were covered by mildew. 'How would you know?'

Having briefed the team on Petr Nowakowski, Kate had chosen to bring Laura with her for support. It was hard enough breaking the news that a relative had died, but they needed to ask Nowakowski's sister, Ana, some questions about her brother's recent activities too.

Laura was first out of the car, darting to the door and ringing the bell, relieved to get out of the rain and under the porch cover. She was just turning to shrug at Kate in the car when the front door opened and a large woman in a pink tabard appeared. Kate watched as Laura and the woman spoke, before the door was closed and Laura hurried back to the car.

'I take it that wasn't Ana?' Kate asked when Laura was back inside.

'No. That woman owns the house, and Ana rents a room from her. The woman said Ana's at work, in the Sainsbury's in Portswood, just up the road.'

Kate took another look at the rundown property, before starting the engine and completing a U-turn.

'Oh, I see,' said the store manager, the blood draining from his face as they informed him why they wished to speak to Ana Nowakowski somewhere private.

'Y-y-you must take my office,' he offered.

'That's very kind,' Kate said with an appreciative nod. 'Would you mind bringing Ana in here? It would be more discreet if you collect her from the floor than us.'

He stood and made his way to the closed door. 'Of course, of course, don't want to set tongues wagging.'

Kate waited until he'd left before closing the door. 'I'll break the news to her, but I want you to watch her reactions as I do. Is she shocked, or does she already know; that kind of thing. Okay?'

Laura nodded, taking the store manager's chair, allowing Kate to sit next to the remaining vacant chair where Ana would sit.

A knock at the door a moment later was followed by a frightened looking young woman entering. Ana Nowakowski couldn't have been much older than twenty-five, a slight, gaunt frame with dark blonde, greasy hair pinned back in a ponytail. With no makeup, the skin on her face was smooth, but the supermarket uniform hung from her body.

'Is everything okay?' she asked, clearly sensing they were police.

'Please take a seat, Miss Nowakowski,' Kate encouraged.

Ana looked back at her store manager, terror in her eyes. 'Have I done something wrong?'

He rubbed her arm. 'No, Ana, it's nothing like that. These detectives just need to ask you a few questions.' He looked over to Kate. 'I'll make myself scarce,' he said, closing the door behind him.

Ana stared at the door, as if trying to determine whether she should run. Was it the reaction of someone with a guilty conscience or someone with too many brushes with the law? 'What sort of questions?' she finally asked, looking back at Kate.

'It's about your brother,' Kate said, patting the cushion of the vacant chair. 'Please take a seat.'

'Petr? Is he in trouble again?'

'What makes you think that?'

Ana perched on the seat, ready to bolt for the door at the first sign of trouble. 'Why else would you be asking about him? Once a criminal, always a criminal: that's what you people think, isn't it?'

'Actually, that isn't a view I subscribe to, despite the common level of reoffending we witness in this country.'

'What's he done this time, then?'

'When was the last time you saw your brother, Miss Nowa-kowski?'

A dimple formed in her chin as she considered the question. 'Two weeks ago? He was due to sail the Thursday before last and we went out for dinner the night before. If you're looking for him, he isn't due to dock until Thursday morning.'

Kate reached out and took the young woman's hands in her own, surprised by how cold they felt, but forcing eye contact. 'I wish there was an easier way for me to say this, Miss Nowakowski, but your brother Petr has passed away. I'm so sorry.'

Ana's expression remained blank.

'Miss Nowakowski? I really am sorry for your loss,' Kate persevered.

Ana pulled her hands away and stood, but couldn't move away from the chair. 'There must be some mistake. Petr is away with work… how… he can't…'

Kate rose to join her. 'I appreciate this isn't easy for you to hear.'

Ana's eyes registered her confusion. 'It's not possible. You must have the wrong person. Petr Nowakowski? My brother? He isn't dead.'

'I'm sorry, Miss Nowakowski, but we've confirmed it through a DNA match. There's no doubt.'

A single tear escaped down Ana's cheek, halting at the edge of her top lip, before continuing down her chin. 'I don't understand. How…?'

Kate took Ana's arm and lowered her back into the chair. 'We're still investigating exactly what happened, but we have reason to believe that his death occurred under mysterious circumstances.

You've said several times that you believed he was away somewhere. Can you explain where?'

Ana continued to blink, her vision focused on the wall beyond Kate. 'He was a sous chef on board a cruise ship… they set sail on Thursday for two weeks. Did he die on the ship?'

'We really don't have any more information we can share at this point.'

'Can I see him?'

It was the question Kate had been dreading. Having discussed Ben's findings with the supe before leaving the station, they'd decided it was best not to mention the circumstances under which they had arrived at the news themselves. 'We don't require you to formally identify your brother, Miss Nowakowski, as the DNA test has already confirmed it.'

'But for me, I'd like to be able to say goodbye.'

'I will see if that's possible at some point in the future, but right now I want to concentrate on finding out exactly what happened to your brother and how he came to die.'

Ana frowned. 'I don't understand… are you saying he was… murdered?'

'We don't know for sure, but it's an avenue of enquiry we're following. I appreciate this isn't easy for you, but I'd like to ask you some questions about your brother if you're happy for me to do so?'

'If you think it will help.'

'Thank you,' Kate said. 'If there is anything you don't feel comfortable answering at the moment, just say, and I'll move on. Okay?'

As Ana nodded, a second tear ran down her cheek.

'When you last saw your brother, how did he seem within himself?'

'He was… fine. He was telling me how this next cruise would pay well, and that when he was back we would look to see if we had enough deposit to get a place of our own to rent.'

'He didn't live with you, then?'

'After his release from prison he stayed in a halfway house, but then he got the job with the cruise company and spent a lot of time on the sea. But I think he was growing bored with the job. He was really keen to lay some roots, I think.'

'You were close, then?'

'He's my only family. After our parents died, he looked after me.'

'How long ago did they pass away?'

'Twenty years ago this year.'

'So, you would have been—'

'I was five and Petr was eight. We went from one foster family to another, but he was always there, watching out for me, making sure nobody took advantage, and ensuring I always ate. I owe him my life.'

'He sounds like a great brother to have.'

'He was, and apart from that stupid robbery, we never fell out.'

'Do you know if he had any contact with the gang after his release from prison?'

'Are you kidding? He wanted nothing to do with them. He knew he never should have agreed to help that day, but he was desperate for money and it seemed so easy. He regretted that decision every day. So, when he was released from prison he swore he would never allow himself to get into that situation again.'

'Did your brother have any enemies that you know of, or had he received any threats he told you about?'

'No. None. That gang he helped put away swore they would get revenge, but he... oh God, is that what happened? Did they get to him?'

'We're investigating *all* possibilities at this time. So far there is nothing to directly implicate any of his old crew in what happened. But we will look into the possibility.' Kate paused, keen to avoid saying too much. 'Can I ask you to write down your brother's address, and the name of the cruise liner he worked for?'

Ana nodded, and took the pad of paper and pen that Laura offered.

'Is there anyone else you'd like us to inform?' Kate asked when Ana had finished.

'No, it was just the two of us. Will you let me know when I can sort out funeral arrangements, and anything else I need to do?'

It was never easy breaking this sort of news, but Kate felt for this young woman. In losing her brother, her whole world had been turned upside down. 'I'll be in touch,' Kate assured her, handing her a business card. 'This has my mobile number on it. You can call at any time if you remember anything else, you have any questions, or if you just need someone to talk to. Would you like me to tell your boss that you should go home for the rest of the day?'

'No, please don't. I'd rather finish my shift; I don't want to be alone.'

Kate watched her leave the office, captivated by Ana's resolve against such adversity. And in that moment, Kate made a silent promise that she would bring Petr's killer to justice.

TWENTY-NINE

Kate stuck Petr Nowakowski's mugshot on a clean board, writing his name in thick black letters beneath it. 'Here's what we know so far: he told his sister he was about to come into a small windfall, enough to put down a deposit on a flat for them to rent. But where was the money coming from? He had form for armed robbery – his sister swears blind he'd turned his back on crime – but I want one of you to follow up on it. Check his room for any sign of planned activity; has he been scoping any areas out for a smash and grab job?'

Freeborn raised his bony arm into the air. 'I'll take that, ma'am. I'll ask my contacts on the streets too, see who's planning what.'

'Thanks, Ewan. Next, Ana said he was working for a cruise company as a sous chef. I can't see that a company dealing with such a wealthy clientele would hire a former thief as a chef, but we need to make contact with them to be sure. Ana's provided the address. If he *was* employed, find out why he wasn't on board the ship like he'd told his sister. That brings us on to the box the heart was in: who sent it? And why?'

'No usable security footage of our suspect at the depot,' Freeborn said glumly. 'And no sign of him at Bitterne train station either, or on any buses that stopped there or nearby in the time around when the box was left on Saturday. It's like he appeared out of nowhere, left the item, and then vanished like a ghost.'

'We can't give up on this, Ewan. That depot is our only confirmed sighting. Go back to the depot, check every business and residence nearby for additional security cameras. Someone, somewhere must have picked him up. We need to know what he looks like so we can narrow our search.'

Freeborn knew she was right, and nodded to hide his embarrassment for not already having made those calls.

'Where are we with the air fresheners? Any prints?'

Rogers raised her hand into the air. 'SSD said no. The ink used to write the message to you is the same as you would find in any dry wipe board marker, commonly found in schools, offices and,' she nodded towards the board, 'police stations. No prints on the air fresheners in the gymnasium either. In fact, no discernible prints have been found in the gymnasium. There are smears on the walls where the technicians believe his hands may have brushed, but they believe our suspect was wearing gloves. All they can confirm is that the air fresheners at the gym *are* the same brand as those in the box.'

Kate sighed. A foot from a female victim left at the school, and a heart belonging to a male victim sent in a box. The air fresheners suggested a connection between the crimes, but little to steer them towards identifying their suspect. 'What about stray hairs? Anything?'

'They're still processing the scene, ma'am.'

'What about the box and gift wrap?'

'The box was the sort used to store paper for printers and the like. This particular brand is quite common, available wholesale to local authorities and businesses.'

'And schools?' Kate asked.

Vicky nodded. 'I checked and St Bartholomew's currently has ten boxes of the stuff in storage. It's possible our suspect collected the box from there, though we may never be able to prove it for certain.'

'Where are we with chasing down Ismael Vardan?'

'Vardan was at the school this morning,' PC Barnes interjected. 'Family wedding in Leicester, which is why he was away at the weekend. Spoke to his sister on the phone and she confirmed he was there.'

'What did he have to say about Friday night's discovery?'

'I was at the school when he arrived. He hadn't even got the message that the school would be closed until further notice. Took the opportunity to question him about his movements on Thursday and Friday. Interestingly, he didn't have any classes between midday and three on Thursday, and when I asked where he was and what he was doing, he said he was reading alone in his classroom. I asked if anyone could verify that, but he said he couldn't be sure. He said it's possible someone could have come past and seen him working inside, but nobody stopped to say hello.'

'You believe him?'

'I think it would be hard to disprove. I can reach out to the rest of the faculty and ask if anyone saw him during those times, but that will mean revealing to the rest that he's a suspect.'

'Why was he in his classroom and not the staff room?'

'I asked him about that,' Barnes said, 'and he told me it's quieter in the classroom. He says he doesn't have too many friends in the school and prefers the solitude of the classroom.'

'We know that TUTD Surveyors had vacated the sports hall by that time, so it's possible he could have been in the sports hall all that time.'

'Doesn't explain how he got the victim in there, though, ma'am. Plus, why do it on school property, unless he wants to get caught?'

Kate fixed Laura with a hopeful look. 'Any news on the photocopy engineer?'

'Chris Jackson was called out to the school on Thursday morning to fix the machine in the administration office, which he did, by all accounts, leaving just before midday. But when I asked the administrators why Jackson had been called back on Friday, they said he hadn't.'

Kate narrowed her eyes.

'Camera has his van entering the school grounds at three on Friday afternoon,' Quinlan added, 'as the school was kicking out, and the van is seen leaving just before five, but he wasn't signed in for that period, and he hadn't been called out to repair anything.'

Kate's pulse quickened. 'What does Jackson have to say about that?' Kate asked.

'Phone still going to voicemail, ma'am,' Laura confirmed. 'You want me to get vehicle recognition to run a search?'

Kate nodded.

'What about the company he works for? Have you managed to—'

'Self-employed. According to his website, he's a sole trader and although there are images of other people in the banner on his site, he seems to be the only person listed as employed by the company.'

'So, where is he?'

Laura opened her mouth to speak when the phone behind her burst to life. Kate nodded for her to answer it, when a second phone rang, and then a third and then a fourth. Kate searched the faces of her team for answers, as they moved off to answer the disturbances.

Laura lowered the phone, covering the mouthpiece. 'Shit! Ma'am, you need to get the television on now. BBC One.'

Kate frowned, but strode across the incident room to the dust-covered set in the corner, switching it on at the wall and flicking through the channels. Behind her, the room was suddenly buzzing with conversations and the distant sound of phones ringing. Kate turned up the volume, recognising the view of St Bartholomew's over the reporter's shoulder.

'News of this discovery was broken by local newspaper reporter, Zoe Denton.' The camera panned round to reveal Zoe, clutching the arm of an umbrella, her face taut. 'Thank you for joining us, Zoe. Can you confirm what's going on just behind us? We've seen technicians from the Scientific Services Department coming and going through the school gates since Friday.'

'From what I understand, the police were already on site when the human foot was discovered on the property after hours. Access to the school has been restricted ever since, but my source tells me the focus of the activity is in and around the old sports hall.'

Kate's head snapped round, looking at her team, all now manning one phone or another as the news filtered out to the general public and terrified parents reacted. Kate turned back to stare at Zoe Denton on the screen. A talented and determined journalist, their paths had first crossed when Kate had been transferred to Southampton and Kate had called on Zoe for support when hunting Amy Spencer's killer last year. But who was Zoe's source this time? Kate didn't want to think that anyone in her team would have leaked these details.

'And this, of course, is the school missing teenager Daisy Emerson attended,' the reporter continued. 'Why do you think this discovery is being kept under wraps? Do you think the foot belonged to Daisy?'

The skin around Zoe's eyes tightened further. 'It would explain why no formal statement has yet to be made to the public, and why the school will be closed for the next few days.'

Kate wasn't even aware that the supe had reached a decision about closing the school, thought it was definitely the right call.

Laura sidled over. 'We're going to need help manning these phones. This story is now on the BBC news site, and starting to trend on social media. This is just the start.'

Kate gritted her teeth. 'If I find out who leaked this information…' She didn't need to finish the sentence. 'Do me a favour. Go down to the switchboard and have them stop filtering calls up here. We don't have time to be manning these calls. Finding Daisy is still our priority.' Taking a deep breath, Kate added, 'I'd better go and brief the supe.'

THIRTY

Heading into the corridor, Kate caught sight of Hendrix disappearing into the supe's office. She hurried down the corridor, reaching the door just as it was closing, but forcing her hand in to keep it open. 'Is this about our girl with the removed tattoo?'

Hendrix pulled at the door, allowing Kate to enter with a look of resignation. Once the three of them were seated, she nodded. 'I just met with a source who works the streets in St Mary's and as soon as I asked her if any of the usual girls had recently gone AWOL, her face filled with panic.'

Kate glanced the supe out of the corner of her eye, but he seemed happy for her to take the lead here. 'Panic?'

'You've got to understand that these women, whilst they're rivals for the business they operate in, they're like a family, looking out for each other, recording registration numbers of the cars the others go off in, so that if anything bad happens they can pinpoint who is responsible.'

'Is that what happened here? Was she able to give you the details of someone who took our girl?'

Hendrix shook her head. 'That's just it. She wasn't taken, at least not that my source knew of.'

Kate's brow furrowed. 'Are you saying she just didn't turn up one night?'

'Not exactly. My source says her friend Maria wanted out; she wanted to jack it in and try and lead a more normal life. But to do so, she needed to buy herself out of the contract with her pimp.

My source said Maria was determined to go clean, kicking the drugs, giving up smoking and drinking in an effort to save every penny to earn what she needed to get free.'

'And did she manage it?'

'According to my source, yes. She didn't know how Maria managed to get her hands on the ten grand needed to buy her freedom, but apparently she did, and was last seen a week ago.'

'Where does a sex worker get her hands on ten thousand pounds?'

Hendrix just shrugged.

'Who's your source? I want to speak to her,' Kate tried again.

'No. Impossible.'

Kate fired a look at the supe, looking for support.

'I'm sorry,' Hendrix continued, 'but my source has already put herself in enough danger just talking to me.'

'Why? She hasn't told you anything; not really.'

'Even so, just talking to me could be enough to get her killed by the people she works for. I'm sorry, but she's off limits.'

'Sir, if I'm to find out what really happened to this woman, then —'

The supe sat forward. 'Our primary duty is to determine what happened and ensure justice is served.'

Kate began to smile, but then he continued.

'That said, we also have a duty of care to DI Hendrix's Confidential Informant, and if allowing her to speak to DI Matthews puts her life at risk, then it's an avenue we can't pursue.'

'What?' Kate demanded. 'But, sir, if—'

'I'm sorry, Matthews, but we can't risk the CI's life too. That's the end of it.'

Kate fixed Hendrix with a stare. 'Did your source say if she saw Maria *after* she'd paid her debt?' Kate pressed.

'No. When she last saw her, Maria said she'd managed to secure the money she needed and would deliver it to their pimp that night when he surfaced. My source did say she was surprised Maria had managed to get the cash so quickly, but was just happy that she was going to get a shot at a new life.'

'Did she not phone Maria after, to find out if she'd been successful?'

'She said she tried to phone Maria to see if they could meet for a chat last Wednesday, but the phone was off and doesn't appear to have been switched on since.'

'Didn't your source find that odd? Did she report her concerns to anyone?'

'She figured Maria had dumped the phone, so she could turn her back on the old life; not wanting anyone to remind her of where she'd escaped.'

'And the pimp? Did he have anything to say about it?'

'I haven't spoken to him.'

Kate puffed. 'Well, I will then.'

'He won't talk to you.'

'He will if I arrest him.'

Hendrix grunted. 'No, he won't. He'll lawyer up, give you "no comment" answers and be out in under an hour. These people are used to fending the police off. Unless you have hard evidence linking him to a specific crime, he won't utter a word. And he'll probably take it out on women like my CI, assuming one of them has spoken to us. Organised crime is a different beast to what you're used to, Matthews. Our suspects don't crack in the same way as common criminals. These people know the rule books inside and out and know exactly how to avoid detection.'

'What if Maria went to pay the pimp, he kept the money and then killed her. A body being chopped up before disposal isn't uncommon in the world you're describing.'

'And if you can find evidence directly linking him to something – evidence that will stick – I'll drive you down there myself so you can arrest him. But until that happens, you need to stay clear of St Mary's.'

'At least give me a surname. Let me find out whether this Maria is our vic.'

'Alexandrou,' Hendrix huffed. 'Her name is Maria Alexandrou.' Hendrix handed Kate a piece of paper with an address on it. 'My source said Maria rented a room here. The landlady says Maria hasn't been back there in over a week.'

Kate accepted the piece of paper begrudgingly, and both women began to stand.

'Matthews, hang back, please,' the supe said. His neck tie was again pulled down, his sleeves were rolled up, and it didn't look like he'd shaved in at least two days. She wondered how much of the stress on his shoulders was coming from above, and how much was being driven by the turmoil Tara was kicking up at home.

He waited until the door was closed. 'Assuming for a moment that this Maria Alexandrou is our vic, it begs the questions, how *and* why was she at the school?'

'You're suggesting one of the staff is responsible.'

'I can't think of any other reason the body would have been chopped up there. Who are your suspects?'

'Nobody obvious jumping out yet, but we're interested in two. The first – Ismael Vardan – is a form tutor at the school, but our interest in him stemmed from believing the foot may have belonged to Daisy. But now that that line has been closed—'

'What made you suspect him?'

'He is Daisy's form tutor and English teacher. One of the teachers we spoke to last week suggested we could look more closely at their relationship.'

The supe raised his eyebrows. 'And?'

'*And* at his previous school, one of his pupils made allegations of inappropriate advances against Vardan, but despite an extensive investigation, no charges were brought, and the pupil later retracted his statement.'

'What does Vardan have to say for himself?'

'We spoke to him about Daisy on Friday morning, but unsurprisingly he denied anything untoward, and accused us of trying to fit him up for her disappearance based on the lies of the previous pupil.'

'And now?'

'His whereabouts are unaccounted for three hours on Thursday, which we believe was the day the body was chopped up.'

'You think he did it?'

'If I knew he'd already be in custody.'

'Anybody else?'

'Chris Jackson, a photocopy engineer. Was apparently seen on camera at the school on Thursday and Friday, but was never signed in on Friday. He is AWOL and I want vehicle recognition and phone signal tracking launched.'

'Do either this Vardan or Jackson have form?'

Kate shook her head.

'Anyone else we should be looking at?'

'Liam Phillips' company has access to the sports hall, but denies any wrongdoing. I want to look into his background more, because there's something about him that just didn't sit right for me.'

'All right, you'd better get cracking. We need this completed as soon as possible. I'm getting heat from the Chief Super. He's agreed to the school being closed for the first three days of the week, but on the understanding that we deliver him a suspect in that time.'

Kate scrunched her nose, not wanting to share the news, but knowing she had to. 'There's something else you should know. My reason for coming in here originally was to advise that BBC news is reporting the discovery of the foot at the school. Someone has talked to the press.'

'Someone in your team? Who?'

Kate fixed him with a certain stare. 'I'm sure it's not anybody from within my team, sir. I would vouch for all of them.'

'Your loyalty to your team is one of your strongest character traits, Kate, but don't allow that to blind you from the truth. You know how lucrative such stories can be. Nip it in the bud. I will speak to the Media Relations team and get some sort of statement released.' He nodded towards the door; her cue that the meeting was over.

THIRTY-ONE

Freeborn rushed over to Kate as she stepped back into the incident room. 'Hot off the press, the IP address—'

'What is it?'

'Hold on, sorry, their written English isn't great. Uh, it seems they managed to trace the IP address to a server in a building on the outskirts of Amsterdam… inside the building they found multiple servers… building owned by a company specialising… oh… they don't think the profile was accessed in Amsterdam.'

Kate frowned. 'What? I don't follow, what are you saying?'

Freeborn lowered his phone. 'Okay, um, listen, so when surfing online every internet-capable device, be it laptop, phone, tablet, or whatever has an IP address – basically a code that identifies the network you're linked to and the device being used. Think of it as a return address so that every time you go online you leave a trail of breadcrumbs back to your activity. Now, in this day and age where everyone is so privacy-obsessed and individuals want to mask that trail of breadcrumbs or return address, it's possible to get hold of software that will alter your IP address to make it seem like you are somewhere totally different. There are loads of companies offering this service at a cost, but it's pretty easy to set it up. According to the Dutch police, the building they visited was a base unit for one of these companies, allowing the user to pretend they were in Amsterdam when Daisy's profile was accessed.'

Kate was struggling to keep up, technology not her strong suit. 'So, whoever liked Hannah's photo—'

'Probably wasn't in Amsterdam, ma'am.'

'So, where were they?'

'They can't say for certain. We'll need a warrant to get the user's true IP address from the company, but the company isn't based in the UK or the Netherlands, so we're going to need to track their actual address and apply for an international warrant to access that information. It's not going to be easy, ma'am. This is why so many of these internet pirate download sites manage to evade prosecution.'

'So, it's possible that Daisy's profile was accessed from the UK all along?'

'Yes, ma'am.'

Kate sighed. 'Would Daisy know how to use this masking software to hide her actual location?'

Freeborn sighed. 'Maybe, I'll speak to her teachers and find out how IT-literate she is. *If* she knew how to use it, it would make sense that she would like the post so her friends knew she was safe, knowing that her true location wouldn't be discovered. But it's a big if.'

'This must be the place,' Laura commented, as Kate opened the wooden gate, weathered and chipped by time and the elements.

Kate double-checked the address Hendrix had given her. 'Yeah, this is it.'

'Do you think the foot belongs to Maria?'

'We'll know soon enough,' Kate said, pressing the doorbell.

The frail old lady with a purple-rinse perm, beige cardigan and checked skirt who opened the door was a far cry from what Kate had anticipated.

'Yes, dear,' the old woman said, squinting behind jam-jar-thick glasses.

Kate passed her identification to the woman who studied it, practically touching it to the lenses. 'I'm Detective Inspector Kate

Matthews,' she added, speaking slowly and sounding out every vowel, 'and this is my colleague Detective Constable Laura Trotter. May we come in?'

The woman smiled broadly, handing the identification back. 'Please do, would you like a cup of tea?'

'That would be lovely, thank you.' Kate replied, knowing they didn't have much time.

The old woman showed them to a small living room, where a halogen heater glowed orange in the corner. Kate and Laura both removed their jackets and opted for the sofa furthest from the heater. The old woman reappeared a few moments later, the tea cups and saucers rattling as she struggled to carry the tray through. Kate quickly stood and offered to take the tray, placing it on a coffee table closest to the woman, and handing out the cups.

'Lovely cup of tea,' Kate offered, kindly.

The woman nodded graciously, her hand trembling as she placed the cup to her lips. 'How can I help you?'

'We were told you have a lodger living with you? A young woman called Maria?'

'Oh, not any more, dear, I'm afraid.'

Kate glanced nervously at Laura. 'But you did have someone called Maria living with you?'

'Yes, she was a lovely wee girl, but unfortunately not very good at paying her rent on time. I had to let her go.'

'Did she leave a forwarding address?'

The woman frowned with disappointment. 'No, I'm afraid not, dear.'

'When was the last time you saw Maria, Mrs Owen?'

The old woman paused, thinking back. 'Must have been two weeks ago. She was already a month in arrears, and it was the day she was due to pay February's rent, and she said she didn't have it. I hate to say we got into a bit of a disagreement, and she left, promising she would find the money and come back, but she never did. My son wasn't happy. He's been saying for months that she was taking advantage of me, but it was nice to have some company around this old place. It's not like I needed the rent money, but my son insisted.'

'Would you mind if we take a look around her room; maybe she left some clue where she'd moved on to?'

A look of guilt spread across Mrs Owen's face. 'Ah, I wish you'd come around sooner. My son was here on Friday and bagged up the few things she'd left in the room – mainly clothes and makeup – and took it to the dump. He said if she hadn't returned to pay what she owed, I was better off dumping her stuff so the room was clean of her. I want to rent it out again, but he doesn't think I should.' She scowled. 'He's started mentioning retirement homes, but I'm not going anywhere.'

Kate thought about her own mother in a care home in Romsey, and made a mental note to visit her as soon as they'd found Daisy.

'Do you know if your son took the bags straight to the dump? He didn't leave them in your bin outside?'

'He was already planning to take some of his own stuff to the dump, so I assume he went straight there. I can phone and ask if you'd like?'

'Thank you,' Kate said, standing. 'While you're doing that, would you mind if I used your bathroom?'

'Of course, dear. It's upstairs, first door on your left. You can't miss it.'

Kate thanked her again, signalling for Laura to keep Mrs Owen busy while she had a snoop in what had been Maria's bedroom. As Kate reached the top of the staircase, she realised what Mrs Owen had meant about not missing the bathroom. The overpowering scent of potpourri was enough to make your eyes water.

Closing the bathroom door loudly, Kate tiptoed along the hallway, ignoring the first room, the biggest, which had a single bed and its own unique odour, and pushed open the door to the remaining room. It was brighter than the first, the curtains wide open and no net curtain to block out the sky at the front of the house.

All that remained was a single bed, a chest of drawers unit and a rickety-looking flat-pack wardrobe. Kate carefully opened each of the four drawers in the unit, but all were empty. Moving across to the wardrobe, the door squeaked as she opened it, but save for half a dozen wire coat hangers, it too was bare.

Allowing her eyes to scan the room one final time, she noticed something poking out just behind the bedroom door. Stepping across and pushing the door to, she saw the wastepaper basket, still containing a translucent plastic carrier bag. Bending closer, Kate could see something in the bottom of the bag. Lifting the bin and resting it on the mattress, she nudged the coloured items with a pen, realising they were nail clippings. Mrs Owen didn't seem the type to paint her nails. Tying the ends of the plastic bag, and squeezing out what air she could, she carefully placed the sealed bag into her jacket pocket.

Moving quickly down the stairs, Kate nodded for Laura to finish her drink. 'We'd best be on our way, Mrs Owen. Thank you for your time this morning.'

Mrs Owen pushed herself up unsteadily, disappointment in her voice. 'Do you really need to go so soon?'

'I'm afraid so, criminals won't arrest themselves.' Kate would have spent the rest of the day keeping Mrs Owen company if she could, but in truth she needed to get back to SSD. 'Thank you for your generosity, but we really do have to be on our way.'

Mrs Owen showed them to the door, and once outside, Kate passed Laura the bag. 'Possible nail clippings from Maria Alexandrou. Can you get these to SSD immediately?'

Laura nodded, seeing Kate staring at a woman across the street. 'You know her?' Laura asked as the Latino woman stared daggers at them.

Kate took in the woman's appearance: spotless makeup, figure-hugging skirt and jacket, designer handbag draped around her shoulder. 'No,' Kate said, as the woman suddenly upped her pace and headed towards the bottom of the road. 'But she clearly knows who we are.' Without a second's thought, Kate raced through the weathered gate in pursuit.

THIRTY-TWO

Kate took the corner at pace, closing the gap with every step, and was soon grabbing the woman's arm to stop her.

'What' you want?' the woman demanded, out of breath, her accent Hispanic.

Kate released her. 'Why were you running?'

'Is free country… I do exercise.'

Kate already suspected exactly who the woman was, but needed confirmation. 'You were coming to see, Maria,' Kate said, finally getting her breath back.

'Who?'

There'd been a flicker in her eyes at the mention of Maria's name. Kate was about to press on when Laura caught up, still holding the evidence bag.

'Everything okay, ma'am?' she said, barely out of breath. 'Who's this?'

'Unless I'm very much mistaken we all have a mutual friend. Naomi Hendrix says hi, by the way.'

A second flicker in the woman's eyes. 'I don't know who that is.'

'Of course not. Listen, I just want to ask you a few questions about Maria. Will you let me buy you a drink so we can talk?'

The woman looked beyond the detectives, as if she was contemplating whether she'd be able to outrun them. She eventually sighed. 'Okay, but we need to get off the streets before someone sees us.'

*
**

With some coaxing, the woman revealed her name was Sofia. The pub she brought them to was dark and grimy. Although it was barely midday, the bar was already being propped up by four men drinking in pensive silence. In the background, Phil Collins sung quietly from the stereo speakers.

'You were the one who told DI Hendrix that Maria was missing, right?' Kate asked when they'd collected their drinks and were squashed around a small table as far from the bar as they could be.

Sofia nodded, placing the straw delicately between her thick red lips, and slurping the double vodka and orange juice she'd ordered. 'She's dead, isn't she?'

Kate considered the question. 'I don't know for certain, but it's looking probable. My colleague is taking nail clippings we believe to be Maria's to be examined. If it's a match, then I'd say it's a strong possibility that she is. I'm sorry.'

'At least she is out of the life; that's all she wanted.'

'Can you tell me about her? I'd like to know as much as I can, so I can catch whoever is responsible for her death.'

'Sure. Wha' you want to know?'

'Everything – her full name, how old was she, where was she from, how the two of you met?'

'We – the girls I work with – we don't use last names; I think most don't use real names. I am Sofia now, but was not always the case. You understand?'

Kate nodded.

'But Maria, she was different. She knew who she was and she didn't hide that. I know her... three years, I think. She's like a sister to me; we share experiences and help each other. She was born in Serbia, I think, come to this country to study, but drop out of university, because too expensive. She didn't want to leave UK, so she did what she had to stay. That's how we meet.'

'You told my colleague that Maria was trying to buy her freedom?'

'Is true. She decide she want to pay the boss to go free.'

'You told my colleague that Maria managed to raise ten thousand pounds to buy that freedom. Did she give you any clue as to how she got that money?'

Sofia shook her head despondently.

Kate chose her next words carefully. 'In your line of work, how could you lay your hands on that amount of money quickly?'

'I wish I knew… In my experience, girls who earn biggest money either do the parties, or they take on other jobs.'

'Other jobs?'

'You know, like, delivering drugs, that sort of thing.'

'Do you think she was working as a mule?'

Sofia shook her head. 'I think not. Listen, everybody take them to get by – it goes with the job – but Maria turn her back on all that last year. When she decide she want to buy freedom, she get herself clean. I don't think she would do those jobs to make the money.'

'You mentioned parties?'

'Sometimes a client speak to the boss because he want to hire several girls for friends at party. Me and Maria never do that. Some of the stories make us feel sick. But maybe Maria did decide to do it, I don't know.'

Kate had heard plenty of horror stories but she'd need Hendrix's support to go much deeper into that line of enquiry.

'Have there been any of those parties recently, do you know?'

'I don't know. The boss, he know I won't, so he not ask me. Maybe, Maria ask him and not tell me, or maybe she get money another way. I don't know, I'm sorry.' Sofia finished the last of her drink. 'I need to go.'

Kate reached for her hand across the table. 'No, please, stay a bit longer. I can buy you another drink.'

But Sofia placed her free hand over the top of the glass. 'I have had enough. I can't be late or the boss not be happy.'

'Okay, quickly then, do you know if Maria actually managed to pay off her debt? Did she give your guy the ten grand he wanted?'

'I don't know. Last I see her, she say she has the money and going to take it to him, and then she gone. I never see her since.'

'We believe she had a tattoo removed from her ankle last week. It's been described as a brand of some kind.'

Sofia raised her own foot, allowing Kate to see the full scorpion and the initials C and E.

'I think maybe the partial scar we saw resembles that.'

'All of us are forced to have it, so we marked as his property.'

'Would he have allowed her to have it removed?'

'If she had bought her freedom, then I suppose so.'

'Sofia, is there a chance that she took the money to your pimp, and he killed her for it?'

Sofia chewed on the straw, suddenly conscious of anyone who might walk in and see them talking. 'I have to go. I'm sorry.'

She teetered to her feet, knocking the table as she went. Kate watched her leave, tempted to go after her, but not certain what additional information Sofia would be able to give her. In her gut, Kate now had no doubt that the victim dismembered in the school grounds was Maria; everything she'd learned till now steered her in only that direction.

But that left the bigger question: how had Maria managed to get her hands on ten thousand pounds so quickly, and had she been killed because of it?

THIRTY-THREE

Seated in the incident room, Kate's mind raced to try and figure out what could have connected Maria Alexandrou and Petr Nowakowski, and driven them into the path of a killer. Two victims from the wrong side of the tracks, striving to make amends, but ultimately failing. There had to be something she was missing.

The incident room was virtually empty. Patel was on his way back from the prison, Laura was waiting at the lab for the DNA results and the rest of the team were out on calls. The only detectives at desks were Humberidge, deep in conversation with someone on the phone, and Olly Quinlan, who seemed practically asleep as he stared at his monitor. With his head propped up by his arm, looking anything but motivated, she couldn't help but wonder whether she had somehow led to this deterioration in his personality. One thing was for sure: she couldn't afford to carry any passengers if she was to manage all three investigations under the supe's nose.

'Olly,' she called out. 'Walk with me.'

He jumped at the sound of his name, and he frowned as his brain slowly processed where he was. 'Sorry, ma'am?'

Kate stood, grabbing her jacket. 'I need fresh air. Walk with me.'

Humberidge was oblivious to the brief exchange, growing angrier with whomever he was addressing on the phone.

Quinlan, pulled the leather jacket from his chair and followed Kate out of the room.

*⁎⁎

'I didn't realise you smoked, Olly,' Kate said when they were outside the station, and he had sparked up.

'I quit, but I've recently started again.'

It was another indicator that something was wrong, but she wasn't sure how much to pry. 'Are you okay, Olly?'

'It's just a cigarette, ma'am. I've quit before, and I'll quit again.'

'That's not what I meant. I don't need to be a detective to see that there's something wrong. You *can* talk to me, you know. I don't bite.'

He watched her as he inhaled deeply, before shaking his head as he exhaled a plume of smoke. 'It's just family stuff, ma'am. Nothing for you to worry about.'

'It's in my nature to worry, Olly. I'm a mother, and my instinct is telling me that something is off with you, and I need you working at full capacity if we're to find Daisy and solve the two murders.'

'I'm sorry, ma'am, but everything is okay. I know I screwed up the other day, but—'

'This isn't about you missing the morning briefing on Saturday. Look at you. The Olly I know is the life and soul of any party, a bubbly character whose cheeky approach to life helps motivate the rest of the team. Something's changed.'

He crushed the cigarette underfoot. 'If there *was* something I'd tell you, ma'am, but I'm fine. A bit grumpy maybe, but I'll try and cheer up. Okay?'

Kate knew anything else she said would potentially overstep the mark of her role as his superior. 'Where are you with speaking to Nowakowski's employers?'

'Oh, I spoke to them, but it'd be more accurate to refer to them as his *former* employers. They dismissed him a month ago.'

'Really? What for?'

'The lass I spoke to couldn't say for certain. It was recorded on her system as "impropriety". I asked her what that meant and she said that was all it said, but in her experience, impropriety usually means that the employee had either been caught taking drugs, or shagging one of the passengers on board.'

'Drugs?'

'Just her opinion.'

'So if he was sacked, why did he tell his sister he was due on a cruise this week? And where was he planning to be really?'

Quinlan raised his eyebrows. 'Exactly!'

'You think he'd fallen back into old habits? Maybe dealing to fund the deposit on the new flat?'

'It's not unheard of. I think we need to look a little closer at his movements in the days leading up to his death to establish that.'

Kate nodded her agreement. 'Do me a favour, see if you can track his activity through mobile phone coverage, but also track it against the mobile number for Maria Alexandrou. I want to know whether they came into contact with one another.' Kate paused to answer her phone. 'Matthews.'

'Ma'am,' Laura said. 'SSD have confirmed the match. The foot belonged to Maria Alexandrou.'

As darkness spread across the sky outside the office, it was hard to ignore the tension on the faces of her team, as Kate gathered them around the board, and asked for their updates in the Daisy Emerson disappearance. Tonight marked the tenth full day since Daisy had last been seen. Given the media attention, countless hours of overtime – some paid, some not – and the team's determination to bring her home safe and well, they were no closer to really knowing where she was or why she'd disappeared. The pain of failure was etched on each of their faces, and Kate knew nothing she could say or do would alter that; at least not tonight.

'Our orders remain unchanged,' Kate informed the group. 'Our focus is on finding Daisy Emerson. Where are we with tracking her movements on that Friday night?'

DC Rogers raised a weary arm into the air. 'I've been at the Highfield campus since lunchtime, ma'am, showing Daisy's picture, stopping groups as they walked past. But nobody claimed to have seen her that night. A couple of guys were happy to offer opinions on what might have happened, based on nothing but a keen sense of imagination.'

'What about the Avenue campus?'

'Hitting that first thing, ma'am, but finding anyone who can help is like looking for a needle in a haystack.'

Kate could feel her dejection, and knew how frustratingly fruitless the leg work could be in challenging investigations such as this. 'We need to keep looking, Vicky. One person out there could have the vital piece of the jigsaw we're missing. Don't give up. Were you on your own up there today?'

'Inspector Bentley sent a couple of uniforms up with me.'

'Good. See if you can get any additional support tomorrow too. In fact, if any of the rest of you are scratching your heads, I want a team going door-to-door again along Daisy's route home. She can't have just disappeared into thin air. Someone knows something. I also want someone to dig into Ismael Vardan's movements in the past week. That three hours when he was supposedly reading in his classroom doesn't sit well with me. Ewan, where are we with tracking that IP address?'

'We've got the original signal narrowed down to the UK, but that's as much as they claim they can tell us at the moment.'

'Who's *they*? Who's tracing the address?'

'The company who supplied the masking software, ma'am.'

'Why are we relying on them for this information? Surely one of the techie guys in SSD can trace it quicker?'

'The company are anxious to protect their customers' identities. Their head office is in Shanghai, so we're having—'

'They must have the individual's credit card information for this software. That would do to begin with. Don't take no for an answer, Ewan. If it's some weirdo from the back of nowhere, we know we're looking for more than a runaway girl.'

His head dropped, crestfallen. 'Yes, ma'am.'

'Come on, people, we need to think smarter. I appreciate you're all exhausted, and every avenue we pursue is leading to a dead end, but we can't give up on her.'

Quinlan cleared his throat. 'I checked on Alfie Caplan's alibi, ma'am. He *was* at his brother's halls of residence in Kingston on Friday night, like he said. His brother confirmed Alfie arrived around eight o'clock and stayed until after lunch on Sunday. We have traffic-camera footage of the car arriving in Kingston just before eight o'clock. Mobile phone signal has him in West London for the entire period.'

'Okay, so he didn't pick her up from Georgie's road, but I still think he's hiding something. Keep digging. What else?'

'Speaking of mobile phone activity,' Laura offered, 'I was looking at Daisy's mobile activity for the Friday night. Georgie said Daisy left at quarter past nine, right? The phone company puts her in Georgie's road at that time, but the phone signal isn't lost until twenty past nine. The whole time it doesn't leave Abbotts Way. You and I have walked that road and it would only take two minutes at most to walk from Georgie's house to Highfield Lane. So why hang around? Georgie was adamant that Daisy left at that precise time, and hasn't mentioned that Daisy was waiting for anyone, or that they continued talking in the street after she'd left. I just don't understand what she was doing for that five minutes. Even if she did eventually walk to Highfield Lane, that still leaves three minutes unaccounted for.'

'Maybe she called someone for a lift?' Rogers suggested.

But Laura had already considered the possibility. 'We know she didn't call anyone, from her phone records. Her last internet activity was just before she left Georgie's house, and then there's no other text messages sent or received, or phone calls made or received, and then the phone signal just disappears at twenty-past. So, what was she doing for all of that time?'

'Maybe she'd arranged for someone to collect her, and she was waiting for a lift,' Rogers suggested.

'But who?' Laura countered. 'Certainly not her parents, and her boyfriend was in London.'

'I wouldn't be so quick to rule out her parents,' Humberidge interjected. 'Barry said he was out with friends on Friday night, but that's not what one of his friends says.'

'What?' Kate blurted, before she could stop herself. 'But we've already checked his alibi. Two of his friends confirmed he was with them playing pool and drinking until the early hours.'

Humberidge fired her a knowing look. 'I know all that, but a third friend who was at said engagement, told me off the record that Barry was *not* there.'

'Who?'

'My source doesn't want to be named, as he doesn't want to be seen to be the one to let the cat out of the bag.'

'Humberidge, we don't have time—'

'Seems Barry has been having it away with one of his former employees behind Val's back. His mates all know about it and have frequently provided him with an alibi so he can see this other woman. My source says Barry contacted them all and swears blind he was with his mistress all night, until he returned home, and asked them to stick to the story so Val won't find out he's been playing away.'

'Who's his lover?'

'The guy didn't want to give me a name, but did say it was someone Barry used to work with. I'm still digging, but I'll find out who. I told you there was more going on with them than they were letting on. Of course, the question is, if he wasn't where he said he was, can we really be sure he was with that other woman all night, and didn't stop by to collect Daisy?'

'That's a big leap.'

'Not as big as you thought though, hey, ma'am?'

Kate could feel her cheeks starting to redden. 'Okay, keep digging, but be discreet, Humberidge. We don't want to add to Val's heartbreak for no reason. As for the rest of you,' Kate continued, 'I want you to go home and spend what time you can with your families. Do your best to switch off all thoughts about Daisy Emerson, just for the night, and try to relax. Tomorrow, we'll be back on it.'

As the team pulled apart, computers were turned off and coats grabbed, Kate remained where she was. She'd been so sure that Barry and Val Emerson were innocent bystanders in the unfolding circus, but could she have been wrong about Barry?

'You should take your own advice, ma'am,' Laura offered, tying a scarf around her neck.

Kate smiled warmly, appreciating Laura's concern. 'You're probably right. I'll just finish up here...'

'Well, don't stay too late. And don't forget to eat! Even the world's best detective has a proper meal every now and again, you know.'

Kate gave her a tired smile which ended the moment she felt her phone ringing in her pocket.

'Tara? What's wrong?' But she could barely make out the words through the sobs. 'Just tell me where you are, and I'll come at once.'

THIRTY-FOUR

Pulling into the car park of the fast-food restaurant on the outskirts of Southampton, Kate quickly fired a message off to Ben, apologising that she would be late for dinner. Inside the restaurant's main window, Kate could see Tara staring forlornly into the milkshake in front of her, her face in stark contrast to the excitable and vibrant girl she'd first met last summer.

Kate knew deep down she should call the supe and ask him to meet her here, but she wanted to give Tara one last chance to do the right thing. Tara nodded as Kate approached, but made no effort to smile.

Sliding in behind the table, Kate passed Tara a paper napkin to dab her eyes with. 'What am I doing here, Tara?'

Tara picked up the napkin and wiped her swollen cheeks as fresh tears fell. 'I'm sorry, I didn't know who else to call.'

'Why are you so far from home?'

Tara stared out of the window as she tried to blink away the tears. 'I went home after college, and the place was empty, but when Mum came back at lunchtime she had another go at me about staying out. She accused me of wasting my education, of trying to throw away all the hard work she and Dad have done for me. I tried to explain but she wouldn't let me get a word in edgeways.'

Kate was sure she was the last person who could judge another mother on her parenting technique. 'I'm sure it's only because she's worried about you,' she tried, weakly.

'She's the reason I'm not right,' Tara spat back bitterly.

Kate was tempted to remind Tara that her mum wasn't the cause of Tara's current predicament, but opted for a more civil approach. 'You need to try and put yourself in your mum's shoes. She loves you and she's worried about you and fear makes people behave in strange ways.'

Tara's head snapped round, rage in her eyes. 'If she loved me, she wouldn't have locked me in my room!'

Kate looked surprised. 'She did what?

Tara's gaze returned to the window. 'She was going on and on, saying how I would be lucky to get into *any* university if I didn't get my head down, and I'd had enough, so I told her I was going to my room and slammed the door. The next thing I know, I hear a key turning. What kind of person does that?'

One who is terrified of losing their daughter, Kate wanted to say, but she could already see the hurt in Tara's eyes. 'What happened next?'

'I banged and banged on the door, but she refused to open it. She even put on the radio to drown out my screams. So I escaped through my window.'

'The window? You're on the second floor!'

Tara gave Kate a half smile that said it wasn't the first time she'd left the property undetected and Kate tried not to think too hard about the risk to the little life now growing inside Tara.

'That still doesn't explain how you wound up all the way out here. We're miles out of the city.'

'I ran from the driveway and caught a bus to town. I decided to take your advice and called the father. He works in town, so I phoned him and told him we needed to meet. I figured it was about time I told him. I know he has his own flat, so I thought if I spoke to him about what's going on with my parents, he'd let me crash at his for a bit – I didn't want to keep bothering you, because I know it's awkward for you and my dad – but he refused to take my calls at first. So I went to where he worked and kept calling until he came out to meet me. He drove us here so nobody we knew would see us.'

Kate wasn't sure she wanted the answer to the next question, but her imagination was already performing somersaults. 'How old is he?'

'What difference does it make?'

'You said he works in town, has a car and his own flat. I'm guessing he's not someone you met at college.'

'He's in his twenties, so not that much older than me.'

'You're seventeen, Tara.'

Tara glared at her. 'And?'

Kate bit her lip. 'Is he married?'

'No! What do you take me for?'

Kate breathed a sigh of relief. 'What happened when you got here?'

'He drove us through the drive-thru, and then parked up. I told him we should go inside, but he had this... this look of revulsion on his face, like he didn't want to be seen dead with me. And then when I explained what had happened with Mum, he told me I should have an abortion. He just came out with it: *you should have an abortion*. Like it was so simple, like it was his choice. What an arsehole!'

Kate was tempted to agree, but stayed silent.

'I was so angry that I told him I'd decided to keep the baby and would be naming him on the birth certificate, and then he'd *have* to support the two of us. He called me a stupid little child, shoved me out of the car and left me stranded. I never should have involved him in the first place. I'm better off without him in my life.'

Kate's anger simmered. 'Where does this guy work?'

Tara frowned. 'Why?'

'I want to have a word with him.'

Tara reached out for Kate's hand. 'No! Listen, I wish I'd never told him. I don't want him involved anymore. Besides, I've decided I'm going to have an abortion anyway.'

Kate's heart sank.

'It's the right thing to do,' Tara continued. 'I'm not ready to be a mum, and it would mess up me going to university, and moreover I won't have to tell my parents about it.'

And there it was. Kate winced.

'Have you discussed this with any of your friends?'

'Uh, no, I don't think so.'

Kate couldn't help but think of Georgie's previous statement that Daisy couldn't be pregnant because she was saving herself. 'But don't you have a best friend who you share everything with?'

'*Not this*. You and… *him* are the only ones I've told.'

Kate reached for the milkshake and took a sip. 'Whatever decision you reach, it affects more than just you. I know it's *your* body, and therefore *your* choice, but if you were my daughter, I'd want to know about it and to help you reach a decision having discussed all your options. Please, Tara, don't shut out your mum and dad. Despite everything, they mean well, and you really should be open with them first.'

'They don't need to know. And I'm sure they would agree that it's the best decision anyway. I'll make an appointment with my GP in the morning and take it from there.'

'I'm begging you not to rush into anything without speaking to your parents. I'll drive you there now, and I'll stay with you for moral support.'

'I was hoping you'd let me stay at yours for tonight; once I've had it done, I'll go home, and everything can return to normal.'

Kate could feel Tara's eyes burning into her, but she had to remain firm. 'No, Tara, I'm sorry, but I can't keep this from them any longer. Grab your coat, I'm taking you home.'

*✳✳

The gravel crackled beneath the Audi's tyres as Kate parked on the large driveway in front of the detached property.

'You don't have to come in,' Tara repeated. 'I'll tell them.'

But Kate could sense the lie. 'They need to know that you're safe and I think it's probably time I came clean with your dad about where you've been the last couple of nights.'

Tara sighed in frustration as she pushed the car door open and headed to the porch. She'd barely put her key in the lock when the door was opened and the supe appeared, dressed in chinos, shirt and sweater, pulling Tara into his arms. 'Oh, thank God you're safe.'

Kate locked the car, the bleep causing the supe to open his eyes and register her presence.

'Kate? What are you—'

'Tara phoned me,' Kate responded. 'I said I'd bring her home.'

The supe released his daughter who hurried inside and hugged a tearful Judith, saying how sorry she was. 'I appreciate you bringing her home, Kate. You know what teenagers can be like.'

'Think nothing of it, sir. I'm glad she felt able to reach out to me.' Kate continued to watch Tara, willing her to tell her relieved parents exactly why she had left. But as Kate waited, Tara's lips remained sealed.

'Was there anything else, Kate?' the supe asked, curious as to why she hadn't moved.

Tell them, Kate urged herself, but the words wouldn't leave her lips.

Tara turned to face her, shaking her head just enough so Kate would see it.

'I'll see you in the morning,' Kate finally exhaled, angry at her own weakness.

'Thanks again, Kate,' he said, as he closed the door.

Getting back into her car, she was relieved to see Ben had messaged to tell her he would slow down the cooking until she arrived. Maybe Laura was right: what she needed was a night off.

THIRTY-FIVE

ELEVEN DAYS MISSING

'Morning, ma'am,' Patel said, with far too much cheer for this time of the day.

Slumped in her chair, struggling not to yawn, Kate looked up at him. 'It's not even half past six, what are you doing here?'

'Same thing as you, I presume,' he said, switching on the coffee maker. 'You want a drink?'

She nodded, handing him her mug as he approached.

'There's some pastries in my bag, if you fancy?' he said, busying himself at the machine. He really had become her rock since joining the team. Methodical to the last, and with a moral compass that pointed true north, he was like her Jiminy Cricket.

'Great minds must think alike,' Laura cooed, as she entered and removed her coat and scarf. 'Morning, ma'am. You on the drinks, Sarge?'

Patel grabbed Laura's mug from her desk in answer.

'Don't you both have beds you could still be in?' Kate said, genuinely surprised to see them so early.

'We can't let you have all the fun,' Laura said, dragging over her chair and resting a fresh pad of paper on her lap.

'Help yourself to a croissant, Laura,' Patel said, placing three mugs on Kate's desk.

Laura's eyes widened with excitement, as she reached for his satchel and unzipped it. The smell of fresh pastries filled the air around them, and even Kate couldn't resist revelling in the buttery warmness for just a moment.

'All right,' Kate said, dabbing pastry flakes from her lips, 'start with telling me what Nowakowski's former crew told you when you stopped by the prison.'

Patel reached for his notebook. 'I spoke to the leader of the group initially. Career criminal called Ash Thomas. You've probably not heard of him, ma'am, as he's been inside since the failed armed robbery at the security depot. He was a right piece of work, though, back in the day; tattooed from head to toe.' He sighed at the memory. 'Anyway, it seems prison life agrees with him. He's certainly not the thug I remember.'

'In what way?'

'He's found religion. Reckons he's repenting his sins and wants to devote the rest of his life to God.'

'Bet he's just saying that to get in with the parole board,' Laura added, sceptically.

Patel shook his head. 'Straight up. I spoke to the prison warden and he said Ash has been on his best behaviour for the past twelve months, spending part of every day in the library, either reading or helping fellow inmates to study. It's quite the switch from all accounts.'

'What did he have to say about Petr Nowakowski?'

'He went quiet for a bit and then told me he regretted his troubled past every day and is grateful that Petr helped him find the right path.'

'Oh, please!' Laura exclaimed.

'I disagree,' Patel continued. 'He seemed genuine. I don't think he had any involvement in Nowakowski's death.'

'What about the rest of the group?' Kate pressed. 'There were four plus Petr and Ash, right?'

'I managed to speak to one of the others who was locked up in Parkhurst too, but he claimed not to have heard anything about Petr since his arrest.'

'Don't tell me he's turned over a new leaf as well?'

Patel snorted. 'No, he was very clear about what he'd like to do to Petr, but I doubt there is much he could have done from the inside. Ash was the leader of the group – the one with all the contacts.'

'What about another crew in the city? If he was desperate for money, maybe he fell back into old ways.'

But Patel shook his head. 'I had a quiet word with a friend in Hendrix's team. She said Nowakowski's name hasn't come up in any conversations on the street. They keep detailed files on known associates of all gangs in the city, and he's not been named since his arrest. I think his sister was right: he'd been making an effort to keep his nose clean.'

'Quinlan mentioned the cruise company sacked him for some sort of impropriety,' Kate told them. 'There's something about a convicted armed robber managing to secure a job on a cruise ship that doesn't sit right with me. Given their clientele, would they really take a chance?'

Laura lowered her croissant. 'You reckon he lied about his conviction?'

Kate nodded. 'More than likely, and then maybe someone found out and that's why they let him go. Can you follow up on that, Laura? Go down to the head office when they open and ask to see a copy of his job application.' She turned back to Patel, as Laura answered a ringing phone. 'Have the vehicle recognition team managed to track Chris Jackson yet?'

Patel nodded, firing up the nearest workstation. 'Had an email overnight. Two seconds and I'll read it to you.'

'Ma'am,' Laura interrupted. 'That was a call from downstairs. Apparently someone decided to put a brick through the front window of Neil Watkins' home last night.'

'The gardener?'

Laura nodded. 'They scrawled the word killer on his driveway and then hurled the rock, apparently. Uniform are on the scene now, but his mother Imelda is demanding to speak to you. Blames the news report about the foot and thinks her son is being targeted.'

That was all Kate needed. 'But the Media Relations team have now confirmed that we aren't focused on any one individual.'

'I guess not everybody got the message. You want me to go down there and speak to her?'

Kate sighed. 'No, ask uniform to pass on that I will stop by to visit her when I get a moment.'

Laura relayed the message over the phone.

'Here you go,' Patel said. 'His van was seen leaving the teachers' car park at St Bartholomew's just after four last Friday... It is then picked up on the traffic camera at the north end of Hill Lane by the Winchester Road roundabout... It is then seen heading up the A35, from where it then joins the M3 at junction fourteen, but it is last seen at junction thirteen, before we lose track of it.' He paused. 'Junction thirteen is the exit for Eastleigh and Chandler's Ford, but we don't know where he goes after that. Given that his home address is in Lordshill, we know he wasn't going home.'

'So where was he going and where is he now?'

'PC Barnes went by his residence yesterday morning, but there was no sign of his van. He called on a couple of his neighbours, but nobody could recall seeing him over the weekend. Jackson's mobile phone is switched off, so we can't monitor him via that, and I have put out a description of the van and its registration plates to our colleagues in Wiltshire and Dorset, but as yet no sightings.'

Kate turned to Laura. 'What else can you tell me about Jackson?'

'I managed to track a page for his engineering business on Facebook, but no personal page,' Laura said. 'My understanding is you can't have one without the other, which suggests he has his privacy settings fixed so that he cannot be located by strangers.'

'Okay, go with what you've got.'

Laura passed her the print outs. 'The business page is pretty basic with its content: he doesn't ever post on it, just contains basic company information, mobile phone number and email address.'

'Have you found a photograph of him?'

'Next page, ma'am,' Laura said.

Kate pushed the business page to the back of the pile. The image was grainy, but his strawberry-blond curls were greased back over his head, and small dimples formed in his cheeks where he was forcing a smile. His eyes were dark, but she couldn't tell if that was just the quality of the print out. He had to be in his mid-thirties at most, and his chin looked freshly shaven.

'You reckon he still looks like this? How old is the image?'

'Hard to say. I pulled it from his business website. I'll check with the administrators at the school.'

Kate raised the picture. 'What does that face say to you?'

'Honestly? He's actually quite handsome, in a goofy sort of way.'

'Do you know what I see when I look at him? I see the face of someone I *want* to trust. He looks like butter wouldn't melt, but I've underestimated people for less than that. We need to find him.'

'Do you want me to put his description out to uniform?'

'Please.'

'His criminal history is clean. He has three points on his licence for speeding two years ago, but otherwise, he's not in the system.'

Kate closed her eyes, trying to process their next steps. If this was a brand-new murder investigation the decisions made in the first hour – the golden hour – would pay dividends later on. But in this situation, Maria and Petr had been dead for days already, giving Jackson a head start. While not conclusive, she couldn't shake the coincidence of the heart being sent in the type of box he would have access to as a photocopy engineer.

'First things first: get his last known location from the mobile provider, and then get his image to the school and ask them how it compares to when they saw him on Thursday. When you've done that, take his description to the mail depot in Bitterne and see if the staff there recognise him as the guy who delivered the heart.'

THIRTY-SIX

Staring out at the one-bedroom maisonette, just off the main road through Shirley, Kate could see Imelda, brush in hand and bucket of soapy water at her feet, as she scrubbed at the red paint on the grimy brickwork. Parking up, Kate exited the car and hurried across the road.

Imelda welcomed the distraction, dropping the wire brush into the suds with a splosh. Despite the chill in the air, her cheeks were flushed. 'I ought to charge you the cost of cleaning this mess up.'

'Is Neil okay?'

Imelda wiped the hair from her eyes with the back of her hand. 'He was so shaken when the brick came through the window. He kept asking me what he'd done wrong. I came around as soon as he called, and as I arrived I could see the curtain-twitchers across the road taking it all in.'

Kate stepped back and took in the wooden board now covering one of the windows. 'Was there any damage caused inside?'

'No, thankfully,' Imelda sighed. 'It was lucky he wasn't looking out the window at the time, or walking past. God knows what could have happened then. Fortunately he was in bed in the back room.'

'He lives alone?'

She nodded. 'It's not very big inside. A small front room with a couple of armchairs and a small dining table, then a bedroom at the rear, a small kitchen and a bathroom. But it's enough, and I just want him to have as normal a life as possible. He needs structure and routine.'

'I'm sorry to ask this, Mrs Watkins, but why do you think somebody targeted Neil?'

'I'd have thought that was perfectly obvious.'

'I saw the news report and I've read Zoe Denton's article, and Neil isn't mentioned in either.'

'Maybe not, but she said the police were considering all associated with the school.'

'I still don't see why anyone would reach the conclusion that Neil would have anything to do with it.'

'People are small-minded, detective. They see a grown man with learning difficulties and they leap to conclusions. I blame myself for putting him in that position. I thought that the role at the school would be good for him; giving him a level of trust he's not experienced before. I thought with him there, I could keep an eye on him, and Mrs Kilpatrick understands that he needs protection, but now I wish I'd kept him safer.'

'This isn't your fault,' Kate offered. 'We will get a formal statement out clarifying matters, and warning people not to jump to wrong conclusions. In the meantime, is there anywhere else Neil can stay? With you perhaps?'

'I've already packed some things for him and he'll be at my place tonight.'

'Whereabouts do you live, Mrs Watkins?'

'North Baddesley. Do you know it?'

Kate nodded. 'On the way to Romsey. It's a very pleasant village.'

'Yes, well, I don't feel right him being here on his own while all this is going on. Do you know when your people will be finished at the school?'

Kate tightened her lips. 'We're working as quickly as we can.'

Mrs Watkins reached down for the brush again, slopping more suds onto the brickwork and scrubbing fiercely. 'The sooner all of this is over, the better.'

'Where's Neil today? With the school closed, I thought he might be home?'

'He loves the sound of the ocean,' she replied, her eyes focused on the brickwork. 'When he's not working, he likes to drive to the coast and just sit and listen to the waves crashing.'

'Bit cold to be at the beach today.'

Imelda frowned. 'He doesn't go into the water; he can't swim. He likes to sit nearby, just listening.'

Kate could imagine how calming that would be. 'I am sorry for what happened. Was there any note attached to the brick?'

'They'd left their message out here in paint.'

'Do you still have the brick? If I could take it with me, I could see if—'

'I threw it in the skip down the road,' Imelda replied. 'I assume that's where the perpetrator got it from.'

Kate looked up to where Imelda was pointing, seeing the battered metal skip on the driveway of a neighbouring property, where it looked like extension work was ongoing.

'I didn't think you could get fingerprints from stones anyway?' Imelda continued.

'There's been some success with it in recent years,' Kate confirmed, excusing herself and walking over to the skip, but on looking inside, she knew her search would be a waste of valuable time. Dozens of rough and broken bricks lay entwined with garden waste and other rubble.

'I doubt you'll ever catch the idiot who caused this damage,' Imelda said, when Kate returned to the maisonette. 'I just worry about the emotional damage it will have caused my little boy...' Her words trailed off as she began to cry.

Kate offered her a tissue, and could only apologise, knowing her words were worthless. She was grateful when her phone began to ring and she excused herself to take it.

'Is Sofia... can you meet me? Is about Maria. I need to see you.'

*
**

'Thanks for coming,' Sofia said, as Kate perched on the stool by the window.

'I was surprised to get your call. Are you not worried that someone might spot you?'

'In this neighbourhood? I doubt it.'

Kate stared out at the sea beyond the road below them. 'I have to admit, meeting an informant in the restaurant of IKEA is a new one for me.'

'The people I know, they don't buy flat pack furniture, if you get me?'

Kate could believe it. 'What did you want to speak to me about?'

'After our chat yesterday, I decided to go and ask my pimp about Maria's payment.'

Kate's shoulders tensed. 'I don't want you to do anything that will put your life at risk.'

'Is okay. I tell him one of Maria's regulars was asking after her, and whether she would be back. He tell me that she clear her debt and is gone. I act surprised, but he show me picture on his phone. It was selfie of him and Maria from the Monday night. They are both smiling, and she not look worried or scared. I ask him about the money and he say she pay ten grand and left. He tell me he think she be back working for him again when she realise how hard real work is.'

'So he didn't know she was dead?'

'No. The way he speak about her, is like she alive. He ask me if I have spoken to her, and I say no, and he ask me to call her and see if she ready to come back yet. I don't think he kill her.'

The admission didn't surprise Kate, particularly in light of what Laura was investigating. Kate fished into her pocket and pulled out her phone, loading Jackson's website, and locating the image Laura had printed off. Kate passed Sofia the phone. 'Do you recognise this man?'

Sofia studied the image, before handing the phone back. 'I don't think so, who is he?'

'You don't remember seeing him with Maria? Maybe one of her customers?'

Sofia took the phone again for a second look. 'I'm sorry, I don't know his face.'

Kate locked the screen, before a new thought hit her. 'You girls make a note of who each other goes off with, right? Do you remember seeing Maria getting into either of these vehicles?' Kate opened the email Laura had sent with the images of Jackson's two registered vehicles.

Sofia studied the two vehicles. 'I think maybe this first one – the car, *not* the van – I maybe see it before, but I no remember registration number.'

'You saw Maria in the car?'

'I no remember. I *think* maybe car has been around, but who with, I'm not sure. Sorry.'

Kate offered her an appreciative smile. 'You have nothing to be sorry for. I appreciate you letting me know what you found out.'

'Oh, other thing I remember. I ask him if Maria work any of those group parties. You remember I say yesterday? He say no. He not know where she get money from either.'

Kate thanked Sofia and waited for her to leave the restaurant, before heading back into the car park to collect her car. The question of how Maria had managed to raise ten thousand pounds in such a short period of time still rankled with Kate. Could Jackson have given it to her? If so, for what reason? And why then kill her after she'd given the money to her pimp? Surely if he planned to kill her he could have done so without handing over the money? And where did Petr Nowakowski fit in to all this?

Despite the certainty in her gut that they were finally making progress with both investigations, she couldn't shake the doubt that there was still so much more they didn't know.

Kate had just started the engine when her phone rang. 'Hi Patel, go ahead.'

'I thought you should know, ma'am, uniform were just called to Alfie Caplan's house after neighbours phoned to report a fight.'

'Between who?'

'Apparently, Daisy's brother just assaulted him. Should I tell uniform to bring them in?'

Kate closed her eyes in frustration. The last thing Barry and Val needed was for Richard to be arrested too. 'No, tell uniform to try and calm the situation and that I'm on my way over.'

THIRTY-SEVEN

The screeching of Kate's brakes as she skidded to a stop caught everyone's attention. Richard Emerson took one look at her before continuing to hurl insults at the house where Alfie Caplan resided with his mum and younger sister.

'You too chicken to face me?' Richard shouted, oblivious to the neighbouring residents sending disapproving looks from the safety of their porches and front windows. 'Get out here, you fucking cheat!'

The front door flew open and Alfie charged at Richard, sending the two of them to the ground as they tussled and fought to get the upper hand. Kate leaped from her car and charged towards the gate, taking it in a single bound, landing on the grass and springing forward to get between the two young men. She took a blow to the ribs from one of them, rolling away and feeling the damp mud soaking into the elbows of her suit jacket. She went for them again, trying to drag Richard off Alfie, but he was too strong and remained where he was, sending punch after punch into Alfie's sides.

Kate nodded for the two waiting constables to intercept them, and when Alfie and Richard had been separated, she told the officers to escort Richard to the car and wait for her return.

'He assaulted me,' Alfie shouted, as Richard was led away. 'I want him charged. A dozen witnesses saw him punch me in McDonald's car park.'

'You deserved far worse,' Richard fired back over his shoulder.

'Enough!' Kate shouted, pushing Alfie towards the house. 'You can tell me about it *inside*.'

The front door was still open from when he'd emerged, so he pushed it with his foot, stomping to the kitchen and filling a glass with water. He put it to his lips, the water spilling at the edges as he chugged it down.

Kate pulled out a chair at the small kitchen table and sat. 'You ought to put some ice on that,' she said, pointing at the red lump forming on his cheek.

Refilling his glass, he plonked down on the chair across from her. 'I'll live.'

But Kate wasn't prepared just to sit there and let him sulk. Pushing herself up, she moved to the combined fridge-freezer unit, and searched the lower half until she found a bag of peas. Pulling it out, she reached for a tea towel from the radiator, folded it in half over the packet and wound the ends tightly before pressing it to his cheek. 'Hold this in place. It'll help the swelling go down and bring the bruise out sooner.'

He reluctantly pressed the pack where she'd put it.

'I'm still waiting for you to tell me why your girlfriend's brother just assaulted you.'

'Ask him!'

'I will in a moment, but for now I'm asking *you*.'

'I don't know what to tell you. I was at the McDonald's in Swaythling getting a late breakfast, when he comes out of nowhere and starts attacking me.'

'Attacking you how?'

'I was heading back to my car as he was driving in, and the next thing I know, he's pulled over and is out of his car shoving me.'

'He must have given you a reason why.'

'He started accusing me of mistreating Daisy, but I kept saying I had nothing to do with her disappearance. I haven't seen her. It's hard on all of us.'

'How did you get back here?'

'I drove home, and the next thing I know he's pulling into my road and starting again. I came inside for my own protection.'

Kate fixed him with a stare. 'You're still holding back on me, Alfie, and I *will* get to the bottom of what's going on.' She stood.

'Where are you going?'

'I'm going to have a word with Richard now and see what he has to say for himself. You want to tell me anything else before I do?'

He looked as if he might speak, but then shook his head.

She pointed at the ice pack. 'You should keep that on for twenty minutes, remove it, then give it twenty minutes before reapplying. Might be worth putting it on your knuckles for a bit too.'

Back outside, Kate's breath swirled in condensation as she stretched out her ribs, certain she'd have her own bruise as a memento of the day.

Kate tapped on the patrol car's window, until the constable lowered it. 'Can you get him out for me? I want a word with him in my car.'

The constable exited and dragged Richard from the back seat, helping him into the front of Kate's Audi.

'Thanks for your support, guys,' she called to the constables. 'You can head on, I've got this now.'

With the patrol car pulling away, Kate climbed back into her car, and started the engine so the heater would come on. 'Well?'

Richard shrugged. 'What did he say?'

'He said he wants you charged with common assault; that you jumped him for no reason in the car park and then followed him home so you could have another go.'

'He was giving as good as he got.'

Kate could see a similar red mark forming below Richard's right eye. 'So you've nothing to add? No mitigating circumstances

I should take into account? What's your mum going to say when she learns you've been arrested?'

'She'll understand when she learns *why*.'

'So, tell me too. Why did you go after Alfie in the car park?'

Richard studied her face and then grunted. 'He didn't tell you who was with him in the car park, did he?'

Kate's shook her head. 'Who?'

'I thought he'd be too spineless to admit what a cheating scumbag he is. I lost it because I saw him in the car park walking with his arm around Georgie Barclay. When he leaned in and kissed her, I saw red.'

'Alfie and Georgie…?'

'And before you start giving him all the benefit of the doubt bullshit, I think it was going on long before my sister disappeared.'

'How did Georgie react when she saw you attacking Alfie?'

'She ran off in tears; I've never seen her look so upset. When he scarpered from the car park, I followed behind and saw him drive back to her house, to try and catch up with her, but she must have taken a different route as I didn't pass her.' He sighed in frustration. 'Look, I know I shouldn't have hit him, but I can't stop thinking that *this* is the reason my sister ran away that night. She was at Georgie's house and maybe she'd found out about the fling and felt she just needed to get away.'

'You've changed your tune. When we first met you were adamant that some pervert had snatched her. If it's because her Facebook profile was accessed, you should know we don't believe your sister did it. Whoever accessed her profile was using software to mask their IP address, but we're tracing it back to the source.'

The blood drained from his face. 'I suppose I might as well admit it was me, then.'

Kate coughed as the spittle caught in her throat. 'You?'

He shrugged sheepishly at her. 'I'm sorry. I thought if you had proof she was still alive it would encourage you to make more effort to find her.'

Kate looked away so she wouldn't be tempted to tell him what she really thought. 'Do you realise how much time that wasted? Where did you get the software from?'

'A friend of mine uses it to download movies and games and stuff. He swore it was impossible to trace, so I didn't think it would be a problem. Are you going to arrest me for wasting police time too?'

Kate looked at him, and for a split second recognised the frightened child beneath the shaved head and muscles. 'I ought to, but that wouldn't do you, your parents or my investigation any good, would it? Can you see the trouble a little lie can cause?'

'I'm so sorry. Are you going to tell my parents what I did?'

'No, Richard, but you are. I'll drop you back there in a minute, but first I think you owe someone else an apology too.' She nodded at Alfie's house.

'I'm not going to apol—'

She raised her hand to cut him off. 'If you don't want him to press charges, you'd better apologise. And I'd make it good if I was you.'

THIRTY-EIGHT

'Richard Emerson is our mystery Facebook liker,' Kate concluded, and she echoed the groan that emanated from the team members who were in the office. 'I know, I know, but at least we can draw a line under the surreptitious activity. Ewan, can you pass on our thanks to our Dutch colleagues?'

Freeborn raised his thumb in the air.

'I'm going to go and speak to Georgie Barclay this afternoon and find out whether Daisy knew about her fling with Alfie. My money is on that she did, and it adds weight to the theory that she did run away, but doesn't help us pinpoint where she is. Humberidge, where are you with confirming Barry Emerson's movements on the Friday night?'

'Mast activity puts his mobile phone in the vicinity of Lordswood. I've been digging into his list of former employees, and have found a Cheryl Oliphant, who lives in Lordswood, and I believe is the woman he's been seeing on the side.'

'Have you spoken with him about it yet?'

'No, ma'am, you said he was off-limits. Besides, I'm pretty sure he'll deny the affair, and put pressure on Cheryl to keep her trap shut as well.'

'What are you suggesting, then?'

'I'll go and speak to her first, tell her what we believe to be true and see if she confirms it. One way or another, I'm sure she'll tell Barry about the visit, and then he'll come to us.'

'How long was his phone in Lordswood?'

'From seven that night until approximately eleven.'

'That puts him in the clear for picking up Daisy, then.'

'Not necessarily, ma'am. Just because his phone was there, doesn't mean he was. Let me keep digging.'

Kate really didn't believe that Barry could be involved in his daughter's disappearance, she'd learned never to make assumptions. 'Fine, but I want something solid by tonight, or you've got to let this go.'

He nodded his understanding, but scowled all the same.

'Patel, any word from the guys up at the university?'

'We finally have a possible sighting,' he said, smiling for the first time in a week. 'Vicky said when she showed Daisy's picture to one student, he said he thought he might have seen her at a bus stop in Portswood crying.'

Kate's mouth dropped. 'When?'

'Well, that's where the problem lies, the student reckoned he saw her on the Friday night, but couldn't give a precise time as he was already drunk when he passed the bus stop, but he remembered she was definitely crying. Vicky has got him to show her the bus stop and she's now trying to get hold of traffic-camera and private security-camera footage, and will check it. It may be nothing, but it could also be a huge break.'

'But we've checked the on-board footage of every bus in the Portswood area that night and at no point did she get on a bus,' Ewan said.

'Just because she was at a bus stop doesn't mean she got on one,' Patel corrected. 'She wouldn't have caught a bus to get home, because it was quicker to walk. We know her phone was switched off after she left Georgie's house, so she couldn't have used it to phone for a taxi, but that doesn't mean she couldn't have flagged down a passing one. I'll keep you posted, ma'am.'

'Let's keep our fingers crossed then,' Kate finished. 'Thanks, everyone.'

The team returned to their desks, but Kate's attention was caught by the sight of Olly Quinlan rushing past the incident room door and along the corridor.

Kate called Patel over. 'I thought Olly was up at the campus with Vicky.'

'He is,' Patel nodded.

Kate left the room without a word of explanation, spotting the door to the viewing suite closing up ahead. She walked quickly, not wishing to draw unwanted attention to her movements. The blind was drawn shut, but as she pressed her ear to the door, she could just make out Olly's voice on the other side, and he didn't sound happy.

'I told you not to call me again... I don't care... oh please, do you not remember what I do for a living? Making idle threats isn't going to—'

As Kate continued to listen to Olly's side of the conversation, the anxiety gripping her tightened.

'Where the hell do you think I can get that kind of money from?'

She'd known something was off about Olly, ever since he'd turned up late on Saturday morning. But had there been signs before that? She tried to remember back to before the discovery of Maria's foot at the school. Had he been withdrawn? Lack of sleep and too many hours in the office meant the days were blurring into one.

'Listen, you don't have to remind me what will happen if this gets out,' Quinlan half shouted.

Kate's fingers brushed the door handle as her hand hovered above it. She'd already confronted him about whatever was going on outside of work and he hadn't been willing to discuss it with her. She'd tried the soft approach and the firm approach, so would barging in on him produce a different result? Although she felt overwhelming responsibility for her team members, she was in danger of overstepping the mark. But if he was having money troubles, had he succumbed to leaking information to Zoe Denton?

'Okay, okay,' Quinlan continued, quieter now. 'I'll sort something... no I can't afford that much... no, wait, don't do that... please, leave it with me, I'll sort it.'

'Ma'am?' Kate jumped as Patel touched her shoulder to get her attention.

Peeling herself away from the door, Kate inhaled deeply.

'I didn't mean to startle you,' Patel continued. 'What were you doing?'

Kate pressed a finger to her lips and ushered for him to move further along the corridor.

Patel eyed her suspiciously. 'Everything okay?'

She nodded. 'You wanted to speak to me?'

'Laura just phoned and asked me to pass on that she's spoken to the administrators at the school, and they confirmed Jackson still fits the image she printed off. She said she's on her way to the courier depot now to show his picture around.'

'Great,' Kate said, as the door to the viewing suite flew open and Quinlan hurried down the corridor. Kate called out to him, but he was already tearing down the stairs.

'I guess Olly wasn't at the school, then,' Patel concluded. 'Is everything okay with him? He doesn't seem right.'

With too many balls to juggle already, Kate waved away Patel's concerns. 'He's just dealing with some personal issues. It's all in hand.'

THIRTY-NINE

'Wondered when you'd be round here,' Georgie Barclay said, wiping her cheek with the back of her hand.

'You won't mind me coming in, then, will you?' Kate said, keeping the disapproval out of her tone.

'My mum won't be back until six, so yeah, you can come in.'

Kate wiped her feet on the door mat as the light dusting of snow began to settle on the ground outside. Taking a final look up at the clouds, Kate could only hope the imminent blizzard would be short.

Georgie grabbed her smart phone, as she settled into the cushion of the sofa in the back room. 'Alfie said you're not planning to charge Daisy's brother.'

Kate's heart went out to her. With her legs curled under her, cheeks puffy from crying all afternoon, and undoubtedly the stress brought on by the revelation of her guilty secret, Georgie looked every part the frightened child, and not the young woman she professed to be.

'How long have you and Alfie been seeing each other?' Kate asked delicately.

Fresh tears filled Georgie's eyes as she raised her head and looked straight at Kate. 'About three months. We got together just before Christmas. Neither of us meant for it to happen, but it just kind of did. The first time we kissed, I knew it was wrong, and I told him that we'd both betrayed Daisy, but as much as we tried to fight it, the attraction was too strong.'

'When I spoke to you on Sunday, and you said Daisy wasn't sleeping with Alfie, was that the truth?'

A tear escaped as Georgie nodded. 'I know she wasn't sleeping with him, because… Oh God, I might as well tell you… I'm sleeping with him.'

'How old are you, Georgie?'

'I'm sixteen, and we didn't hook up until after my birthday. Daisy was one of the youngest in our age group. So, before you start accusing Alfie of doing anything he shouldn't have—'

Kate raised her hands defensively. 'My intention is just to make sure you're okay. When individuals have sex under the age of consent, our concern is only for the safety of the minor. You are old enough to give your consent, but that doesn't mean you can't still feel pressured into engaging in activity that you don't want.'

'It isn't like that. Alfie isn't like that! He would never pressure me into having sex. The first time we slept together it was because we both wanted to.'

Kate's relief was genuine. 'I'm pleased you've told me that, but that doesn't mean I'm not still concerned about you, Georgie. Can you tell me how the two of you first realised you liked each other?'

'It was after my birthday party. We'd gone bowling in Millbrook, and there must have been a dozen of us there, just hanging out, bowling, playing on the arcade games. Daisy asked if Alfie could come along too and I said that was fine, and he gave us a lift home. He dropped me first, and then went on, but messaged me to say I'd left my jacket in his car and did I want him to drop it off. I came out to meet him and thanked him for being so nice. I leaned in to kiss his cheek, but we both lingered and then kissed properly. I felt so guilty all the next day when I was with Daisy, and every time he replied to one of her messages I just wanted to tell her what a terrible friend I was. But she seemed so happy, and I didn't think it would happen again, so I kept quiet. I didn't see him again for a week, but the following weekend we were both at a party and we couldn't keep our eyes off each other. Daisy wasn't at the party as she'd gone to an aunt's birthday meal or something. I kept looking over to see if he was still watching me dancing, and when I went to use the bathroom he followed me upstairs, and one thing led to another.'

'Did you sleep with him that night?'

'God, no! What do you take me for?'

Kate chose not to answer the question.

'No, when we were in the bathroom I told him that we shouldn't have kissed; that it was wrong and we should put it behind us. He agreed it was wrong, but said he hadn't been able to stop thinking about me all week, and to be honest I'd been thinking a lot about him as well.' She shrugged apologetically. 'I don't know what else to say. We both gave in to temptation and made out in the bathroom.' She paused as her phone beeped. She read the message and then looked back up. 'It's from Alfie, asking if you've shown up yet. Should I reply?'

'That's up to you.'

Kate watched as Georgie quickly typed a message, before lowering the phone again.

'Neither of us meant for this to happen. After that party, we arranged to meet up on the nights when Daisy wasn't allowed out because she was studying. I really got to know him, better than any other guy I've ever known. Most of the time we'd just hang out and talk. He's a really nice guy, I swear.'

'So why carry on behind Daisy's back? If he's so decent why not come clean and tell her the truth?'

'He wanted to, but it was me who told him to keep quiet.'

'Why?'

'Because she's my best friend. Even if he broke up with her, there's no way she'd ever be happy with me then dating him. I didn't want to lose her friendship, and the only way I could see that I could keep her as a friend and him as a boyfriend was if she never found out.'

Kate scratched her head. 'That doesn't make sense. Why couldn't he end it with her and you continue to see him privately?'

'Because if she was single again, she'd want to hang out with me *all* the time, and then I wouldn't have time to see him too. This way, he would hang out with her a couple of nights a week, I'd see him a couple of nights a week, and we'd see each other at school and hook up on a Friday night. Then at the weekends I'd get to see them both.'

'It sounds like Alfie was the one getting the best of both worlds: stringing Daisy along while sleeping with you behind her back.'

'No! I told you: if he'd had it his way, he'd have come clean after that party. He only kept seeing Daisy to please me.'

Kate studied her, trying to determine whether Georgie genuinely believed she was in control of the relationship or whether she was being a naïve teenager. 'And Daisy never suspected? The whole time the two of you were carrying on behind her back?'

Georgie bit her lip. 'We were so careful, but on the day she disappeared, she confronted Alfie.'

'The argument in the café: that's what that was about.'

Georgie nodded. 'I think she suspected he was seeing someone else. She had no idea it was me, but she accused him of cheating; said his behaviour had changed. Something about him being less affectionate towards her. She hadn't mentioned any of these suspicions to me or Hannah, but it must have been playing on her mind. Alfie denied anything was going on, but she raced out of the café in tears. When she turned up at mine later, I had no idea what had happened at the café.'

Kate sat forward. 'Tell me about that night, and for once, please tell me the truth.'

Georgie's hand subconsciously rose up to her mouth and she chewed on a nail. 'My parents had gone out for dinner to celebrate their wedding anniversary, leaving me babysitting my little brother. Daisy came round as planned at six, and we were just going to drink some wine and watch a film. But about an hour into the movie, I went to the toilet, and that was the moment Alfie decided to text me and tell me what had happened at the café. Daisy saw the message and when I returned she'd put two and two together and laid into me. I guess she saw through my attempts to lie and cover it up.'

'What time was this?'

'About half eight, I think.'

'But she didn't leave here for another forty-five minutes?'

'I tried lying at first and denying that anything had been going on, but she didn't believe me, so I came clean and told her what had happened. We were both sobbing our hearts out, but I was crying because I was worried she'd never speak to me again. She eventually stormed out, saying she was going home. I begged her to stay, to let me explain, but she was so upset. I'd *never* seen her look so hurt. And it really hit home what a terrible friend I'd been. I wanted to go after her, but I couldn't because my brother was asleep in his room. I called after her, and tried phoning, but she turned her phone off. I tried calling her a couple of times on the Saturday, but figured she was ignoring me. And it wasn't until her parents called and said she hadn't been home that I realised something must have happened.'

'What do you think did happen? Where do you think she is now?'

'I have no idea. I genuinely thought she'd run away, but if she had, you lot would have found her by now.' Fresh tears streamed down her cheeks. 'I don't know what happened to her, and it kills me to think that what we did led to whatever it is. I would give *anything* to see her again and beg her forgiveness.'

Kate moved forward and, crouching down, wrapped her arms around Georgie's shoulders. Having been on the receiving end of a cheating partner, Kate had never considered the stress and upset it could cause the other parties. 'Do you know if she made it to the end of the road on Friday night, or whether she hung around for a lift from anyone?'

'I didn't see. When she stormed off, the shouting woke my brother so I had to come back inside. You should ask the guy down at number forty-eight.'

Kate pulled away. 'Why?'

'He was busy loading something into his car as she headed down the road. I think he asked if she was okay just as I was going back in.'

Chris Jackson's face popped into Kate's head. 'Who's the guy at number forty-eight? Describe him for me.'

Georgie wiped her nose with her hand. 'Um… I'm not sure… big nose, fat face, and an even fatter belly. He looked like an egg in a leather jacket.'

'An egg?'

'Yeah, he had this line of hair like a bird's nest just above his ears, but I could see the street light reflecting off the top of his head.'

Kate frowned, as the description didn't fit the picture they'd pulled from Facebook, but it didn't rule out the possibility he wasn't an accomplice. 'This person who spoke to Daisy: you'd seen him before?'

'Yeah, a couple of times mowing the lawn, but never spoken to him. He'll probably be able to tell you which way she went.'

FORTY

Several centimetres of snow had already fallen on the path down to the road and the dark sky above them suggested the flurry was set to remain a while longer. Kate wrapped the scarf tightly around the lower half of her face and pulled the lapels of her coat up.

She turned and took a final glance at Georgie. 'You shouldn't blame yourself for what happened. We all make mistakes. The key is learning from them. You'd better get back inside before you catch your death.'

Georgie forced a smile, which quickly evaporated as she closed the door.

Kate continued down the path, her footprints indenting the snow as she made her way carefully along the pavement. It was barely three o'clock, but the sun was nearly out of sight, and it felt much later. She could just make out a queue of traffic on Highfield Lane at the end of the road, as panicked workers battled to make it home before their routes would be blocked by snow. It would be a nightmare getting back to the station.

Kate glanced at her Audi as she shuffled past. There was already snow gathered on the roof, and she could barely see the windscreen wipers beneath their blanket of white. There was no point in moving it the short journey to number forty-eight. Lights were on in most of the houses, making number forty-eight stand out as a property with no sign of life beyond the snow-covered lawn and empty driveway.

Kate closed her eyes and tried to imagine Daisy walking this way on that Friday night. Was this why she'd stopped and waited before switching off her phone? If Georgie was right and the owner of the house had asked her if she was okay, had they engaged in conversation? Would an upset fifteen-year-old really talk to a stranger while on her way home?

Kate looked back at the house: semi-detached, with a satellite dish hanging from the chimney pot. Probably a three-bedroom property, at a guess, but the exterior brickwork looked like it had seen better days. There was no gate on the path leading to the green front door where the paint was beginning to flake. Net curtains hung in each of the windows, but pressing her face against the glass, she couldn't see any furniture inside, the only light coming in from the window.

Pulling out her phone, Kate dialled the office. 'Ah, Laura, you're back. Great. Can you do me a favour and check HOLMES2 for the reports on the house-to-house enquiries? I want to know whether anyone managed to speak with the residents at forty-eight Abbotts Way.'

There was a pause on the line. 'One sec, ma'am.' Another pause. 'No, it seems three attempts were made to contact the residents of number forty-eight, but there was never an answer. After the third attempt, a search was run for a phone number, but there is no telephone line connected to the property. Conclusion was that the property is vacant.'

'Who reached that conclusion?'

'Olly's name is on the report, ma'am.'

'Do me another favour, Laura, and see what you can dig up on the owner of the house. Check council tax records, whether it's listed on any estate agent sites as available for sale or rent. Call me back as soon as you have something.'

Kate hung up and moved back to the property. Finding no sign of a doorbell, she thumped a gloved hand against the door, leaning closer to listen for the sound of noise. Her footprints on the path were virtually gone already. She thumped the door again, and this time crouched down so she could lift the flap of the letter box.

The overpowering smell of bleach hit her immediately and then something else, something terrifyingly and unmistakably familiar: strawberries. Her heart began to beat faster as the adrenaline kicked in.

Kate dialled the office again, but this time her call was direct to the supe. 'Sir, I'm seeking authority to attempt entry to a vacant property in connection with the Daisy Emerson disappearance.'

'Reasoning?'

'A witness puts her in the vicinity of the property the night she went missing, and there is a stench of cleaning products coming from within; the same kind left in the school gymnasium. I've attempted to establish contact with the property's occupant, but without success. I believe there's a chance Daisy could be inside.'

'How secure is the door?'

Kate rested the phone between her good shoulder and cheek, pushing against the door, but it didn't budge. 'At a guess, it's double-locked. I'm going to need the battering ram, sir.'

'I'll get someone over there ASAP and have paramedics and SSD standing by.'

The door frame splintered on the third heave, and the second officer managed to manoeuvre it out of their way. The syrupy stench of strawberry was far worse inside, and Kate was grateful to have the scarf over her mouth and nose, to block some of it out.

Kate rested her foot on the bottom step of the staircase. 'One of you wait outside in case our guy suddenly returns, the other check downstairs; I'm going up. Be careful not to disturb any evidence, and shout if you find anything.'

Taking a deep breath, Kate delicately moved her foot to the next stair. With each step up, the cocktail of chemicals and artificial flavours grew more intense. The carpeted stairs strained and whined as if each was carrying the weight of Kate's dread.

At the top of the staircase, she found four closed doors, and based on the downstairs layout, she predicted that the two central doors would be to bedrooms, and then it was a toss-up to determine which of the other doors led to the bathroom, and which to the third smaller bedroom. Composing herself, Kate opened the door immediately to her left. Despite the dim light filtering through the frosted glass, she could see the shower cubicle and cistern, where several flies flickered about.

Leaving the door ajar, she crept along the hallway, ignoring the two central doors, and reaching for the furthest one. Threadbare carpet aside, the small room was empty, a thick layer of dust clinging to the window ledge.

'Nothing going on down here,' the constable called up from the foot of the stairs, startling Kate. 'Place is empty: no food in the cupboards, and no sign of a fridge. Looks like it has been empty for some time.'

'Thanks,' she called back. 'Stay where you are until you hear from me.'

'Ma'am? Snow's laying heavier outside, just letting you know.'

Kate coiled her fingers around the handle of the door where the fresh candy-floss aroma permeated most strongly. She closed her eyes and prised it free. The hinges creaked, as it slowly swung open, rustling against something on the floor. Kate forced her eyes open, already anticipating the scene before her, but nothing could have prepared her for what she saw: bright red sprays of blood covered every wall; all around her thick, sticky, crimson puddles of blood had dried on the plastic sheeting which covered every inch of the carpet; overhead, the ceiling was covered with a poppy field of dangling rose and strawberry-scented fresheners. The gymnasium had been horrific, but here the blood covered every possible surface, as if less care had been taken, as if the blood had been fresher.

Kate stepped back, crashing against the hallway wall, holding her breath and willing herself not to pass out.

The constable must have heard the thud, as he called up. 'Is everything okay, ma'am?'

Kate focused on her breathing, summoning the strength to say her next words. 'Get SOCO here *now*!'

FORTY-ONE

By the time the scene-of-crime vans arrived, the snow had stopped and there were several children skipping and playing in it beyond the perimeter that had been set up. Blue swirling lights lit up the entire street and almost all of the houses had their lights on, and Kate could spot the occasional curious face at the window in her periphery as she worked. It was understandable: it's not every day that this many police officers turned up at the house next door.

Kate shuddered against the memory of what she'd just seen. What kind of monster was she dealing with?

'Kate, Kate,' Ben called from his car, as he looked for a space to leave his vehicle. With three SSD vans already abandoned in the road, space was at a premium.

Ducking beneath the cordon she approached the passenger side and climbed in. 'I think there are some spaces further up the road,' she said, pointing where she meant.

'Is it as bad as they're saying?' he asked, switching off the stereo, so they could talk without interruption.

Kate felt the sting of tears at the corner of her eyes, and opted to nod, fearful he would pick up on the crack of emotion if she dared speak.

'As bad as Friday?'

'Worse.'

He spotted a space and drove straight into it, before killing the engine. Turning to face her, he gently brushed the fringe out of her eyes. 'How are you holding up?'

She nodded.

'I know you have to remain strong in front of your team, but you don't need to do it in front of me. I know how brave you are, and it's okay to admit that something like this has—'

She looked away to avoid the temptation to break down. 'I'm fine.'

'Were there any parts left up there?'

'I-I-I didn't stay long enough to notice. Maybe.'

Reaching out he placed his large warm hand over hers and squeezed it. 'I'd better go and take a look. You know where I am if you want to talk.'

'I need the blood processing as quickly as possible. I need to know if Daisy Emerson was… was one of the victims.'

'I'll work with SSD to compare the profiles.'

She manoeuvred her thumb so it could gently squeeze the back of his hand. 'I'd better get back to the office and update the team. Our work's only just beginning.'

Staring out at the city covered in a blanket of snow, it looked so picturesque; festive, almost. With the sun long since set, and the street lights reflecting off the tiny crystals of ice, it would make a warming holiday photograph, and it amazed Kate how a sprinkling of snow could help mask the evil lurking beneath the surface of her city.

'You okay, ma'am?' Patel asked, handing her a fresh mug of coffee, while the rest of the team began to gather in the incident room for the final catch-up before she sent them home to their families.

'It was another bloodbath,' she whispered. 'I never thought I'd ever witness anything as gruesome as Friday night, but this… we have to catch whoever it is. Promise me we'll catch him.'

'With you running point, ma'am, he doesn't have a chance of escape.'

She forced a thin smile to acknowledge the support, but smiling was the last thing she wanted to do.

Standing to address the team, she wasn't even sure where to begin. 'I'm guessing most of you have heard about the horror show at forty-eight Abbotts Way? If you haven't, picture the crime scene photographs captured at the sports hall at St Bartholomew's and you'll have a pretty good guess of what I've just come from. Someone out there is hard at work dismembering bodies. This could be the worst case any of us will ever deal with in our careers.'

She paused and reached out for the printed image of Chris Jackson, sticking it to the board. 'We know that Daisy Emerson was seen in the vicinity of forty-eight Abbotts Way the night she went missing, and SSD are rushing through testing the bloodwork at the scene to see if any is a match for Daisy. Until those results are in, we need to keep all of this in-house. The last thing I want is more leaks to the media adding to the speculation.' She glanced at Quinlan. 'We need to let SSD process the scene. But, while we're waiting for that, our priority must be to find Chris Jackson, the self-employed photocopy engineer who we have on site at the school on Thursday and Friday, and who hasn't been seen since the discovery was made in the sports hall. Laura, where are we with tracing his vehicle?'

'Nothing back from the neighbouring counties. It's as if he just up and vanished. Mobile phone is still off and there's been no activity on his debit or credit cards.'

'Thanks, Laura,' Kate said. 'Commit this face to memory, people. It is not in my nature to jump to conclusions, but when a person of interest in a murder investigation goes dark like this, it usually means he is planning to strike again. We know our killer dismembered Maria Alexandrou at St Bartholomew's, and someone else at Abbotts Way. That second victim could be Petr Nowakowski, or it could be Daisy Emerson, or worse still, an as-yet-unidentified victim. Ladies and gentlemen, we are going to have to do everything within our power to stop him. I want a patrol car at Jackson's home in case he shows up there. Ewan, he has a Facebook page for his business, which must mean he probably has a private one too. Do your magic and find it. I want to know who his friends are, whether he's married or dating, where he likes to go on holiday. Somewhere in there will be a clue as to where he's currently hiding out.'

Freeborn nodded.

'Vicky, check his phone activity for where he's been prior to switching it off. If he's been scoping out somewhere he can stay, maybe he's been dumb enough to leave a trail we can follow.'

Rogers fixed Kate with a nervous look. 'I was just called by the student who'd claimed to have seen Daisy at the bus stop in Portswood. He's now retracted his statement, admitting he was nowhere near the area that night. Seems one of his housemates dared him to do it.'

'So Georgie Barclay is confirmed as the last witness to see her.'

Rogers nodded.

'CCTV, ma'am?' Patel piped up.

'Yes, of course. I know vehicle recognition can't find him now, but let's see where Jackson was the night Daisy went missing. Can we place him in the area of Portswood? What about near the homes of Maria Alexandrou and Petr Nowakowski in the days before their disappearances? The man Georgie Barclay described at number forty-eight did not match Chris Jackson, but that doesn't mean he doesn't have an accomplice.'

'I'll take that, ma'am,' Laura volunteered.

Kate nodded her thanks. 'Humberidge, I want you to stop looking into Barry Emerson's activities for that night, and focus on finding anything to tie Jackson to Daisy, Nowakowski and Maria, as well as anything that directly links our victims. Cover every possible scenario. We need to establish whether he's hunting them, or whether they've been opportunistic crimes.'

For once Humberidge didn't argue, and Kate was grateful for that.

'It's getting late, and they're threatening more snow overnight. Work for as long as you feel you can and then get home and get your heads down for a few hours and get in as early as you can tomorrow.'

Kate dismissed them and turned back to face the picture of Chris Jackson, wondering just how long he'd been planning this spree.

FORTY-TWO

As the clock hit nine, Kate had nothing but pride for the half dozen detectives who were still feverishly busy working the phones and their computers. Fuelled by Patel's strongest coffee blend and adrenaline, everyone was working flat-out. Kate herself would happily work through the night if it brought them to their killer sooner.

'Ma'am,' said Laura, approaching the desk, and stifling a yawn, 'number forty-eight has been on the market for nearly a year.'

This was news Kate had been half-expecting, owing to the lack of furniture in any of the rooms, and the thick layer of dust on each of the windowsills.

'For sale or to let?'

'Sale. Found it on Zoopla, but it's very low down the list.'

'Is there an estate agent listed? I didn't see a For Sale sign in the garden.'

'Local firm in town is listed, but their office is now shut, so I'll have to go see them in the morning.'

'Do we know whose name the property is currently registered in? Who's selling it, I mean.'

'I tried contacting the land registry people, but again their offices are closed for the day, so have sent them an email, which I will follow up first thing.'

'Council tax?'

'Will also have to be contacted first thing, I'm afraid.'

Kate fought back her own yawn and failed miserably.

'You ought to get home, ma'am. It's been a long day.'

'I'm not going until the last of you have given in,' Kate smiled, appreciating her colleague's concern.

'You do realise that none of the team will leave here until you go, or you send us home. Nobody wants to feel like the first to turn in, because that would mean giving up on Daisy and the others. In fact, you might need to order breakfast now.'

Kate looked around the office. Patel was pinching the bridge of his nose, straining to keep his eyes open as his head rested on his flexed arm, the phone pressed to his ear. Beyond him Vicky was mid-yawn, and next to her Ewan was stretching his arms high over his head. In fact, the only one who didn't appear to be feeling the fatigue bug was Olly, who was pacing back and forth behind his desk, also with a phone glued to his cheek.

Laura was right: not a single one of them would stop unless she forced them to, and in her role as their leader it was time to make that call. Ultimately the enquiries they were trying to make now would be largely met by office answering systems, as the rest of the city had long since gone home for the night.

'Thanks, Laura,' Kate said, relieving the young detective before standing herself and moving to the middle of the incident room floor space. 'Listen up, folks,' she called out. 'I want to personally thank you for all your efforts today, but I'm calling it to an end for now. Go home and rest; we've done all we can and we're all running on close to empty.'

Kate returned to her own desk, briefly looking at the photograph of Chloe which was stuck to the bottom of her monitor, vowing she would catch up with Jackson before the weekend.

The phone ringing on the edge of the desk snapped Kate back to reality.

'Kate?' Ben said down the phone. 'I'm up with SSD and they asked me to call you. They still have technicians processing the scene, but we've definitely found Petr Nowakowski's blood at the scene. It will be some time until they finish processing the remaining samples, but they've positively identified four of them so far, with plenty more to test.'

'So Nowakowski is the victim this time?'

'It's looking likely.'

Kate closed her eyes as she silently nodded. It confirmed what they'd suspected, but since his heart had been delivered in the box, it had been evident that he was dead, so this didn't feel like news.

'Have they found any other DNA in the room yet?'

'As a matter of fact, they have. That's why I'm calling.'

Kate's pulse quickened. 'Who?'

'Unidentified, I'm afraid. SSD found a patch of dried mucus on the carpet beneath the plastic sheeting.'

'Which could have been left by a previous visitor to the property presumably?'

'Maybe. They were able to confirm that it was fairly recent, but that's not the exciting part. This second DNA profile was also discovered at the gymnasium.'

Kate frowned. 'I wasn't aware that a second profile had been identified at the school.'

'It was literally just found; minutes before the mucus profile was assessed.'

'Are you sure the samples weren't cross-contaminated?'

'Couldn't have been. Packaged separately and were being worked on at exactly the same time by different technicians in different laboratories. There is no way they could have been contaminated.'

'So what you're saying is we have an unidentified person present at both crime scenes?'

'Told you you'd be excited.'

'Tell me about this new profile from the gymnasium. Where was it discovered?'

'You remember the box of cleaning products that was located in the corner of the gymnasium? The box that was hiding the foot from view. It had blood spatter on it so naturally was brought to the lab for examination. The technician working on it, found a dried sweat secretion in the bottom of the box, beneath the bottles of bleach and whatever else was in there. Whoever's DNA it is, they had contact with that box at some point prior to the dismembering. And they had also coughed up mucus on the carpet in number forty-eight. At the very least it ties this individual to both scenes, whether or not they were present when the crimes were undertaken.'

'But this profile doesn't match anything on the National DNA Database?'

'Not so far. What I can tell you is the sample belongs to a man. We also believe he may have ginger or strawberry-blond hair.'

Kate turned and stared at Jackson's hair in the profile picture. 'How the hell can you tell that?'

'There's a test for it. Some redheads have a different version of a gene that prevents pigment-producing cells called melanocytes responding to a hormone that instructs them to make dark pigment. In samples such as this where two of the mutated genes are identified, there is a ninety-six per cent probability that the person will be naturally red-haired.'

'No hits on Daisy Emerson's profile in the room?'

'Not so far.'

Kate allowed a small sigh of relief escape. 'Thanks, Ben. I'm sending the team home now, but if you get anything else that needs sharing, I want you to call my mobile straight away.'

'You need to rest too, Kate.'

'I'll stop when the bastard is behind bars.' She paused. 'I don't suppose there's any clue where he's disposing of the body parts, is there?'

'Well, that's the big question, isn't it? Nothing so far, but the team will be excavating the garden first thing. Burying the bodies would be the easiest solution for disposal.'

Kate scribbled the note on her pad. 'When are you finishing?'

'Soon. There isn't a lot more I can do to help them here.'

The drive home was largely completed on autopilot, with Kate suddenly surprised to find herself parked up outside the small block of flats. A dusting of snow remained on the lids of all the bins in the street, but the road and large sections of pavement had cleared. The further flurry had yet to arrive, but as Kate stepped out of her car, the bitter chill that greeted her exposed cheeks warned her that it might not be far away. Locking the car, she hustled through the front door, grateful that the communal areas were benefiting from the heat coming from the ground floor flats.

Charging up the stairs to the first floor, Kate only stopped when she heard her name being called from the second floor. Leaning against the bannister, she looked up and saw her neighbour staring down.

'Hi, Trish.'

'Give me one second and I'll be down,' Trish replied, disappearing from view.

Kate wanted to call after her and try to explain that she wasn't in any state to stay up drinking and chatting, though it had been too long since they'd last had a proper catch-up. But there was only one place Kate wanted to be now, and that was in bed, squashed up next to her pillow.

Kate was unlocking her front door when she heard Trish join her on the landing. 'This came for you today,' Trish began. 'The delivery driver was just going to leave it on your doormat, but I said I would take it in for you in case it was something expensive.'

Kate's eyes widened, as she realised what her neighbour was saying. Kate knew she hadn't ordered anything that would require delivery, and as she slowly turned, the overpowering scent of strawberry confirmed her worst fears.

Gripping the large box tightly, Trish was clearly oblivious to what she might be holding.

'Are you all right, honey?' Trish asked. 'You look like you've see a ghost.'

Kate pushed her door open, asking Trish to carefully carry the brown cardboard box through to the kitchen to avoid further contamination. Resting the box on the counter, Trish stepped back uncertainly as Kate moved closer to the box. Reaching for a pair of Marigolds and a large kitchen knife, she carefully broke the tape sealing the lid and slowly lifted the flaps, gasping as she recognised the glittery wrapping paper around the box inside. Sliding it out, the sweet smell of artificial strawberries filled the room.

'I bet it's from Ben,' Trish giggled, missing the seriousness of the discovery.

Carefully removing the wrapping paper, Kate used the tip of the knife to lift the lid a fraction, dropping it as soon as she saw the bloody contents, and pushing the box further away from them.

'What is it?' Trish asked, perfectly reflecting the fear in Kate's eyes.

A second delivery, but this time to her house. All day her team had been hunting for Jackson, and the whole time he'd been looking for her. How the hell could he have found out where she lived?

Grabbing Trish's arms, Kate gently shook her startled friend. 'Who delivered this, Trish?'

'I-I... just some guy.'

'A courier?'

'Yeah, I guess.'

'Was he, or not?'

'Yeah.'

'From which firm?'

'I-I-I don't know. He was wearing a brown uniform of some sort... doesn't the box say who delivered it?'

Kate carefully spun the brown box around, checking each surface for any kind of postage label, but finding none. 'You need to think carefully, Trish, what did the uniform look like?'

'I-I don't know.' Trish closed her eyes as she tried to focus on the memory. 'His trousers were a dark brown colour, I think, but... oh wait, his bomber jacket wasn't brown, it was navy blue.'

'What about a logo, or badge? Anything to help us find out who he used to send it this time?'

'*He*, who? What's in the box, Kate?'

But Kate knew she couldn't answer that question. And then another troubling thought fired into her mind sending shivers down her spine, as Jackson's goofy smile flooded her mind's eye.

'Describe the courier to me. What did his face look like?'

'I don't understand why you're asking that, Kate. What's in the box? What's going on?'

Kate didn't have time for questions. Gripping Trish's arms once more, Kate stared into her friend's terrified eyes, and spoke calmly, yet methodically. 'I need you to *remember*, Trish. Forget about the box. Close your eyes and remember what the courier looked like. Was he tall, was he short? Was he thin, was he fat? What colour were his eyes?'

Trish's breaths were coming in short, shallow bursts, but she closed her eyes as instructed. 'He was short... well, shorter than me.'

'How much shorter?'

'Six inches maybe.'

'Good, Trish. What else can you remember?'

'He was wearing a dark baseball cap, but I could see wisps of brown hair peeking out beneath it, and over the tops of his ears.'

Jackson's hair in the photograph was strawberry-blond, but in a dimly lit room, could it pass for brown? Maybe.

'Keep going, Trish.'

'He wasn't fat, but certainly bulky... he had a round belly. Oh, and his nose was huge, not long, but spread right across his face.'

Kate froze. The man Trish was describing wasn't Jackson, but possibly the man Georgie had seen speaking to Daisy outside number forty-eight.

'Is there anything else distinctive you can remember? Did he speak? How did he sound?'

'He told me the parcel was fragile, and that he appreciated me volunteering to look after it for you. He made me promise that I pass it on to you today. I didn't even think about it until now, but he never asked me to sign for it.'

Kate released Trish's arms, and disposed of her gloves, before pouring two large glasses of wine. She took a long sip, before pulling out her phone and calling Ben. 'I need you at my place now, and bring SSD. I just got another delivery.'

FORTY-THREE

TWELVE DAYS MISSING

Kate woke as her elbow slipped from the arm rest that had been supporting her on the chairs outside the SSD labs. Glancing at her watch, she was amazed to find it was almost six a.m.

Ben had told her not to bother staying, and had promised he would phone as soon as he was finished examining the second heart, but she had insisted, knowing she wouldn't be able to rest properly until she knew whether Daisy was alive or dead.

Kate released a huge yawn, and was just resting her face on the back of her hand, when Ben emerged from the labs looking as exhausted as she felt. Sitting up, Kate blinked rapidly to clear the sleep from her eyes.

'You're here,' he said, looking disappointed, but not surprised.

'What did you find?'

Ben nodded towards the door. 'You'd better come in with me. You can put on overalls in the lab.'

Once inside and covered, Ben removed the metal tray containing the second heart from the small refrigeration unit. He lifted the lid from the tray and used a scalpel to point at the main arteries. 'I believe the same tool was used to sever the pulmonary arteries and vena cava, as was used on Petr Nowakowski's heart. Based on the jagged nature of the cuts, some kind of scissors were used again.'

'And the bloodwork? Whose heart is it?'

'At only 171 grams, and looking at the thickness of the vein walls it definitely belonging to a female. We've tested the DNA against the two prominent profiles, and I can confirm this was Maria Alexandrou's heart. The DNA matched the extract from the foot you discovered on Friday night, and the nail clippings you brought in on Monday.'

'How long ago did she die?'

'Based on what I determined from the foot and what we know now, realistically about a week ago, maybe slightly less.'

'So, who died first? Nowakowski or Maria?'

'Oh, definitely Nowakowski.'

'So is it possible that Nowakowski was killed and dismembered the Friday that Daisy went missing?'

He considered the question. 'It would probably be impossible to say for certain, but I'd say that's probably a reasonable deduction. What are you thinking?'

'Nowakowski and Maria were both desperate for money; that's the only thing we've found that links the two of them, but there's nothing to link either to Daisy. Georgie Barclay puts Daisy outside number forty-eight on the night she went missing. What if she saw something she shouldn't have? Or maybe she heard the victim screaming, or the sound of the power saw? I don't know, but we know she remained on Abbotts Way for five minutes after leaving Georgie's house, and she definitely stopped outside number forty-eight.'

'You think the killer attacked her too? So far we haven't found any evidence putting her inside the house.'

Kate pulled a face, and sighed. 'It's just a theory. If he did grab her, it's only a matter of time until we discover a third bloody scene.'

'I hope for all our sakes that you don't.' He paused, and fixed her with a look. 'I don't want you going back to your flat alone tonight. He knows where you live and I'm not prepared to let you become his next victim. Either you stay at my place until this thing is over, or I'm coming to yours. I won't take no for an answer.'

Kate was too tired to argue, and secretly a little relived; she didn't want to be home alone, either.

'Maria Alexandrou is confirmed as our second victim,' Kate declared, marching into the incident room. 'Her heart was hand-delivered to my flat yesterday. We have another apology from our killer. Again scrawled on one of those air fresheners. The handwriting is a match for the original note according to SSD, so we're looking at the same killer for both Petr Nowakowski and Maria Alexandrou, but there may also be an accomplice. I want someone checking all the cameras around my home looking for Jackson's van, or his face. Let's follow him if we can.'

'Ewan, can you search through his confirmed friends list and see if any match the description of the accomplice? Does it say if he's in a relationship with anyone?'

'No, ma'am. All he's listed about himself is that he's self-employed.'

'Thanks, Ewan. Laura, where are we with tracing the owner of forty-eight Abbotts Way?'

'On hold with the tax office now, ma'am,' Laura replied, holding the phone to her shoulder.

'Great, let me know the moment you have—'

'Ah Kate,' the supe said, interrupting. Kate turned and saw him standing at the door, still wearing his overcoat. 'Have you got five minutes?'

He looked more serious than usual. Kate hoped it wasn't more trouble with Tara, and put on her most accommodating smile. 'Certainly, sir,' she said, as she followed him through the door and over to his office.

The supe removed his coat and gloves before sitting. 'I heard about what happened at your flat last night. Are you okay?'

His concern shouldn't have come as such a surprise. 'I'm fine, sir.'

'I'd understand if you wished to be removed from the case.'

Kate held his gaze. 'Absolutely no way, sir.'

He broke first, looking over to the window. 'I'm glad that's how you feel.'

'We have reason to believe Daisy may have come into contact with the killer as well, sir. We are focusing on locating our prime suspect now.'

He tilted his head in surprise. 'They're connected?'

'Possibly. We have her in the vicinity of the bloodbath.'

'Anything to put her inside the house?'

'Not yet, but they're still processing the scene.'

'Keep me posted.'

Kate made to leave, before turning back. 'How is everything with you, sir? Is Tara okay?'

His forced smile told her more than he was prepared to. 'All fine now, but I'll tell her you were asking after her.'

Kate was just closing the door behind her when Laura came tearing down the hallway. 'House is registered to an Imelda Watkins, ma'am.'

'Watkins?' Kate coughed. 'The school *governor*?'

Laura nodded. 'The very same, but what I also found out is that twelve months ago, Chris Jackson was paying the council tax on forty-eight Abbotts Way.'

Kate's blood ran cold.

'There's more,' Laura said. 'Vehicle recognition has his van in Portswood the night Daisy vanished.'

Kate stared back at her open-mouthed, shuffling the abundance of dots joining together and presenting her with Jackson's face.

'The deeds to the property are in Imelda's name, but it looks like he was paying the council tax and was listed as the sole resident of the property for a year before Mrs Watkins reverted to paying it herself.'

'He was renting the place from her?'

'That would be my guess, but I'm sure she'll be able to confirm.'

'So that puts him in the property, but not recently. That means if any of his DNA is found inside that bedroom, his defence could argue that it was from when he lived there.'

'Not if the patch of mucus turns out to be his.'

'But why would he do it there?'

'Maybe because he knew the property to be vacant. It's the ideal location if he didn't expect to be disturbed.'

Freeborn burst out of the incident room, almost colliding with the two of them. 'Ma'am, ma'am,' he gulped. 'Jackson's credit card was just used to gain admission to a National Trust site near Romsey. We have his location.'

FORTY-FOUR

Kate abandoned her car right outside the entrance to the Mottisfont National Trust site. Behind her, Laura and Patel's squad car was coming in fast, and beyond that at least two more vehicles.

Forcing her way to the front of the queue at the sales desk, Kate slapped her ID on the window of the ticket both and demanded to speak to whomever was in charge.

'I-i-if you would go to the back of the—' the young man behind the glass said.

'There isn't time,' Kate interrupted. Realising she wasn't going to get any traction out of the kid, she called out. 'I need a manager and security. NOW.'

A woman in glasses wearing a bright red fleece appeared from nowhere, a look of confusion on her face. 'Can I help?'

Kate fixed her with an urgent stare. 'Are you in charge?'

The woman nodded, looking increasingly alarmed as Laura, Patel, Humberidge and Freeborn gathered behind Kate.

Kate passed the woman the profile shot of Jackson. 'We believe this man entered the park this morning and we need to apprehend him urgently. What kind of security do you have around this place?'

The woman steered Kate away from the queue of customers who were now muttering in shocked whispers. 'We have CCTV up at the main house, restaurant and at the café, but the park is spread out over several hundred acres, and we don't have the facilities to monitor everything.'

'The CCTV: that's monitored somewhere?'

'Yes, we have a security office at the rear of the main house where all the feeds go.'

'Good. Laura, go with this lady to the security team and have them go back to the moment Jackson's card was used to pay, so we can be certain he's on site.' She turned to the manager. 'Do you have a map I can use to direct my team?'

The woman reached behind the desk where the young man was doing his best to serve the next customer while eavesdropping on the unfolding scene. 'Here you go,' she said, unfolding a thick paper pamphlet.

Kate spread the map flat. 'Okay, what have we got?'

The manager leaned over and pointed. 'This is where we are now. Visitors can go in any direction and take any path they choose, but the most common are up and to the north-east point which runs along the river.' She moved her finger over the map to show where she was indicating. 'Or, for those who come to look at the main house, it can be accessed heading north along this pathway, avoiding the wooded area. From there the pathway is clearly marked to the chapel, café and gardens to the west of the site.'

'But realistically, our guy could be anywhere on this map?'

The manager nodded.

'Okay,' Kate sighed. 'Not ideal, but we'll have to make it work. Laura, get onto the CCTV and let us know if you spot him or what direction he might have been heading in. Patel, you also head up to the main house along the pathway, but bend off towards the gardens. Ewan, you and I will take a side of the river each. And that leaves Humberidge to wait here at the entrance in case he leaves before we catch up with him.' She turned back to the manager. 'There are no other exits, right?'

'The perimeter is fenced off, but if someone was determined to leave, then...'

Kate wondered whether she should call for backup, but there was no way they'd be able to cover every possible exit, even with the entire force surrounding the estate. She would just have to make do with what they had.

'This man,' the manager began nervously. 'Is he dangerous? Should I warn my staff to look out for him?'

'Please,' Kate nodded. 'Get a description out to all of your team and ask them to notify us the second they see him. But they are *not* to approach him. Is that clear? I also want you to temporarily close the park, and encourage as many of your visitors to leave as possible.'

'I'm at the security station,' Laura said breathlessly into the radio. 'One of the guards is going to look back at the earlier footage to see which way Jackson went after paying, while the other guard and I look at the current footage.'

'Keep us posted,' Kate said, as she crossed the bridge to the opposite side of the river, and proceeded along the hard ground, past the occasional patch of ice where muddy puddles had frozen over. Over the other side of the water, Freeborn was now moving in line with Kate, with both scanning their eyes over the wooded areas beyond the pathway.

In her years since moving to Southampton, Kate had never visited the Mottisfont site, but as she saw the occasional dog walker and single mother struggling to manoeuvre a pushchair through the wild grasses, she couldn't help but think how Chloe would probably enjoy a trip here. But why had Jackson come here? He'd been off the radar since Friday night, so to suddenly use his credit card and draw attention to his movements was either incredibly naïve or maliciously calculated. Given the temperature and the fact most children were at school, the site was relatively quiet, but was that the attraction? With so much natural woodland and unkempt heath in the vicinity, it would be easy for someone to come in and dump all manner of things undetected.

The thought sent a shiver through Kate.

The River Test, running forty miles from Ashe to its estuary in Southampton, bisected the Mottisfont estate, essentially cutting a third of the land from the rest, save for the couple of footbridges allowing visitors to cross.

Maybe he'd come here to dump parts of the bodies he'd chopped into the river? In a bag and with just the right weight, it would make the short journey to Southampton Water in a matter of hours, were it would be lost forever.

But why draw attention to himself by using a credit card and not cash?

'Ma'am,' Laura's voice squawked over the radio. 'I have him on screen. It's definitely him. Jackson is on the site. Over.'

Kate's pace increased subconsciously. 'Anyone spotted him yet? Laura, can you tell us what he's wearing? Over.'

'He's in a large khaki-coloured coat, ma'am, hanging down past his thighs. Beneath the coat he's sporting a grey woollen pullover, and his jeans are either navy blue or black. It's difficult to tell from the video. Over.'

'All units, bear in mind he may have ditched the coat. Laura, anything else we should look out for? Over.'

'He had a rucksack on when he paid. The strap is black, but I cannot see the colour of the main body of the bag as it isn't in shot. Over.'

'Which direction does he take when leaving the entrance? Over.'

'Can't be determined from this camera, ma'am. Checking for him on the five cameras inside the main house now. Over.'

Kate silently cursed, desperately hoping he hadn't already slipped out of their clutches.

'Nothing to report here. Over,' Patel offered. 'Do you want me to wait by the gardens or keep looking? Over.'

'Wander the area, but don't go too far. Over,' Kate called back, as she reached the opening to the final bridge. Beyond it, the path cut away to a small clearing. Kate signalled for Freeborn to stay put until she'd checked it out. The clearing led to a small hut, which was empty, and then off further into woodland. Kate did her best to look beyond the trees, but she couldn't see any movement. Leaving the clearing, she began to cross over the bridge, telling Freeborn to make his way back along the opposite side, when they passed each other midway.

And that's when she saw him.

Bold as brass, maybe a hundred yards further up the bank, heading straight towards them, his khaki-coloured coat billowing in the wind and the satchel strapped to his back.

Kate froze, grabbing Freeborn's arm. 'Pretend we're talking about something,' she whispered as loud as she dared. 'Act casual, and whatever you do: *do not look around.*'

Freeborn's eyes widened as he continued to look away from where Kate was staring in her periphery.

'What do you want to talk about?' Freeborn asked out of the corner of his mouth.

Kate lowered the volume of her radio, willing Jackson to move closer so they could intercept him unawares. If they gave him any reason to suspect, she knew he would run.

The wind continued to blow ferociously around them, but it was like he was moving in slow motion; Kate feeling every single second of the wait for him to get close enough for them to spring into action. She didn't dare message the others to confirm his sighting, in case he overheard and panicked.

'Just a little closer,' she whispered under her breath. And then she set off, striding down the footbridge, and marching straight towards him. He smiled affably as he made to move past her, but as he passed by her, she grabbed his arm, yanking it behind his back, pushing her foot into the back of his knees, sending him hurtling to the muddy bank.

'Hey, what the…?' he managed to stammer, before Kate wrapped the cuff tightly around his wrist.

'Christopher Jackson, I am arresting you on suspicion of the murders of Maria Alexandrou and Petr Nowakowski. You do not have to say anything, but it may harm your defence if you do not mention when questioned something which you later rely on in court. Anything you do say may be given in evidence. Do you understand?'

'Murder? What the hell are you talking about? Who are you?'

But Kate wasn't listening. Securing his second wrist, she hoisted him to his feet, and waited for Freeborn to grip the other arm, before they triumphantly marched their suspect back along the river bank.

FORTY-FIVE

Tapping her hands against the steering wheel as she drove back to the station, Kate's mind was already racing with the actions the team would now need to take to ensure they had the evidence required to charge Chris Jackson.

He certainly hadn't been expecting to be apprehended; that much was clear from his reaction when she'd grabbed his arm and sent him crashing to the ground. As they'd walked him back towards the waiting transport van, he had threatened to sue for wrongful arrest, until she'd reminded him that it was safer to remain silent until seeking legal advice. He hadn't uttered a word after that: was that a sign of a guilty conscience, or was he just being shrewd?

The tyres whooshed through the piles of slush gathering at every kerb side and Kate needed the car's heater firing at the windscreen to keep it from fogging up. She desperately wanted to sit in on the interview, to watch Jackson crack, and to be there when he finally answered the most pressing question: where is Daisy? But the next few hours needed someone headstrong to coordinate, and both Laura and Patel were experienced enough to deliver what was needed.

Kate was eager to call for the search of his home as soon as she was back at the office, but she didn't want to send the team in without direction. They needed to be efficient here, and target specific items: phones, computers, tablets, and any kind of cutting apparatus he could have used to sever the arteries to the heart so

Ben could run a comparison. The receipt for the handheld power saw discovered at the school would be ideal, but unlikely. But they needed to know exactly what had been going on first: how and why he chose his victims, where he'd held them. Most importantly of all, they needed to know if he had Daisy, and where she was. Or, if they were already too late.

The Emersons would need to be notified that someone had been arrested in connection with Daisy's disappearance, but Kate hoped to delay that conversation until they had formally charged Jackson and knew where she was.

The supe would want to be updated as well, but again, he had enough on his plate, so she would defer telling him until the raid on the premises was underway.

'When it's time, I want you to let Patel lead the interview,' Kate said, as she indicated at the roundabout. 'He is calm and methodical, but you're great at reading body language. I want you to watch him like a hawk. You know the kind of tells we're after. Then once the first round of questions are complete and we move to disclosure of our evidence, return to those sensitive areas and press again. And again. We want it all on record so it can be used in court if necessary. But – and I can't stress this enough, Laura – make sure you do *everything* by the book. I don't want this bastard slipping through our fingers on a technicality.'

'Oh, don't worry, ma'am, we've got him. Nobody is going to let him get away with this, least of all me.'

Kate's fingers continued to dance on the wheel. Today was a good day.

'This is where the hard work really starts,' Kate reminded the team as they stood around the picture of Jackson, slapping each other on the back and exchanging congratulations. 'I know you're all eager to get on, so we'll keep this brief. Laura and Patel will be busy interviewing Mr Jackson, when he *finally* stops gassing to his solicitor – always a good sign when they're paranoid enough to have a solicitor on call at short notice. Anyway, I want Humberidge running things at the property. Work with SSD to secure any blood, hair and tissue samples. Bag up *all* electronic devices, address books, maps, and also check the garden for any recent disruption. I know the cold weather won't make it easy, but this is vital.'

Humberidge nodded at her.

'We secured his van at Mottisfont this morning and SSD have promised to rush through the processing of both vehicles. He's in custody now, so we have twenty-four hours to secure what we need to charge him. The clock is ticking, people. Let's make every second count.'

The crowd dispersed and Kate was about to stop by the supe's office when her desk phone burst to life. She answered it to hear the familiar voice of the front desk constable. Her heart skipped at the prospect of another the package.

'I have a Barry Emerson in reception, ma'am, asking to speak to you urgently.'

'Tell him—'

'He says he wants to make a complaint about one of your team, and that if you won't come and speak to him he wants me to call Detective Superintendent Williams.'

Kate rolled her eyes, this had to be about Humberidge speaking with his mistress and Kate really didn't need the supe being dragged into things right now.

She sighed. 'Tell him I'm on my way down and stick him in one of the soft interview suites.'

**⁎
⁎⁎**

'And if your team had spent more time *looking* for my daughter instead of snooping around in my private life, then maybe she would be home already,' Barry Emerson shouted.

He'd been laying it on thick since she'd stepped into the room ten minutes ago.

'You have to understand, Mr Emerson,' Kate tried again, before he cut her off for the third time.

'Twelve days she's been missing! *Twelve bloody days!* And you still haven't a clue what happened to her or where she is.'

'I assure you, Mr Emerson, we are doing everything—'

'I suppose I should have expected this,' he spat. 'Putting a woman in charge.'

Kate flared with anger and she slammed both hands on the desk, standing and leaning towards him. 'That is *enough*, Mr Emerson. You have no idea how hard my team have been working on this case over the past week, how much time with their own families they have given up to work tirelessly on this investigation. When the victim's father *lies* about his whereabouts on the night his daughter went missing it wastes our valuable time and sets off alarm bells. I wouldn't be doing my job if I didn't check that he wasn't in some way connected to the disappearance.'

Kate took a deep breath and lowered herself back into the chair, knowing she'd overstepped the mark. He stared wide-eyed back at her, clearly not used to having people stand up to him.

Kate offered out her palms passively. 'It is none of my business who you choose to carry on with behind your wife's back. I'm not a marriage counsellor, I'm a detective. From what I've been told, Miss Oliphant has corroborated that you were with her all evening, and given what's happened this morning, I'm inclined to accept that you had no involvement with Daisy's disappearance. I think it's best if we both draw a line under this mess and move on with finding Daisy.'

He narrowed his eyes. 'What happened this morning?'

'We've made an arrest, but I can't discuss anything with you until we're sure we've got it right and all the evidence stacks up. I promise I will be in touch with you and Val as soon as I have something I can share.'

'The man arrested in Romsey earlier?'

'Wait, how did—'

'The radio news reported a large police presence at Mottisfont this morning.' His hand shot up to his mouth as his brain made irrational calculations. 'Oh God, was she there? Has he buried her there?'

Kate had already said too much, and wasn't about to make matters worse by continuing. 'Mr Emerson, all I can tell you is we have arrested a man this morning in connection with Daisy's disappearance, but as of now we still do not know where Daisy is. Please don't read anything into that. We are still treating Daisy as a missing person and striving to do whatever we can to bring her home *alive* to you.' She stood, hating herself for the slip. 'I've really said too much already. Please, Mr Emerson, go home and wait for me to contact you.'

Leading him back to the front desk, Kate bumped into Patel as she was heading up the stairs back to the incident room. 'Jackson's solicitor has said he's ready to be interviewed, ma'am. Laura's setting up the room now.'

Kate upped her pace, determined to get into the viewing suite and see just how their suspect would play it.

FORTY-SIX

Kate blew on the top of the coffee that Patel had left for her in the observation room; he was beginning to know her better than she knew herself. On the screen before her, Jackson was holding his face, both elbows pressed into the table, while the grey-haired solicitor next to him idly tapped his fountain pen against his own notepad.

Laura offered Jackson and his solicitor a hot drink, but the solicitor declined for both, muttering how his client was keen to get matters underway as quickly as possible. With the introductions made for the purposes of the recording, Patel kicked off by asking Jackson if he knew why he'd been arrested.

Jackson glanced nervously at his solicitor who gently nodded, a signal to do as instructed. 'No comment,' Jackson offered, though it was difficult to hear with his hand blocking his mouth.

'Please speak loud and clear for the recording,' Patel reminded him. 'It's here for your sake as much as ours.'

Jackson lowered his hand. 'No comment.'

'Does that mean you don't know why you've been arrested?'

Another glance at the solicitor. 'No comment.'

The solicitor leaned forward as Patel was opening his mouth to speak again. 'I have recommended my client not to comment on any of your questions until you've disclosed what evidence you believe you have to connect him to these preposterous accusations.'

'Is that what *you* want to do, Mr Jackson?' Patel pressed, ignoring the solicitor.

Jackson flinched at the sound of his own name and began to nod, before remembering his instructions. 'No comment.'

'The thing is, Mr Jackson,' Patel continued, 'I *need* to ask you questions to establish whether you're the man we believe murdered two innocent people. So, by *not* answering my questions, it makes it difficult for me to rule you out as a suspect. Do you understand?'

'No comment,' said more confidently this time.

'Okay, for the purposes of clarity, you were arrested as we believe you are responsible for the murder of Petr Nowakowski and Maria Alexandrou. Do you understand what that means?'

'No comment.'

Patel nodded, aware of how the next few minutes would progress. 'Did you kill Petr Nowakowski and Maria Alexandrou?'

'No comment.'

'Did you know Petr Nowakowski and Maria Alexandrou?'

'No comment.'

'Had you met Petr Nowakowski or Maria Alexandrou?'

'No comment.'

Kate continued to focus on the monitor. The main image was of Jackson and his solicitor, while a smaller view of Laura and Patel occupied the top corner of the screen. Kate was studying Jackson's body language. She'd observed and undertaken more interviews in her career than she could ever recall, and no two had been the same. When dealing with suspects who had been interviewed or previously charged, the delivery of the 'no comment' was often with confidence or ennui, but with first-timers, more often than not, there was fear in their response. Jackson's shudder every time Patel used his name was telling her a lot. He looked uncomfortable, but that didn't necessarily confirm guilt or innocence, just that he wasn't prepared to be interviewed today. Or, of course, it could all be an act; a cover story he'd concocted and was sticking to. She concentrated harder.

Patel made eye contact. 'You sometimes work at St Bartholomew's school on Hill Lane, don't you?'

Jackson's brow furrowed. 'No comment.'

Kate leaned closer to the screen. Was that a clue? The mention of the school had clearly triggered something behind those dark eyes, but what?

'We know you work there, Mr Jackson, because we have your van on their CCTV footage, and your name in the visitor's book.'

'No comment.'

'Why won't you comment about working at the school? That isn't a crime.'

A glance at the solicitor. 'No comment.'

'You were called to the school last Thursday, weren't you, Mr Jackson?'

'No comment.'

'Why were you called to the school, Mr Jackson?'

'No comment.'

'Was it to fix a photocopier?'

'No comment.'

'Tell me about your business, Mr Jackson; what do you do for a living?'

'No comment.'

'Does it pay well, being an engineer?'

'No comment.' Frustration was starting to kick in.

'I'm pretty good with my hands,' Patel mused. 'I love doing a bit of DIY at the weekend. Are you good with your hands, Mr Jackson?'

'No comment.'

'I bet you are. I mean, you'd have to be to be an engineer, right?'

'No comment.' Delivered through gritted teeth.

Kate smiled to herself, pleased she'd chosen to send Patel in. She'd never known an officer as good at asking the same question a dozen different ways. The repetition and fast delivery could be a useful tool to upset the suspect's rhythm, particularly when they desperately wanted to reply, but were remaining quiet under their solicitor's instruction.

'Did you always want to be an engineer?'

'No comment.'

'I imagine if we looked in the toolbox we recovered from the back of your van we'd find screwdrivers, wire cutters maybe, possibly a socket set.'

'No comment.'

'What about a power saw, Mr Jackson?'

The furrows in Jackson's forehead sunk deeper. 'No comment.'

'Do you own a power saw, Mr Jackson?'

Jackson was now sitting further forward, growing increasingly worried. Was that a sign?

'No comment.'

'What else are we going to find in your toolbox?'

'No comment.'

'Blood?'

Jackson opened his mouth to reply, but the solicitor pressed an arm across him; a simple reminder to stick to the script.

'No comment.'

'Will we find Petr Nowakowski's blood on any of your tools?'

'No!'

'Sorry, Mr Jackson, are you saying we won't find any of Petr's blood on your tools?'

He opened his mouth to speak again, before shaking his head, his lips trembling as he fought against the urge to say whatever he was holding back. 'No comment.'

'What about Maria Alexandrou's blood?'

A shake of the head again. 'No comment.' Anger was becoming exasperation.

'Because, Mr Jackson, the thing is, even if you've cleaned your tools, our forensics team are so good at finding the traces that are missed. So even if you think you've done a good job of cleaning them up, I wouldn't count on it.'

Jackson rose from his chair and leaned in, 'No comment!'

Both Patel and Laura instinctively sat back in response, playing up to the shock of his aggression. The solicitor tugged on Jackson's arm, dragging him back to the seat.

Patel waited until Jackson had taken several breaths to calm himself before continuing. 'Blood gets everywhere. It gets into the hinges and joints, particularly in scissors where the blades pivot. You think warm soapy water and a brush will be enough, but that doesn't clean the microscopic traces unseen by the human eye. Those are the traces that help us nail killers. And sometimes that's all it takes. Just a trace of Petr or Maria's blood on your tools and we'll have enough to press charges.'

'I didn't kill anyone!' Jackson erupted, the first splash of a tear hitting his cheeks.

'We believe you did, Mr Jackson. And the evidence we're currently searching for in your house is going to confirm that. I know it was your solicitor's idea not to answer any of our questions, but it won't be your solicitor in the dock with a jury deciding his guilt. It'll be you and you'll be on your own to face their verdict. Hiding the truth now might seem like a good idea, but it really isn't. The sooner you tell us the truth of what you did to Petr and Maria, the sooner we can all move on.'

'I'm not a killer,' he sobbed, burying his head in his hands.

The solicitor put the lid on his fountain pen and rested his pad on the table. 'I think now would be an opportune moment to give my client a break, don't you?'

Laura suspended the interview, leaving Kate to watch Jackson from the viewing suite, as he broke down into shuddering sobs beside his lawyer. She had to admit it was a convincing performance, but she'd seen better. Switching off the monitor, she headed to the incident room to discuss tactics for the second round of questioning, and to check in with Humberidge to see what progress they'd made at Jackson's house.

FORTY-SEVEN

'Go ahead, Humberidge,' Kate said, leaning towards the conference phone in the supe's office. 'You're on with the supe, Patel and Laura. How's the search going?'

Humberidge's voice crackled through the speaker. 'We've bagged up his computer, but no sign of a tablet device or mobile phone yet.'

Kate muted the receiver so she could fill in the supe. 'Jackson didn't have a phone in his possession when we picked him up, and has yet to confirm where it is. From what we've managed to ascertain he uses the same phone for business as personal use.'

'I've taken a picture of the pages in his address book and have emailed it over,' Humberidge continued. 'There's only a couple of dozen entries, but might be worth checking those nearby.'

'Patel will take a look at those when we're through here,' Kate said, catching eyes with Patel. 'Anything else of interest we can use in the interview?'

'Only been inside for half an hour, ma'am, but will keep you posted. The only other find of any significance is a box containing four unopened packets of photocopy paper. It's the same brand of box and paper as was used to deliver the victim's hearts.'

Kate clenched her fist in satisfaction. SSD had already confirmed that the brand used was generally stocked for both commercial and educational facilities to purchase. It wasn't a smoking gun, but at the very least an uncanny coincidence. If only SSD had managed to locate a fingerprint on either of the boxes Jackson had covered in the wrapping paper, they might be a step closer to charging him.

'I want you to check and see if he has any of the wrapping paper he used left. Check every room and all bins inside and outside, even for a scrap of it. Also, check for any glues or adhesives, so we can compare to what was used to attach the paper.'

'Will do, ma'am.'

'What's the garden like? Anything unusual?'

'There's no garden at the front of the property, just a concrete driveway. The back is like a forest: overgrown and not cared for. No recently disturbed patches of soil as far as I can see, but I've got Vicky out there doing a closer sweep as we speak.'

'Any sign that he might have burned the remains of the bodies? Ash, maybe, or charred patches on the concrete?'

'Will have to let you know. I've got three constables trying to make contact with the immediate neighbours to see if anyone noticed any suspicious behaviour in the last couple of weeks, but I'll keep you posted.'

'Thanks, call me back as soon as you have anything else so I can coordinate with the rest of the team.' Kate disconnected the line and straightened up.

The supe removed his glasses and chewed at one of the arms. 'And presently there is no forensic evidence linking him to either victim?'

'No, not unless we find something in his home or where he's disposed of the rest of the bodies,' Kate confirmed. 'I have officers and dogs still at Mottisfont combing the grounds, but it's such a large estate to cover that it could take days to find anything. But I'm not even convinced that's why he was there this morning. On the security feed he is seen entering with the satchel we apprehended him with, but it only contained a packed lunch when we checked it. Plus, he didn't have any digging equipment with him, and there was no trace of dirt on his hands or beneath his nails. As tough as it is to admit, I think he was only there to see the sights today.'

The supe paused to consider what she'd said. 'Well, you need to work as quickly as you can. If the evidence isn't strong enough by the morning, you know you'll have to release him.'

'You're absolutely right, but I think we need to leave him to a stew a little longer. We need to buy Humberidge and the team as much time as possible to thoroughly examine his home. If we disclose the circumstantial evidence we have at present, his solicitor will be laughing.'

'I think he wants to speak,' Patel countered. 'If we could just get him away from his solicitor, I'm sure he'd come clean.'

Kate agreed. 'But his solicitor will have been working to reel him back in since his last outburst.' She paused and tried to focus on finding the solution. 'Right, you two go back to the incident room and see what else you can dig up about his background. I want to know what school he went to, whether his parents are still alive, who he knew at college, I mean, anything that tells us more about him as a person so we can better focus our search for his victims.'

'I think Quinlan is still in the incident room trying to identify the people in Jackson's social media photos,' Laura offered. 'I'll see if he can fill in any of the other blanks.'

'Good. I'm going to go and visit Imelda Watkins, the owner of number forty-eight Abbotts Way. I want to know why he used her property to do what he did. Maybe she can shed some light on what drove him to kill Petr and Maria.'

*
**

Imelda Watkins' four-bedroom detached property was in a sprawling cul-de-sac, in the large village of North Baddesley, situated halfway between the Lordshill and Romsey suburbs. The front of the property was protected by a small brick wall enclosure and a large wooden farm gate, beyond which Kate spotted a Mercedes, sparkling despite the recent run of bad weather. Parking up directly outside the gate, Kate followed the small pathway that ran down the side of the wall, where a smaller wooden gate led past the bay window to the front door.

Kate casually glanced through the window as she proceeded, but the blinds were partly closed and obscured most of the view. Kate hadn't called ahead to check whether Mrs Watkins would be home, so was relieved to hear her approaching the door when Kate had clattered the letterbox.

'Detective Matthews, this is a surprise. Please, come in.'

Kate followed Imelda out to a conservatory at the rear of the property, politely declining the offer of a drink. The room looked out onto a long lawn, bordered by several conifer trees at its end, which caused a dark shadow to spread over the grass, which still had patches of white from the previous evening's snow. Inside the conservatory, the walls were adorned with pictures of Mrs Watkins and a man.

'Is that you and your husband?' Kate asked, nodding at one of a younger Imelda standing beside a blue beach hut with a tall man, dressed in shorts and a T-shirt.

Imelda looked up at the image, and a sorrowful smile graced her face. 'That's my Graham, yes. I'm sure that's where Neil gets his passion for the ocean from. Graham was in the navy when I met him, before resigning his commission when I fell pregnant, and taking a job at the local hospital.'

Kate watched as Imelda continued to stare at the image, the memories of that time playing silently behind her eyes. 'I'm here about the discovery we made at your Abbotts Way property last night,' Kate continued. 'I believe one of my team has been in touch?'

Imelda's focus returned to Kate. 'Good heavens, no. What kind of *discovery?*'

Kate perched on the wicker chair next to Imelda. 'You haven't spoken to anyone from my team today?'

'No, I've only been home for about ten minutes. Neil and I went and laid flowers at my late husband's graveside. What's going on? Oh God, tell me someone hasn't vandalised it as well? It took me hours to get the paint from Neil's brickwork.'

'Not exactly. One of the rooms upstairs, Mrs Watkins, we are treating as a murder scene.'

Imelda gasped, and covered her mouth with her hand. 'Murder?'

Kate tried to read Imelda's face, but could trace no sign of deceit. This news really was a shock to her. 'When were you last at the property, Mrs Watkins?'

Imelda puffed out her cheeks. 'I-I-I don't know. I can't remember.'

'It's been some time, then?'

'Well, yes. It's been vacant for nearly a year. It's on the market, and I really can't remember when I last called in there. Supporting the school takes up much of my time and I... goodness me. Would you mind fetching me a glass of water?'

Kate stood and made her way back to the kitchen, locating a glass on the draining board and filling it at the sink, before returning to the conservatory. 'Here you go.'

Imelda accepted the glass and sipped from it slowly.

'Can you confirm who has access to the property, Mrs Watkins?'

'Um, let me see. Well, I have a set of keys, of course, and the estate agent has a set so they can show prospective clients around, but I don't think there have been any interested parties in several months.'

'Anybody else? What about your son, Neil?'

'No, he doesn't have a set of keys. He mows the lawn there sometimes, but I don't think he's been over there since before Christmas. I can call him and ask if you like?'

'Is he not here now?'

'No, he dropped me home and then said he wanted to go for a drive. I don't imagine he'll be much longer.'

'You were renting the property out last year, weren't you?'

'That's right. To a man I met at St Bartholomew's, as it goes.'

'Chris Jackson?'

'That's right. Do you know him?'

'What can you tell me about him?'

Imelda lowered the glass of water to a small table adjacent to the wicker chair, considering her answer. 'He paid his rent on time.'

'Is that it? There's nothing else you can tell me?'

'Apologies, detective, but I was raised not to gossip behind other's backs. What is it you want to know?'

Kate had to be careful not to inadvertently lead Imelda as a witness. 'He was renting the property for a year according to council tax records. Why did the tenancy agreement end? Was it his choice or yours?'

'Mine.'

Kate remained silent, waiting for Imelda to elaborate. She eventually sighed. 'After my husband passed, things became difficult... financially, I mean. That was why I first agreed to Chris leasing the property. It was such a big place, and not in a good state of repair, so I didn't charge him top whack. I thought it would be good having someone capable with their hands on site. With all the best will in the world, Neil isn't good at that kind of thing. He can't jump unless I tell him, and I didn't want to spend money on a third party to maintain the place, so Chris just came along at the right time.'

Kate thought back to the threadbare carpets in number forty-eight, and wondered exactly what kind of maintenance Jackson had done. 'So why end the agreement? There's something you're not telling me, and I need you to be open.'

'The house was becoming more of a burden, and I decided to put it on the market. I offered Chris the chance to buy it, but he said he wouldn't be able to secure a mortgage and so he moved out.'

'But he still works at the school?'

'He's self-employed, but I think the school calls on him when required. I really don't get involved in that side of school affairs.'

'So you expect me to believe that your landlord-tenant relationship ended amicably?'

Imelda reached for her water again, studying Kate's face. 'Why would you assume otherwise?' Her eyes widened. 'Wait, you think Chris has something to do with what you've found at the house? You think he's murdered somebody?'

'I can't go into detail, Mrs Watkins, but we have reason to believe that the crime scene at your house is linked to what was discovered on Friday night at the school.'

Mrs Watkins' hand shot to her mouth again. 'You think... Chris? Oh my.'

'Let me ask you again: why did you not extend his lease?'

Imelda suddenly stood and moved to the window, staring into the garden. 'It will probably sound prudish... but he was *into* things.'

'What sort of things?'

'I don't understand the correct vernacular, but... whips and chains and that sort of paraphernalia.'

'Bondage? Sadomasochism?'

Imelda nodded, still stood by the glass. 'I called round to the house one day, and walked in on... suffice to say it was embarrassing for all concerned. I hadn't realised that... it came as quite a shock, I can tell you.'

Sadomasochism wasn't a crime, nor was it an indicator of psychopathy. 'Can you be more specific, Mrs Watkins. I'm sorry to ask. Was he tied up? Was he alone?'

'There was a girl there; I didn't know who she was... but she was tied up... to a chair... she was naked, and her wrists and ankles were tied to the chair with some kind of rope. There was a gag around her mouth as well. When I first saw it, I didn't know what I'd stumbled into, but he explained, and when he untied the girl, she verified that she had chosen to be tied up. Not the sort of thing that happened in my day, let me tell you.'

'How long ago was this, Mrs Watkins?'

She turned back and looked at Kate, her face white as a sheet. 'Just before Christmas the year before last. I was already considering putting the house on the market, and that was the final straw. It's none of my business what people practise in private, but I couldn't forget the look of terror in the girl's eyes when I walked in on them.'

Kate helped Imelda back to the wicker chair. 'What were things like between the two of you afterwards?'

'I didn't really see him much after that. He's been at the school on a couple of occasions as I've been passing through, but I don't think we've spoken.'

'Would you say there's animosity?'

'He certainly hasn't gone out of his way to say hello, and I've been too embarrassed.'

'There was no sign of forced entry at number forty-eight. Is it possible that Jackson still has a key?'

'I wouldn't have said so, but now that you say what's gone on in there, I suppose he could. I never changed the locks when he moved out, so maybe it's possible he had a spare key cut before moving out. I really can't say for sure.'

'We believe the victim was a man named Petr Nowakowski. Does that name ring a bell with you?'

Imelda reached for the water again. 'I don't think so.'

'Did you ever see Jackson with any male friends at the house?'

'No, the only person I ever saw him with was that *girl*.'

Was it possible that the girl Imelda had stumbled in on was Maria Alexandrou? Had Jackson paid her to indulge his sexual fantasies? It still didn't explain how or why he'd chosen to mutilate her at the school. But if he knew number forty-eight was vacant and still had access, he wouldn't have expected to be disturbed... until Daisy.

'Would you be willing to make a formal statement about what you saw?' Kate pressed.

'If you think that would help?'

Kate stood. 'Would you like me to call anyone to be with you?'

'My Neil will be back soon.' She paused. 'When will I be able to see the house?'

Kate's heart went out to her. The mess could be cleaned: walls could be painted and carpets replaced, but it would forever be remembered as the house where Petr Nowakowski was carved up. Over time the names of the victim and perpetrator would be forgotten, but the act was now embedded in folklore. Mrs Watkins would be lucky to receive half the value of the property after this.

'We'll keep you informed. I'll send one of my team around to take that statement from you.'

Kate thanked Imelda, leaving her in the conservatory, and showed herself to the door, keen to get back to the station and secure Jackson's confession and find out where he was holding Daisy.

FORTY-EIGHT

Passing through the security barrier back at the station, Kate was anxious to get into the incident room and find out what progress Humberidge and the search team had made. But as she parked in her regular space beneath the building and got out of the car, the sound of Quinlan's raised voice caught her attention. Looking around to see where the noise was coming from, she soon realised Quinlan was on foot, heading out of the station directly above her. Ordinarily she would have given him his privacy, but it was what he was saying that piqued her curiosity.

'I told you before to stop calling. I'll get you the money. I'll come now.'

Remembering the conversation she'd overheard yesterday, she wondered if he'd been running up gambling debts – or worse, a drug habit. She'd seen too many officers too proud to ask for help who'd lost everything. She knew only too well how thin the line was between right and wrong.

Rather than allowing him to slip away, Kate followed the car ramp back up to the ground level where she saw Quinlan nervously making his way from the building, across the road towards the train station, the mobile phone glued to his ear. He was at least a hundred metres ahead of her, which meant she could no longer hear the conversation, but the way he kept glancing about to check he wasn't being followed set alarm bells ringing in her head. He had to be going to meet whoever was causing him so much distress. If ever Kate had a chance to help him, this was it.

Proceeding along the pavement on the opposite side of the road, Kate kept him just in sight as she followed. As he reached the car park on the south side of the train station, she saw him duck inside and had to dart between the oncoming vehicles to cross the road and keep eyes on him. She lost him. Had he spotted her tailing him and double-backed? She was certain he couldn't have seen her. She looked around, then spotted him at the opposite side of the building, near where the buses dropped passengers.

His back was to her, but he seemed to be staring down and talking to someone seated on a bench. Kate couldn't see who, without getting closer.

She paused for a moment. Was this really the right approach to take? She'd already reached out to Quinlan and he'd rejected her support. Would he thank her for confronting him, or push her further away?

Quinlan suddenly took a step back, and Kate caught her breath as she finally saw who was on the bench and the jigsaw pieces slotted into place. She now had no choice but to intercept.

It was Tara who spotted Kate first, her eyes widening. 'Kate? What are…?'

Quinlan spun round as soon as he heard Kate's name, the shock on his face almost comical.

She spoke before either of them had a chance to. 'Olly's the father?'

Quinlan's face dropped and he collapsed down onto the bench next to Tara, burying his face in his hands as his secret was exposed. He clearly had no idea how to explain himself. Tara could only manage a slow nod before lowering her eyes.

So, that was why Tara hadn't wanted to discuss the father with Kate, because she knew how Kate would react, him being a member of her team. She had to give it to her, Tara had done a pretty good job of coaxing Kate into protecting part of the secret and simultaneously manipulating Quinlan into paying to keep his involvement under wraps.

Kate wanted to bash their heads together for being so stupid and irresponsible, Quinlan especially, but she resisted. 'Does this place have a café? I think we all need a quiet chat.'

*
**

The station café was quiet and warm, allowing them to find a small table and three chairs in a corner where they could talk discreetly.

Kate looked from one to the other. 'Which one of you wants to tell me how this mess started? Olly?'

But Tara was the first to speak up. 'It isn't what you think.'

'No? Tell me what I'm thinking, Tara.'

'We're not dating or anything. It was a one-time thing that unfortunately resulted in…' her words trailed off, but her hands gestured towards her belly.

'I don't understand how the two of you even met,' Kate said, frowning.

'It was at your work's Christmas party,' Tara said, looking away. 'I was supposed to be meeting some friends in town and Dad said he'd give me a lift as he had to make an appearance at your drinks do. I came in for a drink, and Dad was away talking to you I think, Kate, when Olly came and we started talking.'

'I wouldn't have gone near her, if I'd known she was the boss's daughter, and she told me she was nineteen!'

Tara snorted. 'As I recall, you didn't seem all that interested in asking too many questions before inviting me back to your place…'

Kate stared at Quinlan. 'And I take it this was the news you received on Friday night, and why you were hungover when you arrived at the office?'

'I'm sorry, ma'am, it's all come as a bit of a shock. I'm not ready to settle down, let alone be a father—'

'I'm not asking you to be a father,' Tara fired back.

'Well, you can't have a feckin' abortion either,' Quinlan defended.

Kate shushed the two of them, as a woman from a nearby table looked over. 'Now is not the time to make decisions. In all honesty, I don't think either of you are ready to fully understand the implications of what you've done, but this is the situation we find ourselves in, so we're going to have to find the best path forward for everyone, and that includes the little life growing inside you, Tara.'

'I'm going to have it terminated,' Tara said stubbornly, 'and there's nothing either of you can do about it.'

Kate could see Quinlan was about to react, so jumped in first. 'I think the best thing we can do today is to make a plan of where and when you are going to break this news to your parents, Tara. I know you are worried about how they will react, and I'm sure you're just as terrified, Olly, but there's absolutely no way around it. None of us can keep something this big from them; they deserve to know, so they can be supportive. And believe me, Tara, they might be shocked by the news, but they love you and that will never change. I know that if my daughter ever comes to me in your situation, I'll give the support she needs. And your parents will be the same.'

'I'll lose my job,' Quinlan said.

'You're both over the age of consent, so you haven't done anything illegal. He'll be upset, of course, but the supe is a consummate professional and he won't allow this to get in the way of work.' She paused and checked her watch. 'Speaking of which, you and I should be heading back, Olly. Tara, how did you get down here?'

'Caught a bus.'

'And are you okay getting home, or do you need a lift?'

'I can catch the bus.'

'Good. All the secret phone calls and messages between the two of you need to stop. And I think the three of us need to sit down with your parents at the weekend, Tara. I know you're both scared, but this secrecy ends here.'

Neither Quinlan nor Tara looked up, but both reluctantly nodded.

'Good,' Kate said, standing and leaving the café with Quinlan in close pursuit. 'Olly, we won't mention this again until we've nailed Jackson. But I need your head in the game. Understand?'

He stopped her and fixed her with a stare. 'I'm sorry you got dragged into all this, but thanks for having my back. I swear I'll work night and day until we have the evidence we need against Jackson and find Daisy.'

FORTY-NINE

Kate clapped her hands together for the attention of the incident room. 'What's Humberidge saying at the site? Any updates?'

Patel grabbed a note from his desk. 'They've found a shed packed full of garden equipment: spades, forks, buckets, and a lawnmower covered in rust. More interestingly, they've also found a patch of lawn that looks recently turned over.'

Kate didn't want to ask the next question. 'How big is the hole?'

Patel tried to allay her fears, spreading his arms wide. 'Humberidge reckons about a metre deep, and half a metre wide.'

'Not big enough for a body,' Laura offered.

'Not in one piece,' Kate agreed, but they all understood what she was alluding to. 'Are they digging?'

Patel frowned. 'The ground is pretty solid from what Humberidge said, but SSD are down there and will excavate the hole as soon as they can.'

'Can we get sniffer dogs down there? Maybe they could at least indicate if there's a scent of blood in the ground?'

'The dog unit is already at the Mottisfont site, ma'am. To be honest, by the time we'd get them to the house, SSD could already be through the top layer.'

Kate nodded, glancing at the clock. 'It's nearly two o'clock, so that gives us nineteen hours until we have to release him; unless of course the supe agrees to extend his custody. But he'll only extend if he believes we have a genuine opportunity to nail the bastard, and as it stands we only have circumstantial evidence at best. Is Jackson still in with his solicitor?'

Patel nodded. 'Yeah, they broke for half an hour for Jackson to eat lunch, but reconvened immediately after. I've no idea what they're discussing, but if he's as innocent as he claims, I don't see why he'd need to talk for so long.'

Kate sighed, feeling they'd never been closer to confirming what had happened to Petr and Maria, but no closer to finding out why. The psychology of the criminal mind fascinated her, particularly when she came up against someone with a psyche as twisted as Jackson's.

Kate focused back on the three of them. 'How are we with progressing *why* Petr and Maria were picked by Jackson?'

Laura shuffled forward on her chair. 'I've been looking into the financial side of things, ma'am. We know that both Petr and Maria weren't in professions that would make them a lot of money, but we have witnesses who say that both had either received or were about to receive a windfall, right? Sofia said Maria managed to raise ten grand to pay off her pimp, and Petr's sister said he was going to put a deposit down on a flat for them to rent together. I've been going through Jackson's recent bank statements, courtesy of what Humberidge has scanned and sent over from the house, and there are multiple ATM withdrawals from his personal account. Not in the region of ten grand, but over time, a couple of grand here, a grand there, it could add up. However, we have yet to lay our hands on his business records. From what I can see, he was taking home a considerable monthly sum from the business, which would suggest the company has been doing well.'

'Define *considerable*,' Kate said.

Laura grabbed the statements from her desk and handed them to Kate. 'I've highlighted the figures in question. This month, the company paid him just under four thousand, the month before, just over that figure, and the month before that well over six thousand.'

'Where are his business accounts?'

'Humberidge hasn't found them at the property yet, but is still searching. I've put a call in to his bank to request access and am waiting for a call back.'

Kate narrowed her eyes. 'But even *if* we can establish he made significant withdrawals from his business account in order to pay them, what was he paying them for?'

'Maybe he set up business as a loan shark?' Quinlan offered.

Kate furrowed her brow. 'I don't think it fits.'

'Drugs then?' Quinlan countered.

'No evidence to suggest that Jackson has any involvement in that world.'

'Well, that only leaves sex, ma'am,' Quinlan concluded. 'You reckon he goes both ways?'

Kate considered it. 'We know that Maria was used to selling her body for money. Could he have offered her the money she needed in return for something sexual? According to Imelda Watkins he had an interest in sadomasochism. But the only evidence we have that Maria received the money is Sofia saying their pimp had released Maria from their contract. The money never touched a bank account.'

'Maria Alexandrou hadn't used her account for several years,' Patel advised.

'And Petr? What do his accounts say?'

'In the last six months, his only account transactions were the monthly payments received from the cruise company, which he withdrew in whole almost immediately after. No direct debits or debit card payments on the account. There's obviously a mattress stuffed full of money somewhere.'

Kate fixed Patel with a look. 'Have we been through Nowakowski's accommodation yet?'

He shook his head. 'Humberidge was supposed to be heading there this morning, but with Jackson's sudden appearance, it hasn't happened.'

Kate fired a look at Quinlan, who grabbed his coat. 'On it, ma'am. What are we looking for?'

Kate joined him at the door. 'Anything that might tell us how he crossed paths with Jackson: computer, tablet, phone, sexual paraphernalia, anything and everything.' She glanced back at Laura and Patel. 'Keep digging. We need something to tie our victims and suspect together. I'm sure we're missing something obvious; I just can't work out what.'

A twenty-minute walk from the city centre, Mountbatten House bordered Southampton Common. Built in the early twentieth century and with gardens to the front and rear of the property, it could house up to twenty individuals and was open to anyone who had fallen on hard times, but was primarily used by former offenders and those trying to kick addiction. A charitable organisation, all residents were required to pay a minimum weekly rent to cover the cost of utilities.

Kate and Quinlan showed their identification to the woman manning the front office, and asked to be taken to Nowakowski's room.

The woman gave them a sceptical look. 'We had to give Petr's room to someone else after he didn't return a fortnight ago.'

'What about his possessions? Did he leave anything behind?'

The woman nodded, leading them to a locked door beneath the large staircase. 'All unclaimed property is locked away in here, and if the individual doesn't return for it within six months, we reserve the right to reuse or sell what is left.' Unlocking the door, she held it open for them. 'That large box is what we collected up, and that large suitcase was also in his room.'

Quinlan leaned in and pulled out the cardboard box, passing it to Kate before drawing out the suitcase.

'And there's nothing else?' Kate asked.

The woman shook her head. 'The people that stay with us don't tend to keep a lot of possessions.'

'Is there somewhere we can look through all this stuff?'

The woman looked at her watch. 'I'm due on a break. You can use my office for now.'

'You search the case and I'll do the box,' Kate told Quinlan when they were alone.

Reaching in to the box, Kate first pulled out a framed picture of Ana Nowakowski, captured mid-laugh, looking far removed from the distraught woman they'd spoken to at the supermarket on Monday. Beneath that was an antique-looking cigar box, the corners mottled and the label fading. Opening the lid, several loose photos fell to the desk. Kate scooped up and returned them to the cigar box, resting it on the desk. The remaining items in the box included a brown-stained mug, a toothbrush, toothpaste and a dog-eared copy of a spy novel. Kate held the book aloft, looking for any hidden notes between the pages, but nothing fell out.

'Library book,' she commented, noticing a stamp inside the cover. 'What you got?'

Quinlan lifted a pair of underpants from the case with the end of a biro. 'Underwear, T-shirts and work shirts; none of which smell clean.'

'No phone, tablet or laptop?'

He shook his head, closing the lid of the case. 'Maybe SSD can find fibres on some of his clothes. What have you got?'

Kate passed him the cigar box of photos and moved across to the noticeboard hanging from the wall, advertising various support groups for addiction, anxiety and depression. Kate snapped a photograph of each showing dates and times. Both Maria and Petr were trying to improve their lives; was it possible Jackson had met them in such a support group?

'Ma'am?' Quinlan suddenly called out. 'You'd better look at this.'

Kate turned and saw him holding a pile of photographs in one hand, but just one aloft in his other hand. Stepping across, Kate gulped as she stared closer at two of the men in the group shot. 'Nowakowski knew Liam Phillips?'

Phillips' cocksure grin stared back at her, an arm draped around Nowakowski's shoulders, both dressed in shirts and ties, while five other similarly dressed men looked on.

'Does it say when it was taken?'

Quinlan shook his head. 'No date or time. Small world, huh?'

She cocked an eyebrow. 'Getting smaller by the day. Come on, let's go and ask Liam how he knew our victim.'

FIFTY

Kate didn't wait for Phillips to come to them in the waiting area of the offices of TUTD Surveyors, marching straight to his private office and knocking on the door. She heard voices from inside, and as Phillips opened the door, she saw his cheeks flush as he quickly apologised to the Asian man seated at the desk.

Phillips didn't even acknowledge Kate, as he turned back to his prospective client. 'Apologies, Mr Yamamoto. Could I ask you to step outside for just a moment? If you head down to the waiting area, my secretary will fix you a fresh cup of tea.'

The client bowed his head as he passed through the door, and made his way towards the waiting area, tightly gripping his briefcase.

Phillips ran a hand through his hair as he closed the door. 'Don't you people ever make appointments?' he said testily, as he retook his seat.

'Not when I'm investigating a double murder and the disappearance of a vulnerable child,' Kate fired back, remaining on her feet.

Phillips switched off his monitor, resting his hands flat on the desk, and forcing a thin smile. 'What is it I can do for you this time?'

Kate raised the photograph they'd retrieved from the cigar box. 'How did you know Petr Nowakowski?'

'Petr? We used to play football together. Why?'

'Used to?'

'Yeah, he stopped playing three or four years ago I think. He got pinched for armed robbery, as I recall. Never saw him much after that.'

'Have you seen him recently?'

Phillips frowned. 'What's all this about?'

'Have you seen him recently?' Kate repeated.

The frown deepened. 'About a month ago, I guess. He asked me for a job.'

'And?'

'And I told him I wasn't hiring at the moment.'

'Where did the two of you meet?'

'I told you: playing football. A couple of friends and I signed up to play in a five-a-side league, and I met him there.'

'You were on the same team?'

'No. I was on a team with friends from university, and he played for one of the others.'

'You seem very friendly in this photograph. Where was it taken?'

He studied the image for a moment, before staring straight at Kate. 'As far as I remember, it was at an awards ceremony organised by the league sponsors. Our team had won the league and Petr's were runners-up. There was a big party, loads of booze, and we were presented with our trophy.'

'Did you ever see him socially outside of football?'

'No. But I'd see him every couple of weeks when we'd have matches at the same time.'

'Where did you play?'

'The five-a-side place along the Millbrook Road.'

Kate knew the place. 'When did you stop playing?'

'I busted my knee a year ago, and the doctors warned me not to risk playing again. I now work off my stresses at the gym instead.'

'Why did Nowakowski ask *you* for a job if you hadn't seen him in so long?'

'I don't know. He showed up here out of the blue and asked. I wasn't sure that he'd be able to do anything to help us, and told him we weren't hiring.'

'How did he seem when you spoke?'

'Listen, are you going to tell me what this is all about? Why the interest in Petr?'

Kate kept her lips tight.

'He seemed all right, I suppose. Looked like he'd put on a few pounds since I'd last seen him.'

'Did he seem desperate for money?'

A flicker in Phillips' eyes.

'What is it?' Kate pressed.

Phillips shrugged. 'He asked whether he could borrow some money. Said he'd fallen on hard times and would do anything, but I said things were tough for all of us, and I couldn't help.'

'And afterwards, did you see him again?'

'No. Seriously, what is all this? Why all the questions about Petr? Is this something to do with that girl's foot you found at the school?' A pause. 'Oh God, do you think he was responsible?'

Kate watched Phillips closely. 'We're asking all males with access to the sports hall at St Bartholomew's to provide a DNA sample for comparison. Would you be willing to come down to the station and provide a voluntary sample?'

Phillips looked from Kate to Quinlan and then back again. 'Unless you want to arrest me, I think I'll decline your offer. Certainly until I've spoken to my lawyer.'

Kate nodded at Quinlan. It was time to go.

Holding the phone to her ear, Kate tapped her fingers against the desk as she waited for Humberidge to answer.

'Ma'am?' he finally said as it connected.

'Anything to link Jackson to Nowakowski or Maria?'

'One of the technicians is going through his computer now, but it's taking time.'

'What about the disturbed earth in the garden?'

'For a minute I thought we were on to something when I heard someone shout that they'd found bones—'

'Bones?' Kate interrupted, suddenly sitting up.

'Turned out to be a decomposing cat, ma'am. It wasn't buried too deep. Probably been in the ground a few months.'

'Any other signs that he may have buried or cremated Nowa-kowski or Maria there?'

'Nothing, ma'am. I'm sorry. We have found pornographic material in one of the upstairs rooms: magazines, a couple of DVDs, and a sports bag with bondage gear shoved in a wardrobe. It's all being sent back for analysis.'

'Ties in with what Imelda Watkins told me.' Kate thanked him for the update, adding, 'Let me know if you find anything on his computer.'

Kate dropped the phone into its cradle as she struggled to contain her frustration. Six hours had passed since they'd brought Jackson in for questioning, and they were no closer to evidentially tying him to the crime.

FIFTY-ONE

Retaking her seat in the viewing suite, Kate watched as Jackson was escorted in, head bent low, and shoulders sagging. He certainly didn't resemble a confident, cold-blooded killer, but then that could all just be part of his carefully crafted act.

Kate had called in every favour she could to ensure SSD prioritised processing the tools from the back of Jackson's van and any new evidence being brought in from the unfolding scene at his house. But with two bloody crime scenes still being analysed, she knew the technicians in SSD were already spread thin.

Nothing persuaded a jury as successfully as clinical evidence, but a confession made during a police interview could be just as persuasive, even if it was later retracted in an open court.

'How much should we disclose to the solicitor?' Patel had asked after Kate had directed them to re-interview Jackson.

Sharing all the evidence or suppositions too early, and the suspect would be given time to formulate his excuses. But holding too much back could mean the suspect not feeling worried enough to tell them what they needed to know. Kate had told him to tread carefully.

Patel cleared his throat as Laura reintroduced those present and restarted the recording. 'Given the information we've disclosed to your solicitor, is there anything you wish to say before we begin our questions, Mr Jackson?'

Jackson eyed the solicitor, who produced a handwritten piece of paper. 'My client wishes to read a statement in response to the allegations made against him this morning.'

Kate saw Patel and Laura exchange glances, and knew what they were thinking: was he was about to confess?

The solicitor slid half-rimmed reading glasses over his ears. 'I will read Mr Jackson's words as he has written them, and you will be allowed to take a copy when it is finished.' He paused, before beginning to read. '"I, Christopher Thomas Jackson, make this statement of my own free will. I understand that I do not have to say anything but that it may harm my defence if I do not mention when questioned something which I later rely on in court. This statement may be given in evidence. I wish to put on record that I do not know, have never met and did not kill Petr Nowakowski and Maria Alexandrou. I am making this statement against my solicitor's guidance, but wish to set the record straight.

'"I understand,"' the solicitor continued reading, '"that my presence at St Bartholomew's school last Friday is one of the reasons for my arrest today. Whilst I was not formally called to visit the school for business purposes, I was in fact there for personal reasons. If you contact Miss Sally Chalmers who teaches at St Bartholomew's, she will confirm that I was at the school to collect her. I was with her from the moment I arrived until the time I left. Sally and I then spent the weekend together at her parents' home in Poole, before we returned early this morning."'

Kate jotted the name down to pass to the team to check against the list of teachers Mrs Kilpatrick had sent over. It didn't surprise her that Jackson had instantly provided an alibi of his actions leading up to the discovery of the foot. But they would need to follow up with this Sally Chalmers to see if she could verify his statement.

'"I also understand that at present you are searching both my home and business van for evidence to link me to these absurd allegations,"' the solicitor read. '"I am certain you will find no such evidence. I am happy for you to ask me any further questions about my recent activities, but I reserve the right to answer 'no comment' if I believe you are trying to misinterpret my answers."'

The solicitor folded the piece of paper and handed it to Patel, a self-satisfied smile spreading across his face.

'Where's your phone, Mr Jackson?' Patel asked.

'I switched it off on Friday as I didn't want our weekend away to be disturbed. I thought it was in my bag until we got back today, and realised I must have left it at Sally's parents' house.'

'And, of course, you won't mind us contacting them to verify that the phone is there?'

Jackson no longer looked the broken man who'd first walked into the interview room. 'I'll give you the address and you can bloody go and collect it yourself!'

Kate knew he was right to be so confident. Unless Humberidge and SSD came through with something soon, he was going to walk, and with him would go their chance of finding Daisy alive.

Kate rapped on the interview-room door and Patel pulled it open, stepping out when he saw it was Kate and closing the door behind him. 'Ma'am?'

'Ask him about Daisy.'

'We were going to get to that, but there isn't anything to—'

'Just ask him. Find out what he was doing in Portswood on the night she disappeared; ask him when he was last at number forty-eight. I want to see his reaction when he realises we've rumbled him. Don't tell him anything has been discovered to connect him to her disappearance but intimate that we have something. See if he bites.'

'Is there anything?'

'No, but I know he's holding back. He's far too confident in there. We need to knock him off his stride.'

'Ma'am, we can't mislead him.'

'It isn't misleading. You're not saying we've found anything, but just hinting that we expect to. Give me five minutes to get back upstairs and then go in. He'll wonder what's taken you so long out here. Every minute you're out here, is another minute for him to squirm.'

'What about the teacher he reckons he was with?'

'Quinlan is verifying that, but it wouldn't surprise me if the reason he was away with her was to establish an alibi.'

'Ma'am, you're not making any sense.'

Kate fixed him with a stare. 'I think he has an accomplice.'

'Who?'

'That's what we need to find out. The figure that Daisy stopped and spoke to outside the house; what if he and Jackson are up to something together?'

Patel offered her a sympathetic look. 'Ma'am, I know you're desperate to find Daisy, but you're making huge leaps here.'

'Just ask him. SSD will find the link soon enough.'

Patel re-entered the room on the screen and took his seat. Kate smiled as he whispered something unintelligible to Laura, who nodded. It didn't matter what he'd said, it was enough to unnerve Jackson.

Laura restarted the recording, and sat forward; Patel must have instructed her to take the lead. 'Where's Daisy, Mr Jackson?'

A look of confusion gripped him. 'Daisy who?'

'Oh, don't try that with me,' Laura continued, opting for bluntness over gentle probing. 'We know you were in Portswood the night she went missing. What did you do with her?'

Jackson was looking at his solicitor who in turn looked bewildered. 'I don't follow.'

'Daisy Emerson. You remember? The fifteen-year-old that you and your pal snatched nearly two weeks ago. We have a witness who saw your mate speaking to her outside number forty-eight Abbotts Way. You know that address don't you, Mr Jackson?'

'What? No—'

'Oh, so you've never lived at forty-eight Abbotts Way? You were listed as the registered tenant according to council tax records.'

'What? Well, yes, I… I *did* live there once, but—'

'When were you last at that residence, Mr Jackson?'

'I-I-I don't know.'

'In the last month?'

'What? No.'

'Really, why were you in Portswood on the second of February, then?'

'February second? I-I-I can't remember where I was on that day.'

'Your van was clocked on a traffic camera heading towards Portswood at nine p.m. on February second, why were you there?'

Jackson looked away, his eyes darting as he tried to access his long-term memory. 'Um, I don't know… I can't remember.'

'Where's Daisy now, Mr Jackson?'

'I don't know. I don't know who you're talking about.'

'Like you don't know Petr Nowakowski and Maria Alexandrou? What did you do with their bodies, Mr Jackson?'

Jackson nodded at his solicitor to interrupt.

The solicitor removed and folded his glasses. 'Detective, I don't know where this new line of questioning has stemmed from, but unless you care to disclose your evidence, I will be instructing my client not to respond to any of these wild accusations.'

Laura ignored the solicitor, keeping her eyes firmly fixed on Jackson. 'We found your stash of pornographic materials; we know the sort of thing that turns you on, Mr Jackson. It's time for you to come clean and tell us where Daisy is.'

Jackson's face contorted with desperate anguish, and Kate couldn't keep the smile from growing across her face. They had him.

FIFTY-TWO

Kate's eyes fell on the framed photograph of Chloe smiling back at her, and the breath caught in her chest. Snatching it up, she held the frame to her chest, clamping her eyes shut so Laura and Patel wouldn't see the tears that were slowly building. It could have been her little girl out there.

But she couldn't allow her own feelings to cloud the actions she was charged to undertake. Lowering the frame to the desk, and setting it at just the right angle, she turned to her two most loyal companions. 'Whatever it takes. We get them. We get them both.'

Neither Laura nor Patel needed any further encouragement, both feeling the same emotional response to the possibility they'd been dreading since Daisy Emerson had been first reported missing.

Humberidge's call couldn't have come soon enough. 'It's Ismael Vardan, ma'am,' he said breathlessly. 'We've found an exchange of emails between the two of them going back several months.'

Kate called Laura and Patel over, switching the phone to loud speaker.

'The technician managed to get into Jackson's Hotmail account,' Humberidge continued, 'and it seems the two of them have been openly discussing shared fantasies. Some of it is pretty intense, but the crux is they've been planning a trip abroad where they can – and I'm quoting here – *indulge our desires without fear of British law.*'

'Abroad where?' Kate asked urgently.

'They discuss several places: all outside the EU. Ma'am, there's mention of Daisy too.'

Kate gripped the edge of the desk. 'Go on.'

'Well, it's Jackson that mentions her first. It's hard to judge the tone of the email at first, but three months ago he starts making references to *that girl who likes you*, and Vardan ignores the jibes to begin with, but then it must get to him as later he starts warning Jackson to stop. And then last Monday, Jackson asks whether Vardan is stashing Daisy somewhere.'

'He mentions her by name?'

'Yes, ma'am. It's the first mention of Daisy but the email alludes to their previous discussions.'

'What does Vardan say?'

'That's the last email, ma'am. Vardan has yet to reply, and from what the techie says, Jackson hasn't accessed his emails since Thursday.'

Kate steadied her breathing. 'Bring Vardan in now.'

'Already on my way, ma'am.'

Kate disconnected the call, and looked over to Laura. 'Go through HOLMES2 now. Who gave Vardan an alibi for this weekend?'

Laura rushed over to the computer and began to search, before calling over her shoulder. 'Barnes spoke to his sister who confirmed he was at a family wedding in Leicester.'

'You think she's lying?' Patel asked calmly.

Kate closed her eyes and focused. 'We have Jackson in Portswood the night Daisy disappears, and we know he has access to the school and was familiar with the Abbotts Way address. If he was at the house with Vardan when she stopped... no, wait, neither Vardan nor Jackson fit the description of the man Georgie Barclay said was with Daisy.'

'Plus, why would Jackson tease Vardan about Daisy's disappearance if they were both at the house?' Patel countered.

'A third accomplice?' Laura offered. 'Someone we're yet to come across? Or maybe Georgie made a mistake; it was dark by then.'

Kate's eyes remained clamped shut. 'Apart from the two crime scenes, we still don't have anything to directly connect Jackson to Maria and Nowakowski. We hypothesised that he might have paid Maria for sex, but we have no proof, and that still doesn't tie him to Nowakowski.' She paused. 'What do we know about Vardan? Can you pull that up next please, Laura? Is there anything to tie Nowakowski to Vardan?'

Laura obliged, and began to read. 'Born in Leicester… graduated from university with a degree in English Literature, but then he spent a further year converting it to a PGCE… spent three years at a school in Gosport… then there were all those rumours and accusations… he was cleared and has been at St Bartholomew's… this is his second year.'

Kate's eyes flew open. 'Wait, go back, which university did he graduate from?'

Laura reread the screen. 'Degree in English Literature received at Leeds University.'

Kate sighed.

'But,' Laura continued, 'his PGCE conversion was undertaken at Southampton University.'

'What year?'

'It was 2013,' Laura said, clicking her fingers together. 'The same year as our building inspector, Liam Phillips, graduated. I saw the date on his certificate on Saturday.'

'Doesn't mean they knew each other,' Kate interjected.

'That's why we need to check whether their paths have crossed,' Laura pressed, her eyes twinkling with excitement. 'We can check university graduation records, student housing records, social media activity, and anything else that might establish a connection. We should cross match with everything we've found on Jackson too.'

Kate couldn't argue, as the pieces seemed to fall into place, but it was one thing to speculate on links; proving they were real was a different challenge altogether.

⚹⚹

A sudden burst of whistling was swiftly followed by Olly Quinlan breezing into the incident room. 'She backs up his story,' he said, hanging his jacket on the back of his chair.

'Did you get her statement in writing?' Kate checked.

He nodded, and lifted the sheets of paper into the air. 'She's given dates and specific locations they visited. She's also provided her parents' contact information for us to check with them. Apparently, her parents paid for them to go out for dinner on Friday, Saturday *and* Sunday night, which is why Jackson didn't use his card at any point over the weekend. She was shocked when I told her he'd been arrested, and is adamant that we've made a huge mistake and that Jackson is really squeamish. She reckoned he nearly passed out once when she cut her finger while chopping onions.'

Laura fixed him with a frustrated stare. 'Did you believe her?'

Quinlan nodded, staring at Kate. 'I did, yes. She says they've been dating for two months, and he wouldn't hurt a fly. She said he came to the school late on Friday to collect her before they drove to her house in Chandlers Ford and then on to her parents' place in Poole. She swears blind he never left her sight at the school.'

'But we know that the body could have been disposed of when he was there on Thursday,' Laura challenged. 'It still doesn't explain his presence in Portswood when Daisy disappeared.'

'She was able to confirm he was there to pick her up,' Quinlan countered. 'Apparently, she was at a friend's birthday at The Mitre pub, near the big Sainsbury's. He arrived shortly after ten, collected her, before they returned to her place, where he spent the night.'

'Vehicle recognition has him in Portswood an hour before that,' ma'am,' Laura said. 'What was he doing there for an hour before he met his alibi?'

'Phone the pub now,' Kate demanded. 'If he was in there, they should have him on their security footage. Also, chase SSD. We need to know whether the DNA sample we took from Jackson matches the mystery profile from the two scenes. Finding this connection is our only way to find Daisy.'

FIFTY-THREE

'Tell me again,' Kate said, staring at the notes Laura had been scribbling on the board, hoping it would make more sense second time around.

Laura, nodded, replacing the lid on the marker pen, so she could use it as a pointer. 'It's all connected, ma'am, rather, *they're* all connected. Vardan and Jackson both work at St Bartholomew's, and both had access to the sports hall.'

'But how? The caretaker Mr Linus had the only key to the hall.'

'That's why they changed the padlock. Or maybe they somehow managed to make a copy of Linus's keys. Probably wouldn't have been too difficult. Anyway, we also have this exchange of messages between Vardan and Jackson, discussing their urges and whatever else, so we know they have a relationship of some sort. Right?'

Kate nodded for Laura to continue.

'We know that Phillips also had access to the sports hall, because he's got the contract to knock it down and build the pool this summer. He was at the school on Thursday, but we only have his word that he didn't go inside. We also have Vardan and Phillips graduating from Southampton University in the same year. Okay, we don't have anything concrete to suggest they were friendly back there, but we'll explore those avenues when the offices are open again in the morning.'

Kate pulled an apologetic face. 'It still feels pretty thin.'

'Not so, ma'am,' Laura continued. 'We have the photograph that shows Nowakowski knew Phillips and they'd been in touch recently because Nowakowski had asked for a job and money. How do we know Phillips didn't agree to provide the money Nowakowski wanted in exchange for—'

'And that's where the theory falls over, Laura. We don't know what any of them could have promised Nowakowski and Maria, and whether the intention was always to kill them. Plus, how does any of this tie back to Daisy?'

'Phillips lures Nowakowski with the offer of a payment to do *whatever*. Jackson does something similar to entice Maria, offering her ten grand for some kind of kinky bondage fantasy he wants to play out. And that leaves Vardan and Daisy. Jackson's emails suggest Vardan knew Daisy had developed some kind of school-girl crush on him, so maybe he brought her into whatever was planned. It's like that Hitchcock film *Strangers on a Train*. The story concerns two strangers who meet on a train: a young tennis player and a charming psychopath. The psychopath suggests that because they each want to get rid of someone, they should *exchange* murders, and that way neither will get caught. It allows them both to have strong alibis in place when the acts are committed.

'Jackson knew the Abbotts Way address was vacant, and chose that as the first murder scene, and he carries that one out, killing Nowakowski for Phillips. Vardan is then unaccounted for, for three hours on Thursday because he's busy dismembering Maria for Jackson. And that leaves Phillips taking care of Daisy.'

'You're making a lot of assumptions, Laura. We don't have any evidence suggesting Jackson wanted Maria dead, or that Phillips wanted Nowakowski gone. And why the hell did Vardan want Daisy killed?'

'Could be blackmail, ma'am?' Patel offered, having been observing the exchange.

Kate raised her eyebrows at him.

Patel sat forward. 'Let's say Jackson previously hired Maria to participate in a sordid fantasy, but she threatens to expose his little secret if he doesn't pay her the money she needs to get free of her pimp. He initially pays, but then fearing she will blackmail him again, he ties up the loose end, or maybe she came back and demanded more. Similarly, maybe Nowakowski had some dirt on Phillips from their previous working together. Maybe Nowakowski – in his desperation to make enough money for the deposit for the flat he wanted to get with his sister – blackmails Phillips. And finally, we know what Vardan has been accused of before. Maybe he tried something on with Daisy and she threatened to blow the whistle on him. Three strong motives for murder, if you ask me.'

Laura was nodding enthusiastically. 'Let's get Vardan and Phillips into custody, but let slip to each of them that the others are talking and the first to spill could get a lesser sentence than the others. Then we'll see how loyal they remain to each other.'

Kate narrowed her eyes. '*If* you're right, *if* the whole purpose of this pact was to keep it a big secret, why throw an enormous spotlight on their activities by sending me the hearts?'

Laura opened her mouth to speak, but closed it again as no answer would come.

'Maybe it was guilt?' Patel suggested. 'We know that Jackson and Vardan went through with their murders, but there's been no sign of Daisy's heart or a bloodbath with her DNA, so maybe Phillips bottled his end of the bargain. So in order to ensure he follows through, one of the others sends the hearts to get us sniffing around: put the frighteners on Phillips, so he knows his only way forward is to follow through and off Daisy.'

Kate shook her head. 'I don't buy that: it's too risky for Vardan or Jackson to do that. Isn't it?'

'Whatever the reason,' Patel continued, 'it's worth exploring. You're the one who doesn't believe in circumstance, ma'am.'

Kate glanced back at the photo of Chloe on her desk. 'If Daisy is still alive, where the hell is he keeping her?'

'He's a surveyor and property developer,' Laura suddenly shouted. 'His company must have a string of developments yet to complete. I'd bet money he's stashing her in one of those.'

Kate pointed at the computer. 'Find me that address.'

*
**

Humberidge looked exhausted as he stumbled into the incident room, his cheeks flushed, and the bags enormous beneath his eyes. 'Vardan wasn't at home, ma'am,' he sighed.

Kate looked at the large clock hanging above the door. 'It's just gone eight, where is he?'

'With your authorisation, I'll ask the phone company to run a trace.'

Kate nodded and Humberidge reached for the nearest desk phone.

Laura returned from the printer, presenting a page to Kate. 'Here's a list of TUTD developments I managed to find on their website. They have a residential housing project of a hundred new homes out near Winchester, which isn't due for completion until 2019. It doesn't say how far along they are with building the estate. Then there's a redevelopment of an old factory works down by the docks. It's going to be developed into a new luxury hotel.'

'Because that's what Southampton needs: another hotel,' Kate said, rolling her eyes.

'The hotel is due to open in 2019 as well.'

'Could he really be holding her at one of those addresses? If the developments are ongoing, he'd be running a huge risk that someone would find her. Where does he live?'

'Owns an apartment down by Ocean Village, ma'am,' Patel confirmed. 'Hardly surprising: fits in with the polished image he tries to present.'

'Please, ma'am, let's bring them in. We have Jackson already, but he'll be released in the morning unless the supe will authorise extending his custody by a further twelve hours. With all three here, I'm sure one of them will crack.'

'My money's on Phillips being the first to blab,' Patel agreed.

Kate looked at her two most-trusted allies and finally relented. 'Fine. Have the phone company pinpoint Phillips' phone and go and get them.' She looked over to Humberidge as he hung up the phone. 'Take Quinlan and the two of you get Vardan. Laura and Patel, have uniform check out the two developments while you bring in Phillips. We'll give them just enough rope, and then see which hangs himself first.'

The four of them bustled out of the room, the echo of their excited chatter drifting down the corridor, until silence descended on the incident room once more.

Standing, Kate made her way to the board and silently reread Laura's notes, still trying to shake the voice of doubt that continued to niggle at the back of her mind. Reaching for the reports Ben had produced following his post-mortem analysis of Maria's foot and the two hearts, she began to read, hoping the final piece of the puzzle would present itself.

According to the report, the foot was severed at the joint where the tibia met the plantar calcaneonavicular ligament, but described the cut as succinct and efficient. Ben's notes also confirmed that the cut was completed in one go with a powerful electric circular saw. Yet the vena cava, pulmonary arteries, and pulmonary trunk of both hearts were cut using some kind of shearing instrument. She still couldn't believe that Phillips would have sent the hearts. On neither occasion she'd met him had he demonstrated any kind of emotion or guilt, nor had he attempted to confess his actions.

A knock on the incident room startled her. Turning, she saw DI Steve Hardy, wearing his usual white lab coat, leaning in. 'Ah, Kate, I was hoping one of you would still be here. I've just been processing the belongings of Petr Nowakowski that you collected from Mountbatten House. We're currently testing fibres from his clothing, but I thought this might interest you.' He thrust out a small plastic wallet, carrying it over to the desk. 'Found it folded and hidden inside the framed photograph of the young woman—'

'His sister, Ana,' Kate confirmed. 'What is it?'

Hardy rested the wallet on the desk. 'Looks to be a printed copy of a chat room conversation between Nowakowski and someone with the username Guardian Angel. I guess he must have wanted to keep it as confirmation of what was discussed.'

Kate stared down at the page, reading the exchange between the two parties. Her eyes widened with every word. 'He was trying to sell a kidney? Is there any more? Can we see what website this chat occurred in? Or who this Guardian Angel person is?'

'Afraid that's all there is. Looks like the conversation occurred two weeks ago, about a week before he died.'

Kate's mind raced. Could one of Vardan, Phillips or Jackson have been trying to buy a kidney from Nowakowski? It didn't fit with Laura and Patel's blackmail motive. Did it? She couldn't see the angle.

'There's nothing else? Just this page?' Kate urged.

'Unless you managed to find a computer and printer at his address that you forgot to drop off, I'm afraid that's all I have.'

'He didn't own a computer... where else could he have printed this off?'

Hardy considered the question. 'A library? Internet café? An office he worked at? Maybe a friend's device? Could be any number of places.'

Kate reread the messages. 'He was offered ten grand in exchange for his kidney.'

Hardy nodded. 'Quite a lucrative market, the unofficial transplant of organs. Most people can survive with just one kidney, and these predators will pay good money for one if you can find them. Doesn't tend to be a big thing in the UK, mind you. It's a much bigger issue in the developing world, but I thought it might give your investigation some steer.'

'Is there any way to find out where this page was printed? If we could trace the original printer and computer you'd be able to find the website and possibly this Guardian Angel, right?'

'In theory, but being able to narrow down exactly where this was printed could take a lot of hours and even more luck.'

Kate looked at him pleadingly.

'All right, all right,' he sighed. 'Leave it with me and I'll see what I can do. You look exhausted, Kate. Don't you ever go home to rest?'

'No,' she smiled back, as he left the room.

Kate was about to lift the phone and call Laura, when it suddenly rang. 'DI Kate Matthews,' she said, answering it.

'Ma'am,' Freeborn said urgently. 'I was just called by the mobile phone company. Daisy Emerson's phone was just switched on. They have its location.'

Kate grabbed a pen and paper. 'Talk to me.'

Freeborn relayed the coordinates. 'I'm at my brother's in Portsmouth at the moment. You want me to meet you there?'

But Kate was already grabbing her car keys and coat, racing out of the door.

FIFTY-FOUR

Throwing her coat onto the passenger seat, Kate dived into the Audi and started the engine, punching the coordinates into the Satnav and flooring the accelerator as she shot out of the car park, her blue lights and siren warning other drivers of her urgency. Her wipers squawked as they battled with the falling snowflakes but Kate was oblivious to the noise, her heart pounding and mind racing as her subconscious pieced together everything she'd seen and heard in the days since Daisy had disappeared.

'Laura, where are you?' she called out as her phone connected via Bluetooth.

'We just got to Phillips' office, but he's not here. His phone is on charge, but there's no sign of him. Security had to let us in.'

'Daisy's phone was just switched on at a place called Old Harry Rocks off the Dorset coast.'

'She's alive?'

'That, or he's messing with us. I'm en route now, but I need backup. Freeborn can send you the coordinates.'

'Wait, and we'll join you.'

'There's no time. I need to get there before the signal goes. Have Rogers double-check he's not at home, but get there as quick as you can.'

'I know the place you're going,' Laura said. 'My dad used to take me there as a child. Three chalk formations jutting out to sea. According to legend, the devil used to sleep on the rocks. Go careful, ma'am, the pathways up there are precarious, and in this weather, make sure you're not ambushed.'

'Do me a favour, Laura. See if you can get any kind of air support over that way. I'm not sure they'll be able to fly in these conditions, but explain it's an emergency and see what they say. Have you heard from Humberidge yet?'

'No, ma'am, but I'll follow up with him and let you know as soon as Vardan is in custody.'

'We need warrants to search each of their homes and offices for evidence of their involvement in illegal organ transplants.'

'Ma'am?'

'Nowakowski was trying to sell a kidney to someone called Guardian Angel. We need to check their hard drives, phones and tablets for confirmation of who Guardian Angel is.'

'I'll get Humberidge and Quinlan on it.'

Kate disconnected the line, focusing on the road ahead, the traffic starting to clear, but the dark night sky enveloping the horizon.

*
**

The air was heavy with the smell of sea salt as Kate pulled into the South Beach car park, the uneven ground crackling beneath the tyres as she strained to see anyone who might have turned on Daisy's phone. Completing a circle of the car park, she spotted two empty cars, parked at the far side, and as she continued around, the headlights finally fell on a shadowy figure just beyond the wooden railing that ran the perimeter of the cliff top. Parking as close as she could, Kate left the lights on as she forced open her door against the rushing wind, feeling the bitter chill as soon as it scraped her cheeks.

Shielding her eyes from the snow that continued to fall, though not settle, she moved unsteadily forward, turning on the torch from her phone, trying to make out whether Vardan or Phillips had summoned her. But as she moved closer, the headlights causing her shadow to shrink as she neared the figure, the breath caught in her lungs as she recognised the blue and green woollen lumberjack's coat, and the fur hat with the ear flaps pulled firmly down. If Neil Watkins had noticed her arrival, he hadn't shown it.

'Neil?' Kate called out over the wind. 'It's Detective Matthews. Do you remember me?'

His shoulders tensed, and he looked back at her over his shoulder. 'Yes.'

'What are you doing here, Neil? Are you okay?'

'I'm cold.'

Kate took a tentative step closer, not wishing to cause him alarm, remembering what Mrs Kilpatrick had told her about Neil's apprehension around people he didn't trust. 'It *is* cold, Neil. Why don't we get into my car where it's nice and warm?'

'No,' he said pulling an angry face.

Kate took another step closer, her legs brushing the wooden railing. She wouldn't be able to get any closer without climbing over it, and to do so, might raise alarm, and he was far too close to the edge of the cliff to risk sudden movement.

'Will you at least come away from the edge, Neil? It's dangerous.'

'No. I like it here.'

Kate struggled not to shiver as the wind continued to blow snowflakes into them. 'Just take a couple of steps backwards. I'm worried you might fall.'

His head turned back to the sea beyond the cliff face, but rather than moving away from the edge, he carefully sat down, dangling his legs over the edge. It wasn't ideal, but was a fraction safer.

'What are you doing out here, Neil?'

'I like it here.'

'But it's so dark and cold. It's not a very safe place to be.'

'I come here to think.'

'Yeah? What do you think about?'

'Stuff.'

'Like what, Neil?'

'Can't tell you.'

'Why not?'

'Not allowed.'

'Why aren't you allowed?'

'It's a secret.'

'What's a secret, Neil?'

'Can't tell you,' he said, the anxiety growing in his voice.

'But I'm a detective, Neil. Do you remember? Like Sherlock Holmes. You're allowed to tell me secrets.'

'No. Not allowed to tell *you*.'

'Someone told you you're not allowed to speak to me?'

'Yes.'

'Who, Neil? Who told you not to speak to me?'

'Can't say.'

Kate began to slowly lift her leg, but he noticed the movement of the shadow in the light, and turned back to face her. Kate quickly lowered the leg, holding her hands out passively. 'Do you remember what you told me when we first met, Neil? You said you wanted to be a detective. Do you remember, Neil? You said you were smart enough to be like Sherlock Holmes.'

'I am. I am smart.'

'I know you are, Neil. You *are* smart. That's why you turned on Daisy's phone, isn't it? You wanted me to find you.'

He didn't answer, but his eyes told her she was on the right track. It triggered a fresh flurry of thoughts in her mind: someone connected with the school *and* Abbotts Way; someone who would use a shearing implement – like secateurs – to cut out Petr and Maria's lifeless hearts; someone who wouldn't be able to cope with the guilt of his actions; someone who couldn't communicate what had happened because he had been manipulated into keeping quiet; someone who, in a final cry for help, did the only thing he thought would bring the police to his door.

'You sent me the hearts, didn't you, Neil?'

Again, he remained silent, but his eyes began to water.

'You can trust me, Neil,' Kate beckoned. 'I'm one of the good guys. Like Sherlock Holmes. He does what's right, doesn't he?'

Neil nodded slowly.

Georgie Barclay's description of the man she'd seen speaking to Daisy in the darkness echoed through Kate's mind. 'Do you know where Daisy is, Neil?'

Another nod.

'Will you tell me?'

'Can't.'

'You *can* tell me, Neil. I want to help Daisy. Is she still alive?'

'She's not safe.'

'Not safe from whom?'

He screwed up his face as he fought against the building tears. 'Can't say.'

'Is that why you took Daisy? To keep her safe.'

He nodded rapidly.

'I want Daisy to be safe too. I promise you, Neil, I can protect her against whomever you're afraid of.'

He blinked against the tears, his expression softening slightly.

'You can help me make her safe, Neil. You could take me to her, and then we could protect her together. What do you think?'

He was starting to nod when a squeal of tyres shattered the silence behind them. Turning, Kate saw the flashing blue lights of Patel's car skidding into place alongside hers. When she turned back to reassure Neil that there was nothing to worry about, he gave her one final look, shuffled forward and was gone. Kate's scream disappeared with him into the darkness below.

FIFTY-FIVE

Staggering forward, Kate's legs were like jelly as she hoisted them over the wooden railing, stumbling perilously across the uneven ground, craning her neck forward as much as she dared. She held her arms out to maintain her balance, her feet edged slowly forward, but the buffeting wind wouldn't allow her conscious mind to move any closer. Daring to look down at where she could hear waves crashing against rocks, she could see nothing but the abyss-like darkness, stretching forever.

Kate finally let air back into her lungs, as loose rocks trickled off the cliff face, as her foot edged her closer to peril.

'Ma'am, ma'am?'

Kate wobbled at the calling of her name.

'Ma'am – Kate – come back!'

Kate stumbled backwards, adrenaline flooding her system as her outstretched arms made contact with the wooden railing again.

Laura gripped Kate's arms and held her in position. 'Ma'am, I thought you were going to… never mind, what's going on? Why were you staring over the edge? Who was here? Where's Daisy?'

Kate stared wide-eyed at Laura. 'I-I-I don't know. He didn't…'

'He? He who, ma'am? What happened here? Was it Phillips? Was Phillips here?'

Kate shook her head vigorously.

'Was it Vardan?'

Kate searched Laura's face for answers. 'Didn't you see?'

'See what, ma'am?'

Kate gesticulated to the edge of the cliff, but the words couldn't escape her mouth. 'He-he-he…'

Laura leaned over the railing as much as it would allow. 'Someone went over?'

Kate nodded frantically, not even believing her own memory of events. 'One minute he was there, and then…'

'Ma'am, you should come back to this side of the railing. It's not safe out there.'

Patel rushed over to them, each taking one of Kate's hands and helping her back over the top. Kate bent forward, away from the cliff, willing herself not to throw up, as the adrenaline began to subside and her mind came to terms with what had happened.

Patel crouched down in front of her, tiny glitter-like snowflakes catching in his beard. 'Can you tell us what happened? Take your time.'

The image of Watkins leaping flashed through her mind again, but she still couldn't bring herself to admit what she'd witnessed.

Laura lowered Kate so they were sitting on the railing. 'Who was here? Where's Daisy's phone?'

'W-w-watkins. It was Neil Watkins. He had the phone… he sent the hearts… it was Watkins.'

'Watkins?' Laura checked, her face cloaked with confusion. 'The groundsman from the school?'

Kate was nodding, but the memory was swiftly becoming a blur.

Laura looked over Kate's shoulder. 'You saw Watkins here? Was he leaning over? Did he lose his footing?'

Kate shook her head, blinking back the tears that were beginning to pool at the edge of her eyes. 'Didn't you see? He jumped.'

'He jumped?' Laura repeated, unable to keep the surprise from her tone.

Kate straightened up, feeling lightheaded. 'One minute we were both here, and then he-he-he was over the railing and gone. Where were you two? Didn't you see him?'

'When we reached you, you were leaning over the edge,' Laura said. 'I thought you were going to fall, so I raced from the car, screaming your name. Didn't you hear me?'

'He must have panicked when your car approached. He was terrified. He wanted to tell me what's been going on, but he couldn't. Someone was making him keep quiet.'

Patel straightened, staring into the gulf of black. 'I don't understand, ma'am. What does Watkins have to do with Jackson and the other two?'

Kate clamped her eyes shut trying to order her thoughts into a logical sequence. 'All I know is: Neil had Daisy's phone, and he came *here* to switch it on. I think he wanted me to find him. He was terrified that whoever's been manipulating him was a danger to Daisy. He said he was trying to keep Daisy safe.' Kate's eyes snapped open. 'She must be close. That must be why he chose this place. We need to get everyone here straight away. We need the Coastguard, Search and Rescue, SSD, we don't have long.'

The floodlight on the boat bobbed up and down as it rode the waves, lighting the foot of the cliff as a team of divers worked just beneath the surface of the water. Kate, Patel and Laura watched from the viewing platform nearby, as close as they could be without getting in the water. Kate's eyes fell on the awkward shape of Neil's body, his legs at opposite angles, splayed on three jagged rocks sticking out of the sea, waves crashing against them, sending white foam into the air and landing like snow on his torso. The drop must have been eighty feet at least, but she couldn't remember him making a sound as he'd vaulted into the open air, like a trapeze artist expecting to be caught by a partner who didn't appear.

At least he was at peace now, oblivious to the activity carrying on around him. The divers were working to identify whether he could have buried the chopped body parts of his victims nearby, but they wouldn't be able to excavate properly until morning when the sea had moved back to reveal its secrets.

'Coastguard has been up and down the shoreline,' Patel advised, coming off the phone, 'but there's nowhere obvious he could be holding her. If this wind passes soon, the chopper is ready to go up and use heat-seeking equipment, but they're still not cleared for take-off. Apparently, there's a maze of caves around these parts, but with the tide in, it's virtually impossible to search them. There's not a lot else can be done until morning, ma'am. The supe wants us to get back to Southampton and wait for news. Personally, I think that's the best idea. It's freezing out here.'

Kate knew he meant well, but she didn't want to leave until she found Daisy. 'You two go. I want to wait.'

'Can you remember anything else he said?' Laura tried. 'Any kind of clue where specifically he could have taken her? Given how cold it's been this week, would he really hide her somewhere so exposed to the elements?'

'He was too trusting,' Kate said. 'He was easily duped. A couple of boys convinced him to buy alcohol for them at the school once. It wouldn't have been hard for one or all of the others to convince him to do their dirty work. But which one? What if Daisy witnessed what was going on at Abbotts Way? He couldn't let her go to the police and blab everything, but if he told his partner what she'd seen, would the partner have ordered him to kill Daisy? He wasn't a killer, I'm certain of it. Someone else is behind all this, and was using Neil. But who?'

Patel held his phone up. 'Word from Humberidge is Vardan and Phillips are now in custody. Rogers picked up Phillips at his apartment. Why don't we head back to the station and ask them all?'

Kate stared back out at the Coastguard's boat, knowing she wouldn't find the answers here. But determined that she would do whatever it took to bring Daisy home.

FIFTY-SIX

The cool-persona, polished grin and carefully coiffed hair were gone. Liam Phillips looked terrified as Kate entered the interview room and took her seat across the table from him. All they'd disclosed to the solicitor so far was that Phillips was involved in a double murder enquiry.

Kate had insisted on leading the interviews. She had to be in the driving seat as the finish line loomed in sight. Patel was alongside her to ensure she didn't stray too far, and Laura had taken her place in the viewing suite. Both Jackson and Vardan had been set up in the next two interview rooms, and she would stalk from one to the next until she had the truth, and more importantly, the location of Daisy. According to Watkins, Daisy was alive, but she wouldn't remain so for much longer. Jackson, Vardan and Phillips all had access to the school, and all had demonstrated they had the skills to manipulate a vulnerable man like Watkins who longed to be accepted. The question was: were they all involved or was it just one of them?

Kate watched Phillips as Patel started the recording and introduced them all. Phillips' solicitor had objected to the lateness of the interview, but Kate had waved those concerns away. With a child's life at stake, every second counted. The sweat shining off Phillips' forehead confirmed he was worried about some sordid secret being exposed.

'We know about you and Watkins,' Kate began, watching his every twitch and jar. 'And we know why Petr Nowakowski and Maria Alexandrou had to die.'

His eyebrows had almost formed a single line at the mention of Nowakowski's name.

'We also have two other suspects in custody, just down the hall, and the first to confess… well, the courts are usually kinder to the one who shows remorse sooner. So, is that going to be you, Mr Phillips? Are you going to save us all a lot of time and admit your involvement?'

The solicitor, her hair as dark as night scraped back into a bun, and her designer glasses perched on the end of her nose, leaned in and whispered into his ear.

'No comment,' Phillips offered.

'You've already told us you knew Petr Nowakowski, and that the two of you met up a month ago. What you haven't confirmed is why you agreed to give him the money he desperately craved. What did you get in return?'

'No comment.'

Kate suddenly sat forward. 'Can we cut the crap, Mr Phillips? We don't have time to slowly tease out information. I need to know what you know and where that girl is.' She rested her hands on the table, splaying her fingers. 'So, here's what I'm going to do: I'm going to lay all my cards on the table; I'm going to tell you everything we know, and then – if you have any sense – you'll fill in the blanks.'

The solicitor reached for her pen, primed to scribble notes.

Kate took a deep breath. 'We know you were using Neil Watkins.'

A flicker, almost impossible to see, but Kate had spotted it.

'My team are currently confiscating the computers from your offices and your home. They will check every megabyte of data until they find the proof of what you've been up to.'

Phillips leaned over and whispered something into the solicitor's ear. She covered her mouth as she whispered something back.

'Watkins confessed what he'd done to Petr Nowakowski and Maria Alexandrou less than an hour ago. But we know that he wouldn't act of his own volition; he didn't have it in him. But oh, he was scared of someone. I saw it in his eyes: he was terrified! You see, his partner didn't know where he'd stashed Daisy. Why was he so scared of you, Mr Phillips? What did you have over him? Or what did you threaten to do if he talked? He told me, you see, he told me he'd been told not to talk to me. Did you give him that order, Mr Phillips?'

'I don't know what you're talking about,' he said through gritted teeth.

Kate slammed one of her hands against the desk. 'A precious child's life is at stake!'

'I don't know anything about a girl.'

'Her name is Daisy, Mr Phillips. You're a man of the world, you watch the news. You know *precisely* who Daisy Emerson is.'

'Yes, okay, I know there is a girl missing, but it has nothing to do with me.'

'Did you tell Neil to kill her?'

'What? No!'

'Did you tell Neil to kill and chop up Petr Nowakowski?'

'No! He was a friend. I didn't even know he was dead until you told me a moment ago. Jesus! What is all this? You think because I'm from South Africa that I'm just going to cop for something I haven't done?'

'This has nothing to do with where you were born, Mr Phillips, and everything to do with how you manipulated Neil to do your bidding.'

'That's absurd!'

'What about Maria Alexandrou? Was it your idea to have her killed at the sports hall? The same sports hall that was under your supervision?'

It was Phillips' turn to raise his voice. 'Are you fucking stupid? Why would I do anything to delay that project? I have sunk almost everything we have into that redevelopment. Every day we fall behind schedule I risk my company going under. If that's your best theory then have a look at my books! You'll see how counter-productive such an act would be!' He rested back, straightening his blazer, and running a nervous hand through his damp hair.

Kate continued to watch him in silence, until it became uncomfortable. 'You haven't denied knowing Neil Watkins.'

'Yes, okay, I knew the groundsman. That doesn't mean I was colluding with him to commit murder.'

Kate turned to Patel. 'You know there's been something bothering me about Mr Phillips here since the first time we met in his office. I asked you at the time why the school had opted to use a third-party building inspector, rather than one provided by the local council. You claimed it wasn't uncommon… but now I think I understand. *Now* I understand how you managed to offer the winning tender for the work; how much of a backhander did you offer to secure the project, Mr Phillips?'

Phillips was whispering to his solicitor again.

'You said yourself it was a huge stepping stone for the company, and could bring in a lot of new business for you,' Kate said, as the hushed conversation continued. 'And that must be the case if you've ploughed most of the company's resources into it.' She paused, chancing her luck. 'Was Neil the middleman between you and whoever benefited from the bribe?'

More hurried whispers.

Kate nodded for Patel to suspend the interview. 'We'll leave the two of you to chat,' Kate informed them, 'while we go and talk to the person I think will come clean first. We'll be back, Mr Phillips.'

*
**

Ismael Vardan had surrendered his right to legal counsel, and was sipping from the plastic beaker of tea as they entered. His cheeks bore the scars of childhood acne and his chin sported a thin black goatee.

'We've got your friend Liam Phillips next door,' Kate began when Patel had started the recording. 'He's speaking with his solicitor at the moment, probably trying to work out a plea bargain. You've opted not to seek legal counsel, Mr Vardan. Are you sure you shouldn't review your options?'

Vardan glared at Kate, folding his arm, daring her to break him.

'All right,' Kate acknowledged. 'Where's Daisy?'

Vardan rolled his eyes. 'I have told you before, I don't have a clue where she is.'

'Can you tell me what she was like to teach?'

He sighed loudly. 'She was a good student, with a keen interest in literature, as I told you when you asked me these questions last week.'

'But you knew she had a crush on you, didn't you, Mr Vardan? You didn't tell us that last week.'

His shoulders tensed. 'I wasn't aware that—'

'Bullshit!' Kate interrupted. 'We have emails between you and Chris Jackson confirming you were more than aware of her infatuation with you.'

For the first time since he'd been arrested, Vardan looked uncomfortable. 'No… well, I-I-I couldn't be sure… I, uh—'

'I forgot to mention we have Chris Jackson in custody as well,' Kate said, raising her eyebrows suggestively. 'He's been here since this morning, and our IT specialists have been pouring all over his computer and emails. We found the conversations between the two of you, Mr Vardan, and, in a moment I'm going to go and interview Mr Jackson and I expect he's just about to tell me everything I want to hear. But I thought I'd give you the chance to come clean first.'

Vardan looked at the door, as if he was considering making a dash for it. His hand trembled as he lifted the beaker of tea to his mouth.

'I'm waiting, Mr Vardan. You knew Daisy had a crush on you, didn't you? You knew because you've been in that position before, haven't you? Last time you managed to cover up what had happened, but maybe things went too far again. Did Daisy threaten to tell what had happened?'

'No, nothing happened… okay, look I knew she acted differently around me, but I didn't do *anything* to lead her on. School girls develop crushes on their teachers all the time, but I *swear* I didn't go near her.'

'What were you and Jackson discussing in your emails then? You were planning to go abroad together, weren't you? Why?'

'Chris is… Chris is a friend. That's all.'

Kate gave him a knowing smile. 'It was a bit more than that, wasn't it, Mr Vardan? Remember, we *have* read the emails.'

'No, listen, it has nothing to do with Daisy.'

'Why did he mention her in the emails, then?'

'He was just trying to wind me up! He knew what had happened in my last school, and knew that you lot would assume I was somehow involved in Daisy running off. It was playful banter, that's all.'

'Where were you for three hours on Thursday when we believe Maria Alexandrou's body was being mutilated in the sports hall at St Bartholomew's?'

'I was reading in my classroom.'

'Don't lie to me! Your whereabouts are unaccounted for. Were you helping Neil? Is that why nobody saw you?'

'Neil? The gardener?'

'That's right. He confessed his involvement in the two bloody crime scenes we discovered. He also told me he had a partner who had sworn him to secrecy. That was you, wasn't it, Mr Vardan?'

'What? No! I don't know what you're talking about.'

Kate sighed. 'I'm about to go and interview Chris Jackson. If he confirms that all of you were involved, he'll probably get a lesser sentence than the rest of you. This is your final chance, Mr Vardan. Tell me what happened.'

His hands flew up to his eyes, as he began to gently sob.

'You, Jackson, and Phillips,' Kate continued, 'you're all in this mess up to your necks, but all I want to know *right now* is where Daisy is. We know about Phillips paying you to win the swimming pool contract. Whose idea was it to exchange murders? Whose idea was it to try and sell the victims' organs to the highest bidder? Talk to me, Mr Vardan. Where the hell is Daisy?'

An urgent knock at the door interrupted proceedings. Kate leaped from her chair and yanked the door open.

Freeborn leaned in. 'Ma'am, the supe wants to see you upstairs *now*.'

FIFTY-SEVEN

Knocking twice, Kate entered the supe's office, but it was only when she saw who was seated across the desk from him that she understood the summons.

'Mrs Watkins,' Kate said, moving quickly over to her. 'I'm sorry for your loss.'

'How could you let my little boy *die*?'

'I couldn't stop him,' Kate pleaded. 'We were talking and then the next thing I knew he'd leaped from the edge.'

'I warned you about speaking to him alone! He was a wonderful boy, but he didn't know his own mind. You should have called me!'

'There wasn't time, Mrs Watkins. I was trying to coax him back from the edge of the cliff, but I had no idea what he was planning to do.'

'What were you even doing there with him so late at night? And on your own too? Is this how the modern police operate? Threatening the life of a vulnerable man until he breaks?'

'Whoa, whoa, whoa, our being there had nothing to do with me. I didn't even know he was there until I arrived.'

Imelda eyed her cautiously.

'Please, Mrs Watkins, I understand this is an impossible time for you, but if you'll hear me out, I believe I can shed some light on what's been going on. Please?'

Imelda retook her seat, reaching into her handbag for a tissue and dabbing her eyes.

Kate glanced over to the supe, who looked like he'd been getting it in the neck since before Kate arrived. He nodded for her to proceed.

Kate sat next to Imelda, and adopted a non-threatening stance. 'Neil had Daisy Emerson's mobile phone, Mrs Watkins. That's how we traced where he was.'

Imelda blinked back tears, shaking her head in disbelief. 'No, there must be some kind of mistake.'

Kate fixed her with an empathetic look. 'I'm so sorry, but it's the truth. I have reason to believe that Neil has been the unfortunate victim in all this, and that somehow, Daisy inadvertently stumbled onto what was going on, and that it was Neil who took her—'

'Absolutely preposterous! My Neil wasn't like that. Just because he was *different* doesn't make him a paedophile!'

Kate raised her hands apologetically. 'Nobody is accusing Neil of being a predator. If anything, I believe he took Daisy because he believed it was the only way to keep her safe.'

'Ever since you met my son, you've been trying to pin something on him.'

'It isn't like that, Mrs Watkins. Neil was the one who told me he was trying to keep Daisy safe. I know it can't be easy to hear, but I assure you it's the truth. We have three men in custody who we believe may have been responsible for manipulating him.'

Imelda's eyes suddenly stared at Kate. 'Three men?'

'I'm not able to say much more than that for now, as we're still investigating, but it seems like they duped Neil into carrying out activities for them and when he tried to confess what he'd done they threatened him into silence.'

Imelda looked to the supe for confirmation, and he nodded gravely back at her.

'But I don't understand,' Imelda continued, 'who are these men? How did they know Neil?'

'We think they met him through the school. I'm sorry, Mrs Watkins, there really isn't any more I can say at this time.'

Imelda dabbed at her eyes, as she continued to look at the supe. 'I cannot believe this has happened again. He was such a sweet-natured boy. All he wanted was the best for everyone, and there are people out there who will take advantage.' She turned back to Kate. 'Did he... did Neil say anything before...' her words trailed off as fresh tears filled her eyes.

'I think he was very troubled at the end,' Kate said kindly. 'I don't think his conscience was able to cope with what he had done, that's why he wanted me to find him. He wanted to know that the truth would come out. Turning on Daisy's phone was his one final act of defiance against whoever was threatening him.' Kate paused. 'Mrs Watkins, Neil told me that Daisy is still alive, but we haven't been able to find her, and it seems unlikely she was being held where I found him. Can you think of *anywhere* Neil might have taken Daisy? Somewhere quiet, where nobody would notice him taking a fifteen-year-old girl, and somewhere where she wouldn't be heard?'

Imelda blew her nose. 'I'm so sorry, detective, I really have no idea. I still can't believe he had anything to do with that poor girl's disappearance. Up to this point, I thought she was just another runaway. Are you sure he had her phone, and wasn't given it by one of these other men?'

'The way he spoke to me, he realised that what he'd done was wrong. I am truly sorry for your loss, Mrs Watkins.'

'Kate,' the supe interrupted, 'would you mind stepping outside for a moment so Mrs Watkins can have some alone time?'

Kate stood and followed the supe out of the room, down the corridor and into the incident room. 'Where do we go from here, Kate?'

'We know that Vardan and Jackson knew each other and as much as the teacher denies it, I can't help thinking he was planning to instigate something with Daisy if he hadn't already.'

'What about the other man? The building inspector?'

'I think Phillips used Neil to pay a bribe to Vardan to help him secure the swimming pool project at the school. Phillips has admitted he is in serious money trouble, and that makes sense.'

But the supe was frowning. 'Vardan is Daisy's form tutor, isn't he?'

'Yes, sir, form tutor and English Lit teacher, I believe.'

'Then I very much doubt he's the person Phillips was bribing. He wouldn't have had any say in which bids were accepted for contract. Mark my words, as a former school governor myself, I know that the teachers have very little sway or influence over such matters, if any at all. Did Phillips admit to paying off Vardan?'

Kate thought back. 'Well, no, not in so many words, but it…' her words trailed off as an impossible idea floated to the surface. 'Sir, would you excuse me? There's something I need to check on.'

'Very well, very well. I'll see if a patrol car can give Mrs Watkins a ride home. We should assign a Family Liaison Officer too.'

'No, wait. Can you keep Mrs Watkins in your office for now?'

His brow furrowed. 'Why?'

'Please, sir, just trust me. I'll speak to you as soon as I've got this sussed.'

**

'What exactly are we looking for?' DI Steve Hardy asked from the confines of his office.

'I'll know it when I see it,' Kate replied, as he continued to recover the deleted internet history from the hard drive. 'Have you managed to download the emails yet?'

Hardy pointed at the printer in the far corner. 'They should be printing as we speak.'

Kate rose and moved across to the printer as the final page spurted out. Carrying them back to Hardy's desk, she stifled a yawn.

'My wife must think I'm having an affair,' Hardy chuckled, glancing at the clock.

'I promise I'll let you go as soon as you've finished. I really do appreciate your support.'

'Right,' he said, sitting up. 'That's all the partitions scanned. I should warn you, a lot of this data will be fragmented, depending on what software was used to erase the original information. Think of it as a book where all the pages have been shredded. I do have software that can painstakingly find the fragments and try to stick them back together, but that'll take time.'

'Time is the one thing I don't have.'

'And you're sure we're allowed to extract this data? From what I understood, the suspect didn't live at this address.'

'He was staying there at the time of his death,' Kate confirmed, 'which means he had access to this computer, and we're therefore within our rights to review the contents.'

Hardy cocked a sceptical eyebrow. 'If you say so. Okay, what terms do you want me to search for?'

Kate looked him straight in the face. 'Guardian Angel.'

Hardy frowned. 'You think the guy who jumped was the one offering Nowakowski money for his kidney?'

'Humour me,' Kate replied.

Hardy pulled up a search window and typed the words.

FIFTY-EIGHT

THIRTEEN DAYS MISSING

'Ma'am, you look awful,' Patel said, as he entered the incident room, removing his coat and scarf. 'Don't tell me you were here all night?' But he didn't need her to confirm it. 'Coffee?'

Kate gave him a nod as she continued to file the pages before her. 'I'm going to need you downstairs this morning. I've finally figured out what's been going on, but whatever happens in there, I need you to back me.'

He passed her a fresh mug of coffee. 'You don't need to ask. We've only got a couple of hours until we have to release Jackson.'

'Forget about Jackson. We have bigger fish to fry.'

Patel gave her a curious look, but followed her out of the room, as she carried the box of papers down to the interview room.

Imelda Watkins looked far from impressed to find herself seated across the table from Kate and Patel. The duty solicitor who had been called to attend the police station didn't look too pleased by the early wake-up call either.

'The first time we met,' Kate began, 'you told me that people have been taking advantage of Neil's kind nature all his life; that people assumed because he struggled to communicate, there was something wrong with him. And then when those vandals defaced his property you told me you blamed yourself for putting him in harm's way. I thought you meant by helping him get the job at the school, but that wasn't what you meant, was it, Mrs Watkins? What you meant was you blamed yourself for asking him to clean up your mess. The only thing I don't understand is how you wound up in such a mess to begin with.'

'I don't understand what you're talking about, or why you have detained me—'

Kate raised a hand to cut her off. 'We have your computer, Mrs Watkins. We found the conversations you conducted online with Maria Alexandrou and Petr Nowakowski. Unless you're going to pretend that Neil was the individual offering them ten thousand pounds each a kidney? I'll be honest with you, Mrs Watkins, I can't prove for certain that you are Guardian Angel, and that it wasn't Neil involved from the outset. My team are currently requesting access to your bank account information, which should quickly establish whether you have been paying out large sums of money to desperate people, so it's only a matter of time until we know everything.

'But,' Kate paused, 'I don't believe you will allow Neil's name to be dragged through the mud any more than it already has been. Why did you involve him?'

The duty solicitor leaned in to talk to her client, but Imelda brushed her away. 'I plan to sue you for wrongful arrest and I will be having a very stiff word with your Superintendent. I am a grieving mother! You cannot arrest me and start throwing accusations.'

Kate removed the lid of the box she'd brought into the room, pulling out the pages and dropping them onto the table in front of Imelda. 'These are printed copies of what we have recovered from your hard drive, Mrs Watkins. More than a dozen conversations with individuals in which you – or Neil – clearly offer money in exchange for their organs. Just because you deleted it from your computer, doesn't mean it disappears forever. This alone is sufficient to allow us to turn your world upside down. It's over, Mrs Watkins.'

Imelda's eyes fell on the pages.

Kate softened her tone. 'I don't believe you did this by yourself; neither you nor Neil could have surgically removed the kidneys adequately enough for transplant. Who are you working with?'

Imelda looked up and met Kate's eyes and something in her broke. 'Can I see him? I'll tell you everything if you allow me to see my son one final time, to say goodbye.'

'I give you my word.'

Imelda nodded in acknowledgement. 'For a long time I refused to accept that what had happened at St Bartholomew's had anything to do with Neil. I suppose he thought he could do it there because the old building was going to be torn down. He probably didn't think that anyone might go inside in the meantime. I should have been clearer in what I asked of him.' But then she shook her head. 'No, what I should have done is not involved him at all. That day in the school when you were talking to him, as we left he told me he was going to tell you what had happened, and I told him he couldn't as we'd both get into serious trouble. I swear I was less worried about myself than I was about him. He couldn't have coped with going to prison, not understanding why. It was my fault, but I thought that if I could just keep him quiet, everything would blow over. I knew if you found any of his DNA at Abbotts Way that we could explain why, given he used to tend the gardens there, but I could see he was struggling with something. You need to understand that Neil was only acting upon my instructions, and that he did *not* kill either Petr or Maria.'

Kate's eyes widened at the mention of their names. 'You admit to knowing Petr Nowakowski and Maria Alexandrou, then?'

Imelda nodded. 'Yes, I knew them. I only met them the one time when I handed over their payments, so you can imagine how shocked I was when Petr contacted me days after the surgery to complain of abdominal pain and nausea. I knew he couldn't go to an NHS doctor for care because then the whole situation would be exposed, so I contacted the men responsible for the operation. I told them they needed to help him, but they told me they had what they wanted and it was up to me to deal with him. I didn't know what to do. They said if I didn't take care of matters they would sever our partnership and make Neil suffer.

'So, I invited Petr to my house. I was going to call a doctor and just hope for the best, but before I got the chance, he died, right there in front of me. I swear I didn't kill him, but I fear my indecision indirectly led to his passing.'

'Who are your partners?' Kate asked.

'We never use real names, for everybody's protection.'

'But how did you become mixed up with them?'

Imelda closed her eyes. 'It was only after my Graham passed that I learned just what a terrible situation he'd left us in. He used to deal with all the finances, and I assumed everything was okay until I discovered the truth. The bank was threatening to sell our family home. I tried selling the place in Abbotts Way, but nobody wanted the dilapidated building. I was about to lose everything, and I knew Neil would need continued financial support. I was desperate, and that's when I stumbled across a couple of emails Graham had received shortly before his death. He was a retired surgeon, you see, and they were asking if he would be interested in performing surgeries off the books. They were offering enormous sums for what amounted to a few hours' work.

'All I did was vet the seller, check their medical history and then organise where the exchange would take place. I was just the go-between. And it was going well: we were helping to save lives. People can live with one kidney, so why not allow those willing to sell one do so. Petr and Maria were handsomely rewarded for their donations, and those kidneys went on to grant a new lease of life to those in need. I know what you must think of me, but

I really never thought anybody would suffer because of what we were doing.'

'Until Petr contacted you.'

Imelda wiped a stray tear from her eye. 'When my partners threatened mine and Neil's lives, I felt like I had no choice but to cover up the crimes. I panicked and told Neil that I needed him to dispose of the body: burn it, bury it, or whatever it took. I never had any idea he would take Petr to Abbotts Way and dismember him.'

FIFTY-NINE

Kate watched Imelda carefully. 'What did you tell Neil about Petr?'

She stared off into the distance. 'I told him that Petr worked for some bad men and had come to the house to hurt us, but had died suddenly. I said we couldn't go to the police because they would arrest me, and then he would be on his own. I felt so bad lying to him. But he hugged me and said he would do whatever was necessary to keep me safe. I told him he needed to get rid of the body. I never realised he would chop up their bodies, but then he does read a lot of crime and detective stories, so something in one of them must have inspired him. He said he'd taken care of it, and I was desperate to believe him and move on.'

'What about Maria Alexandrou?'

Imelda's voice cracked under the strain. 'Ah, that poor girl. She had such high hopes for the future. She messaged me, saying she had a fever and couldn't keep food down, as Petr had said. I knew I only had a small timeframe to get her treated, so I reached out to my partners again, and I begged them for help; I didn't want Maria to die too. But again they told me just to deal with it. The threat from before still hung over me, and I had no doubt they would follow through.' She paused and blew her nose. 'So, I told Maria to come to my home and that I would try to help her. I researched symptoms and suspected she had contracted septicaemia. And then I saw what a botch job they'd done with her stitches, and suddenly I realised exactly the sort of people I'd been dealing with. She had no memory of where they'd taken her or who had operated, only that she'd been met by a van, and had woken up in a hostel.'

'Did she tell you where the hostel was? Maybe there is CCTV nearby.'

But Imelda shook her head sorrowfully. 'I insisted she stay with me until she felt better, and she seemed to be improving, but then last Thursday morning I couldn't wake her and I realised I'd failed again. I swore from that moment I would have nothing more to do with them, but I still needed to deal with Maria... Neil had done a good job with Petr's body – or so I thought – and I asked him to help me again. He was on his way to work at the school when he called round. I never imagined he would take her in with him, or what would unfold thereafter. I-I-I never should have left it to him.'

'What about when we sealed the place off? Did you never suspect what he'd done?'

'Why would I? He told me it was taken care of and I believed him. As far as I knew, you'd found Daisy's foot. It's not like you or your team have been particularly forthcoming with information. Until you came to my house and started asking about Abbotts Way and Chris Jackson, I hadn't connected the dots.'

Kate paused. 'After I visited you yesterday, did you confront Neil about what had happened?'

Imelda's head dropped and she wiped at her eyes with the tissue. 'He'd just come in and I sat him down, and asked how he had disposed of Petr and Maria. Until the moment he spoke I was desperately hoping he would say he'd buried them, or he'd hired someone to deal with it, but he told me... about... oh God, my poor boy. What did I put him through?'

Although she knew it would be an eternity until Imelda forgave herself, Kate couldn't help but empathise with the position she'd found herself in. 'What more can you tell me about these partners of yours?'

Imelda's face shot up, gripped with panic. 'You have to find them. They won't hesitate to come for me when they hear about my arrest. They'd rather I die than give them up. You have to promise to protect me. I'll tell you everything I know, but you have to take into account the huge risk I'll be taking.'

A knock at the door interrupted proceedings. Pausing the recording, Kate exited the room and found Laura in the corridor.

'Ben just called,' Laura advised. 'They've just discovered two compost bags stuffed with Petr and Maria's bodies buried beneath the sand where Watkins jumped.'

'What about Daisy?'

Laura shook her head. 'No sign. They've checked the caves in the area, but she's not there.'

Imelda practically leaped out of her skin as Kate burst back into the interview rom. 'Where is Daisy? Where would he take her?'

Imelda raised her arms defensively. 'I-I-I don't know. I *swear* to you. Do you really think I want to see another innocent person come to harm?'

Kate's cheeks burned with the frustration of being so close to an answer, yet no nearer to actually discovering where Daisy was being held. 'You must be able to think of somewhere he would have taken her? Do you own any other properties?'

'Apart from Abbotts Way, no.'

'What about where Neil grew up? Did he always live in Southampton?'

'We bought the bungalow in North Baddesley when Graham left the service. Neil didn't know any other home. The only places I can think of are his place in Shirley or the school.'

'We have covered every inch of the maisonette, and there's no sign that Daisy was ever there. And she's not at the school. Come on, Mrs Watkins, you need to think long and hard. Where would he take her? A favourite place? He buried Petr and Maria at Old Harry Rocks, but Daisy isn't there. Did he have any other favourite spots?'

'I-I-I don't know…'

'You told me he loved going to the seaside, but couldn't swim. Did he have any one particular place he would go to? Somewhere he wouldn't be disturbed? Somewhere he could hide a vulnerable child for nearly two weeks without being caught?'

'No, no, no!' Imelda screamed, her face awash with tears. 'I just don't know. I never used to ask him about where he went. So long as he came home and had had a good time, I didn't worry about it.'

'But there has to be *somewhere*. Somewhere he felt safe; somewhere he thought she would be safe,' Kate paused, her voice rising. 'He never told you about Daisy interrupting him at Abbotts Way because he was terrified *you'd* tell him to kill her too. That's why he took Daisy, Mrs Watkins. He wanted to keep her safe from you and your partners.'

'I'm so sorry.'

'We don't have time for apologies. Help me find her.' A fragment of memory flashed behind Kate's eyes. 'In your conservatory, there was an image, a photograph of you and your late husband by some beach huts.'

'And?'

'Where was that picture taken?'

'Um…'

'Come on, Mrs Watkins. Neil would have looked at that picture every day of his life. A picture of the two people he cared for the most, in a place where they looked so happy. Where was it taken?'

'Mudeford… Mudeford Spit… but—'

'Would Neil know where the hut was?'

'Well, yes, he would, but—'

Kate picked up her phone and dialled Laura. 'I want units to check *every* beach hut at Mudeford Spit.'

'Wait, detective, you don't understand,' Imelda persisted. 'We only rented that beach hut, and it was nearly forty years ago. I doubt the original hut is still there. He wouldn't…'

'Mudeford's only a forty-minute drive from here; seems close enough for him to visit and check on Daisy every day. You said yourself, nobody really goes to the beach at this time of the year, so he wouldn't have been disturbed.' Kate nodded at Patel. 'Get *her* back to the cells and meet me in the car park.'

SIXTY

'The hut in the picture was right on the sand,' Kate told the three units gathered with Laura and Patel. 'Mrs Watkins was right, the original hut will be long gone by now, but that doesn't mean Neil wouldn't have looked for something similar. Again, the hut in the image was painted blue, but we need to check every hut. Initially, I want you to knock on every door and listen for movement inside. People aren't allowed to live in beach huts, so if you hear anything I want you to call it in immediately. There are over a hundred to check. Start at the opposite end of the beach and work back towards the car park. Laura, Patel and I will start this end and work towards you. Let's find our girl.'

The group disbanded.

'I spotted CCTV in the beach car park,' Patel commented as he zipped up his coat. 'Should be able to confirm if Watkins' van was here.'

'Let's find her first,' Kate replied, unable to keep the concern from her voice. If they didn't find Daisy here, there was a chance she would never be found. Not that she needed to tell Patel and Laura this; they both already knew how high the stakes were.

Jogging along the pathway down to the beach, Kate sent Patel to the left where half a dozen huts stood, boarded up and padlocked for the winter. Meanwhile Kate and Laura ducked to the right, with Kate taking the row of huts on the sand, and Laura heading to the row directly behind. Kate's memory of staying in a beach hut as a child was of a rickety old shack, not much larger than a garden shed. But these huts looked big enough to sleep a couple, were freshly painted and all had power cables leading inside.

Kate's heart raced as she mounted the stairs and thumped her fist against the wooden boarding, calling out Daisy's name. Laura's and Patel's voices carried on the wind. Pressing her ear against the wood, Kate strained to hear any sound over the crashing of the waves behind her. If they had no luck hearing Daisy's desperate pleas, they would need to make contact with the owners of the huts and ask for them to be unlocked.

Thirteen days locked in a hut: no light, no fresh air, and no human contact other than with her captor. Even if they managed to find Daisy alive, there was no way of knowing what state she would be in.

They had to keep going.

Moving to the next hut, Kate hammered again. 'Daisy? Daisy, can you hear me? This is the police, you're safe now.'

Laura's words echoed in the distance.

The next hut along, still silence. Kate looked off into the distance. She desperately hoped the uniform units had reached the end and were making their way back. No word on the radios yet.

Onto the next hut. 'Daisy? Daisy? This is the police. Make a noise if you can hear me.'

And then there was a noise. Faint. Somewhere nearby, but not this hut.

Kate ran to the next hut, and banged again, straining to hear anything else. Was it just her imagination?

Onto the next hut, daring the sound to grow louder, and not certain it wasn't the racing rhythm of her own heart.

And there it was again: a persistent banging but barely audible over the sound of the water.

'Ma'am?' Patel asked breathlessly as he arrived next to her.

She shushed him. 'Can you hear that?'

He cupped his ears and closed his eyes. 'I can't hear anything but the sea.'

Was it just Laura's feverish banging on the next row over?

Avoiding the next hut, Kate raced up the steps and listened again.

'I can hear it,' Patel suddenly declared. 'It's coming from just up here.'

Again skipping a hut, Kate suddenly found herself at a hut painted sky blue, with white shutters pulled down and a newly fastened padlock hanging down. Thumping the boarding Kate called out Daisy's name, and the banging was reciprocated.

'Daisy? Daisy?' Kate called excitedly. 'It's the police. Knock if you can hear me.'

The banging started again, quicker now. Urgent.

'Quick,' Kate demanded. 'Pass me the bolt cutters.'

Patel obliged, reaching for the padlock. 'This looks like the same type used at the sports hall.'

Kate recognised it too. Jamming the lock into the tool's jaws, Kate and Patel worked together until it snapped in satisfaction, dropping to the floor with a crash. Patel yanked open the closed shutters, holding it aloft so Kate could prise the door open, and as she did the shuffling and scraping inside chilled her heart.

Scurrying to the far corner, amongst a carpet of crisp packets and sweet wrappers, a gaunt and timid creature blinked against the bright light flooding through the door; her lips dry and chapped, wrapped in a dirty blanket. Despite the strawberry fresheners stapled to the inside of the door, the smell of stale faeces was overpowering.

Crawling in on her hands and knees, Kate forced the terrified child to make eye contact. 'Everything is going to be okay, Daisy. My name is Kate and I'm going to take you home.'

The girl didn't move at first, and for a moment Kate couldn't believe she was looking at the face of the girl whose every line and dimple she'd memorised. Kate continued to crawl forward ever so slowly. 'The man who took you is gone now. You have nothing to be afraid of, my darling.'

And as if the spell was broken, the girl rushed forward, wrapping her tiny arms tightly around Kate's neck, refusing to let go. Kate fought the stinging in her own eyes, knowing she had to stay strong. She had to get Daisy to safety. She'd made that promise.

Daisy finally released her grip on Kate's neck when the paramedics gave her a sedative and strapped her into the stretcher.

'I'll stay with you,' Kate promised, as they carried the gurney across the sand. 'I promise you have nothing else to be scared of.' Looking back at Patel as SSD's head, DI Steve Hardy, arrived on scene, Kate instructed, 'I want every inch of the hut processed. You're to run point while I'm at the hospital with Daisy. She is in a bad state, and my guess is he was drugging her somehow. Check the water bottles, and I'll have the hospital run her bloods for cross-examination purposes. Let's make sure we tie up the loose ends for Daisy, for Petr Nowakowski and Maria Alexandrou.'

Patel nodded, before extending his hand to shake. 'You found her, ma'am. If ever there was a time to take a pat on the back, this is it.'

Kate shook his hand, but it would be some time before she accepted any credit for her part. Over the coming days her rigorous self-examination would assess whether she could have done more to identify Neil's and Imelda's activities sooner, and whether Daisy's nightmare could have been avoided.

EPILOGUE

TWO DAYS LATER

Sitting down at her desk, Kate wasn't surprised to find the incident room empty. After the discovery of Daisy on Thursday, she'd promised the team the weekend off, subject to any major case breaking.

'Ma'am, what are you doing here?' Laura asked, as she entered the room and began to unravel her scarf.

'I thought I'd make an early start on some of the paperwork,' Kate smiled back. 'I gave the team the weekend off, why are you here?'

'Snap,' Laura said. 'I was bored at home and figured I might as well do something constructive. I thought you were going to your daughter's birthday party?'

Kate smiled. 'I will be, but I have a couple of bits and pieces to sort out first.'

'Any news on whether the CPS will be pressing charges against Phillips for bribing Imelda Watkins to secure the swimming pool job?'

'The Fraud team are now handling that, and despite a thorough examination of both Jackson's and Vardan's hard drives, no indecent images of children were identified, which is a relief.'

'And Imelda Watkins?'

'Is on remand, awaiting a trial date. She's kept to her word and is chirping like a canary. Hendrix's team are looking to build a case against Watkins' silent partners. I guess we'll just have to watch this space.' Kate paused. 'What's that?' she asked, pointing at the large box on Laura's desk.

'It came for you last night,' Laura replied, lifting and carrying it over.

Kate's eyes widened as she saw how neatly it was decorated.

'Don't worry,' Laura teased. 'I checked inside. Open it and see for yourself.'

Kate stood and tentatively lifted the lid. The perfume from the flowers hit her nose before she'd even spotted the petals inside.

'Val Emerson dropped them round,' Laura confirmed. 'She wanted to personally thank you for finding Daisy, but I said I'd pass on the flowers. They're in a pot of water, so should last a few days.'

Kate lifted out the vase and put the roses to her nose and inhaled deeply. 'They're beautiful. I think I might leave them here, though. They brighten the dreary walls, don't you think?'

'They'll help block out the smell of Patel's latest coffee bean mash-up too.'

'Did Val say how Daisy is doing?'

'The hospital want to keep her in for observation,' Laura confirmed, 'certainly until she's at a more stable weight. Apparently she'd lost nearly a stone since she disappeared. She hasn't been able to say much about her experience in that hut, but SSD believe he was drugging the water he was bringing her each day so she'd remain compliant, and wouldn't make a noise to attract anyone to her location. It's amazing that she didn't freeze to death out there. She's lucky to be alive, and owes you her life, ma'am.'

'Owes *us*, Laura. The whole team contributed to finding her. Remember that.'

Laura smiled. 'I will. I'm going to go and fix a drink. Do you want anything?'

Kate shook her head, as she heard her guest approaching. 'I have an errand to run, but I'll check in with you later. Don't work too hard: that's an order.'

Kate waited until Laura had left the room, before gathering her own coat and meeting Quinlan in the corridor. 'Are you ready to do this?'

'Are you kidding? I've never been so scared my entire feckin' life, ma'am.'

'It'll be okay. The supe knows I'm coming over to see him, but he doesn't know what for. It's better that we meet away from the office and prying ears.'

'What if he fires me on the spot?'

Kate had never seen Quinlan looking so terrified. 'He can't dismiss you. He'll be upset, angry too, I expect, but he'll respect you more for coming clean, before he finds out what's happened. Try not to worry. I'll be with you the entire time, and I'll make sure things don't get out of hand.'

'I appreciate everything you've done for me, and for Tara. She told me you'd let her crash at your flat a couple of nights. It should have been me offering her support. If I wasn't such a coward...'

'Hey, look at me. Parenthood comes as a shock to all of us, even those who have been trying for a baby for years. Believe me, it takes some getting used to. What counts is what you do from here. Whatever decision you and Tara reach, you need to be grown-up about it.' Kate rubbed his shoulder. 'Now, come on, are you ready to get the shit kicked out of you?'

He forced a smile of gratitude, and led the way down to the car park.

A MESSAGE FROM STEPHEN

Thank you so much for taking the time to read *Cold Heart*; it really does mean the world to me. As a character, Kate is never far from my mind. Whenever I find myself facing a difficult decision in my life, I now ask: what would Kate Matthews do? And I usually find I arrive at the right conclusion. If you want to be kept updated about Kate Matthews and my other novels, you can sign up to the mailing list on my website.

You can also get in touch via Facebook or Twitter. I genuinely read and respond to every message I receive. Writing can be such a lonely business, and nothing thrills me more than hearing from a reader who has enjoyed my books; I promise I won't bite!

If you enjoyed *Cold Heart*, I would be so grateful if you could leave a review. It doesn't need to be long, just a few words, but it makes such a difference. It will help new readers discover one of my books for the first time. I cannot overstate the importance that book reviews play for authors. Every review has the potential to lead to an extra sale, and every extra sale encourages a writer to work on their next story.

Thank you again for reading my book. I hope to hear from you soon.

Stephen Edger

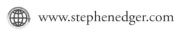 www.stephenedger.com

 AuthorStephenEdger

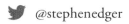 @stephenedger

ACKNOWLEDGEMENTS

I'd like to say special thanks to the following people, without whom *Cold Heart* wouldn't be in existence today:

Parashar Ramanuj, my best friend for more than twenty years and my first port of call whenever I have strange questions about medical procedures and body parts; Joanne Taylor, who has been reading and providing feedback on my novels since the beginning; Elaine Emmerick for reading and championing my work; and my incredibly supportive family, in particular my wife Hannah, who puts up with my mind wandering mid-conversation as a new plot twist strikes.

As ever, I'd also like to thank my eagle-eyed editor Jessie Botterill and the incredible team of editors, cover designers and marketers at my publishers Bookouture. I've learned so much and everyone has made me feel so welcome. I'd also like to give a shout out to the other Bookouture authors who are massively supportive and super talented.

Final thanks must go to every reader of my books for encouraging me to follow my dream and not to give up.

Printed in Great Britain
by Amazon